GOLDEN KEY

THE DOUGLAS FILES: BOOK EIGHT

NATHAN BIRR

Published by BEACON BOOKS, LLC

Cover Images Copyright ©
VR_Studio/iStock/Thinkstock

THE HOLY BIBLE, NEW INTERNATIONAL VERSION®, NIV®
Copyright © 1973, 1978, 1984, 2011 by Biblica, Inc.®
Used by permission. All rights reserved worldwide.

The Holy Bible, King James Version. Cambridge Edition: 1769;
King James Bible Online, 2018.
www.kingjamesbibleonline.org.

ISBN: 978-1-7321373-1-8 (hc)
ISBN: 978-1-7321373-2-5 (sc)

www.nathanbirr.com

Also by Nathan Birr

The Douglas Files
Overnight Delivery
Three's a Crowd
All an Illusion
Shot List
Chasing the Wind
Blood and Treasure
One Life to Lose

Douglas Files Shorts
Black Male – Short
WinterKill – Short
Short Sail – Short

Last Resort Series
Fire & Ice

God, Girls, Golf & the Gridiron
(Not Always in That Order) . . . A Love Story

All is Calm? – A Christmas Novella

The Book of Levi

For Caleb, Gabey, Chloe, and Sophie . . .
I hope you always know how much laughter
and joy you bring to Uncle "NayNay."

Chapter One

JACKSON DOUGLAS HAD yet to spot the ocean, but he knew it had to be close. The air rushing in through his car windows was heavy with the smell of the sea, and it left the tang of salt on his lips. The car had A/C, but the breeze was refreshing as it cut the otherwise humid air. And this was Florida, so a little mugginess was in order.

Jackson took a deep breath, basking in the fact that for the first time in weeks it didn't hurt his ribs to do so. He'd been on the road for almost an hour, first through suburb after suburb on Florida's Turnpike, now on U.S. Route 1 through miles and miles of swampland. Every so often a billboard broke the barrenness. They advertised restaurants and bars, hotels and motels, souvenir shops, various local businesses, and an assortment of beach attractions. Most of them included a catchy slogan welcoming travelers to the Florida Keys.

He had departed his native Los Angeles before dawn, fueled by coffee and expectation. Vacation, by definition, brought with it a certain level of excitement. And this being his first trip to Florida—even if he was just swapping one coast, one ocean, one beach for another—he felt drawn to the Gulf of Mexico and the Caribbean. Vacation also, by definition, meant getting away, and he really needed to get away.

A five-hour flight had put Jackson in Miami just before two o'clock local time. Half an hour later, having picked up his luggage, a quick lunch, and a rental car, he had started on the three-hour journey to Key West. Having once seen a History Channel documentary on the Overseas Highway that connected Miami to Key West, Jackson had chosen to drive the last leg of his journey rather than fly directly to Key West's international airport. So far, the much-acclaimed road had yet to cross anything but a few sounds and marshes.

1

That changed suddenly as Jackson rounded a corner on the highway. He found himself traversing a long corridor of dive motels, restaurants, bait shops, gas stations, and convenience stores, along with small retailers selling everything from T-shirts to seashells to fresh produce. There were also residences, most of which were rundown, and the standard assortment of small businesses. All the buildings had a decided beach community feel, but everything was surrounded by green. Trees and underbrush encroached everywhere, and Jackson assumed the locals fought a constant battle against the swamp's efforts to reclaim its ground.

He still hadn't seen any open water, even though signage told him he was in Key Largo and thus the Florida Keys. He was starting to wonder if he'd been duped by the History Channel when finally, after almost forty minutes of driving through beach communities without seeing any beach, Jackson crossed a bridge over a small inlet. To his left was nothing but brilliant, wide-open blue water.

As he continued west, the beachside sprawl thinned out as the Keys became smaller and the distance between them longer. Soon Jackson's views were of open water as often as not. The color of the water ranged from deep blue to jade to brownish tan in spots where the sandy bottom was just feet beneath the surface. The ocean breeze had become a wind, flapping through the windows and reinvigorating Jackson as he cruised under a vast blue sky. On the horizon, fair-weather cumulous clouds towered like masts of distant ships. Actual sailboats dotted the seascape, darting among the islands and reef formations that comprised the Keys. This was the Florida Jackson had envisioned and anticipated, just what he needed to shake him from the doldrums.

*   *   *

One day ago . . .
Saturday, May 11
6:38 p.m.

JACKSON STARED at the sun's reflection on the dark bluish-gray ocean. Sunset was maybe an hour away, and the Pacific was lit with a golden yellow ribbon that danced on the surface directly in line with the low-hanging sun. It was mesmerizing.

"Gonna miss sunsets in Florida," Reggie Cameron said. They stood in the sand, equidistance from the crashing surf and the restaurant Reggie owned and that bore his name. He'd long ago promised Jackson as many on-the-house meals as he wanted, and Jackson didn't believe in wasting good. Especially since there was so little of it of late.

"Been a while since my last science class, but pretty sure the sun sets in Florida too."

Reggie grinned. "I meant over the ocean."

"Depends what side you're on, I guess."

"Where you going again?"

"Key West."

"Yeah, I guess they'll have some sunsets there."

"Yeah."

Reggie said nothing. He was not the strong silent type, although definitely strong. He stood six-three and weighed two-fifty. A former all-conference defensive end at Nebraska, Reggie's NFL career hadn't panned out, and he'd turned—with an assist from Jackson—into an entrepreneur. As to being silent, he'd never shied away from telling Jackson what he needed to hear. But he also knew when there was no point in saying much more.

"Why Florida again?"

"Ben, an old buddy of mine lives down there. Said he wanted to pick my brain."

"This old buddy not have a phone?"

Jackson shrugged. "He's been bugging me to come for a while. Seemed like a good time."

"Your birthday?"

Jackson shrugged again.

"I know it's a rough time for you, J. You sure you want to be alone?"

"I won't be alone."

"Your old buddy."

"Right. Besides, it's not just my birthday."

Reggie took a breath. "This still about Maggie?"

Jackson pursed his lips. He and his sort of girlfriend Maggie had broken up six weeks ago. No, not broken up. She'd dumped him for the preacher's kid. But it was all good because they were going to still be friends.

"It's not just Maggie," he said.

"Something else happen while I was gone?"

Jackson sighed. "It's been a long . . . well, life actually."

Reggie again said nothing.

"I need a change of scenery, Hoss."

Reggie looked at him and waited until Jackson met his dark brown eyes. "You mean temporarily, don't you, J?"

"Unless I meet a Ving Rhames lookalike who owns a seafood restaurant on the beach."

"Man, I don't look nothing like Ving Rhames."

Jackson shrugged.

"You tell your grandpa about your plans?"

Jackson nodded.

"How is he?"

"Same as ever."

"Connie?"

"Better to ask forgiveness than permission," Jackson said in reference to his overbearing if not well-meaning neighbor.

"You in trouble again?"

"She's just kind of stifling, trying to nurse me back to health and all. What with my best friend in Nebraska for three weeks."

"Ten days."

"Whatever."

"And we didn't hardly talk for two weeks before that."

Jackson shrugged. "How's your grandma?"

"Still kickin'."

He nodded.

"What about you? You back to health?"

Jackson slowly raised both arms over his head, and did so with only a minimal wince.

"Good as new," Reggie said with a smile.

"Such a high standard."

Reggie clapped him on the back. "Maybe you do need a change of scenery. Recharge the batteries."

"Worth a try," Jackson said.

"Need a ride to the airport?"

"I'll leave the Granada. I gotta leave before decent people are awake anyhow."

"How long you staying?"

Jackson shrugged. "Week. Ish."

"Stay in touch."

"Sure."

They resumed staring at the sunset. They chatted a little about the Lakers, who had been bounced in the first round of the NBA Playoffs, and the Dodgers, who were playing .500 baseball to start the season. A rumor had floated that the Rams might be considering moving back from St. Louis to Los Angeles, which was as close to buoyed as Jackson's spirit had been in a while. Other than for thoughts of Florida.

When darkness fell, Jackson headed home. He still had to pack and be up well before sunrise. As usual, he and Reggie slapped hands as they said goodbye. Reggie clasped his hand for a few seconds.

"Take care, J."

Jackson nodded, noting a depth and intensity in the big man's eyes. Concern, and not just about a cross-country flight.

"Yeah. Yeah, I will."

Then he turned and headed into the night.

*   *   *

Sunday, May 12
4:56 p.m.

THE JEWEL of the Overseas Highway was Seven Mile Bridge, stretching from Marathon on Knight's Key to something called Little Duck Key. Spanning its eponymous length, it connected the Middle Keys to the Lower Keys, meaning Jackson was about three-quarters of the way from Miami to Key West. That was good, because despite his desire to make this drive and despite the beauty of the Keys, he was sick of sitting and sick of traveling.

But he had to admit, the views were spectacular. He was flanked on both sides as he drove, on the south by power lines and on the north by the old Overseas Railroad. Built in the early 1900s by Henry Flagler, its concrete arches had served as the base for the original Overseas Highway until the road was rebuilt in the 1980s. Now the arches stood as reminders of a previous era, and while they took from the natural serenity of the Keys, they added an ambiance of sorts. Almost as if Jackson was traveling into a different world and a different era.

The speed limit certainly supported that premise, and with heavy traffic, Jackson felt like he was crawling along. Large spans over open water had given way to quick hops between numerous islands that resembled paint splatter on an ocean canvas. From the highway, Jackson couldn't tell where one island ended and another began, just that he kept passing key after key.

Finally, he saw the giant white radome of Boca Chica Key's Naval Air Station and knew that he was close. Crossing one more overwater span, Jackson turned onto the lone road leading to Key Haven. Situated on Raccoon Key just east of the city limits of Key West, Key Haven was a small community built around a series of canals and harbors. Several streets branched off the main drive, each leading to more streets that ran between the canals so that the majority of the properties in the community had both road and water access.

The houses themselves were a complete hodgepodge: large and small, two-story and single level, gated and open to the street. Some were little more than rundown bungalows; others bordered on palatial. Parking options ranged from in garages to under carports to on the street. A few houses were built on stilts with parking beneath them. Lawns were a combination of grass, dirt, or landscaping of all skill levels and varieties. Palm trees of one shape or another grew on most of the lots, and they would have been the dominant feature on Raccoon Key if not for the power lines. They ran along every street, the poles sticking out of the pavement itself, with feeder lines running to each property.

Jackson navigated past streets all named for flowers—Amaryllis, Arbutus, Azalea—before finding Angelonia Terrace. He stopped at the end of the street at a property surrounded by a three-foot-high wall lined with short, stubby palm trees. He drove through an open gate and followed the curving driveway to a carport covered with flowering bougainvillea. Blooming azaleas lined a walkway that mimicked the driveway, curving to an arch-spanned front entrance. The columns of the arch were draped with more flowering vines. Jackson didn't remember Ben being such a green thumb. He also didn't remember him saying anything about being gone, but the carport was empty. Then again, Ben did live on a canal. Maybe he got around via gondola.

Jackson parked and got out. He spent a moment admiring the property. He didn't remember what Ben's dad had done, but he knew even back during their time in San Diego, the O'Reillys had been fairly well off. And Ben had mentioned something a while back about an inheritance, which explained how a history teacher could afford a place so, well, palatial.

The house was square, with a pyramid metal roof that featured a cupola in the center. Large windows looked out from rooms on either side of the entrance, which was recessed several feet. The homes Jackson had passed on the way in were a mixture of old and new, well-kept and rundown. Ben's place didn't look new, but it was in show-home condition. That wasn't a surprise. Ben was meticulous to a fault.

Palm trees surrounding the lot isolated it from the neighboring properties, blocking out views of the power lines and cars on the street, and adding to the sensation that Jackson had stepped back in time. The satellite dish on the roof kind of cancelled out that notion. Even so, all that was missing was the hammock stretched between a pair of palms and a cat on the front step. Weren't cats prominent in Key West? Or maybe that was just a famous house that had a lot of cats. Or maybe the sun was already getting to Jackson.

Leaving his one duffel bag in the car, he approached the front door. It appeared to be made of solid oak. Jackson rang the bell and waited, then thumped on the door with his fist when no one answered.

Ben had a tendency to get distracted at times, but Jackson doubted he had forgotten a guest was coming. He rang the bell again, waited a couple more minutes, then decided to circle the house and see if Ben was out back. He meandered through the carport, which led him to a patio that was just yards from a canal. The view across it was of an undeveloped portion of Raccoon Key and, in the far distance, the open waters of the Gulf of Mexico.

Retracing his steps, Jackson circled around the other side of the house, along the boundary with the neighbor to the south. It led him to another canal, across which were more homes on another peninsula. He circled all the way to the patio again, which spanned the entire backside of the house. No pool, but there was a hot tub and a built-in grill to put most restaurants to shame. Three sets of double doors led into the house, one on either side of the patio, presumably to bedrooms, and one in the middle, beyond a recessed section of the patio that was sheltered beneath the square roof, making room for a full patio table and chairs. Ben lived in a resort.

Seeing no signs of his old friend, Jackson retreated back to the front of the house. He rang the bell once more, for good measure, then sighed and reached for his cell phone. He dialed the programmed number and squinted against the afternoon sun.

A computerized female voice answered. "Your call has been forwarded to an automated voice message system. The number you dialed is not available. Please record your message at the tone and when you are finished, hang up, or press 1 for more options."

Jackson snapped his phone shut and sat down on the front step. "All right, dude, now what?"

Chapter Two

6:31 p.m.

IN JACKSON'S DAY at USC, the unwritten rule was that tardy professors were given ten minutes before students excused themselves from class. Fifteen if the prof had a Ph.D. Jackson gave Ben—who neither was a professor nor had a Ph.D.—an hour before he struck out in search of food.

Breakfast had been granola bars in the car and lunch a sub sandwich in the airport. By six o'clock—even though it was only midafternoon California time—Jackson was starved.

He had done some brief research online before leaving, so he knew the basics of Key West. The airport and newer residences were on the eastern half of the island, much of which was actually built on top of landfill. Historic Old Town, the tourist sites and cruise port, and the Truman Annex military installation were on the western half. So were the majority of the original restaurants, which, by the time Jackson got there, would likely be hopping. He didn't really feel like battling touristy traffic, so he hoped he could find something on the eastern half of the island.

Between Key Haven and the island of Key West was Stock Island, half of which was within the city limits and half of which wasn't. After passing a golf course and more sprawl, Jackson crossed one last bridge and was finally on Key West.

He immediately turned north, driving along the coast and passing chain hotels and restaurants, commercial properties, and a mall. Key West looked very much like Miami. Jackson drove until North Roosevelt Boulevard/Highway 1 narrowed and turned into Truman Avenue. The neighborhood had taken on a residential flavor, so he headed back the way he had come, ultimately stopping at a Denny's inside a Quality Inn almost back to the eastern end of the island.

An Indian woman with a bindi between her eyes seated Jackson at a window table where he was able to look out at the water while he pondered the menu. It had plenty of options all for a good price, which made up for the fact that Jackson had not come all the way across the continent to eat at Denny's. But somehow, given the circumstances, he wasn't in the mood to put on board shorts and flip-flops and wander into Jimmy Buffetville or some such place.

He ordered a burger and fries and sipped an iced tea while waiting for his food. It had been a month and a half since he had been rescued from Russian terrorists looking for a nuclear weapon. They had beaten the tar out of Jackson over a period of twenty-four hours, bruising and breaking bones and damaging several internal organs. He'd lost ten pounds because he'd been too sore to eat much, then put them and an additional five back on thanks to Connie's cooking and his inability to exercise.

Although he no longer had any physical restrictions and the pain was mostly gone, his doctor still advised taking it easy. This trip was supposed to, among other things, be a healing balm. Ben had invited him to visit numerous times, and Jackson had always found some or other excuse. But after Ben's latest call a week ago, Jackson had decided some deep sea fishing, sightseeing, and seafood—and maybe a little flirting with some cute Florida girls—were just what his sore ribs and wounded psyche needed.

"Here you are," the waitress announced, setting a huge open-faced burger and a plate full of fries in front of him. "Can I get you anything else?"

"No, thanks."

"More tea?"

Jackson looked at his glass, about half full. "Sure."

She smiled and promised to be right back.

Jackson waited until she returned with a second glass before he sampled his burger. It hit the spot. He munched a few fries while looking out at the water where a fishing trawler was headed for the marina on Stock Island.

Then there was the puzzle Ben had asked Jackson to help him solve. He hadn't given any indications what it was, just that he wanted to pick Jackson's brain about something. He'd used those words specifically. He had also promised not to strain Jackson too much and assured him he could spend most of his time lounging in a hammock drinking lemonade. Jackson had no idea what the puzzle could be. Ben was an author and a history nut, but that didn't narrow things down much.

It did, however, make Ben's absence at his house a little disconcerting. Ben could be somewhat forgetful and had a tendency to become overly focused on one thing to the exclusion of all others. So it was distinctly possible that he had made some other appointment without realizing it conflicted with Jackson's arrival. Or maybe he was just operating on island time.

But Jackson couldn't shake the small, niggling fear that maybe something was wrong. Ben wasn't the kind to get into trouble, and he hadn't hinted that his "puzzle" involved anything dangerous. In fact, he'd stressed that he only needed Jackson's brain. And there hadn't been any signs of anything amiss at Ben's house, other than for the lack of a car and his not answering his phone. Both were easily explainable, although the generic message Jackson got when he called was a little odd. Then again, Jackson's recent experiences as a private investigator had made him somewhat jaded toward, well, life. He shook off his concern, chalked it up to a long day, and concentrated on finishing his burger.

A family of four was shown to a booth opposite Jackson, and their bubbly conversation made it impossible not to eavesdrop. They had taken the ferry to Dry Tortugas National Park, home to the massive but unfinished Fort Jefferson, dazzling coral reefs, and plentiful sea life. Located some seventy miles west of Key West, the uninhabited islands marked the true geographical western end of the Florida Keys. Ben had said something about taking the trip out, if time permitted.

Jackson finished his burger to stories of snorkeling, bird watching, clambering around the fort, and the daughter getting seasick on the trip over, despite the tranquil seas. Spotting a giant sea turtle while snorkeling had made up for it, and she was fine now, judging by the way she flipped through her menu while reliving the day. Jackson's waitress stopped by to take their order, engaged them in a story about spotting a shark off Dry Tortugas, and then came to see if Jackson needed anything else.

He declined one more refill, and she gave him his check. He paid and headed back outside, where the sun was low in the sky but the heat of the day was still hanging on. Jackson tried to view it as tropical, which made it a little less unpleasant. So did the hope that Ben would be waiting for him with an air-conditioned house and a bowl of orange sherbet for dessert.

Jackson got into his car and headed back toward Key Haven, thinking back on the day he had first met Ben O'Reilly. Ben's family had moved into Jackson's neighborhood, and Jackson and his dad had been part of a group from church that helped the O'Reillys unload their U-Haul. At that time, Jackson had never expected that he would someday be friends with Ben. He was tall, lanky, a little awkward in his dress and mannerisms, and quiet. Jackson, though not extroverted, was casual and carefree, smooth around girls. Ben seemed almost disinterested in the opposite sex. Jackson was a smart-aleck; Ben was no-nonsense. Jackson loved sports; Ben couldn't tell Tommy Trojan from Joe Bruin. Jackson had been born in Hawaii and lived in California all his life; Ben and his family were originally from North Dakota.

But over time, Jackson had come to appreciate a soundness of character in Ben, sincerity, a hunger for truth. It manifested itself in Sunday school, discussions with the fellas, and in school, where Ben was an honor student. He loved knowledge, loved history. Whereas most teenage boys had shallow preoccupations with girls or sports, Ben was someone with whom Jackson could have a serious discussion. And despite his own preoccupations with girls and sports, Jackson appreciated that.

Ben had never become a best friend, a Trapper to Jackson's Hawkeye, but he'd been part of Jackson's inner circle, one of the few he trusted. Then in Ben's senior year, his dad's company had transferred him to Atlanta. Ben had followed his family with plans to attend the University of Georgia in Athens, and Jackson hadn't seen him since.

They had stayed in touch, however. Ben had earned a B.A. in history and gotten a job as a teacher in Tallahassee. He had moved to Key West a few years ago and had written a book about the Civil War's effect on American society. His parents had both passed away (his mom in a freak bicycle accident and his dad from a heart attack), and he seemed to be taking it as well as could be expected. Then again, it was hard to tell such things from biannual e-mails. Ben had never married, although his e-mails had mentioned a girl named Lisa a few times a year or two back. Nothing since. Maybe she'd dropped him for a pastor's kid too.

Reminiscing was getting depressing. Jackson had come to Florida to forget, so he turned his mind to other things. Like what he was going to do if Ben wasn't home.

The carport was still empty as Jackson pulled into the driveway, and since a car couldn't get around him in the driveway anyhow, Jackson parked under its shelter. For diligence's sake, he rang the doorbell and got the expected lack of an answer. So he tried Ben's cell once again. He got the same generic voicemail.

With a sigh, Jackson sat down on the step. The sun had set behind the trees, but the sky was still plenty light. He checked his phone. It was quarter to eight. How long did he wait before checking into a hotel? Or going back to the airport?

After five minutes of unproductive thinking, Jackson decided to try the door before leaving Ben a note and heading to some dive named the Surf and Sand or the Ocean Breeze.

It opened.

Tentatively, Jackson stepped inside. "Hello?" His voice trailed off into the darkness.

The living room was in the center of the house, opening to the patio on the far side. The ceiling was vaulted to the cupola, the windows in which let in enough light for Jackson's eyes—once they grew accustomed—to see. There were five doors leading out of the living room, other than the front entrance and the double doors to the patio. Two on the left, on the near corner and the far corner, flanked a stone hearth fireplace. They were matched by two in the corners on the right, but instead of a fireplace in the middle, there was a doorway to the kitchen. Eight feet of countertop opened to the living room, which added to the open concept of the house. Jackson's house in Pacific Palisades offered views of the Pacific Ocean, but even he was a little envious of Ben's pad.

"Ben, you here?" He let his voice echo through the empty house. "It's Jackson."

He concluded the house was empty and did some brief exploring, working his way around the living room. The doors on the left opened to bedrooms, a master in the back, and a guest room—and guest bath that was accessible from the bedroom or the stub of a hallway leading to it—in the front. On the right side of the house, a wide archway opened from the kitchen to a formal dining room at the front of the house. And in the back, a third bedroom had been converted to a home office/study. One entire wall was filled from floor to ceiling with books, and even had a rolling ladder to access those on the top shelves. Jackson read quite a bit, mostly Grisham or Cussler novels, but couldn't imagine owning half that many books. There were maps and seascapes—both photos and paintings—on the walls, a separate desk featuring a desktop computer with dual flat screen monitors, and half a dozen model ships—modern aircraft carriers, a Civil War-era ironclad, several sail-powered vessels—on staggered shelves on the far wall. Jackson didn't remember Ben having a fascination with ships or models, but the proof was in the pudding. That, or he had the wrong address and had entered the home of a retired admiral.

Jackson studied a few of the maps, then checked out the desk in front of the bookshelf. It was huge and old, the wood nicked and scratched and clearly worn. An antique, green-shaded banker's lamp was mounted on one corner of the desk, the rest of which was covered with books, papers, notebooks, and a rotary telephone. Ben was meticulous to a fault, unless he was knee-deep in a project. Then, everything became secondary to his singular objective.

Jackson clicked on the desk lamp and scanned the desk, looking for anything that might tell him where Ben was. The papers and notebooks were full of Ben's somewhat sloppy handwriting, and Jackson didn't feel that motivated. After all, he was in the house; he had a place to sleep.

A pad of sticky notes by the phone grabbed his attention, and he picked it up. Two words were written on the top note: "The Point." Jackson frowned. He had no idea what "The Point" was supposed to reference. If it was a meeting place, it lacked a time. He shrugged and set the pad back down.

He turned and studied the hundreds of spines on the bookshelves lining the south wall. Seriously, how did a guy even acquire so many books? Had he looted Key West's library?

Jackson clicked off the light and turned to leave. Then he thought better of it. Orange, pink, and purple streaks filled the northwestern sky, and Jackson opened the French doors and stepped outside. The corner of the house was no more than twenty feet from the canals behind and to its right. Jackson stood where he was on the edge of the patio, admiring the view in the sky, the quiet marsh across the canal, and the serenity of it all. Once again, he felt a million miles away from civilization.

As the colors faded and the sounds of the swampland grew a little more ominous, Jackson reached into his pocket for his phone. He gave Ben's number one final call and again got the generic voicemail. That really was odd, unless Ben had never set up his voicemail or his battery had died or something else had happened that was beyond the scope of Jackson's technical understanding. He clapped his phone shut with a sigh and headed back inside.

Immediately, he got the sense that something wasn't right. He couldn't identify what . . . the study was still dark and the house silent. As quietly as possible, he eased the door behind him shut.

A thud sounded from the living room, and Jackson tensed. He moved around the desk, creeping over a large rug that covered the wood floor. He stopped beside the bookshelf and listened for footsteps. For a moment he thought he was mistaken, his senses over-stimulated, turning random noises into intruders. But then he heard a slight creak in the floorboards, followed by a couple of soft footsteps.

Chapter Three

JACKSON'S FIRST THOUGHT was to grab a book off the shelf and whack the intruder over the head. The cooler half of his head prevailed, and he waited quietly as the figure took another step into the room and stopped, turning right and then left.

"Hey there."

"Aaagghhh!"

It was either a girlish yell or a manly scream, and the figure jumped back, stumbling and retreating against the wall. Jackson edged to the desk and felt for the lamp. He found the chain and pulled, bathing the room in a soft, muted light. It was enough.

The figure was a woman, and a fairly attractive one at first glance. A Kelly green T-shirt and denim shorts accentuated a toned body without being immodest. Her bronzed skin was accented by sun-whitened blond hair that was cut at the chin, maybe a little longer. It was hard to tell since sunglasses pushed up on top of her head held it back. Her dominant feature was a pair of dark blue eyes—even in bright sunlight, Jackson guessed—that regarded him carefully. When she realized he was holding his ground, her eyes quickly narrowed, and she regained her composure. She stood a few inches taller, stepping away from the wall.

Jackson quickly scanned her head-to-toe, making sure he wasn't missing anything like a gun or some other concealed weapon. Her hands hung at her sides, and he deemed she wasn't a threat.

He nodded at her slightly. "Mrs. O'Reilly?"

The woman frowned. "Who are you?" she asked, the accent decidedly Southern.

"I sort of asked first."

"I'm a friend of Ben's."

"Me too."

"What's your name?" she asked.

"I asked first."

"You asked if I was his wife. I'm not."

Jackson grinned, admiring the slow, smooth cadence to her voice. And her spunk. He shrugged. "Fair enough. I'm Jackson."

"Sawyer," she said, removing her sunglasses. She shook her hair from her eyes. She turned, found a light switch on the wall, and flooded the room with light from lamps in two corners and in a small fixture in the ceiling. "Are you from around here?" she asked, turning back to face Jackson.

"California."

"You're a friend of Ben's, and you're from California?"

"So once was he."

Sawyer nodded.

"I don't have to ask if you're from around here," Jackson said.

"Did my accent give it away?" she asked with a grin, and maybe a dash more inflection.

Jackson nodded.

"I'm from Alabama."

"And you're a friend of Ben's?"

"Originally from Alabama," she said.

"Aha." He stuck his hands into his pockets. "Roll Tide or War Eagle?"

She practically glared at him. "I am no barner," she said, using a nickname with which Alabama fans frequently disparaged Auburn fans.

"Noted," Jackson answered, leaning against the doorpost. "I guess we should address the elephant in the room, and I don't mean Big Al."

Sawyer grinned at the reference to Alabama's mascot.

"I'm visiting for a week. A little tropical vacation."

"I came to drop off some photos," she said, reaching into her back pocket and pulling out an envelope.

"You and Ben . . . uh, dating?"

Sawyer shook her head. "No. We're just friends."

He nodded.

"Why?"

"You apparently let yourself in."

"I rang the bell, and called out when I entered, but nobody answered. Ben sounded like he wanted the photos right away, so I thought I'd leave them for him. Besides, nobody around here locks their doors."

"Or turns on lights when they enter a home?"

"You didn't turn them on either."

"It was still sort of light when I got here."

"Well, I knew where I was going, and I was only going to be here a minute."

Jackson nodded again. "I see." It made sense, at least in theory. He could have missed the doorbell, what with being on the patio and on his phone trying to call Ben. And he was known to enter his house without turning on the lights. A friend's house was different, but his initial vibe was that Sawyer was telling him the truth.

"So, you know where Ben is?" she asked.

"No. I thought he'd be here when I arrived this afternoon, but I haven't seen him."

"And you let yourself in?" she asked, a smile tugging at the corner of her mouth.

"I thought if I slept outside I might wake up next to a gator."

Sawyer narrowed her eyes. "You're sort of a smart aleck."

"More than sort of, but somehow I get the feeling that doesn't offend you."

The smile broke free. "No."

Jackson exhaled any remaining tension from his body. "So you have any idea where Ben might be? I haven't been able to get a hold of him."

"No. He's usually around at night, so I figured this would be a good time to swing by. You try his cell or home phone?"

"Cell."

She nodded. "He forgets to turn the thing on half the time. And he kind of gets caught up in his work."

"Yeah, I've noticed. I just didn't think he'd get so caught up in something he'd forget I was coming."

She shrugged. "Wouldn't be the first time, I'm sure."

"So what kind of work we talking? Work work, or a hobby?"

"A little of both, usually," Sawyer answered. "He's always researching historical fact and fiction. Some of it's for school, a lot of it used to be for his book. But I think most of it is to satisfy his inner craving for knowledge."

"Any idea what craving he's after lately?"

She held up the envelope she'd taken from her pocket. "Might be related to these."

"Your photos?"

Sawyer nodded. "They're of the *Barracuda*."

"That a code name for an ex?"

"The *Barracuda* is a shipwreck off Sugarloaf Key." She opened the envelope and withdrew the pictures, handing them to Jackson. "She was sunk in 1715 when a hurricane hit the Keys."

Jackson thumbed through the photos, showing large, coral-covered timbers that vaguely resembled the skeleton of an eighteenth-century ship. Taken from underwater, the photos were high-quality, full of vivid colors as schools of brightly-colored fish swam in and out of the wreck.

"You take these?" Jackson asked.

"Um-hmm. I'm a part-time diver, in my spare time."

"So what was the *Barracuda*?"

"She was the ship of legendary pirate James Brackett."

Jackson looked up, wondering if he'd discovered the "puzzle" about which Ben had wanted to pick his brain. "You're telling me Ben's a treasure hunter?"

Sawyer shrugged. "I don't know. He's talked about the *Barracuda* several times, and when he found out I'd dived it, he asked if I had any pictures."

"So are you a treasure hunter?"

"No. Just curious. And the coral was really beautiful down there. Water's some of the clearest in the Keys. And that's saying something."

Jackson handed backed the photos. "Great. I come to visit, and he's using his vacation to chase a three-hundred-year-old treasure."

"I doubt it," Sawyer said. "I don't know what he was like when you knew him, but Ben is less a chaser and more a researcher. If he's going treasure hunting, it would only be after a long, introspective process."

"Yeah, that's true."

"I should get going," she said, dropping the photos on the desk. "When you see Ben, please let him know I was here."

"I will."

She searched for a pen for a moment, then jotted something down. She handed him a sticky note. "My cell, in case you need anything."

Jackson regarded her with a wary look, but her casual demeanor and soft smile diffused it. He took the note. "Thanks."

Jackson wasn't sure about it, but he thought Southern dignity dictated he walk Sawyer to the door. So he did, said good night, and watched her get into a maroon Jeep. A real Jeep, with a roll bar and a soft top that was down. Sawyer gave a wave, threw the Jeep into reverse, and barely missed the gate as she backed out of the driveway.

Jackson closed the door and sighed. The obvious question was whether Ben had wanted Jackson's help finding Brackett's treasure or if his interest in the *Barracuda* was unrelated. Maybe the answer lay in all the notes in the study, but Jackson didn't have the inclination to dive into that tonight. Or maybe ever. He'd spent several weeks back in February chasing treasure. It had been a paying gig—a well-paying gig, in fact—but had ended with no treasure and with him having to go all *Rambo* to save the lives of several members of his party. He wasn't particularly in the mood for another treasure hunt.

He retrieved his luggage from the car and claimed the front bedroom as his own. Then he searched the freezer, found some chocolate ice cream, and settled down in front of Ben's modest TV to channel surf. Ben's couch was comfortable, and Jackson watched the end of one John Wayne black-and-white Western and the first half of a second before the long day of travel caught up with him. He fell asleep, waking for the final shootout. The house was still empty and dark, and when the credits rolled, he headed for the front bedroom.

As he lay in the queen bed and tried to fall asleep for the second time, the day replayed itself in his mind—his flight, the drive across the Overseas Highway, Ben's absence, Sawyer. His detective's mind told him there was more to her showing up at Ben's place to drop off photos. His rather effectual and instinctive gut told him there wasn't. Expecting he would dream about a lady pirate kidnapping his best friend and taking him to a coral palace beneath the ocean, Jackson gave up on figuring her out and drifted off to sleep.

The night went too fast, and Jackson awoke with a start. He sat up slowly, squinting in the darkness. He glanced over at the alarm clock by his bed, an alarm he'd been quite careful not to set. Its red numbers glared 1:11. Jackson's sleep-deprived mind grasped that it was not morning. So what had woken him?

Something thunked. It was muffled and distant. But inside the house.

Was Sawyer back? Did Ben have as many photo-delivering girl friends as Jackson used to have casual girlfriends? Had Ben returned late and was now raiding the fridge for a midnight snack? Or was it someone else? Jackson decided to proceed with caution.

He slipped out of bed and crept across the floor, hoping it wouldn't creak. It only disappointed him once. Jackson inched open his door and listened. At first he heard nothing, but then another thunk sounded. More of a thud.

Jackson stuck his head out the door. The hall and living room were dark. No glow from any lights. Jackson padded to the end of the stubby hallway leading to the living room. He stopped, listened. Now all was quiet.

This was where all the protagonists in suspense movies got into trouble. They investigated and explored instead of going back to bed. Question was, was this the scene where a silhouette with weapon in hand emerged from the shadows or the scene where a raccoon was found eating the garbage?

Go back to bed, Douglas.

He disobeyed and took a step into the living room. The second step on the hardwood floor creaked, and Jackson froze. Nothing.

One foot, then another, then another.

As Jackson sidestepped the couch, the floor groaned as if he had pried a rusty nail from it. He froze again. From the back of the house came a quick series of thuds and thunks and then something akin to a crash. Like drawers being slammed shut.

Jackson retreated to the corner of the room and flailed at the light switch. A pair of ceiling light fixtures blipped on, and he squinted at the onslaught. Only for a second. Then he advanced through the living room, toward the study. Remembering where Sawyer had found a switch earlier, he swiped at the wall. This time, instead of illuminating a good-looking Southern woman, the study lights revealed a slightly ajar French door. Jackson studied it for a moment, trying to remember if he had closed it tightly after slipping back in that evening.

He shut off the light, then reached back into the living room for another switch to do the same with those lights. The house was dark again, enabling Jackson to see out through the windows. He saw nothing. He was too late. If the groaning floor hadn't spooked the intruder, the living room lights had.

They had also ruined any chance Jackson had of spotting the intruder making their getaway outside.

Assuming, of course, there had been an intruder, and Jackson's ears weren't playing tricks on him.

He felt his way around the desk and eased through the dual French doors, onto the patio. He listened for almost a minute, not hearing anything. No engine of a getaway vehicle. No lapping water from a swimmer or rowboat slinking off in the canal. Nothing.

Jackson re-entered the study, closed the door behind him, locked it, and switched the light back on. It was hard to tell if anything had been tampered with in the room, simply because it had been so messy to begin with. The papers on the desk may have been rearranged, but Jackson hadn't paid enough attention to them earlier, and he couldn't spot anything out of order.

Had he imagined a second intruder? The noises had been real, but in the middle of the night, had he confused routine noises for something more sinister? Was the open door his fault from earlier? He'd eased it shut, thinking something amiss as he'd entered the study. Had it not latched? Could that be all this was?

Sighing, Jackson switched off all the lights and made sure the doors off the living room and the front door were locked. If Ben came home late without a key, tough. Then Jackson returned to bed and waited for his nerves to calm so he could get some much-needed sleep.

Chapter Four

POUNDING WOKE JACKSON with a start again. This time, sunlight was streaming in through the blinds, and he blinked it away. The clock told him it was just after eight. Factoring in his middle of the night awakening, he'd slept for roughly eight hours. So why did he feel as if he'd been run over by a truck?

He pulled on yesterday's jeans and trudged out into the living room as the pounding ensued. If he had to guess, it was someone assaulting the front door, and he wondered why they hadn't tried the doorbell. Maybe they had, and he'd been too deeply asleep to hear it. Or maybe the bell didn't work, which would explain why he hadn't heard Sawyer the night before. Either way, whoever was here was persistent.

Jackson brushed his hand through his hair and yawned, then reached for the doorknob. He twisted it open just as a fresh round of pounding resumed.

"Oh. Hi there."

It came out, "Hah thar."

"Morning," Jackson said, squinting against the sun. He was looking at a large, rotund, red-jowled man dressed all in black. Pants, shirt, tie, cap. Everything but the badge and medals.

"I'm Sheriff Hawkins," the man said. Shay-riff Howkans. His accent made Sawyer sound like a Yooper. "Is Mr. O'Reilly here?" he asked.

Jackson frowned, realizing he wasn't entirely sure that Ben hadn't come home during the night. "Um, no, I don't think so."

"No, or you don't think so?"

"I just woke up, Off—uh, Sheriff. But he wasn't here last night."

Hawkins nodded. "Mind if I ask who you are?"

"Jackson Douglas. I'm a friend of Ben's, visiting from California."

The sheriff nodded again. "Do you mind if I come in and verify Mr. O'Reilly isn't here?"

Jackson wondered for a moment if his consent could somehow violate Ben's constitutional rights. It was too early to worry about it, and Sheriff Hawkins didn't look like the kind of guy he wanted to tussle with.

"Yeah, sure," he said, stepping back.

Hawkins nodded and removed his cap to reveal a bald head with only a few fringes of brown above either ear. He sighed as he felt the air conditioning. "Gonna be a hot one out there today," he said.

"Mind if I ask what this is about?" Jackson asked.

"Mr. O'Reilly chartered a boat from Cayo Hueso Charters yesterday," Hawkins answered. "He never brought it back."

"You think he stole a boat?"

Hawkins licked his lips and reached for a handkerchief from his pocket. He used it to dab the shine off his forehead. "A couple of fishermen spotted the boat out near the Reef. It'd capsized. The Coast Guard already searched the area but didn't find nobody."

"So Ben's missing at sea?"

"That's what we're trying to figure out. All we know is he chartered the boat. First thing first, before we start to panic, we wanted to make sure Mr. O'Reilly ain't asleep in his bed."

"Back corner," Jackson said. "Like I said, he wasn't here when I went to bed last night."

Hawkins nodded and ambled across the living room. Jackson sat down on the arm of a chair. Ben had chartered a boat, capsized it, and was missing? If he wasn't bobbing in the transparent Caribbean waters, where was he? And did the break-in the night before—if that's what it had been—have anything to do with it?

The sheriff's boots clacked on the wood floor as he exited the master bedroom. He peeked into the study, then the kitchen and dining room before rejoining Jackson. "He's not here."

"What's next?" Jackson asked.

"The Coast Guard's still searching the grid. They're also righting the boat and towing it back to shore, and we'll take a look at it then." He scratched his head. "You say you're visiting from out of town?"

"L.A."

Hawkins nodded. "Any particular reason?"

"Just a vacation, catching up with an old friend."

The sheriff scratched his head. "You, uh, you mind coming down to the station to answer a few more questions?"

Jackson met Hawkins' dark brown eyes. "Am I missing something, Sheriff?"

"Just covering all my bases. O'Reilly's missing, you're here in his place. I'd rather ask the questions now than wish I had later on."

Jackson nodded.

Hawkins gestured with his thumb. "Station's just on the other side of the golf course. If you don't mind."

"No, if you want to give me a few minutes to get dressed."

"Take your time. Off of College Road. First right after the golf course, then your first left."

"I'll be there shortly."

Hawkins nodded and showed himself out. Jackson frowned at his departure for a moment, then afforded himself a shower, shave, and change of clothes. Less than thirty minutes later, he left Ben's house hungry and confused. And for the first time, legitimately worried.

Sheriff Hawkins was right about one thing: it was going to be hot. At least there was a breeze, stirring the otherwise torpid air. The sky above was blue but a little hazy, and Jackson hoped the Monroe County Sheriff's Department was air-conditioned.

It was, and Sheriff Hawkins promptly greeted Jackson in the lobby and showed him back to his office. As he closed the door, he offered him a cup of coffee. Because he was still a little tired and feeling a little lethargic, Jackson accepted.

"Cream, sugar?"

"Black, thanks."

Hawkins handed him a steaming mug that resembled an oil spill. "Appreciate you coming down here."

Jackson shrugged. "Nothing else to do. Any word from the Coast Guard?"

"Nope."

"What can I do to help, Sheriff?"

"Tell me what you know. Anything, whether you think it's relevant or not."

Jackson briefly explained his relationship with Ben, his decision to visit the Keys, and the events that had transpired since he arrived—namely, Ben not being home. He didn't mention Sawyer, not seeing how it could be relevant. For that matter, he didn't see how much of anything could be relevant if Ben's boat had capsized. But he couldn't blame the sheriff for being thorough.

"Anything else you can tell me?"

"It may not be worth mentioning, but I thought somebody was in the house last night."

Hawkins' brow creased as he leaned forward. "In the house. You mean an intruder?"

Jackson tested the coffee, which had been too hot to drink previously. Oil spill was being kind.

"I don't know what it was," Jackson said. "I heard a noise, came out of the bedroom to check it out, heard more noises. But I never saw anybody or any evidence that anyone had been there. For all I know, it was jetlag and an unfamiliar environment playing tricks with me." He shrugged. "Besides, if this was a boating accident, I don't see how there's a connection. Unless you have reason to suspect foul play."

Hawkins shook his head. "No." He leaned back, his chair creaking. "But I don't have much of anything now. The dang Coast Guard must be towing that boat back by canoe."

"You mind if I ask you a question?"

Hawkins shook his head again.

"Why'd the sheriff come out to Ben's place? Why not send a patrol car?"

Hawkins sat back in his chair. It creaked again. "I know O'Reilly. Consider him something of a friend."

Jackson nodded when he realized that was all Hawkins had to say. He thought about asking a follow-up about the depth and nature of the friendship, but before he could, a knock rattled the glass on Hawkins' door.

"Come in," he called.

The door swung inward, and Sawyer entered. Her hair was pulled into a stub of a ponytail. Sunglasses hung over the V-neck of a crimson shirt with "Bama" scrawled on the front in white. No purse. Just a key on a lanyard that was wrapped around her wrist.

"Miss Collins," the sheriff said, standing at considerable displeasure. Jackson followed suit. This was the South.

"Sheriff." She turned with a pleasant smile. "Hello, Jackson."

"Sawyer."

"All y'all know each other?" Hawkins asked.

"We met last night," she said.

"Uh-huh. Have a seat." They all sat down. "What can I do for you, Miss Collins?"

"I heard Ben O'Reilly's boat was found capsized off the Reef."

"Where'd you hear that?"

"A friend at the marina."

Hawkins nodded, rolling his tongue inside his cheek. Jackson took a drink of "coffee."

Sawyer leaned against the wall. "What do you know?"

"Afraid not much more than you. Fishing boat found his charter capsized this morning. Coast Guard's searching the area but they ain't found nothing yet."

"What kind of boat?"

"Power boat. Sixteen-footer."

"Do you think he was diving?"

"Nothing to indicate it."

Sawyer frowned. She turned to Jackson. "Why are you here?"

Hawkins answered for him. "I stopped by O'Reilly's house this morning to see if he happened to be there. Found Mr. Douglas. Says he's visiting from California."

"And you ran him in?" she asked without accusing.

"Just wanted to ask some questions."

"I can vouch for him, Sheriff."

The tongue-rolling continued. "You want to tell me the nature of your relationship?"

"No relationship," Sawyer said before Jackson could open his mouth. "We're both friends of Ben's."

"Uh-huh. Well, since you're here, you got any light to shed on the subject?"

"No. I stopped by last night to drop off some photos and Ben wasn't in. Now I guess we know why. He was out on a boat."

"Yeah. Either of y'all got anything else to offer?"

Jackson looked at Sawyer, waiting to see if she'd speak up. She simply shook her head. "Maybe," Jackson said. "The reef where the boat was found. Where is that?"

"The Great Florida Reef? It's several miles south. Runs the length of the Keys."

"Where in relation to Sugarloaf Key was the boat found?"

"About twenty miles to the southwest. Why?"

"Ben mentioned that he had something he wanted to pick my brain about, and Sawyer said he'd expressed an interest in the wreck of the *Barracuda*, which is off Sugarloaf Key, right?"

Sawyer nodded.

Hawkins grunted.

"You said anything, whether I think it's relevant or not. Is there any chance Ben was out looking for treasure?"

"I suppose it's possible."

"You said you didn't suspect foul play, but if he was after a treasure, would that change your opinion? Someone else looking for it, maybe? Especially if you factor in the break-in last night?"

Sawyer perked up. "Break-in?"

"I heard somebody in the house last night."

"You thought you heard somebody," Hawkins said.

"Yeah. I looked around but didn't see anybody. Truth is, I don't know what I heard."

Hawkins sat forward. "Look, I'm not blowing you off. It warrants an open mind. But the Keys are full of treasure legends and supposed shipwrecks full of gold. Most of 'em are nothing but myths. If O'Reilly's chasing pirate gold, the only thing he'd have to worry about other than ancient curses would be some loner with a metal detector. Besides, his boat wasn't found anywhere near Sugarloaf Key."

Jackson shrugged.

"Anything else?" Hawkins asked. "Else I'm going to call the Coast Guard and see what's holding them up."

Jackson shook his head, and he and Sawyer stood to leave.

"Thanks for the coffee," Jackson said, setting down the mug by the pot.

"You in town for a while?"

"Kind of open-ended."

Hawkins nodded. "Do me a favor. You leave town, let me know. You're not under any suspicion, and it's a request, not an order. I just like to know what's going on. And I'll let you know as we learn anything more."

"Sure thing, Sheriff. Thanks."

He and Sawyer left the office, pausing in the hallway.

"Somebody broke into Ben's house last night?" she asked, her blue eyes wide.

"Technically, I'm not sure they broke," Jackson said. "I may have left the study doors ajar when an earlier intruder scared me."

Sawyer grinned briefly, then the concern returned to her face. "But you think somebody was prowling around?"

"I don't know. It sure sounded like it, but when I looked around, I couldn't find any evidence of any . . ."

"What is it?"

"The sticky notes."

"What sticky notes?"

"There was a pad, like the one you wrote your number on, with a note on top." He closed his eyes. "I think it was gone last night."

"I tore it off to write my number."

Jackson exhaled. "Oh."

"I set it down beside the phone."

Jackson closed his eyes for a moment, picturing the scene the night before after the alleged second intruder. The note may or may not have been there, beside the phone. He hadn't looked that closely.

They resumed walking. "You know what 'The Point' is?" he asked.

"Yeah. It's a restaurant out on Sugarloaf Key. Why?"

"That's what was on the notepad. Ben's handwriting."

Sawyer frowned. "Anything else?"

"Just 'The Point.'"

"Hmm. Maybe he was going to take you for dinner."

"Had he not capsized his boat, you mean?"

"Yeah," she said, looking down. "I didn't even know Ben was a boater."

"He mentioned going deep-sea fishing while I was here."

"Oh, he'd go fishing. But he wouldn't pilot the boat. That's what's odd."

"You said a friend at the marina told you he was missing?"

Sawyer nodded.

"This friend tell you anything else?"

"No. She just knew Ben was a friend. When she found out the Sheriff's Office was involved, she thought I might want to know."

"You on close terms with the sheriff?"

Sawyer stopped. "I dated his son a few times."

"Why'd you dump him?"

"Who said I dumped him?"

Jackson grinned. "Just a guess."

Sawyer dragged the toe of her shoe along the floor. "He had different standards than I did."

"I see."

She looked down at her watch. "I, um . . . I have to go. Work."

"Okay. Thanks for having my back in there."

Sawyer smiled. "You're welcome. But I don't think you have anything to worry about. I know when the sheriff's got a bee in his bonnet. That is, when someone rubs him the wrong way. I don't think you do."

"Still, thanks."

"Anytime." She smiled again. "You'll call me if you hear anything from Ben?"

"I will." He gave her his number, and she entered it into her phone as they exited the building. The air was like a wet washcloth slapping them in the face.

They said goodbye and Jackson walked to his car, watching Sawyer tear out of the lot in her Jeep. He felt a rumble in his stomach and decided to grab some breakfast. But beyond that, he had no clue what to do. He had assumed Ben would have an itinerary planned. Tooling around the Keys, out fishing, maybe bumming to Dry Tortugas like the family from Denny's the night before. Instead, he was left to grab a couple of breakfast sandwiches at Burger King and return to Ben's empty house.

Some vacation.

Chapter Five

JACKSON ATE HIS breakfast while flipping through channels on Ben's satellite, not finding much to watch. With his breakfast gone and his second cup of coffee of the day lukewarm, he realized he needed a plan.

There were three possibilities. One, Ben had been aboard the boat he'd chartered, it had capsized, and he was dead. Two, he'd been aboard, capsized, but was not dead, and would be rescued. Three, he hadn't been aboard the boat, which brought up the question of why he'd chartered it and which also left his current whereabouts a mystery. Then there was the break-in, real or imagined, and legendary pirate treasure that may or may not have resided in a shipwreck off Sugarloaf Key.

If Ben was bobbing in a shipping channel waiting for the Coast Guard to find him, there was little Jackson could do. But he could try to figure out why Ben had chartered the boat in the first place and if it was somehow tied to the treasure, the break-in, or both. He was, after all, a detective. It would involve rifling through his friend's personal stuff, but what were friends for?

Jackson started in the master bedroom and bathroom. A clothes hamper in the master bath—which also housed the washer and dryer—was empty but for a single set of clothes. The washer and dryer were both empty. All of the drawers and the hangers in the closet were full. The medicine cabinet looked fully stocked. It didn't appear that Ben had packed up and left, but that made sense. Most guys—other than Thurston Howell III maybe—didn't take a suitcase out on a powerboat. Still, like the sheriff, Jackson was covering bases.

Ben's alarm was set for five-thirty, but Jackson didn't know if that was typical or not. Ben taught history at a small, private college whose semester had ended Friday. So had he slept in Saturday and Sunday and not bothered to adjust his alarm, or had he been up early on the weekend too, say to charter a boat?

There was nothing else in the room that grabbed Jackson's attention, so he moved on to the rest of the house. There were no notes by the phone in the kitchen and no messages on the answering machine. The refrigerator was adequately stocked. The milk still smelled good. Jackson decided to leave rifling through the garbage as a last resort.

He checked the study next, starting by sampling some of the titles in Ben's vast collection of books. There was a little of everything—biographies, novels, reference volumes, a lot of historical and geographical works. All that was missing was a card catalog, and that may have only been because Jackson hadn't looked everywhere yet.

Next he studied the maps on the wall. There were several world maps from different eras. Another map, split into four sections, showed the Caribbean at different points in history, color-coordinated according to the European nation that owned the various islands and territories at each time. Jackson checked the segment with the date closest to the sinking of the *Barracuda*. In 1713—two years before Sawyer claimed the ship had sunk—Florida, Cuba, and most of Mexico had all belonged to the Spanish. Not a surprise.

In a corner beneath several maps was a small bin containing at least a dozen rolled up documents. Jackson removed and unrolled one of them, a nautical chart showing depths and tides for the Lower Keys. Jackson rolled up and re-sheathed the chart. With a sigh, he checked the rest of the maps and charts in the bin. More of the same, many of the Keys or the Caribbean, but some from distant locations, like the Horn of Africa. Maybe Ben was after modern-day pirate loot too. Or just had a thing for water depths.

With reluctance, Jackson moved to the desk. He didn't know where to start, and his eyes were drawn to the phone. As Sawyer had claimed, the note with "The Point" scrawled on it was stuck to a rare open patch of desk beside it. So it hadn't been taken by the alleged intruder.

Jackson lifted a couple of books off the desk. Both were general histories of piracy in the Caribbean. He thumbed through them but saw nothing of interest. No bookmarks, slips of paper, or pens stuck in them to indicate where Ben had been reading, and he didn't spot any marks on the pages. Then again, a good librarian didn't scribble in his books.

Under the books were several loose sheets of paper and a few more stapled together. They were computer printouts that had been marked up with notes from Ben. Jackson scanned a few of them. One was a blogger's take on geographical changes in the Keys over the centuries. Another online article was similar, only with a stronger environmental lean. The loose sheets appeared to be more of the same, all with Ben's notes agreeing with or questioning certain points.

"What are you looking for?" Jackson muttered.

He set the papers down and lifted a pair of spiral notebooks. The first was full of Ben's notes on pirate history, listing names, dates, ships, places. A few of them stood out to Jackson, but most of it read like an encyclopedia. There didn't seem to be a real direction to any of it, as if Ben was searching for a particular treasure. It was just general notation, a compilation of data, all of it indexed.

Jackson shook his head. Ben had never been a big computer user. He had a computer, had a cell phone. But instead of keeping his research on a thumb drive or in cloud storage, Ben had it all on paper. Knowing Ben's proclivity for privacy, Jackson guessed it was more a fear of being compromised by a hacker than a lack of technical savvy.

The second notebook was like the first, only the data seemed more limited to what had happened in and around the Keys. Still, it was just a repository of data. Jackson wondered if maybe Ben wasn't hunting a treasure as much as he was preparing to write his second book.

Jackson remembered the thuds and thunks, as if someone had been ransacking drawers, and decided to check the contents of the desk. One drawer contained a stack of bills, some paid, some not. No surprise, Ben received paper statements for his various utilities. Another drawer contained a bunch of knickknacks and random keepsakes. Another held standard office supplies. A fourth, reams of paper and empty notebooks.

He checked out another book from the desktop, this one about ship construction over the centuries. Had Ben actually read all three hundred pages? He sorted through a variety of papers that had nothing to do with piracy or Ben being out on a boat or anything relevant. Still, he took mental snapshots of everything in case it turned out to be important later. Sawyer's photos were right where she'd left them, fitting perfectly with an abundance of data that seemed to have no meaning or purpose.

The last item to catch his attention was a large reference book buried under the rest of the clutter on the desk. Jackson moved and stacked the rest into piles so he could open the large book, *Storms of the Caribbean*. Clever title. Unlike the other books, which appeared to be Ben's, this one had a reference number and a stamp identifying it as belonging to the Monroe County Public Library.

Browsing the table of contents, Jackson realized the book was quite new. It covered Hurricanes Ivan, Katrina, and Wilma while also going back to the earliest days of European discovery of the Americas. Jackson turned to the year 1715, long before the United States Weather Bureau started naming tropical storms. Prior to that, hurricanes had been cataloged by when and where they hit, and details were wide-ranging.

According to the book, the equivalent of a Category 3 hurricane had broadsided the Lower Keys in August 1715. It had then moved up the gulf coast of Florida before curving over what was now Orlando and back out into the Atlantic. Its swath had been narrow but powerful, and it had destroyed a few primitive structures in modern-day Key West, knocked down and uprooted some trees, and made some small alterations to the coast in a few places. There was no mention of it sinking any ships or of the *Barracuda*.

Jackson flipped through the book a little more, pausing at the 1935 Labor Day Hurricane that had ravaged the Keys. Closing the book, he was reassured by mostly blue skies and by the fact that May was not quite hurricane season. He dreaded the thought of the entire city of Key West trying to evacuate via a two-lane highway that spanned water as much as land.

Jackson got up and paced, opting to step outside and sample the late-morning air. He was sorry. It was hot and heavy, with a breeze off the canal that felt like a steam bath. L.A. could be hot, but this was intense. Languid. The blue sky was tinged with thick haze. Either a storm was brewing or another oil well was on fire in the Gulf.

Jackson returned to the climate control and fired up Ben's computer. It was not password protected, and Jackson quickly found out why. There was nothing on it. Standard Windows operating system, standard software, a few games, a combination dictionary/thesaurus, and a few family photos. No folders full of pirate research. No browser history to speak of. Jackson thought for a moment about calling his tech friend Mouse to see if he could hack Ben's e-mail but opted against it. Not yet. Not unless he had more proof that something nefarious had happened.

To that end, Jackson decided to give Sheriff Hawkins a call. He wasn't in, and Jackson left him a message. He sighed. His brain and his gut both told him Ben had indeed capsized the chartered boat, and that every second that went by without word from the Coast Guard via Sheriff Hawkins increased the chance that Ben had come to an unfortunate end at sea. For some reason, Jackson felt distant to the potential loss. Maybe because it was still potential, albeit growing more and more likely. Maybe because he and Ben, while friends, hadn't seen each other in over a decade. Or maybe because he was just growing numb to pain.

*   *   *

5:16 p.m.

JACKSON SPENT the day lounging in the air-conditioned living room, waiting for Ben to return. He didn't. Jackson passed the time by reading Ben's book, *Reconstructing Civility*. Well written and informative, it was not terribly exciting. At least the first half of it. Nor did it trigger some offhanded insight into Ben's psyche that explained all the research in his study or why he had purportedly taken a boat out to sea the day Jackson was due to arrive.

Restless and hungry, Jackson set out to find some food. First, he stopped at the Sheriff's Department. The heat and humidity had not subsided, nor been broken by thunderstorms. Wasn't it supposed to thunderstorm every afternoon in Florida? Just walking from the parking lot to the climate-controlled lobby nearly caused Jackson to break into a sweat.

Hawkins was in his office and made a few minutes for Jackson. Fortunately, he didn't offer him any coffee.

"Afraid there ain't much to tell you," Hawkins said.

"You find anything on the boat he chartered?"

"Not sure yet. We sent a sample to the lab. Might be blood."

"Ben's blood?" Jackson asked, knowing Hawkins had no way of knowing.

"Could be. Could be a fish. Boat was upturned in the water for quite a while, so it compromised the scene. Washed away pretty much anything else we might have found."

"Yeah."

"I'll keep you posted."

"For what it's worth, I looked around Ben's place."

Hawkins raised an eyebrow.

"I thought maybe he'd have a journal or notes on research that would explain what he was up to. He didn't."

The sheriff huffed dismissively. Jackson didn't bother telling him he was something of an accomplished private investigator. It didn't matter.

"You happen to know his next of kin?" Hawkins asked.

"Has it come to that?"

"I figure his momma might want to know he's missing."

"He doesn't have a momma. Died when he was a kid."

"I, uh, didn't know."

"Dad too."

"Yeah, I'd heard that. Heart attack, wasn't it?"

Jackson nodded.

"Any brothers and sisters?"

"No, he was an only child."

"Cousins, grandparents?"

Jackson shook his head again. "I don't know. I never knew any other family members."

"All right. Well, we can find out. Thought I'd save myself the trouble."

"Sorry."

Hawkins again promised to keep Jackson posted, and he returned the promise, should he find something. Hawkins huffed dismissively again. Jackson didn't take offense.

Leaving the Sheriff's Department, Jackson set out in search of food. He again didn't feel like the tourists and crowds and senior citizens looking for tacky souvenirs that he would find on the west side of the island. Nor did he feel like eating at some kitschy, themed restaurant with ship planks for tables or fishing nets as décor. He found a Five Guys and ate his second burger in as many nights. When he was done, boredom barely won out over discomfort, and he wandered around a strip mall and flea market, looking in shops and stores selling items he had no intent to buy. The temperature and humidity had each dropped a few degrees, but it was still borderline unbearable, and he returned home shortly before seven.

Ben still wasn't there.

Jackson spent the last five hours as a thirty-year-old watching TV, then went to bed.

Chapter Six

JACKSON LAY IN bed, staring at the ceiling. Today marked the second anniversary of the worst day of his life. There wasn't a close second. There wasn't even a second. Nothing compared. Or ever could.

The day had been engraved on his mental calendar, drawing inexorably closer like midnight for a man on death row. That was part of the reason Jackson had come to visit Ben when he had, hoping that maybe, just maybe, he could escape the haunting memories and the pain.

He couldn't.

His phone vibrated on the nightstand, giving him a reason to move. He fumbled the phone open and sat up in bed. "Yeah?"

"Mr. Douglas? Sheriff Hawkins."

A surge of hope awakened Jackson. He swung his legs off the bed. Half the covers went with them.

"What's up?" he asked.

"How soon can you get down here?"

"Why, you find Ben?"

"No, but we found something."

"I'll be there in minutes."

"Thanks. I'll put on coffee."

Jackson almost told him not to bother. Instead, he hurried into some clothes and stopped in the bathroom to brush his teeth and wipe gunk from the corners of his eyes. With a Dodgers cap covering a mess of bedhead, he grabbed his keys and wallet and headed for the car.

The morning air was thick as a sponge, and the blue sky was covered in a thin sheen of gray. Jackson missed his beach with seventy-degree days and unfiltered sunshine.

He drove toward the Sheriff's Department for the second morning in a row, wondering what Hawkins had found. Evidence of Ben's survival? Evidence of his death? Fortunately, it was a short drive, and he didn't have much time to ponder.

Jackson parked next to a familiar maroon Jeep and hurried inside. Immediately, he realized something was up. The secretary at the front desk was juggling phone calls while an officer hovered over the desk on a separate line. Several other uniformed officers and people in street clothes scurried around, in and out of offices, all on cell phones, tapping away at mobile devices, or carrying papers and folders. Only the lobby was void of activity or people, except for a tall Southern woman in denim shorts and a loose, peach-colored blouse.

Sawyer stood when she saw Jackson.

"What are you doing here?" he asked.

"I was going to ask you the same thing."

"I beat again."

Just a fraction of a smile turned up the corner of her mouth. "So you did." She stuck her hands into her pockets. "Sheriff Hawkins called me down."

"Me too. He say why?"

She shook her head. "Just that they found something."

He frowned. What had they found? And why had Hawkins called Sawyer? Because she had shown up yesterday morning and thus was involved? Or did the fact that she was Hawkins' former potential daughter-in-law give her insider privilege?

Hawkins appeared at the end of the hallway. He motioned with his hand for Jackson and Sawyer to follow him. He led them back to his office, closed the door, and offered them chairs.

"Coffee?"

"No thanks," Sawyer said. Jackson just shook his head.

"I'll get to it," Hawkins said. "A jogger found a body washed up on Smathers Beach this morning."

"Ben?" Sawyer asked around a lump in her throat.

"No." Hawkins thumped a file onto his desk, opened it, and pulled out a photo. "Either of y'all recognize him?"

They leaned forward to study a pale man, maybe thirty, with dark, wavy black hair. Very dead.

"No," Jackson said. Sawyer echoed him.

"Name's Ted Ryker, a petty criminal from New Orleans."

"New Orleans?" Sawyer asked.

"That mean something to y'all?"

"No, not to me," Sawyer said.

"Long ways to float," Jackson said. "You think he's tied to Ben?"

"Not sure what it's like for all y'all out in Cal-ee-forn-ee-ah, but we don't get a lot of capsized boats or bodies washing ashore around here. Two in forty-eight hours, that's mighty coincidental. When that body's been slashed with a knife, it really gets our attention."

"Slashed?" Sawyer asked.

"Had a pretty nasty gash from just under his neck down across the chest."

"Is that what killed him?"

"Not directly," Hawkins said. "Coroner says he drowned, but the cut and a pretty good knot on his head could have contributed to it. Lucky the sharks didn't get him."

"Not too lucky," Sawyer said.

"You identify the weapon?" Jackson asked.

"Not in particular, but looks to be a hunting knife or maybe a filleting knife. Pretty common on fishing vessels."

"Don't suppose you found any bloody knives on the boat?"

Hawkins shook his head. Then he lifted a sheet of paper from the folder. "Then there's this. Blood they found on the boat was not a match to O'Reilly."

"That's great," Sawyer said.

"Yeah. Lab's still testing it for a match, but they confirmed it was AB negative. Rarest blood type in the U.S. Y'all wanna guess Ryker's blood type?"

"AB negative," Jackson said.

"Less than one percent of the population has AB negative. Smart money says Ryker was on O'Reilly's boat." He looked from Jackson to Sawyer and back. "Either of y'all have a theory on what happened out there?"

"No," Jackson said while Sawyer slowly shook her head.

Hawkins sighed as he dropped the sheet of paper. "Yeah, me neither."

"Are you investigating this as a homicide?"

"Not yet."

"Why not?" Sawyer asked.

"Because we don't have any evidence it's a homicide. We're investigating what happened."

"Fair enough," Jackson said.

"I'll let y'all know if we find anything more," Hawkins said, clearly dismissing them. They thanked him and exited his office. Outside the building, they stopped. Sawyer lowered sunglasses from her hair. Jackson squinted.

"What do you make of that?" she asked.

"I don't know, but I don't like it. Ben charters a boat, now it's capsized, he's gone, and a guy who was likely killed on it washes ashore."

"Ben wouldn't kill anybody."

"Ben wouldn't murder anybody. He might kill somebody in self-defense though."

"Maybe, but I still don't know. And if it was self-defense, where is he?"

Jackson shrugged as they crossed the parking lot to their cars. "Maybe it wasn't very good self-defense."

"And his body just hasn't washed ashore?"

"It's a possibility."

"And the Coast Guard hasn't found it?"

"It's possible."

"Yeah," she said with no conviction.

They stopped at her Jeep.

"What are you going to do?" she asked.

He shrugged.

"You going to hang around?"

"I don't know."

"If you do, and if you need somebody to talk to . . ."

"Yeah, thanks."

She smiled sweetly, in a way only a Southern woman could.

"Hey, can I ask you something?" Jackson said.

"Of course."

"The other day, why'd you vouch for me with Sheriff Hawkins?"

She was wearing flip-flops, and she tipped one foot and thus one flip-flop on end, tapping it up and down on the pavement. "The sheriff tends to have something of a suspicious mind at times. I didn't want him barking up the wrong tree."

"How'd you know I was the wrong tree? We barely know each other."

Sawyer shrugged. "I didn't know. But my sense was you're on the level."

"Fair enough," Jackson said.

They said goodbye, and Jackson sat in his rented car, trying to make sense of everything. He failed. On the verge of passing out, he started the car to get some ventilation going. Then he headed back for the highway and turned east, toward Ben's house.

He again picked up a couple of breakfast sandwiches at Burger King and thought briefly that he should keep going, back to Miami, back to the airport, back to California. Instead, he turned off on Raccoon Key and returned to Ben's empty carport.

Ben's car. Sheriff Hawkins hadn't said anything about it, but it was presumably parked by the boat charter place. Could it contain any clues? Not likely, and Hawkins' people would have thought of that too. On TV, the private investigators always managed to deduce the next clue while the cops stood around with their mouths open. It wasn't that way in the real world.

Jackson whipped up some lemonade from concentrate and took a glass out onto the back porch with the last half of his second sandwich. He sat in the shade and read some more of Ben's Civil War book, interspersed with moments of staring out at the canal and trying to tie Ben's fascination with pirates and treasure and hurricanes and tidal charts to a capsized boat and the dead man from New Orleans. His imagination dreamt up some wild theories, but none were probable or fit with what he knew of Ben.

By late morning he was not only bored but also going stir crazy. Plus the memories were starting to come back. So he got in his car and drove, deciding to explore Key West. On his previous forays onto the island, he'd turned north, following the Overseas Highway. This time he went south on the A1A. He drove past hotels and private homes, then toward the open ocean. Technically, the Straits of Florida. Beautiful, brilliant, greenish blue water as far as the eye could see. Somewhere out there was the Reef. And Ben?

The road curved southwest and then west, following the contour of the island. On the right, several hotels and restaurants gave way to swampland, beyond which was Key West International Airport. Jackson was again tempted to fly home. Or to Jamaica.

He drove past Smathers Beach, where Ted Ryker's body had washed ashore. A short while later, the four-lane highway merged down to two lanes and promptly turned inland. After passing several hotels, Jackson found himself in a compact residential neighborhood that might as well have been in central Florida instead of the Keys. He made a couple of turns, trying to extricate himself, trying to find a better highway or a landmark. He crossed Duval Street. He'd heard of it, knew it was home to many famous eateries and drinking holes. He bypassed it and found himself at the red, yellow, and black concrete buoy marking the southernmost point in the United States.

Jackson gawked out his window and continued driving, ultimately ending at Fort Zachary Taylor Historic State Park, a fifty-four-acre park that covered the southwestern corner of the island. Because he was sick of sitting, and because he'd seen a sign for a café on the park grounds, he found a place to park and got out of the car. More muggy air slapped him in the face.

After downing a pulled pork sandwich and some chips, Jackson spent an hour wandering around the fort named for America's twelfth president and learning of its role in both the Civil War and the Spanish-American War. He couldn't help thinking about how much his dad, a Captain in the U.S. Navy, would appreciate the history of the fort, and how much Jackson would enjoy experiencing it with him.

If he weren't dead.

Suddenly, the fort was another reminder of why he hated this day. Two years ago, on his twenty-ninth birthday, Jackson's parents and brother had been killed in a restaurant explosion. In an instant, his life had been shattered, the things he held most dear ripped away from him.

Jackson wandered aimlessly along the park's trails, taking some respite from the heat of the day in the shade of a copse of Australian pine trees. The trails led him to a rock jetty at the very tip of the island. He walked out on it and sat down. He scanned a few clouds on the horizon, feeling like Jonah and hoping one of them would provide him relief. He watched a cruise ship sailing in toward port, passing through a channel not far from the fort. He looked back at the beach at the park's southern border, at the couples and families enjoying the midday sun.

It killed him, sometimes, watching people have fun, because he knew he was never going to have what they seemed to—an unbridled sense of happiness. Not that he was craving some hedonistic pursuit of pleasure or never had any fun of his own. But it was always shackled by the constant ache, the gaping wound that refused to clot and scab over until it was just a scar.

Time did not heal all wounds—at least not two years' worth of time.

Is this it? Jackson asked in silent prayer. *Is this as far as I go?*

The Great Physician wasn't providing much healing, frankly. And Jackson felt like his supply of faith was running low.

He got up. Mulling and moping weren't good for much. Besides, it was so blasted hot he could hardly stand it.

He trudged back through the trees to the same café where he'd had lunch. He bought an ice cream treat that turned to soup before he could eat half of it, and he ended up throwing the rest in a trash can that smelled like expired food that had been sitting in the heat for too long. Returning to his car, he let out the mother of all sighs.

Happy birthday, Jack.

Chapter Seven

3:07 p.m.

JACKSON'S PHONE RANG as he crossed onto Stock Island. It was Hawkins.

"Yeah?" Jackson said as he slapped the phone to his ear.

"Douglas? Where you at?"

"On the road. Two minutes from the office," he said as he passed the turn to the Sheriff's Department. The view out the left side of the car was filled by a golf course.

"Stop on in."

"You find Ben?"

"No. We got some things to discuss."

"Be right there."

Jackson closed his phone, wondering what there could be to discuss. Had Hawkins found Ben's next of kin? Had he learned something about Ted Ryker? Or would the discussion pertain to what Jackson feared?

Hawkins was waiting for Jackson in his office. So was a deputy and a United States Coast Guard officer in a dark blue uniform, complete with shiny black boots and a blue baseball-style cap emblazoned with "U.S. Coast Guard" in gold lettering. Sawyer was absent. Hawkins introduced Jackson to Deputy Peterson and Lieutenant Riggle. Peterson sat in a chair at the end of Hawkins' desk. Riggle leaned on the desk that held the coffee pot. Hawkins nodded at a chair for Jackson, then sat down himself.

"The Coast Guard is calling off the search for O'Reilly effective at sundown," Hawkins announced.

"Already?" Jackson asked, looking between the sheriff and Lieutenant Riggle.

"It will have been thirty-six hours since the boat was found," Riggle said in a voice without any accent. "Admittedly, we've got a large search grid, but even factoring in the unknown time the boat capsized and potential currents and drifting, the calm seas . . . we're confident that if Mr. O'Reilly were adrift, we would have found him. And if not . . ."

"He wouldn't survive any longer," Jackson said.

Riggle confirmed with a nod.

Jackson sighed. "So is that the official ruling? He's dead?"

"We're not ready to make it official," Riggle said, glancing at Hawkins.

"He could've been picked up by another boat, swum to shore."

"Or sunk."

"Or sunk," Hawkins said.

"And we've still got a few hours of daylight left," Riggle said. "It's possible our search efforts will turn up something in that time. But if not . . ."

"If not, I think it's time we notify O'Reilly's next of kin," Hawkins said.

"You find one?"

"An uncle in Atlanta. Malcolm Bradshaw."

"Doesn't ring a bell."

"Looks like it was his mom's brother-in-law. Her sister, Ben's aunt, died last year."

Jackson exhaled. His wasn't the only family suffering a rash of deaths.

"I'm sorry," Riggle said.

"There nothing else we can do?"

"As Sheriff Hawkins said, he could have been rescued or swam to shore, in which case hopefully he'll make contact soon. But as far as the Coast Guard is concerned, we're confident if he was somewhere to be found, we would have found him by now. Certainly by sundown."

"If you've got any leads as to where he might be on land . . ." Hawkins said.

Jackson shook his head. "I've got nothing."

Hawkins bit down on his tongue for a moment, maybe weighing words.

"What about Ryker?" Jackson asked.

"Like I told you and Miss Collins, he's a petty criminal from New Orleans. A couple B&E's, some low-level fencing. Nothing ever stuck to him."

"What's he doing in Key West?"

"No idea."

"Or on Ben's boat?"

"No idea."

Jackson exhaled again. "Anything else?"

"No. I've contacted NOPD for more on Ryker, see if they can find a tie between him and Ben. Deputy Peterson's been talking to Ben's friends and coworkers, trying to find a connection from that angle. There's nothing so far."

"Anything I can do to help?"

"You still staying at O'Reilly's place?"

"For the time being."

"We might send out a detective to look it over."

Jackson nodded. "Let me know. I can tell him what I've found or I can vacate. Whatever."

"Appreciate it."

Jackson stood, thanked Hawkins and Riggle, and made his way out of the office. He stopped for a moment in the lobby when he saw that it was pouring outside. Florida rainstorms were purported to come out of nowhere, and this one certainly had. Fifteen minutes ago, the sun had been shining brightly. Then again, fifteen minutes ago, before the Coast Guard's decision to call off the search and the sense of finality it brought, Jackson had still held out hope that Ben would be found and life would go on as normal

With a shrug, he trudged out in the deluge. Life going on as normal. He really should know better by now.

*   *   *

7:55 p.m.

SUNSET WAS maybe ten minutes away. The western sky was aglow, thin wisps of cloud catching the reflection of a luminous orange sun that was playing hide-and-seek behind stray cumulous clouds. The ocean similarly blazed with orange and red and pink highlights. Behind Jackson, in the eastern sky, billowing tufts of white were tinged with pink and purple where they caught the sun's departing rays. Occasionally, flashes of lightning caused them to radiate with a peachy, creamsicle-orange color. The air was warm but pleasant, mitigated by a steady but gentle breeze. The night was magical.

And Jackson was miserable.

He'd returned from the Sheriff's Department to Ben's house soaked and had sat on the porch under the overhang watching the rain fall. It had poured steadily for an hour, then off and on for another two hours. Jackson had ordered pizza and mindlessly watched TV until sitting around in a dead man's—presumably—house drove him to leave again. He was the picture of restlessness, not happy anywhere, unsure of where to go or what to do next.

For some reason, feeling almost as if he was on autopilot, he'd driven to Smathers Beach, south of the airport, midway along Key West's southern shore. It was the beach where a jogger had found Ted Ryker's body that morning. Jackson didn't go to find clues or to ponder. He didn't know why he went.

He walked from east to west, trudging through drying sand in his shoes. On some level, his mind appreciated the beauty around him. But Ben's death made him sick. Ben's parents' deaths made him sick. Ben's aunt's death made him sick. Most of all, his parents' and brother's deaths made him sick.

The sun fully emerged from behind the clouds, shining like a laser atop the surface of the water. The sand and palm trees blazed. The crests of the gentle waves lapping at the shore were kissed with color.

Then the sun set and darkness began to settle over the Keys. Jackson turned out to the horizon, the line between sky and water quickly blurring. Somewhere out there Ben's chartered boat had capsized, and Ben had . . .

Jackson turned around. This was pointless. What was he doing in Florida? Ben was gone. He hadn't swum to shore and fallen asleep or been picked up by a fishing vessel with a broken radio. He wouldn't be making contact with Jackson or Hawkins or anyone. He was gone. Jackson had no clue as to what had happened or why, no lead to chase down that the Sheriff's Department hadn't, couldn't, or wouldn't chase. Stalking around beaches and watching Ben's TV weren't accomplishing anything. Time to pack up and head back home. There was nothing here for him.

Problem was, there wasn't anything back home for him either.

*   *   *

Three weeks ago . . .
Wednesday, April 24
8:28 p.m.

JACK BAUER had just infiltrated the Chinese consulate when the doorbell rang.

From where he lay on his couch, Jackson sat up, pausing his DVD player. It took him a few moments to reorient from the dark scenes on his TV to the utter darkness of his living room. By the time he did, the doorbell had sounded again.

He stood with a grimace, made his way around the coffee table, and approached the front door. He couldn't remember his last visitor—they'd sort of died out a few weeks ago. Connie, maybe, bringing more chicken cacciatore? There were worse things, he realized, as he reached for the doorknob.

It was not a worse thing. His visitor was a woman with shoulder-length blond, slightly damp hair, wide blue eyes, and a smile that was a little lopsided but still sweet. She wore a three-quarter-sleeve lavender top and jeans, and looked cold as she stood under the dripping awning over Jackson's front door.

"Sam," Jackson said with a trace of surprise in his voice. He backed up. "Come on in."

Samantha MacRaney stepped through the doorway and out of a drizzle Jackson hadn't realized was falling. "Were you sleeping?" she asked.

"No, TV," he said with a nod at the set.

"With the lights off?"

"Ambiance."

She nodded. He hit the switch on the wall and squinted against the onslaught. "To what do I owe the pleasure?" he asked. "You cut your hair."

Sam looked up at him with a smile. "I did."

"I like it."

"Really?"

"I liked it the old way too, but yeah. It looks good."

"Even better when not rained on."

He shrugged, and they looked at each other for a moment. "What brings you by?" he asked.

Sam exhaled. "I wanted to talk. I haven't seen you in a while, haven't been able to get a hold of you . . ."

"Yeah, I've been . . . recuperating."

Recuperating meaning playing Xbox and watching whole seasons of *24* on DVD. Season 3 had actually been viewed in its entirety in a twenty-four-hour period, for authenticity's sake. Events in real time indeed.

"How are you feeling?" Sam asked.

Jackson motioned her to the couch, and they sat down. "Okay," he said. "Nothing hurts terribly anymore. It's just sore." He winced as he sat back to prove it.

"You look good," Sam said, referencing the bruising and discoloration that had marred Jackson's face for several weeks.

"So do you."

Sam looked down.

"But you didn't come all the way over here to tell me how good I look, did you?" Jackson asked.

"No."

"What's on your mind?"

"This is really hard for me, Jackson."

"Another plea for me to give up the dangerous life of a P.I.?"

"No, although I am concerned about you. This is taking a toll on you, and I don't just mean physical. You seem . . . distant lately."

"Doctor's orders. I'm not supposed to do much."

"I don't just mean laying around watching Bauer every day," Sam said.

"Who told you?"

"Easy guess. And I don't just mean the last month, Jackson. I mean since New Year's, since Nevada, since Ryan. And that's why . . ." She bit her lip. "That's why this is so hard."

Jackson put a hand on her shoulder. "It's okay, Sam. Whatever it is, just say it. I can take it."

Sam looked up as she blinked away a tear. "I can't see you anymore, Jackson."

"See me. You mean, tolerate my presence or go out for ice cream and watch chick flicks at your place?"

"I mean whatever you call what we've been doing. Dating, sort of dating, whatever."

"Kissing on Christmas Eve."

"That too."

Jackson exhaled. "Because I've grown distant."

"No. Well, that's part of it. But no." She stood and paced around his coffee table, to a photo hanging on the wall. It showed Jackson and his grandpa at a Dodgers game a few years back. Sam studied it for a moment before turning around. "Jackson, the last few months, I've realized something. Little things have been getting to me—people in the E.R., moments on TV, little nothings that suddenly mean something—and big things, like my mom's cancer."

"How is she?"

"She's doing good. She's taking Tamoxifen, and initial signs are promising. She's not dealing with many side-effects either. So far, so good."

"I'm glad to hear it."

Sam nodded. "Like I said, things have been getting to me. And then seeing Stephanie holding Mackenzie confirmed it to me." She took a deep breath and looked him straight in the eyes. "I'm ready for more, Jackson. For a family. To be a wife and mother. I've known all along that's what I wanted, but now I think it's time."

Jackson stood. "And I don't fit into that?"

She bit her lip, on the verge of tears. "I don't know, Jackson. I thought maybe you did, but . . ." She shook her head. "I can't be sitting home wondering if my husband is coming back. I can't have a child who might grow up without a father. And I can't ask you to change what you do and who you are, and for all I know, you have no interest in being a husband or a father now or ever. I just . . ." She bit harder on her lip and Jackson moved forward and wrapped his arms around her.

"It's okay, Sam."

She cried for a moment before pulling herself together and stepping back. "I'm sorry, I thought I could do this easier."

"You don't need to be sorry. I understand."

She looked up.

"Really," he said. "And you're right. I'm not sure that I'm ready to be a husband and father or to start a serious relationship with that as the end target. In fact, I'm sure I'm not." He shrugged. "But that doesn't mean I won't someday. And it doesn't mean that someday you and I might—"

He stopped when Sam shook her head. "I met someone, Jackson."

He swallowed.

"It's not serious yet, but . . ." She looked up. "I didn't mean for it to happen, I really didn't. I'm still worried that I'm vulnerable now and . . . I just can't in clear conscience lead you on when I'm involved—to whatever degree—with someone else."

Jackson nodded. He nearly smiled at the irony. First Maggie had found somebody else, now Sam too. Could be just a coincidence, but Jackson had to wonder if maybe Sam was onto something. Maybe it wasn't Maggie and Sam; maybe it was him. Maybe he had driven them away. Maybe he had missed his chance with either of them by choosing neither of them and keeping things too casual.

Sam was right. His life was taking a toll on him, and it wasn't physical.

Chapter Eight

THE HUMIDITY RETURNED.

Ben did not.

The United States Coast Guard officially called off their search for his body. The Sheriff's Department officially ruled him missing at sea. That was not a pronouncement of death, technically. But unless he'd pulled a Captain Jack Sparrow and strapped himself to a pair of sea turtles, it was as good as.

Jackson had cereal for breakfast, then dumped the rest of Ben's milk down the drain. He wondered if Uncle Malcolm from Atlanta would be coming down to take care of all the crap that had to be taken care of when someone died. That should really be a business, offering to deal with everything while the family grieved. Probably would turn in to a rip-off scam like everything else.

Regardless of what Ben's next of kin did or didn't do, Jackson decided he was getting out of Ben's house. Common sense dictated he go back home, but he didn't want to. He couldn't quite explain it, but he felt like he needed some time away from, well, everything. Maybe it was just his way of having a pity party, of pouting on a grand scale. Instead of taking his ball and going home when he didn't get his way, he was refusing to go home. That'd show 'em—whoever 'em was.

No, Jackson knew who 'em was. It was God. He knew it was petty, small-minded, biblically inaccurate, logically fallacious, and contrary to everything he'd been taught and believed, and yet he couldn't help feeling God was to blame. For Ben's death, for Jackson's family's death, for everything that was wrong in life. Even as he recalled Bible verses and principles that countered that thinking, it persisted. Maybe that's what this was, a giant temper tantrum, a protest. Jackson hated tantrum throwers and protestors, and yet there he was, not driving back to Miami but checking into a hotel on the northeast corner of the island.

Or, rather, trying to check in. It was only mid-morning, and the very polite clerk informed him that no rooms would be ready for a few hours. So with his possessions stuffed in the trunk of his rented car, Jackson drove back to Smathers Beach, where he had watched a beautiful sunset the night before. He parked and walked onto the beach, taking a seat in the shade of a palm tree.

How does this end? he asked. Or maybe he didn't so much ask as mimic the question being posed to him.

Did he turn into a Florida beach bum, grow his hair and beard out, end up making another lapse in judgment like the summer after his family died? That had ended with him burning hash with a dopey coworker. Actually, it had ended with him getting arrested, begging his dead brother's fiancée—a beautiful, belligerent defense attorney named Hillary—to get the charges reduced, and seeing a court-ordered shrink.

More than that, how did his life end? Tragically? Bitterly? He couldn't keep going like this, but he couldn't move on. And didn't really want to either. Would time—enough of it—really make things better? Did he just keep trudging along, dodging bullets as a P.I., until things fell into place? He had come to accept that he was the "garbage man" of society, doing the unpleasant work (mostly shooting baddies to save pretty girls' lives) so others wouldn't have to. But he wasn't invincible. Sooner or later, he'd get clobbered. His most recent adventure had been the worst. At one point, he'd resorted to egging on his Russian captors in the hopes that they'd kill him and put him out of his misery. Now, he sort of resented that they hadn't.

He again felt like Jonah, sitting under a tree to avoid the heat of the day. Jonah's tree got eaten by a worm, and the story ended abruptly. Jackson's tree was still subject to a stagnant, torpid lack of breeze, and his ending was just as nebulous as Jonah's.

*   *   *

3:32 p.m.

JACKSON RALLIED somewhat after lunch. He'd grabbed a few sandwiches off the dollar menu at McDonald's and returned to his hotel, by which time he'd been allowed to check in. He'd mindlessly watched an episode and a half of *Fixer Upper*, thinking how idyllic Chip and Joanna's life seemed compared to, say, his. Somewhere in the midst of shiplap and barn doors in a kitchen, he'd concluded that some of his doldrums might be related to lack of knowledge as to what had happened to Ben—and why. And while he didn't distrust the Monroe County Sheriff's Department or fear Sheriff Hawkins would be negligent, he knew he'd feel better if he could at least check a few boxes.

To that end, he left his hotel and drove around the east end of the island, then west on Highway 1, past the Denny's where he'd eaten his first night. He passed a couple other marinas and what looked like military housing before seeing the sign for Cayo Hueso Charters, located inside the island's largest marina and within walking distance of Old Town.

It was not what he expected. A narrow, rutted—albeit paved—drive led to half a dozen ad hoc parking spaces beside a dock. The drive and parking spaces formed a manmade isthmus into the harbor, at the end of which was a single story building, half pink, half white. The shingles were a faded blue. It was the Keys.

Jackson parked and got out, immediately assaulted by the heat and humidity. Storms appeared to be building again, and he took note from the day before how quickly they could come.

The dock to his left formed a T, with the leg sticking out into the marina. One of the arms ran up and around the building, on which hung a sign identifying it as Cayo Hueso Charters. Jackson climbed onto the dock. A couple of sport fishers and mid-sized powerboats were moored at the dock, with slips available for several more.

Jackson found the door to the building open and stepped inside, letting his eyes adjust to the relative darkness. Country music played over a radio on the countertop to his left, which was otherwise covered in papers and a logbook. There was also a desktop computer with an old CRT monitor on the near end of the counter and an oscillating desk fan fighting a losing battle on the other.

In addition to the expected nautical knickknacks, the walls were covered with photos of various ships, from tiny speedboats to luxurious yachts to sailing vessels of every size. On the far wall, a pair of vending machines, a mini fridge, and a microwave functioned as a kitchen. To Jackson's right, several racks of clothing, life vests, fishing gear, sunblock, and snacks and drinks were available to buy or rent. A single restroom was in the corner, its door open and its light off. The building was empty.

Jackson waited a few minutes, noting the absence of a bell to ring. The desk fan was failing miserably, so he stepped back outside. That's when he spotted a woman with a hose and a bucket spraying off the bottom of one of the sport fishers. He clomped down the dock toward her.

She stopped just before he arrived and turned to look at him. "Can I help you?"

"You work here?"

She nodded as she stood, wiping her hands on her shorts. She extended a hand. "Liz Hafer," she said as she chomped on a piece of gum. Or chaw. "You looking to charter a boat?"

"I was actually hoping to ask a few questions."

She squinted at him. "About what?"

"Ben O'Reilly. He chartered a boat on Sunday."

Liz looked him over real quick. She blew a bubble. So it wasn't chaw. "You're not a cop."

"No."

She shook her head. "I spent an hour with a detective the other morning. And I can't reveal client information to anyone else."

"I appreciate that, but I'm a friend of Ben's. I'm visiting from California, where I'm a licensed private investigator." He pulled out his wallet to show her his license. "I won't ask anything confidential. I'm just hoping to figure out what happened to Ben."

She studied him for a moment, blowing another bubble. "Come with me."

Jackson followed her as she carried the bucket around the backside of the building, where she dumped it out and rinsed it from a faucet. "What do you want to know?"

"Ben chartered a powerboat, is that right?"

"Yeah, a 160 Bowrider."

"Had he ever chartered one before?"

"No, but he and a buddy have chartered a sport fisher a few times before. I think the friend was the pilot."

"You know the friend's name?"

"Uh-huh," Liz said as she wrung out a sponge.

"But you aren't going to tell me."

"Sorry. Policy."

"Right. You tell the detective his name?"

"I did."

Jackson nodded. That lead was theoretically covered then.

"Can you tell me if he was with Ben this time?"

"No. It was just him."

"That mean he was going to drive?"

Liz smiled. "Pilot, landlubber."

"Sorry."

"Yes. He signed to pilot the boat. We check to make sure everyone who charters a boat has an active boater's license."

"Could someone else have piloted it?"

She shrugged. "You rent a car, you're supposed to be the only driver, but there's nothing to stop you from letting your girlfriend or buddy get behind the wheel."

Jackson nodded. Liz gestured for him to follow her inside.

"What time did he charter the boat?"

"A little after six. That's when I get here, and I'd just arrived."

"You get here at six on a Sunday?"

"I'm an early riser. And it's peak season."

Jackson nodded. "Did Ben call ahead?"

"Nope. Just showed up and requested a boat."

"He request the Bowrider?"

"He just asked for a small powerboat. I had two Bowriders, so I gave him one."

"How long was he supposed to have it?"

"Just one day."

"Twenty-four hours?"

"Until close. Dusk."

"He file a plan of where he was going or anything?"

"No."

"Rent any other gear?"

"No."

"Have anything with him?"

"Not that I saw, but he could have gotten something out of his car."

"Is it still here?"

"Cops towed it the other day."

Jackson nodded again. Another lead covered.

"Anything else?" Liz asked.

"Yeah. Is the boat here?"

She nodded toward the door. "Third from the end."

"Can I take a look at it?"

"Cops already did, and it's been cleaned since."

"Still, if you don't mind . . ."

Liz sighed, but only minimally. Then she led him out to the boat. The 160 Bowrider was pretty simple, powered by a sixty horsepower outboard motor. Two captain's chairs behind a wraparound windshield, a bench seat for three behind that, and two more bench seats at the bow provided ample seating. The controls were standard—steering wheel, throttle, a couple of gauges.

"How hard is it to capsize this thing?" Jackson asked as he and Liz stood side-by-side on the dock.

"Depends. On the open ocean, you can get some pretty big swells. The reefs can also be tricky. But we're talking extreme situations. Not Sunday."

Jackson remembered the family at Denny's. The girl had gotten sick, despite calm seas. Meaning the Bowrider should not have capsized.

"Pilot error?" he asked.

"Not likely," she said. "He'd have to be crazy or blind drunk to pull that off."

Jackson frowned. "So what then?"

"I don't know." She shrugged. "Fact is, it shouldn't have happened."

"You tell all this to the detective?"

Liz nodded.

"He didn't say anything about suspecting foul play?" Jackson asked.

"It doesn't mean foul play necessarily. Just that I can't think of any reason it should have capsized."

"What about another craft running into it?"

"Possible. Would have likely left a mark, though."

Jackson looked at the hull. There were a few small scratches and dents, but nothing to suggest it had recently been broadsided.

"You have whales down here?" he asked.

"Not a lot, but some. And it's possible but very unlikely."

Jackson nodded. "Any way of knowing how far he drove it?"

"He used about half a tank of gas. Ten gallons."

"What's that translate to in mileage?"

She shrugged. "Just like a car. Depends how fast he went. For that matter, he could have idled in the marina all day and used it up." She looked up at Jackson. "He didn't."

His turn to shrug. "Say he ran at normal speed, whatever that is, would about half a tank get him to Sugarloaf Key and back to where he capsized, out by the reef?"

"If he ran wide-open, he'd burn more fuel, but still would have made that no trouble. Why Sugarloaf Key?"

"Just a theory. Thanks for all your help."

Liz nodded. "Sure. I hope your friend's all right."

He didn't bother to tell her that, unlike the Bowrider, that ship had already sunk.

Chapter Nine

LEAVING CAYO HUESO Charters, Jackson set out on foot. Despite the obscene heat, he decided to take a stroll down famed Duval Street. He had no destination in mind, and no purpose other than avoiding going back to his hotel room. A guy could only watch so much *Fixer Upper*.

He wandered along the sidewalk, watching the pedicabs, trollies, bikes, and standard vehicles vie for space on the streets. Tourists carrying bags from local souvenir shops dodged among them like fish through coral. The shops hawked the typical discounted T-shirts and conch shells and assorted knickknacks and were interspersed with seafood restaurants, bars, various merchants, inns, and a Ripley's Believe It or Not! Local flavor was blended with mass appeal chain stores. The clientele ranged from the post-college crowd on a girls' trip or brocation to the senior citizens from one of the cruise ships docked a few blocks west. Heavy on the seniors.

Jackson waited for the light at Greene Street. He thought some more about packing up and going home. His return ticket wasn't until Sunday, but that could always be changed. Then again, the investigator in Jackson had been roused by his visit to see Liz. He didn't buy Ben's death being an accident, and couldn't bring himself to go home and forget the whole business. But what could he do when the trail was cold?

Several people passed by Jackson, and he realized the light had changed. He walked south another block, glancing at merchandise at several shops but not stopping. He was missing something. How could all these people enjoy roaming around looking at postcards of views they could see a block or two away? Did they really come all the way to Key West to drink beer in front of an oscillating fan? Jackson sighed. Maybe he was just cranky. Maybe if Ben had been there to greet him on Sunday, they would be kicking it in some watering hole, swapping stories and having a great time despite the heat.

Jackson decided to chill out and get some ice cream. His lunch had worn off, but he didn't feel hungry enough given the heat for an actual meal. He found a place serving frozen custard, ordered standard chocolate in a waffle cone, and joined the happy throng on the sidewalk. They had their eyes on the next purchase or the co-ed halfway down the block or the pictures they had snapped on their phone, and he had his on the rapidly melting custard.

He ventured west, saw a Carnival cruise ship at the dock and a Royal Caribbean liner pulling in. The closeness of the open water did little to bring relief from the heat, and Jackson scanned the sky. Still hazy, still some building clouds, no imminent rain or relief. His custard long melted, Jackson pitched the final third of his cone in a trashcan, realizing it was the second day in a row he had done so. Maybe a sign to stop buying ice cream treats while inside a furnace. That resolved, he headed back toward the marina and his car.

Sweat beaded on his forehead and dripped over his brow as he walked. He concluded that Key West, despite its charms, was not for him. Too much humidity, too many tourists, not enough to do. Maybe it could be blamed on the somber occasion. Or because he was by himself. If Sam was with him, or Maggie—heck, even that Christy or Christa lady from the courthouse who'd talked him into seeing some weird twist on *The Wizard of Oz*—Jackson was sure his outlook would be different. But they weren't, and he was alone.

A familiar maroon Jeep was parked next to his rented car. And a familiar woman was hunched under the roll bar, rummaging around, it appeared, in the backseat. Sawyer stood, raking a hand through chin-length blond hair that tumbled back beside her smiling face. "Jackson. I thought that looked like your car. What are you doing here?"

"I was going to ask you the same thing."

"I was first this time."

"I came to ask about Ben's boat," he said, nodding past her at the Cayo Hueso Charters building.

"Did you talk to Liz?"

"I did. Is that why you're here? Is she the friend who told you about Ben?"

"Aren't you the junior detective?"

"As a matter of fact."

She wrinkled her brow.

"I'm a P.I. back in California."

"Get out."

He nodded.

"Is that why you're still here? I thought when they called off the search you'd head home."

"Among other reasons," he said, fudging the truth just a little.

"Did you learn anything, from Liz I mean?"

"Just that Ben used enough gas to get out to Sugarloaf Key."

"You think he went to Sugarloaf Key?"

Jackson shrugged.

"You're sweating," she said.

"Because I'm in a sauna."

"There's that smart-aleck side again."

"Not so much a side. What's in the Jeep?"

"A cooler of shrimp, courtesy of a friend at Captain Carl's."

"Bait shop?"

"Seafood place," she said with a nod across the marina.

"Hmm. Going on a picnic?"

"Fishing. It's past expiration, but the snapper love it."

He nodded.

"Wanna come?"

"Fishing?"

She nodded.

Oddly enough, he did. Not so much because of a burgeoning desire to fish, but to have something to do. And because Sawyer intrigued him. There was more to her than met the eye, he felt, and she kept turning up. First at Ben's house. Then at Sheriff Hawkins' office a couple of times. Now here. The churning in his gut told him there was something about her.

"Sure."

"Hop in," she said, nodding at the passenger side of the Jeep.

He did. Sawyer joined him, grabbing the same pair of silver-rimmed aviator sunglasses she'd worn Sunday night when she'd dropped photos off at Ben's house. That seemed like months ago.

With the windows and top down, air moved pretty well in the Jeep, and for once Jackson didn't feel oppressed by heat and humidity. Nor, as they cruised south through town, did he feel the overwhelming negativity that had plagued him the last few days.

"So where are we fishing?"

"White Street Pier."

"Secret spot?"

"Hardly. But you can't beat the view."

They skirted the cemetery and made enough back and forth turns that Jackson started to wonder if Sawyer was lost. Then the view opened as they reached a palm-dotted park and, beyond it, the open sea. Sawyer parked in a public lot across from the park. She cast a quick glance at the sky and got out. She did not put the top up.

"Sorry, I only have one pole," she said as she reached into the backseat. "Wanna grab the cooler?"

Jackson nodded and lifted out a small blue Coleman cooler.

"We can take turns," she said.

"Don't worry. I'll just hang."

"You can't come to Key West without fishing," she said, emerging around the back of the Jeep. She carried a small tackle box in one hand and a telescopic fishing rod and a small bucket in the other. Wearing faded denim shorts and a loose, bell-sleeve pullover, she did not look like the fishermen on the piers back in California.

The White Street Pier was a concrete structure extending a few hundred feet out into the water, and Sawyer marched to the end of it before setting down her tackle box and bucket. Only a handful of other people were braving the heat of the day out on the pier, leaving Jackson and Sawyer in solitude. While she extended her pole and baited the first hook with a wriggling shrimp, Jackson scanned the view.

Water in three directions ranged in color from deep blue to teal to aqua to so clear he could see the sandy bottom. Clouds towered into the sky, their white puffs and gray undersides contrasting sharply with the vibrant blue sky. Like the night before, it was another magical view. This time, he enjoyed it.

"What else did Liz tell you?" Sawyer asked after casting her line into the water.

"Not much. Ben chartered the boat solo, didn't seem to have anything with him." He shrugged.

"Hmm."

"Also that he's chartered a fishing boat with a buddy a few times, but she wouldn't tell me the buddy's name."

"Hmm." She paused. "You think that's important?"

"It's a contact who might know something about him."

"Are you investigating what happened?"

"Not officially. The sheriff doesn't even know I'm a P.I."

"Why not?"

"Didn't seem relevant. Until a couple hours ago, I wasn't doing much but sulking."

For the first time, she made eye contact with him. "Ben's death hitting you hard?"

"You've concluded he's dead?"

Sawyer shrugged. "The authorities have. I guess I'm just going by what they say."

"Yeah."

She looked at him until it became uncomfortable.

He raised an eyebrow.

"You didn't answer my question."

"Which was?"

"You said you were sulking. Ben?"

"Among other things."

He thought Sawyer's Southern disposition might dictate her pushing and asking more. But she turned her eyes to her bobber some thirty feet out in the water.

"What about you?" Jackson said, sort of changing the subject. "How are you doing with the news?"

"I'm okay," she said. "Ben and I were friends, but we weren't *that* close. I'm sad, but I know where he is. I know he was right with God before he died. I knew him that well."

Her eyes probed Jackson's, and he wondered what his gave away.

"But I am mad."

"Mad?"

"I don't think his death was an accident."

"You don't?"

"Do you?"

Jackson shook his head.

"I suppose a rogue wave or a careless boater could cause Ben's boat to capsize, but that dead guy from New Orleans whose blood they found on the boat . . ." She looked at him again. "You don't have to be a private eye to see that something's off."

"No."

Sawyer looked down at her rod. Jackson had yet to spot a fish, but with Sawyer, he guessed the catch might be secondary to the process.

"Liz tell *you* anything?" he asked.

"No. But I didn't ask much. We just talked."

"How do you know her?"

"Church. We go—went—to the same church."

"She stop or you?"

Sawyer looked at him with a hint of a smile threatening to break out.

"That's what I thought," he said.

"You go to church?"

"Not as much as I should."

He expected her to ask, "Why not?" Instead, she countered with, "How much should you go?"

"According to my parents, as often as the doors are open."

"You bucked against that?"

"Not so much."

Sawyer waited.

"I've been in a rut of late," he said finally, not sure why he was opening up to her.

"With church or with God?"

Jackson exhaled. "A little of each."

She nodded. Then looked down at her rod.

"You got something?"

Sawyer nodded again while deftly reeling in the line. In two minutes, she had lifted a twelve-inch red snapper out of the water. She deposited it into the bucket, letting the fish flap and flop and try to survive. She ignored it.

She handed Jackson the rod. "I'm cooking. See if you can catch yourself some dinner."

Thirty minutes later, he hadn't had so much as a nibble, despite re-baiting and re-casting. That changed suddenly when the rod was nearly pulled from his hand. With some direction from Sawyer, he began reeling in a stubborn, seemingly big fish. He battled for several minutes, long enough to see he had hooked a nearly two-foot-long snapper. As he was wondering if he could hoist it out of the water without the aid of a net, the snapper broke free and darted away.

"Phooey." Sawyer turned his way. "Don't you fish in California?"

"I actually prefer the shrimp."

"Well, me too, unless it's fresh-caught, home-cooked snapper."

"I'll take your word for it."

She baited the hook again and cast her line in a different direction. The pier was mostly empty, still, and Jackson and Sawyer resumed talking while waiting for a bite. She asked about life in California, which she compared to life in Key West. She had never been west of the Mississippi, and he did his best to explain the California condition, as he called it. In turn, she talked about the languid pace of life in the South and explained how she had learned to catch and cook fish—from her dad. From her tone, it sounded like fishing skills only scraped the surface of things she'd learned from him.

The first raindrop pelted Sawyer square in the sunglasses.

She looked up. So did Jackson. The sun had gone behind the clouds a few times over the last hour, but this time the cloud was dark gray on the bottom.

As several more drops splattered on and around them, Sawyer started reeling in her line. She looked at Jackson. "I think we're in trouble."

He looked up at the sky. "It's just rain."

"It's not about to turn your frilly shirt into a negligee."

He replied by bending down to close the cooler on the unused shrimp.

"No, dump them," Sawyer said as she finished reeling in her line and began removing the hook. "Put the fish in there."

He did as she collapsed her rod. The raindrops were gaining rhythm. Jackson picked up the cooler and the bucket. As soon as she'd stowed everything in the tackle box, Sawyer hefted it and her pole. The rain was starting to sizzle, and they hurried down the pier. As they ran, Jackson looked to his left, across the open sea, to where streaks of rain turned the horizon into a hazy white mist.

"Forget the Jeep," Sawyer said when they reached the base of the pier. "We'll never get the top up in time."

As if to echo her point, the sound of the rain intensified and the breeze began to gust. They turned to the right, Jackson following Sawyer down a winding sidewalk through flapping palm trees. The rain was steady now, kicking up dust as the drops pelted the sandy grass all around them. One hundred feet down the sidewalk was a small, palapa-style pavilion. Supported by a single pole, its roof was only six feet in diameter, but it was the only shelter around. With the rain chasing them, they both ducked under its protection.

Seconds later, the sky opened, and the rain fell in buckets. Under the pavilion, Jackson and Sawyer avoided getting drenched, but there was enough wind, spray, and splattering rain to get them wet.

"So can two people eat off a twelve-inch snapper?" Jackson asked Sawyer. He had to borderline shout to be heard over the rain as it drummed on the pavilion roof. "Or do you have some loaves to go with it?"

"'*If any would not work, neither should he eat,*'" she said with a wink.

"Touché."

The downpour abated, but the rain continued steadily.

"So why are you in a rut with God?" Sawyer asked.

Jackson looked into her dark blue eyes. "It's kind of a long story."

"I'm not exactly pressed for time."

"Short version is because I'm an entitled millennial."

She raised an eyebrow.

"I feel like God owes me a happy life. Even though I know it isn't true, even though that's not what I believe, it's what I feel."

"And you operate on feelings?"

"No. I think it's absurd because feelings come and go like the wind. And yet . . ."

"They're powerful."

"Yeah."

There was a moment's pause. "Is your life not happy?"

"Has its moments, but by and large . . . no."

Sawyer had shown a knack for knowing when to push and when to back off. She didn't push, and they listened to the rain. It kept up for another ten or fifteen minutes. Then, as quickly as it had begun, it pattered to a stop. Soon the sun was shining brightly again, and the wet concrete was steaming.

Sawyer stepped out from under the pavilion, raking a hand through her damp hair. She looked at Jackson. "You hungry?"

"I could eat. If there's enough for two."

"May not stuff you to the gills . . ."

She paused, and he groaned appropriately.

"But there'll be enough to go around."

"Okay then."

"I think there's a public grill a little ways down the beach."

"Admittedly I don't do a lot of my own killin' and grillin', but don't you need to gut or debone this thing," he said, lifting the cooler with the fish inside. "At least gouge out the eyes?"

Sawyer smiled. "I've got everything I need in the tackle box."

"Matches?"

"In the tackle box."

"Charcoal?"

"In the Jeep."

"You come prepared."

"We could use a side though."

"A side?"

"Biscuits or rolls or something."

"Nothing in the Jeep, huh?"

"I wasn't expecting there to be two."

"You don't have to feed me, Sawyer. I can head back to my hotel."

"Hotel? You moved out of Ben's house?"

"Seemed prudent. And less creepy."

She reached into her pocket, and before he knew it, threw a dual set of keys at him. "Why don't you run and grab us something while I clean the fish?"

He looked at her. "You're giving me your keys?"

"Why not?"

He raised his eyebrow.

"It's not like I have to worry about you stealing a 2001 Jeep Wrangler and driving it three thousand miles back to California."

Jackson grinned.

She winked as she reached for the cooler. "Pick up some slaw too, will ya?"

Chapter Ten

6:36 p.m.

SAWYER DIRECTED JACKSON to Fausto's, a neighborhood grocery store several blocks north on White Street. After toweling dry the driver's seat in her Jeep, he headed off to buy some rolls and slaw. He had a lot to wonder about Sawyer, a woman who spent her afternoons fishing for dinner off the pier, inviting a relative stranger to join her and then sending him to buy side dishes—all the while probing his feelings and spiritual health. At least, for a while, he was something less than depressed.

He made quick work at Fausto's, buying Hawaiian rolls and generic coleslaw. It was characteristically cool inside the grocery store, and when Jackson re-entered the evening heat and humidity, it felt tropical instead of oppressive. Maybe the effects of the rain or maybe a change in perspective. Or the influence of company.

Jackson drove back toward the pier and parked in the same spot as before. He grabbed his purchases and a half bag of charcoal from the back seat and, after checking the sky, set out in search of Sawyer. The clouds were thinning but not gone, promising another beautiful sunset in a little more than an hour.

He found her a hundred yards down the beach from where they'd ridden out the rain. There was another pavilion nearby, along with a picnic table and a boxy charcoal grill. And a garbage can, into which Sawyer had presumably deposited all but two small filets of snapper. Other than a bloody knife and a similarly soiled rag she used to wipe it down before returning it to the tackle box, there was no evidence she had gutted the fish.

"Good, you remembered the charcoal."

"Yeah, but I forgot to buy utensils."

"I have some in the Jeep."

"I'll run back."

"How about you light the grill and I'll go get 'em. Where'd you park?"

"Same spot," he said, tossing the keys back to her.

She nodded at the Hawaiian rolls in passing. "Good choice."

He muttered a "Thanks" over his shoulder and watched her go. He didn't stare because she was a beautiful woman or because her clothes were draped to her skin, which they weren't anymore; the sun had dried everything quickly. Rather, he watched her go because there definitely was something about her, something appealing. Maybe she was one of those people with a magnetic personality, or maybe she was a charming Southern woman compared to all the plastic and silicone women in SoCal. Unable to place it, he turned his focus to lighting the grill, and by the time Sawyer returned with tongs, a small stack of paper bowls, and some plastic cutlery, he had the coals flaming.

"Can I ask you something?" he said as she sat down at the picnic table.

"You can always ask me something. I may refuse to answer . . ."

"If you hadn't run into me in the parking lot, was this your plan— fishing, eating on the beach?"

She nodded.

So did he.

"Why do you ask?"

"No reason. It's just that most people I know don't eat on the beach alone."

"Can you think of a better place to eat?"

"No, I can't."

"I live in a house that's two hundred square feet."

"A tiny house?"

"Uh-huh. They're becoming more common in tourist places like this with seasonal employees. So I don't spend much time at home. I sleep and shower there, dry off sometimes," she said with a grin, "but that's about it. I prefer to spend my time out under the open sky," she said, looking up at it.

"Yeah, I know what you mean."

She stood up, checked the temperature on the grill, then laid the filets on it. She turned to Jackson. "There should be a small bottle of olive oil in the tackle box. Also some salt and pepper."

He raised an eyebrow.

"Some women have purses, I have a tackle box."

"No, I was just expecting some gourmet recipe."

"You don't want to overdo it." She took the olive oil from him and used her fingers to rub it into the filets. "Thanks," she said as he handed her a folded paper towel. She wiped off her fingers, then took the salt and pepper. "I dated this guy once who suggested we grill some steaks." She lightly seasoned the fish. "He proceeded to apply so many seasonings, rubs, marinades—by the time he was done, I couldn't tell if I was eating steak or microwaved meatloaf."

She stepped back and leaned against the trunk of a palm tree. "I mean, if you want leftover meatloaf, that's fine, but if you're going to have steak, enjoy the flavor of the steak."

"Or freshly caught snapper."

"Right."

Sawyer used the tongs to flip the filets. She monitored them for several minutes while Jackson monitored the sky. No signs of another sudden downpour.

After the filets had spent just a couple minutes on each side, Sawyer removed them, placing them in two of the paper bowls. She forked some coleslaw in each, and added a pair of rolls. She handed one bowl to Jackson, but instead of taking a seat at the picnic table, nodded toward the beach. He followed her a short distance to the sand, where she kicked off her flip-flops and sat down cross-legged, facing the ocean. He dropped to a seat beside her.

Balancing her arms on her knees, Sawyer held her bowl in front of her. She closed her eyes.

"Jesus, thank You for placing this fish in the sea and giving it the poor discernment to eat my expired shrimp. And thank You for someone to share dinner with."

She opened her eyes and looked to Jackson. "Amen," he said, not knowing what else to add. She seemed content with his reply and dug into her snapper. He was a little suspicious of freshly-caught fish cooked on a public grill on the beach, but he too stuck his fork into his bowl. The tender snapper disintegrated. A moment later it practically melted in his mouth, full of flavor, and his suspicions went away.

"Mmm, this is delicious."

"Olive oil, salt and pepper."

"You do this a lot?" he asked after quickly forking in another bite.

"Not a lot. Depends on work."

"Where's work?" he asked, trying the coleslaw next.

"Here and there," Sawyer answered. "I don't really have a job, per se. I do a lot of . . . irregular work."

He tried a roll next, waiting for her to explain.

"For example, this morning I did portraits for the new members at the Wild Boar Lodge."

"Portraits?"

"Um-hmm."

"Photo portraits?"

"Oil on canvas. You know, like the President or the Heisman winner gets."

"You do landscapes too?"

"Yeah. I do a little bit of everything."

"So where do you sell them? Do you have a gallery or something?"

"No. I actually don't sell that many. I usually just paint for fun."

"Let me guess, on the beach?"

"Not much room in a two hundred-square-foot house."

"Where do you keep them?"

Sawyer shook her head. "I give most of them away."

Jackson nodded. "So if you don't sell many paintings, what else do you do?"

"Odds and ends. I do freelance photography, I've published some poems, I sing."

"Sing?"

She nodded.

"Sing how?"

Sawyer looked him straight in the eye and, regardless of who else might or might not have been around them on the beach, sang a few lines of "God Bless America," indistinguishable from Martina McBride's rendition. Her voice was rich and pure, polished yet wholly natural. Her accent came through but wasn't overpowering, adding a dimension without stealing the show. Jackson knew nothing of pitch and timbre or any other fancy musical terms, but he knew this girl could sing.

He waited until the final note had disappeared on the breeze. "Wow."

Sawyer shrugged and picked at her fish with her fork. "I can't take credit for the voice God gave me."

"Most people would."

"My daddy didn't raise me to be most people."

Jackson smiled to himself. It seemed like a perfectly Southern thing to say, and a Southern way to say it. Especially with the accent.

"So where do you sing?"

"Local restaurants and bars, although I don't like the bars. Weddings. Here and there."

"You ever record an album?"

Sawyer glanced at him incredulously.

"I'm serious."

"Southern girls are used to being complimented, but you don't have to go overboard."

"Same's true of Southern girls and modesty."

"Touché."

"So what do you sing?"

"Whatever's in my heart. Which is mostly country."

"So does all that keep you pretty busy? Painting, singing, the like?"

"Usually. Busy enough, anyhow. If not, I wait tables or work at one of the local shops, pick up hours where I can."

"And I'm guessing your mortgage is pretty light."

She grinned and licked off her thumb.

"How long have you lived in Key West?"

"On and off for four years."

"On and off?"

"I spend a few months a year back home, in Alabama."

"Which part?"

"Tuscaloosa. Center west of the state."

He nodded.

"What about you? Which part of California?"

"Pacific Palisades. In the hills just north of Santa Monica."

She raised an eyebrow. "That's a pretty ritzy part of the world, isn't it?"

"You mean for a P.I.?"

"Did it sound like that?"

"I know what you mean. And yes, but I got a steal on a house. Bought it from drug dealers."

"Really?"

"Well, from the bank. They foreclosed on the drug dealers."

"So what's it like being a private investigator?" she asked, setting aside her empty bowl. "Truth be told, I didn't know they existed anymore."

"Just a few of us. We've been outdone by iPhones and apps."

"What kind of cases do you take?"

"You name it. I had an undercover cop posing as a Valley Girl hire me to deliver wood idols that actually, unbeknownst to me, contained cocaine. My former roommate hired me to find his missing girlfriend, who then came and said he was trying to kill her, which was actually a lie she'd manufactured to con me into thinking she wasn't committing corporate espionage, which she was. An actress hired me to find a stalker, and he thought I was her boyfriend and shot me."

"Whoa, what? He shot you?"

Jackson pointed to his shoulder. "New Year's Eve."

"Are you serious?"

"Very."

"Wow yourself."

"I've had kind of an interesting year," Jackson said. "It's part of the reason I came down here, to just get away and recuperate."

"Recuperate," she said. "From what?"

"A number of things. Mostly my last case."

Sawyer looked at him, waiting for him to speak.

"I was protecting a World War II vet from Russian terrorists who thought he knew the location of a nuclear weapon."

"Did he?"

Jackson nodded.

"Did they find out?"

"No, I got in their way."

"What happened?"

"They grabbed me one night and took me to the basement of a safe house where they used me as a human piñata until my friends rescued me."

Sawyer removed her sunglasses. "Are you serious?"

"Yeah. Broke ribs, bruised about everything. I've been on modified bed rest for a month. Ben told me that the Key West climate would be therapeutic."

"Well, shut my mouth. I thought Southern men told good tales."

"You don't believe me?"

"No, I believe you," she said. "I can see it in your eyes. But it's still quite a tale."

And Jackson hadn't told her the worst of his job, about the lives he had taken. About the choices he'd made and things he'd done for the proverbial "greater good." About the demons that plagued him every day.

"Is that why you're 'in a rut' with God?"

"Not entirely."

She waited a beat, giving him a chance to clarify. When he didn't, she leaned forward. "And then you show up, and your friend is missing, and instead of recuperation, you get another chance to play private eye."

"Something like that. Only I haven't been playing much."

"You talked to Liz."

"Yeah. And I looked through Ben's stuff too but didn't find much. Certainly nothing to suggest what he was doing on that boat, how he might have known Ted Ryker, or why someone would want to capsize his boat."

A gust of breeze stirred a nearby palm frond. The sun was low in the sky, but the air was still warm.

"You mentioned asking Liz about Sugarloaf Key," Sawyer said, "and you said something about it to Sheriff Hawkins the other day too. You thinking that's where Ben was going?"

Jackson shrugged. "The only thing I found looking through his stuff was that he'd done a lot of research on pirates, weather, ocean depths."

"By Sugarloaf Key?"

"Not specifically. But he asked you for photos of it, made mention of a restaurant on Sugarloaf Key." He shrugged again. "It's all I've got."

A particular wave, as they sometimes did, made a little more noise than the rest.

"How was your snapper?" Sawyer asked.

"Under-seasoned."

"Shut up."

"It was great."

"I'm glad."

"Thanks for inviting me, Sawyer. I needed a pick-me-up."

She smiled. "What are friends for?"

He smiled back, thinking how refreshing it was to meet someone as open and friendly as Sawyer, someone who considered a guy a friend after nothing more than an evening fishing and eating together on the beach. Maybe that's what it was about her, an authenticity, an openness, a trust in her fellow man that wasn't born of naivety but an innate positivity.

They sat together, mostly in silence, and watched a stunning Key West sunset play out on the placid ocean.

*   *   *

Thursday, May 16
9:20 a.m.

JACKSON'S HOTEL served a complimentary breakfast, which he ate on a small terrace looking at four-lanes of traffic on Highway 1 and, beyond the highway, the shallow, mangrove-lined backwaters that surrounded the Keys. It was hot again, already, but perhaps not quite as humid. Small victories.

Shortly after the sun had dipped into the Gulf of Mexico the night before, Jackson and Sawyer had packed up their small picnic. She had then driven him back to the Cayo Hueso Charters parking lot, where they'd parted ways. He'd driven back to his hotel, feeling a little better about life. He couldn't really explain it, what with Ben still being missing and the assorted issues that had put Jackson in a rut still being unresolved. But somehow, his evening with Sawyer had been cathartic.

He'd sat on the terrace for a while, nursing a coffee from the hotel lobby, thinking about her, about Ben, about life. The moon had been chasing the sun toward the western horizon, and the balmy air had been invigorating. Maybe that was why he'd stayed up until almost midnight. Or maybe it was jet lag finally catching up with him. Whatever the reason, he woke up late and groggy, and again uncertain about his immediate future.

Eating breakfast didn't clarify things for him, so, despite the heat, he went for a walk. As he hiked along the highway with the water on his right and an endless supply of restaurants, hotels, gas stations, and other commercial properties on his left, he tried to figure out what to do. Part of him said go home, there was nothing left for him in Florida. Part of him said he should try to investigate Ben's presumed death. And part of him said he might as well spend the rest of his vacation hanging out at the beach, maybe bumming grilled snapper off charismatic Southern belles.

He thought about calling Reggie, asking his friend for advice. But Reggie would tell him to come home, and for some reason, Jackson didn't want to go home. He also thought about calling Sheriff Hawkins, but what could the sheriff tell him? Besides, he'd promised to keep Jackson in the loop if something broke. Say, if Ben's body washed ashore on Smathers Beach.

The fact that it hadn't bugged Jackson. Sure, there were plenty of reasons why it wouldn't have. He and Ryker could have entered the water at different times and different points, causing Ben's body to drift to some uninhabited spit of land or into the open ocean. Ben could have sunk for some reason, or been eaten by a shark. Or he could still be alive. It was incredibly unlikely, Jackson knew, especially after so much time, but a tiny little part of him hoped against hope that Ben wasn't dead.

Maybe that was what had kept him up so late.

By the time he returned to his hotel, he was sweating through his shirt. He opted for a second shower. He liked to think in the shower, and he realized he had already decided he was staying for the rest of the week. As he showered, then dried off and dressed, passing on shaving for the second time that morning, he tried to figure out, since he was going to spend the next few days in Florida, how to spend the next few days in Florida. Everything from taking a tour of Dry Tortugas to crawling into a bottle at a dive bar off Duval Street passed through his head, some ideas more legitimately than others. He still had nothing when his phone rang.

Jackson found it on the dresser and flipped it open without checking the display. "Yeah?"

"Hey."

It was Sawyer.

"Hey," he said back.

"So I've been thinking since last night," she said.

"Okay."

"You doing anything this afternoon?"

"Absolutely nothing."

"Wanna take a boat ride?"

"Where to?"

"The wreck of the *Barracuda*."

Jackson didn't ask why. And he didn't take the time to think about it.

"When do we leave?"

Chapter Eleven

11:57 a.m.

SAWYER LIFTED HER sunglasses into her golden hair as Jackson approached.

"You not get my text?"

"What text? Why?"

She stood, having been leaning against her Jeep in the Cayo Hueso Charters parking lot. She wore a loose white crewneck T-shirt with "Roll Tide" in large letters on the front. It was tucked in only in front to a pair of distressed denim shorts. The ties of a swimsuit, presumably, stuck out the collar. Instead of flip-flops, she wore white canvas boat shoes. She looked ready for an afternoon at sea.

Jackson, on the other hand, wore a light gray T-shirt with an interlocking cardinal S and C on the front, blue jeans, and his standard tennis shoes. He looked like he did every day of his life, which was suitable for riding the waves, he thought.

"I thought we might want to snorkel around the wreck," she said. "I texted you to wear a swimsuit."

"Sorry. I don't text."

She frowned.

"Or own a swimsuit."

Her mouth dropped. "You're from California."

He nodded.

"And you don't own a swimsuit?"

"Technically, I've probably got one stashed away somewhere."

"And you didn't think to dig it out to come down to Florida?"

He shrugged.

"Hmm."

"You were planning on snorkeling?" he asked.

"It's a good way to see the wreck, and the water isn't that deep. You don't text?"

"Never have."

"You're sure you're from California?"

He smiled.

"Can you even swim?"

"I can stay afloat."

"Wanna try snorkeling? You can pick up a pair of trunks anywhere around here."

"I'm not going to get eaten by a shark, am I?"

"Probably not," she said, emphasizing "probably" with a smirk.

"Okay."

She looked at his jeans. "Small boat, if you catch my drift."

"I'll change first."

"I'll set things up with Liz, get our gear. Meet you back here?"

He nodded, then set off for the nearest beachwear store. He had yet in his life to see a pair of men's swimming trunks that didn't look completely ridiculous and, short of a pair that desecrated the flag, he still didn't. He picked a cheap pair that only sort of made him think of the 1980s, used a changing room to slip them on under his jeans, and hiked back to the Cayo Hueso Charters parking lot, sweating by the time he arrived. A dip in the ocean was sounding better and better.

Sawyer was again by her Jeep. She hoisted a cooler out of the back seat— not the same one that had contained expired shrimp the night before—which she handed to Jackson while eyeing his blue jeans again.

"Underneath," he said.

"Okay."

"We all set?"

"Yep. There are a few storms north of here, but nothing that should cause us any trouble."

"I'll take your word for it, Skipper."

Sawyer led the way onto the dock and to a twenty-eight-foot walkaround boat moored alone at the dock's end. Jackson helped her cast off and then took the passenger seat underneath a hard top canopy as she navigated away from the dock and out of the marina.

Boat traffic was heavy, from ferries to cruise ships to pleasure boaters to fishermen, and Jackson let Sawyer pilot without much conversation until they were alongside Fort Zachary Taylor at Key West's southwestern tip. She opened the throttle and continued south to deeper water.

"So, slow day of work?" he asked.

"One of the perks of my career path," she said. "Flexibility."

"I hear ya."

She turned his way. "Thanks for coming."

"Yeah. I was just trying to figure out which way to twiddle my thumbs when you called."

"I kind of got the impression yesterday you were in a deeper funk than grilling some snapper on the beach could fix."

"Is that why you suggested this?"

"In part." She looked out to sea, the wind taking her hair for a ride. "I also can't let Ben's disappearance go so easily."

"His disappearance?"

She looked back at him.

"Last night you called it his death."

"Whichever."

"Are you like me, holding out some unreasonable hope that he's still alive?"

"Mmm, maybe. More than anything, I want to know what happened." She shrugged. "Not sure what we'll find out here, but he was interested in the *Barracuda*. You speculated this is where he was headed Sunday. Maybe . . . I don't know. Call it a hunch."

"Yeah, I play my fair share of hunches and gut instincts too."

"What's your gut instinct tell you about Ben?"

He pursed his lips. "Not much."

Sawyer veered farther right in the channel to avoid incoming fishing boats. About a mile south of shore, she brought the boat around to port and headed east through bright blue water. She explained that the Great Florida Reef was about five miles south. Cuba, as she was sure he knew, was ninety miles south.

"About how far to Sugarloaf Key?"

"Twenty miles."

"And how fast are we going?"

"Sixteen knots."

"What's that in land speed?"

She turned his way. "Don't you have boats in California either?"

"Not me personally, no."

"Not quite twenty miles per hour."

He nodded.

"So about an hour's ride."

"You Californians all put so much stock in time?"

He shrugged.

"You need to relax," she said. "Blue sky, blue water, a charming Southern woman for company." She grinned. "What's time?"

Jackson grinned back. "Fair point."

"Sandwiches are in the cooler, by the way," she said, referencing the lunch she'd promised Jackson when she'd called earlier. "Water too. And leftover brownies."

"Leftover from what?"

"The other night when I wanted some brownies."

Jackson grinned again as he helped himself to a ham and Swiss sandwich and a bottled water. He also brought a sandwich and a water to Sawyer, rejoining her at the helm. She piloted the mid-sized powerboat effortlessly and comfortably, her eyes behind the silver aviator sunglasses, the breeze swirling her hair and flapping her T-shirt. Once again, Jackson thought there was something about her—something that went beyond good looks or simple charisma. He couldn't place it but didn't much care.

"So what's the deal with the Conch Republic?" Jackson asked as he took a bite of his sandwich. He chewed quickly and swallowed. "I've seen signs and T-shirts . . ."

"Oh, it goes back to the 1980s when the U.S. Border Patrol set up a roadblock on Highway 1, trying to stem the tide of illegal aliens and narcotics coming into the states via the Keys. The City Council said it was a major hassle and a hindrance to tourism. When their complaints weren't getting them anywhere, as a means of protest, they claimed independence and declared themselves the Conch Republic."

"Why Conch?"

"Slang term for natives of the Keys. I think it originated in the Bahamas."

"So what happened? This is still Florida, right?"

"When the Keys declared independence, the mayor was named Prime Minister of the Conch Republic and promptly declared war on the U.S."

"You're kidding."

"They surrendered a minute later and applied for foreign aid."

"These people are crazy."

"It worked. The protest got attention, and the roadblock was lifted. There've been a few other events over the years that stir up the secession sentiment again, but by and large, it's just a tourism marketing ploy now."

"That worked too, apparently."

"Apparently," she said. They'd finished sandwiches, and Sawyer let Jackson man the wheel while she retrieved a pair of brownies. "So yesterday you mentioned looking through Ben's stuff," she said after a bite. "Find anything?"

He recapped his search, highlighting what he'd found in Ben's study, from the books on Caribbean piracy to Ben's notebooks to the giant encyclopedia of storms. He shared his theory that Ben was writing another book.

"It's possible, I suppose. He didn't say anything to me about it."

"Else he's looking for Brackett's treasure."

"Did you find anything to indicate that?"

"Not specifically. But there were your pictures of the *Barracuda* that he wanted to see. And he had all sorts of maps and charts of the area. Depths and tides dating back decades."

"You said you didn't think the intruder you mentioned took anything?"

"Hard to tell," Jackson said. "If there even was an intruder."

"Now you don't think so?"

"I think it was the middle of the night and I can't be sure. At any rate, I didn't notice that anything was missing. But he or she or it could have found something and put it back. Or I could have missed whatever they did."

Sawyer wrinkled her face.

"So this James Brackett," Jackson said. "You familiar with his treasure legend?"

She nodded.

He sighed. "My last case before the one with the World War II vet and the Russians—a guy hired me to find crusader treasure. We chased to France and Greece and Israel and got nothing. So I'm a little hesitant to ask, but lay it on me."

"You went to France, Greece, and Israel?"

"And technically Jordan."

"When?"

"February."

"You have had an interesting year."

"Yeah."

"Well, I'll warn you, the Brackett Legend is just that."

"There's no treasure?"

"There might be. But nobody knows. There's no proof. Just lots of little pieces that nobody has figured out."

"Ben said he wanted to pick my brain," Jackson said. "Maybe this was what it was about."

"That would make sense."

He took a drink of water, leaning against the side of the boat, enjoying the breeze. "So about this legend?"

"You'll have to wait," she said, reaching for the throttle. She cut power. "We're here."

Jackson hadn't been paying close attention and hadn't noticed that Sawyer had angled the boat away from shore. They were now maybe a mile and a half out from a desolate, tree-covered shoreline.

"That's Sugarloaf Key," she said. Then she pointed to the east, to a small strip of wooded island. "That's Lois Key."

Jackson nodded.

"You follow Lois Key to the northwest, it points almost directly to The Point."

"Ever eat there?"

"Uh-huh."

"Any good?"

"The best."

Jackson nodded again. "So where's here?"

Sawyer pointed to a buoy floating about fifty feet to starboard. "That marks the *Barracuda*."

"It has its own buoy?"

"It's a hotspot for divers. You ever dived?"

"No. Snorkeled once, but never dived."

"You should try it sometime. I'm a licensed instructor."

"There anything you don't do?"

Sawyer just smiled. "Come on, we should be over it."

"You can see it from the surface?" Jackson asked, following her toward the bow.

"Uh-huh. Water's clear as a November morn." She leaned over the railing. "There, see that?"

Jackson peered into the water. He couldn't believe how clear it was, allowing him to make out a dark shape amid the otherwise light-colored sand and rock. Nor could he believe he was looking at an actual pirate vessel. Shipwrecks were supposed to be down in the abyss with eels squiggling through them and man-eating sharks circling them to guard what lay beneath. They weren't supposed to be seemingly within reach beneath water clearer than Jackson's tap. "I'd never know it was a ship," he said.

"Maybe not from up top," Sawyer said, "especially with the coral covering it."

"How big is she?"

"About a hundred feet long," Sawyer said. "Beam of twenty-five. The mainmast would have been close to a hundred feet too."

"I assume she's been thoroughly salvaged?"

"Um-hmm. She was discovered in the mid-sixties and identified shortly thereafter. They found cannon, pistols and rifles, swords, kitchen utensils, some other odds and ends."

"No gold though?"

Sawyer shook her head. She returned to the console and eased the boat right and around the outside of the buoy. She backed off the throttle again and dropped the anchor. "Now you can see the outline better," she said, moving to the port railing as the boat rocked in the gentle swells.

Jackson joined her again and looked through the crystal clear water. "How deep is this?"

"Only about twenty-five feet. Over the years, the pressure has compacted the *Barracuda*. Still, it's probably only a dozen feet below the surface at low tide. It's another reason for the buoy."

"I guess."

"Wanna get wet?"

"I certainly didn't buy a new swimsuit because it was stylish."

Sawyer retreated to the stern, where she'd stashed two sets of snorkeling gear—one pink, one blue. She took the blue one with a smirk.

"Hmm, voluntarily wearing Auburn colors," Jackson said as he kicked off his shoes.

"God made blue, and He never sold the rights to that cow college. Besides, this is not Auburn blue."

He smirked in return, then stripped down to his swimsuit. Sawyer did likewise, and even though it was a relatively modest tankini—and the blue stripes interspersed with white stripes were pretty close in color to UCLA's powder blue—it was hard not to stare. Fortunately, he had snorkel fins to focus on.

"You've done this before?" Sawyer asked.

"Once, in Hawaii."

"Quite the world traveler."

"I was born there, actually. Dad was stationed at Pearl Harbor."

"Oh dear."

"What?"

"Daddy was in the Army. He never much cottoned to Navy folks."

She said it with a straight face, and Jackson didn't know if she was serious or not.

"Do I need to spit into this or something?" he asked, holding up a pink-rimmed mask. It was little more than goggles.

Sawyer smiled. "Only if it gets foggy." She fitted her mask over her head. "Ready?"

"Let's roll."

"Follow my lead."

"Okay."

"You know how to expel water if it gets in your snorkel?"

"Dump it out?"

"You can usually clear it by exhaling, but if not, just tip it back slowly and let it drain."

"Got it."

They took seats on a platform at the stern, legs and flipper-clad feet dangling in the water. Sawyer positioned her snorkel and, just before putting it in, looked at Jackson. "If a shark attacks, punch it in the eyes or gills." She inserted the snorkel into her mouth and slipped over the side of the boat into the water. Jackson waited a second, a smile forming as he again tried to figure out if she was serious or messing with him. Then he entered the water.

Even in the ocean, the swells were gentle, and it only took him a moment to orient himself and get comfortable with a basic swimming stroke. He wouldn't chase down Michael Phelps anytime soon, but he could at least keep up with Sawyer. She waited for him to get his bearings, then stroked away from the boat. He followed slightly off to her side.

Brightly colored coral, equally vibrant fish—none of which were large enough to pose a threat—and beautiful blue-green water that filtered bright sunlight almost made him forget about the wrecked ship. Sawyer led him directly over it at first, the rotted wood feeling close enough to touch. Then again, maybe it was.

The *Barracuda* lay on its port side, the broken and sheared masts pointing roughly toward Sugarloaf Key, Jackson concluded after using their boat and the position of the sun as a compass. Several large sections of the hull had disintegrated, and numerous portions had rotted. More of the ship was covered in coral, giving it an otherworldly appearance. So too did several small schools of fish streaming in and out of its myriad openings.

Sawyer kicked for the bow, and Jackson followed. The main mast had cracked in several places but fallen to the seabed almost in line with the prow. Hovering just above it with lifelike expression was a figurehead that resembled a mermaid. Jackson touched Sawyer's arm, signaling to surface. They both popped their heads out of the water and lifted their snorkels and masks.

"What do you think?" Sawyer asked. "Isn't the water great?"

"Yeah," he said, not sure if she was referring to its warmth or clarity. Both were unprecedented. "Is that siren of the sea made of gold?"

"The figurehead?"

He nodded.

"No. Polished and painted wood, probably."

"I was going to say. Still, remarkably preserved."

Sawyer wiped a hand over her face. "Feel like a little freediving?"

"For kicks?"

"There's something I want to show you."

"Not in the pictures you took?"

"I was running out of air and had to hurry, so it was blurry."

He shrugged.

"Follow me, and when I signal, take three deep breaths. Hold the third one."

"Okay."

"We're going straight down, through the opening behind the mizzen mast."

"The what?"

"You sure your dad was in the Navy?"

"You think the Bear's kids could break down film, spot the weakness in a quarterback's throwing motion, anticipate play calls just because his dad was a coach?"

"Probably."

"Yeah, I suppose. Where's the mizzen mast?"

"Back of the ship."

"And we're diving through a hole behind it?"

She nodded.

"Sounds smart."

"It's plenty wide for two divers side-by-side."

"If you say so."

She nodded. "Look to your left when you get through, and watch my signals."

"Okay."

"Ready?"

He nodded. They reinserted their snorkels and swam side-by-side toward the stern of the *Barracuda*. Sawyer turned so she was facing Jackson, then made a sweeping motion with her hand. They each took a deep breath through the snorkel, then exhaled. They repeated. The third time, Jackson filled his lungs and immediately followed Sawyer down toward the hole in the starboard hull of the ship.

She was right. It was huge, and they both fit through and swam into a dark chamber beneath the angled hull and mostly eroded deck of the *Barracuda*. Enough sunlight penetrated the four fathoms of water and shown through the gaps in the wood, enabling Jackson to see Sawyer's outstretched arm pointing to his left. Feeling that he still had plenty of air, he kicked his fins and pushed several feet in that direction.

The combination of disintegrated wood, list of the ship, abundant coral, and comparative darkness was starting to make him feel disoriented. He roved his eyes left and right, wondering what Sawyer had wanted him to see. He was about to give up and head for the surface when she materialized beside him, pointing again. Once more, his eyes followed her outstretched arm, toward a dark corner near an intact section of decking.

At first, all he saw was more wood. That and several silver and black fish. Then he detected a form to the wood, and a discoloration. No, not a discoloration, but a separate entity. Maybe gold, maybe bronze, maybe brass. Bands, holding straps of wood in place, and what looked like a hasp or part of a lock.

He was looking at a treasure chest.

Chapter Twelve

2:41 p.m.

JACKSON LAY BACK, drifting in the warm water, studying wisps of thin clouds in the beautiful blue sky as he drew several deep breaths. After holding his breath for nearly a minute underwater, it took a few minutes to regulate his breathing. When it evened out, he straightened up and tread water, looking for Sawyer. She was positioned likewise just to his left, grinning, her snorkel mask pushed up on top of her head.

"A treasure chest," Jackson finally said.

"Uh-huh."

"But no gold."

"Nope."

He took a few more breaths. "So where is it?"

"You're the detective. You tell me."

"You wanna run the legend past me?"

"There's a reef about a hundred yards this way," she said, pointing toward Lois Key to the east. "Wanna check it out first? Since we're here?"

"Okay, sure."

They spent another half hour in the water, swimming to the reef and back and viewing an assortment of colorful fish, sea anemones, a stingray, and a pair of mid-sized turtles. No sharks, eels, jellyfish, actual barracudas, or anything terribly dangerous.

Jackson's arms and legs were both sore by the time he and Sawyer climbed back onto the chartered boat. They removed their flippers and masks, and Sawyer tossed Jackson a towel before tousling her hair with another.

"Whadiya think?" she asked after stepping into her shorts. "Better or worse than Hawaii?"

"Just as good. Better guide."

"Oh?"

"In Hawaii, it was a dude."

She grinned and pulled her T-shirt on over her swimsuit. Jackson blotted his trunks dry so they weren't clingy and uncomfortable, but let the sun and breeze do the rest. He downed a second ham sandwich and a bottle of water while Sawyer weighed anchor. Then he brought her and himself a second brownie.

"Thanks."

"It's a bribe."

"You want the treasure legend?"

"Uh-huh."

"Let me get us on our way back."

He nodded and consumed the rest of his brownie. Sawyer got the engine going and eased away from the buoy, ultimately turning back toward Key West. The afternoon sun was still high and hot, albeit having begun its westward and downward trajectory, causing the sky to pale in the west. Only a few fair-weather clouds marred the otherwise endless blue. It was as wide open as any place Jackson had ever been, and he was starting to feel the allure of the Keys.

"So, Brackett's treasure," Sawyer said when they were up to speed, the breeze quickly drying her hair and Jackson's skin. "You want the *Reader's Digest* version or the full story?"

"Spare no detail."

She raised an eyebrow. "Remember, you asked for it."

He nodded.

"By the 1700s, most of the gold and silver the Spanish conquistadors had—ahem, recovered—from Central and South America had been shipped back to Spain," she said. "But in 1715, Philip V of Spain sent a convoy of ships to retrieve one last cache of treasure. The Spanish empire was in decline, and he hoped to use the gold to restore Spain to its heyday."

"A stimulus package."

"Of sorts. The convoy sailed to Veracruz, where they met with the Spanish forces stationed there and loaded the gold." She looked at him. "Normally, the ships sailed in fleets or convoys, but for some reason, the *Nuestra Señora de la Granada* set sail solo on July thirty-first, 1715."

"*Nuestra Señorita de* what?"

"*Nuestra Señora de la Granada.* Our Lady of Granada. Granada's a city in southeastern Spain."

Jackson nodded.

"Anyhow, the *Granada* was headed for modern-day Fort Meyers, to a Spanish fort where they were going to pick up reinforcements."

"Reinforcements?"

"Apparently quite a few members of the original crew had succumbed to smallpox while in Veracruz, and they were afraid of not being able to defend the ship in case of a pirate attack. Turns out, their fears were well founded. About two hundred miles southwest of Tampa, they were attacked by Captain Brackett and the crew of the *Barracuda.* They took a huge chest of gold and various other valuables and left the crippled *Granada* adrift in the Gulf."

Sawyer turned to look at Jackson. "That much isn't legend. Several surviving members of the *Granada* testified to what had taken place."

"So the treasure did exist?"

"Yes, it existed. And Brackett at least had it in his possession at one time. So there's a basis for the legend."

"Well, that's something."

"Brackett not only took the treasure from the *Granada* but also kidnapped Liliana de Castaño, daughter of Gabriel Vicente de Castaño, the Capitán General of the Spanish Navy under Philip V."

"I gather that made Brackett something of a wanted man."

Sawyer nodded. "Yeah. The entire Spanish Navy was put on the lookout for him, his crew, and his ship."

"Never found him?"

"No. Brackett attacked the *Granada* on August second or third. The hurricane that sank the *Barracuda* hit the Keys on August sixth. And that's where the facts run out. No one knows what became of Brackett, Liliana de Castaño, or the treasure."

"Nothing ever found with the wreck? Nothing at all?"

"No. Plenty of people have looked. They've studied the tide and the currents and storm tracks and covered every inch of these waters. Never found so much as a piece of eight."

"So what's the theory?"

"Take your pick," Sawyer said. "There are still plenty of people who think the gold went down with the ship and has yet to be found. Some think Brackett and his crew took it ashore and stashed it somewhere in the Keys, or else rode out the hurricane and then went on their way in another ship. Brackett was English, so there's a theory he returned to England—with or without Liliana, depending on your perspective—and spent it there."

Sawyer veered a fraction closer to shore, making way for an eastbound pleasure cruiser that was twice their size. She checked her gauges, then turned back to Jackson. "For a while, the theory was popular that Brackett was captured and rotted in a prison in Seville. Another rumor that gained traction stated that he showed up in the newly founded city Nouvelle-Orléans a few years later, poor as Job's turkeys, looking for another crew."

"New Orleans?"

She nodded.

"Interesting."

"If you travel down to the Lesser Antilles, you'll hear stories about Brackett's crew—without him—causing trouble in the 1720s. There's a claim that Brackett died in Jamaica leaving behind a wife and kids, that he buried his treasure in the Bahamas before disappearing, and my personal favorite," she said, turning to look Jackson in the eye, "is that he still lives on, pirating a magical ghost ship around the Caribbean."

"No doubt staging battles with Captain Hook and Long John Silver."

"With all the theories, it's become increasingly harder to sort the fact from fiction. All of the theories and rumors are based on something, but all have enough holes in them that they've never become the predominant theory." She shrugged. "So it's anyone's guess."

"What's yours?"

She looked at him. "I'm not a treasure hunter."

"You know the legend pretty well."

"It gets passed around. You wait enough tables, make enough friends and acquaintances, and you put the pieces together." She shrugged again. "I tend to think the simplest theory is the most likely, but that would mean the gold went down with the ship."

"Kind of makes me want to do more than freediving."

"Trust me, there's no gold in that ship."

"Have you looked?"

Sawyer shook her head. "No, but like I said, a lot of people have. If it was there, somebody would have found something—other than an empty chest."

Jackson thought for a moment. "You said gold and various valuables. What are the specifics?"

"I don't know. A lot of gold, but it could have been coins, idols, utensils. Maybe some silver and jewels." She shrugged. "That part's sort of murky."

"How much are we talking?"

"Depends what it was, obviously, but a chest full of gold . . . Conservative estimates put it in the millions."

Jackson whistled.

"Now you really want to go diving, don't you?"

"I want to know if Ben was onto something with one of these theories, because if he was, it would add credence to the intruder/foul play theory."

Sawyer bit her lip but didn't say anything, focusing instead on piloting the boat.

"You said earlier that Ben wasn't the treasure hunting type," Jackson said, "that he was more of a researcher."

Sawyer nodded.

"So in your opinion, if he was pursuing the Brackett treasure, how would he go about it?"

"Books," she said. "He'd study history to learn anything and everything he could about the subject."

"Solo?"

She turned. "Unless he had a wingman."

"You know who he'd go to for expert insight?"

"No."

"Somebody at school, church, an old professor?"

Sawyer shrugged. "He's never mentioned anyone."

"Yeah, to me either," Jackson said, thinking through past e-mails. He and Ben generally swapped one or two per year, mostly casual "how's life" communications. If Ben had said something about an academic knowledge source, Jackson didn't remember it.

"What about friends, coworkers? Who would he talk to, if not for advice then just to share what he was working on?"

Sawyer shrugged again. "I don't know. He didn't have a lot of really close friends, at least that I knew. Maybe there was somebody he worked with, a colleague somewhere. But he kept to himself quite a bit."

"Yeah," Jackson said with a sigh. He tried a different tack. "What about you? Let's say you had the million-dollar itch. Where would you go to scratch it?"

Sawyer looked at Jackson with a sideways smirk. "Ben."

"Besides Ben," Jackson said, returning the grin.

"I don't know. Most of what I've heard of the legend has come in bits and pieces, from old guys at a restaurant or fishermen swapping stories or . . . Ben."

"He told you about it?"

"He's mentioned it before, but just in passing. At least, I thought."

"Do you remember what specifically he said?"

"Not really. I think he told me about a few more of the theories as to where the treasure might be. You know, New Orleans, Jamaica, Bahamas."

"Sounds like the Beach Boys."

"Why do you ask? The P.I. in you coming out? You going to investigate what happened?"

"I don't know. Maybe. But there isn't much of a trail unless we dig through all his research."

"We?"

"The royal we. But even so, finding out his favorite treasure theory doesn't tell us what happened out on that boat or who Ted Ryker is and how he knew Ben or anything else. If, on the other hand, we knew who he talked to about it, maybe we can tie that person to Ryker or figure something out."

"You don't trust the Sheriff's Department?"

"I don't not trust them," he said. "Unless you have reason not to?"

She shook her head.

"You do know the sheriff."

"His son didn't respect personal boundaries, but I have no qualms with Sheriff Hawkins or his department's ability."

Jackson nodded. "It's not that I don't trust them," he repeated, "but I just feel like I should be doing something." He sighed. "Unfortunately, I'm not Lance White. I can't just make a clue appear."

"Who?"

"Sorry, obscure TV reference."

"I don't watch much TV."

"How do you kill time on a rainy day? *Guitar Hero?*"

"The real thing. Rain is a great motivator for song-writing."

"You write songs too?"

"Um-hmm."

"So do I get to hear an original Sawyer Collins?"

"When you say it that way, it sounds like malt liquor."

"I was thinking a vintage guitar. Or a watercolor."

"Oil, remember?"

Jackson grinned. "So . . . ?"

"Not until I've known you more than a few days."

"Fair enough."

Sawyer made a slight adjustment to course, then turned her attention to Jackson. "You have dinner plans tonight?"

He shook his head slightly. "We going fishing again, or you asking me on a date?"

"I was thinking of an actual dinner, at a restaurant."

He nodded.

"But to be clear, I'm not asking you on a date. I don't date men I don't know, and I don't know you that well."

"Only a few days."

She nodded.

"Including snapper on the beach."

"Just dinner," she said with the beginnings of a smile.

Jackson wasn't sure what did or didn't constitute a date in the South—or with Sawyer—and didn't much care. "I don't have dinner plans," he said. "You got a place in mind?"

"The Point," she said. "The seafood is incredible."

"Sounds good," Jackson said with his best smart-aleck face. "It's a date."

Chapter Thirteen

6:07 p.m.

SAWYER HAD CHANGED into a pair of jeans, a faded pink tee, and a pair of boots. Jackson was relieved. He'd been afraid she'd show up in a stunning sundress and heels, and he'd feel underdressed in a (clean) tee and his jeans. Her hair was down, very blond in the early evening sunlight, and date or not, Jackson would have been lying to himself if he didn't admit he was looking forward to dinner with Sawyer.

"Sorry I'm late," she said as Jackson closed his hotel room door behind him and stepped out onto the exterior corridor. "But it is a Southern woman's prerogative to be fashionably late."

"Five minutes?" Jackson said. "By what I hear of Southern time, that makes you early."

"Put those away," Sawyer said as Jackson reached for his keys. She nodded at her Jeep, in the parking lot below. "I'll drive."

"Southern woman's prerogative?"

"Just this Southern woman. I hate being a passenger."

With no windows and no roof, the ride in the Jeep wasn't conducive to conversation once they reached highway speed. So Jackson sat back and enjoyed the view. The day had continued hot and sunny, with increasing mugginess as the afternoon wore on. Now, as the sun sunk to the west, the clouds on the western horizon were growing in both size and number, forming a line that was steadily marching eastward. The air had an electricity to it, signifying a humidity-relieving storm was on the way. But for now, the sun was still bright and warm. Jackson was amazed at the texture created as the sun's rays played on the trees and bushes, contrasting sharply with the lengthening shadows it created. Jackson's opinion of the Florida Keys, as well as his general outlook, had definitely improved over a day and a half ago.

Sawyer drove with a carefree spirit, weaving around slower-moving vehicles, waving at pedestrians and boaters, and tapping her palms on the steering wheel all the while. She cranked the radio to a country station, casting one glance at Jackson to see if he minded. He was in the South and thus didn't.

After driving across and past miles of water that seemed only a few feet deep, Sawyer turned off the Overseas Highway. They passed through a small neighborhood, then a patch of scrub and brushwood before turning to the east on a road lined by trees and bushes that blocked the view. A short while later, the pavement ended, and they rumbled along a gravel road for a hundred yards until Sawyer turned off onto a narrower, uneven gravel drive leading through more thick foliage. After a hundred feet, the drive opened into a small parking area. Sawyer parked the Jeep adjacent to a rusty old pickup and killed the radio.

"Tell me this is the honky-tonk where we're stopping so you can punch out your ex and win back some lost pool money to pay for dinner," Jackson said.

"It may not look like much," Sawyer said with a grin, "but trust me, the food here is spectacular."

Jackson nodded as he looked at the faded brown siding, dark windows, and overgrowth surrounding the building. The only identification was a weathered wooden sign hanging on one of the columns supporting the porch. It had a large oak tree in the center with "The Point" painted beneath it. It was so faded that Jackson could barely make it out.

"What are the odds of a Northerner making it out of here alive?" Jackson asked.

"I thought you were from California."

"'Northerner' relatively speaking."

"You'll be fine. We Southerners are known for our hospitality," she said in her best *Gone With the Wind* accent.

Jackson followed Sawyer onto the porch, where a black and white cat scurried out of their way. A young man asleep in a wooden rocking chair didn't.

Sawyer just shrugged as she opened the door.

Unidentifiable reggae music greeted Jackson, along with the aroma of grilled seafood. There was no hostess, and Sawyer walked straight toward a sliding screen door on the back side of the restaurant. Jackson followed, ignoring the patrons at booths and tables and at the bar who all turned to watch them. Sawyer led the way onto a narrow wooden deck that extended over shallow, stagnant water backed by trees. There were a few tables to the left, shaded by umbrellas. But Sawyer turned right, up a set of rickety wooden stairs to a flat roof with half a dozen tables.

The view was spectacular. Behind them, the open sea was visible beyond a tangled mess of bushes and low trees on the far side of the stagnant pond. The water was the most perfect blue Jackson had ever seen, a rich cobalt infused with sunlight. On either side, the treetops were just below eye level, allowing a view down the length of the coast to the west and, for a short while, east until the coast extended into the ocean and then turned north as Sugarloaf Key rounded out. Straight ahead beyond the parking lot, road, and more trees was more of the low, coastal overflow—the sounds and bights on the interior of Sugarloaf Key. The low sun glistened off the water and turned the sand, trees, and distant rooftops a magical golden color. Jackson had a feeling he was in for another legendary Keys sunset.

There was another couple seated in the far corner, so Sawyer picked a table by the stairs and sat down before Jackson could think to pull out her chair. He sat too and spent another minute enjoying the view, sweeping his eyes across the panorama of the distant Keys on his left to the setting sun on his right, with a smiling Southern belle in the middle.

"What did I tell you?" she asked.

"Wait until I taste the food."

"The food will embarrass the view."

A waiter in a blue tie-dyed shirt and a New York Yankees cap (Jackson smirked at the irony) delivered menus and took drink orders. Sawyer ordered sweet tea and lots of it, and Jackson opted for unsweetened tea. The waiter and Sawyer both looked at him as if he'd asked for puppy blood.

The menu was simple: several kinds of shrimp, several kinds of fish—including shark—gator tails, a Cuban sandwich, a few varieties of chicken, a burger, and a couple cuts of steak. Jackson opted for the shrimp, Sawyer the catfish, and she talked him into an appetizer of gator tails. The Yankee promised they would be right up and darted back down the stairs.

"So, I called Sheriff Hawkins before coming over," Sawyer said, squeezing a lemon into her tea.

"Oh?"

"I was curious if his investigation had made any progress, after our talk earlier."

"Has it?"

"No. He said New Orleans police weren't aware of any tie between Ryker and Ben, that they had no idea what Ryker was doing in Florida. Seemed like a dead end."

"Of course."

"He said they looked over Ben's house yesterday, but didn't find anything."

Jackson sighed.

"And none of Ben's friends or coworkers had anything to contribute either, according to Hawkins. Like I told you before, he's a quiet guy and keeps to himself. Whatever he was working on, nobody seems to know anything about it." She sipped her tea through a straw.

"I guess that's that, then," Jackson said. "Since we talked this afternoon, I'd been thinking about whether I should try to track down Ben's coworkers and friends, see if any of them knew anything. But I guess Hawkins has it covered."

He took a pull on his tea. Perfectly unsweet. If he wanted a sugary drink, he'd order Kool-Aid.

"So why'd you become a private investigator?" Sawyer asked. "That isn't something most young men aspire to, is it?"

"No, I can't say it is." He looked up at her. She was looking straight at him, not staring, not in an intimidating way. Like the night before while fishing and eating on the beach, she was simply being authentic. It was refreshing.

"I went to USC out of high school," Jackson answered. "Dropped out. Joined the Army. Dropped out."

"You can do that?"

"I got an Entry Level Separation. It's basically an annulment as opposed to an honorable or dishonorable discharge. It's for people who can't cut it or can't adapt to military life, for a variety of reasons." He shrugged. "Then I went to the University of San Diego for a year."

"Dropped out?"

He nodded. "I worked every job from host at a pizza parlor to shuttle driver at the airport. I wasn't a flunkie or a loser, unless you ask my brother. Or his fiancée. But now we're off topic." He shrugged. "I just didn't feel any direction in life. Nothing felt right. Then I worked at an investigative firm for a few years, gofer work, pushing papers. I started to think maybe I had a knack for it. I've always been decent at figuring out puzzles and solving mysteries or whatever. And I thought this was maybe a way I could do some good in the world."

"Have you?"

Jackson looked at his tea. "Depends who you ask."

Sawyer waited until he raised his eyes. "Suppose I ask you?"

"Yeah," Jackson said. "I've done good. But I've done bad, too."

"Haven't we all?"

"Yeah."

The Yankee returned with a plate of gator tails, little breaded bites that smelled like all other cooked seafood. He set small plates in front of Sawyer and Jackson and went to check on the other couple. It looked like they were finishing up.

"You don't sound convinced," Sawyer said, unfolding her napkin and placing it on her lap.

"My bad's a little worse than the standard."

"Says who?"

"Pretty much everyone."

"Everyone and Anybody are two very bad judges of character," Sawyer said. She lifted several bites of gator onto her plate, then extended her hands across the table.

Jackson looked at her.

"Where I come from, we pray before meals," Sawyer said. "And we hold hands around the table."

"We didn't hold hands on the beach last night."

"That was really more of an evening snack." She made a come-here signal with her fingers, and Jackson placed his hands in Sawyer's and waited until she closed her eyes to do so as well.

"Jesus, I thank You for our food tonight. I thank You for some good company across the table. And I thank You for Ben. We don't know what happened to him or why, but You do. We trust You to reveal truth, because truth is what You do and Who You are." She paused for a few seconds, and Jackson opened one eye to see a tranquil smile on her face. "I ask You, as always, through the blood of Jesus. Amen."

"Amen," Jackson said, opening both eyes. He and Sawyer let go of each other's hands, and he reached for a gator tail of his own. He took a bite and found the meat tough but not overly flavorful. The breading, on the other hand, had some kick.

"Do you want to talk about it?" Sawyer asked. "The good and bad you've done."

Jackson shrugged. "No, but I don't mind talking about it either."

She ate a tail, then dabbed a crumb from the corner of her mouth. "Well, now I don't know what to do. I'm naturally curious, and I love hearing people's stories. But being nosy is terribly impolite."

"And you are a refined Southern woman," Jackson said with a trace of Scarlett O'Hara in his voice.

"Now you're mocking me."

"Teasing. Very different."

"Oh?"

"You mock people you don't like; you tease people you do."

She closed one eye.

"I mean it. And I like your accent."

She opened the eye again, but said nothing.

Jackson had more gator, then sighed. "Being a private eye, I've had to do some nasty things. For example, to save the undercover cop masquerading as a Valley Girl that I told you about, I had to shoot five gangsters."

"Isn't that akin to self-defense?"

"Yeah. And when I killed Noelle's stalker, it was self-defense. When I shot a man in the West Bank a few months ago, it was to save three women's lives."

"Sounds like all the bad you've done has been to accomplish something good."

"Yeah. Even . . . Nevada. And I've always thought that the ends justified the means. But I'm not so sure."

"What was Nevada?"

"I killed twenty people."

"Twenty?"

"They were part of a militia group doing genetic experiments on people. They had kidnapped my brother's fiancée and they were trying to kill me. It was all legally justified again, and I saved her life. But . . . it takes its toll."

"Yeah," Sawyer said quietly.

He looked at her. "Sorry. Kind of brings down dinner."

"You don't have to apologize to me."

"You want to run and stick me with the check, I won't blame you."

"A refined Southern woman wouldn't dream of it."

Jackson grinned.

"Besides, this refined Southern woman keeps a Ruger M77 Hawkeye under the backseat of her Jeep."

"What don't you keep back there?"

She grinned.

Jackson reached for another piece of gator. "Ever shoot it?"

"Plenty of times."

"At someone?"

"Once."

"Really?"

"Um-hmm. He was an Auburn fan."

Jackson raised an eyebrow.

"That wasn't why," Sawyer said as she reached for her straw. She took a long drink. "Entirely."

"This is confession hour," Jackson said.

She smiled. "It was after the game a few years ago, where they came back from twenty-four down to beat us. He was drunk, hollering outside of my friend's house, using a lot of profanity. We asked him to leave, and he made a few crude comments. He was smoking and throwing his butts in my friend's landscaping. He also smashed this little statue of a boy and girl on a swing she had hanging from her tree. So I politely asked him to leave again, and he said some things a Southern woman should not have to hear." Sawyer pinched off half a bite of gator. "So I walked calmly to my Jeep, pulled out my rifle, and fired a round at his feet."

"What'd he do?"

"Made pretty good time, considering he tripped over himself a couple times."

Jackson grinned.

"I didn't shoot anybody, but I shot at him."

"Well, if you're not put off by my Jack Bauer approach to private investigating, I'm okay with you being a gun-toting Southern Miss."

"Fair enough."

Chapter Fourteen

7:27 p.m.

THE ENTRÉES WERE delicious and plentiful, and by the time Jackson was almost done with his shrimp, he had to agree with Sawyer that, despite its appearance and location, The Point provided a quality dining experience.

As they ate, the sun sunk lower and lower in the northwestern sky, eventually dipping behind a wall of dark bluish-purple clouds. The heat and humidity of the day tempered and a steady breeze kicked up, making the evening air bearable. The other couple on the roof finished and left, and except for tea refill trips from the Yankee, Jackson and Sawyer were alone.

"How'd you meet Ben?" she asked.

Jackson explained how he had gone to help the O'Reillys unload their moving truck, how the friendship had slowly formed, and how he and Ben had grown to be really solid friends. Then Ben had moved to Georgia, Jackson had gone off to college and new friends and adulthood, and they had been relegated to swapping e-mails a few times a year.

"And yet you came all the way to see him."

"He said this was the place to get away. And I needed to get away."

"From work?"

"Yeah. And life."

She thought for a moment. "So have you?"

"Gotten away from life? To an extent. The last few days."

Sawyer nodded.

"How about you? How'd you meet Ben?"

"Church," she said. "I was unfashionably late one morning, and the only available seat was next to this tall guy with a tie. A tie, in Key West, in June. So I had to strike up a conversation with him afterwards." She shrugged. "Sort of like you said, the friendship just happened."

"You said you and Ben weren't best friends, weren't *that* close?"

"Not because we don't like each other well enough to be close friends. We just never really had reason to hang out or anything. Plus, I'm only here part time."

"Why's that?"

Sawyer sighed. "I have wanderlust. I can't stand to do the same thing all the time or be in the same place all the time. I don't know how so many people do it. Same job, same routine, same breakfast every morning. I couldn't live that way. Plus Tuscaloosa will always be home."

"So why the Keys in the summer, in the heart of hurricane season?"

"Because it's when they're the most beautiful. And it's not like I'd be escaping any heat in Alabama."

"No, I suppose not."

"And because I don't miss Crimson Tide football this way."

"So the truth finally comes out."

The Yankee returned, asking if they wanted dessert.

"Two slices of key lime pie, to go," Sawyer said. He left, and she sipped the last of her tea.

"Isn't the guy supposed to order for the girl?" Jackson asked. "Or is that not how it works in the South?"

"I was afraid you wouldn't have the courage to try key lime pie."

"In the Keys, are you kidding?"

She shrugged. "And I got it to go because it'll rain before we get back otherwise."

"You're a regular Stephanie Abrams."

"Who?"

"Never mind. Where are we going?"

"I have a thought on that, actually."

"Yeah?"

"I was thinking about what you said earlier, about Hawkins having the investigation into what happened to Ben covered."

"You think he doesn't?"

"No, I think he does. But I remember what you said on the boat too, about the trail being cold unless we dig through all Ben's research." She fiddled with her straw. "How thorough were you?"

"Not very. Enough to uncover something obvious, but that's about it."

"Maybe we should dig a little deeper. I know it's a long shot. Like you said earlier, figuring out what he knew about the treasure won't tell us what happened to him. But maybe . . . it will tell us something."

Jackson shrugged. "Why not?"

"It will at least feel like we're doing something, and it's the one lead I'm betting Hawkins' detectives won't pursue."

"You talked me into it," Jackson said.

The Yankee returned with two slices of pie in clear plastic containers and the check. Jackson reached for it, but Sawyer beat him to it.

"I'm not being forward. I asked you to dinner, so I pay."

"I like Southern women."

"If this had been a date, I'd have insisted you pay."

"Naturally."

Sawyer retrieved a credit card from a small clip in her pocket—no purse—and slid it into the check holder. The Yankee took it, promised to be right back, and headed downstairs again.

"My turn not to be forward," Jackson said. "How is this not a date?"

"For one thing, we are both wearing denim."

"And one of us a pair of boots."

"Two, I asked you."

Jackson nodded.

"And three, a date carries with it the weight of implied romantic feelings and expectations. A date is something serious, something not to be taken lightly. Dinner, on the other hand, is much more relaxed. Dinner is fun."

Jackson nodded. "Well, thank you for dinner."

"You are welcome."

"And for the experience. I've never dined on a roof in the middle of a mangrove swamp before."

"This isn't a mangrove swamp."

"Whatever."

The Yankee brought back the check, thanked them, and left them alone again with the relative silence. Various birds and insects and the occasional clatter of dishes from below kept the night from being totally quiet. So did a distant rumble of thunder, if Jackson wasn't mistaken. They stood, and Sawyer reached into her pocket and withdrew her phone.

"Here, stand by the railing a minute."

"Why?"

She joined him and extended the phone out. "Smile."

Jackson did, and she snapped a quick picture. She showed it to him. The sun was behind the oncoming storm clouds, but enough of its rays still infused the sky with color, making for a beautiful backdrop.

"What was that for?" Jackson asked.

"Because I like to take pictures for memory's sake," Sawyer said. "Places I go, people I meet, experiences."

"Why not. Ready?"

She nodded, and Jackson grabbed their pies. The air was still warm as they headed back toward the Overseas Highway and some signs of civilization. As Sawyer turned west, lightning began to flash on the horizon. The clouds quickly mushroomed into the air, towering plumes behind the initial cloud that was darkening the evening sky. Sawyer pushed her Jeep a little faster across the bridges and open marshes of the Keys.

By the time they reached Ben's house in Key Haven, giant raindrops were plummeting to earth. The driveway was still empty, as was the carport. Jackson asked Sawyer if Hawkins had said anything about Ben's Uncle Malcolm from Atlanta coming down, and she said it hadn't come up.

She parked under the carport, and they took several minutes to put the top up. The wind was gusting, suggesting the carport might not be enough protection. The rain was intensifying as they hurried to the front door. It was unlocked, and no sooner were they inside the house than the rain began falling in earnest.

"You want coffee with your pie?" Jackson asked as he headed for the kitchen.

"Coffee? It's eighty degrees outside."

"I take that for a no."

"No, but thank you."

"Something else? I think there's still some lemonade in the fridge."

"No thanks."

Jackson turned around, then stopped. The red message light on Ben's phone was blinking.

"Hey, Sawyer."

She looked his way. "Yeah?"

"What's the code for refined Southerners listening to someone else's voicemails?"

"It depends," she said, walking toward him. "Are you listening because you're nosy or because you think it might be relevant to what happened to him?"

"It wasn't here last time I was."

"What, you checked for messages each day?"

"I notice things like blinking red ones on a phone's display."

"Probably the library about an overdue book," she said.

A steady growl of thunder rattled the windows, then shook the floor. Jackson looked at Sawyer as he pressed the play button.

"Hey, brother, it's Damon," came a quick, smooth voice. "Hey, I think I might finally have a lead for you. There's a guy named Louviere, a real bigwig around here, whose family goes back centuries. Word is, and I've got it from two different sources, that Louviere owns a logbook of every ship and captain that came or went in the early 1700s. And I think I may even have a line on how to get a look at it. I'll let you know how it goes and if I find anything. Hey, I also wanted to check if you've heard of the Missianna or if the name means anything to you? Might be nothing, but I can give you the full story if you want. And, I thought I should tell you that somebody broke into my place the other night."

Jackson raised his eyes to Sawyer's again as Damon kept speaking. "I keep everything in the cloud so if they were looking for anything, they didn't find it. And there have been a few burglaries in the neighborhood lately, so it may just be coincidence. But given everything, I thought I'd mention it. Anyhow, I'll try you again next week. Hope you're enjoying summer vay-cay, bro. Out."

Jackson looked up at Sawyer as a flash of lightning reflected through the dining room and kitchen and off her face. "Who's Damon?" she asked.

"I was hoping you knew."

She shook her head.

Jackson played the message again, along with the time and date stamp. It had been left the previous evening at a quarter to seven, presumably after the Sheriff's Department's detective had looked over the house.

"The Missianna," Sawyer said with a frown. "A ship?"

"Not familiar from the Brackett legend?" Jackson asked.

"No. Did you see it in any of Ben's notes you looked through?"

Jackson shook his head. "The French dude . . . Louviere?"

"Never heard of him. You know he's French?"

"Sounds French," he said, suddenly feeling as if that detail was important. But he couldn't place why.

Sawyer leaned back on a barstool at the counter. "Well, this muddies things."

"We should call Hawkins," Jackson said. "See if any of the names mean anything to him."

"I'll call him," Sawyer said, reaching for her phone. "You stow the pie. We have work to do now."

Her conversation lasted two minutes, and she joined Jackson in Ben's study. He was already at Ben's computer, looking for a list of contacts.

"It won't be in there," Sawyer said. "He keeps everything on paper."

"What'd Hawkins say?"

"Not much. None of the names meant anything to him."

Jackson tried several desk drawers, digging through them more thoroughly than he had the other day. Outside, the lightning was growing in frequency, its flashes blinding. The thunder was almost constant.

"What all did you look through the other day?" Sawyer asked.

"Everything on the desk."

She walked over to the wall and began checking out the books. "I can't figure out his filing system," she said. "It's not Dewey."

"Alphabetical by title by category," Jackson said.

"So what are the categories?"

"That I don't know. I just know they're in sections." He tried the last drawer and found a rolodex. "Really?"

"What?"

He held up the rolodex as Sawyer looked over her shoulder. "Are there names in it?" she asked.

Jackson nodded and began flipping through the cards. The names were arranged alphabetically, but not knowing Damon's last name, it didn't help much. "You're not in here," he said.

"I move around a lot," Sawyer said.

"Oh?"

"Um-hmm."

"Didn't give him your cell?"

"We weren't that close. It never came up."

Jackson flipped to his name. Ben had an old address for him, back in San Diego. Maybe the rolodex wasn't up to date.

The lights temporarily flickered as a boom shook the house.

"Here we go," Jackson said. "Damon Villars. St. Philip Street in New Orleans."

"New Orleans? Same as Ryker?"

"That explains the French name. Louviere."

"Why, do French people live only in New Orleans?"

The teasing was evident on her face, and Jackson gave her an evil eye.

"There a phone number?" she asked.

"No."

"You think Ben has Caller ID?"

"I'll find out." He trudged back to the kitchen and picked up the phone handset just as the power flicked off. It didn't come back on.

"Awesome. You happen to know where Ben keeps flashlights?" Jackson hollered after waiting close to a minute.

There was no response.

"Sawyer?"

"I'm sort of stuck on the ladder," she called.

Jackson smiled at the thought of her waiting for lightning flashes to take the steps down. He used the flashes to ransack drawers in the kitchen. He didn't find a flashlight, but he did find a lighter and several short, stocky candles. He carried them back into the study, where Sawyer had found her way down to the floor.

"Not big on heights?" he asked with a grin.

"When I was a teenager, I was carrying laundry down to the basement, missed the last step, and severely sprained my ankle. I've been a little leery of suspicious footing ever since."

"What were you looking for anyhow?"

"Just surveying his collection," she said as she lit a few candles.

Jackson set the rest on the desk. "I'm going to check the bedrooms for more."

"And something to set them on."

The bedrooms had none, but in a hall closet, he found a dozen more candles, all of them unburned. Still no flashlight. He stopped in the kitchen to pick up a pack of disposable paper plates, figuring they would collect dripping wax. He returned to the study, and he and Sawyer lit a total of half a dozen candles, spreading them around the room. They gave just enough light for them to continue.

"So how do you want to tackle this?" Sawyer said.

"Wasn't this your idea?"

"You're the detective."

He shrugged. "Presumably, the stuff on his desk was what he was working on. So we can look through that for particulars. But then it's probably wise to find out anything and everything we can on our own about Brackett, the treasure, the *Barracuda*, now Louviere and Missianna, whatever that is. Fact, fiction, anything in between. If nothing else, we'll be well-versed so if we trip over a clue, we'll know it."

"Okay," she said. "You've already been through Ben's research once—"

"I only skimmed."

"Still, it was one set of eyes. How about I take that and you ransack the library this time?"

Jackson nodded. "Works for me."

She smiled. "Then let's get to work."

Chapter Fifteen

10:19 p.m.

THE FLAMES ON Ben's candles were long and flickering, filling his study with orange light. The rain had moved on, leaving distant grumbles of thunder and the occasional far-off flash of lightning in its wake. The power was still out, and Jackson and Sawyer had opened the windows to let in a pleasant post-rain breeze.

Sawyer sat on the floor, open books and notebooks and maps spread around her, along with a plate of mostly consumed key lime pie. Jackson's piece was long gone, tasty as everything else at The Point. He was reclined at Ben's desk, as much as the office chair would allow, his feet propped on the desk. His eyes were long tired of reading in the dim light afforded by the candles, and he finally could take it no more. He slammed his current book shut.

"You give up?" Sawyer asked.

"My eyes are starting to bleed."

She took one last look at the book in her lap and closed it. "Okay, I'm pretty much done too. What'd you find?"

"I now know Brackett better than I know myself."

"Let's hear it."

"He was born in Torquay, England, in 1676 to a third-generation blacksmith. His mother was Spanish, originating from Seville."

"Seville? How'd she end up in England?"

"Didn't say."

"Where's Torquay?"

"On the southwestern peninsula, on the Channel."

Sawyer nodded.

"Brackett enlisted in the Navy when he was sixteen and was kicked out when he was nineteen or twenty. He joined a band of scallywags who made a living raiding the French, Portuguese, and Spanish coasts."

"Scallywags?"

"The author's words."

"So how'd he get from scallywag to pirate captain?" she asked.

"The way all great leaders come to power: he alternated scratching and stabbing backs. By the early 1700s, through a combination of mutinies, duels, fractions, and various deaths, he became the captain of his own ship. He continued to pillage throughout the eastern Atlantic, finally venturing to the West Indies by 1710. By then, he'd upgraded to a frigate named the *Barracuda*."

"You find out why he called it the *Barracuda*?" Sawyer asked, swiping a bite of pie off her fork.

"No, but from what I know of barracudas, it makes sense. Long, fast, aggressive predators."

"I suppose."

"Anyhow, from 1710 to 1715, there are a number of reports of Brackett's raids across the Caribbean. His crew pillaged with no discrimination and made a pretty good living. It also sounds like they *enjoyed* a pretty good living, spending what they stole on rum and prostitutes and other kinds of squalor."

"Well, that's typical for pirates."

"Yeah. So you have to wonder, why would he bury or hide or store away the treasure from the *Granada*?"

"I might have found an answer to that. But you keep going."

"Okay. Anyhow, Brackett made a return trip to Europe in 1713, during which time his crew underwent an overhaul."

"Mutiny?" she asked.

"More like corporate layoffs. There was a split, and instead of letting it turn into anything, Brackett canned the whole business. Sounds like things got pretty contentious, but being the charismatic guy he was, he kept it together." Jackson sat up. "And that's what I keep reading about Brackett. He was charismatic. He was tall, dark, always portrayed in pictures as having a well-groomed beard. He had a sense of humor, was incredibly clever. His crew often overpowered victims with their size and strength, but they also outwitted many a foe, especially the authorities who hunted them across the Caribbean. He was also a master sailor . . . or his crew was, or whatever."

A flash of lightning illuminated the room as Sawyer took another bite of pie. "Brackett was known to be ruthless but not for the sake of ruthlessness,"

Jackson said. "He wasn't overly coarse, just incredibly consumed by his greed. Everything he did was driven by a desire to have more. Which might have been part of the reason for the split in his crew. Maybe he was sick of them all squandering everything right away."

"So he was a pirate with a business mind?"

"Something like that. And he was apparently adored by women."

"Of course."

"Turns out, it wasn't all that common. Pirates are romanticized now," Jackson said, whirling his arms in his best Johnny Depp as Captain Jack Sparrow, "but back in the day, pirates were a dirty, smelly, foul bunch."

"Then what's with all the buxom beauties you see hanging around them?"

"Yeah, but where do you see them?"

Sawyer shrugged in concession. "Romanticized modern accounts."

"Right. And I'm not talking prostitutes at backwater brothels. Prominent women of the day were rumored to have had dalliances—author's word again—with Brackett. He was quite the ladies' man."

"Greedy, ruthless, clever, and charming."

Jackson nodded.

"You find anything about the *Granada* heist?"

"Basically what you mentioned before. Brackett and his crew attacked the *Granada* on August second or third, 1715, in the Gulf of Mexico. Two days later, a hurricane hit Florida, and it is widely considered to have been the storm that sank the *Barracuda*."

"Widely considered. Is there another theory?"

Jackson shook his head. "Not that I found. There just weren't any eyewitnesses."

"I see. What else?"

"Not much. From there it's like you said, all various theories but very few facts."

"Well," Sawyer said, licking the last remnants of pie off her fork, "I confirmed some of what you found about Brackett in Ben's notes." She laid her fork on her plate and set it aside. "It seemed like he did a general survey of piracy more than focus on any one aspect of the legend."

"That's what I thought too."

"You think he hadn't honed in on Brackett yet?"

Jackson shrugged.

"But I suppose it doesn't matter if someone else thought he had honed in."

"No."

"Having said that, he did focus on one thing, and that's the position of the *Barracuda*."

"Yeah, I saw something about that. It was getting kind of technical and nautical, so I didn't pay too much attention to it."

Sawyer flashed him a chiding smile. "I'll spare you all the technical details, but basically, Ben thinks the *Barracuda* had already arrived at Sugarloaf Key before the hurricane hit."

"Arrived how?"

"Was anchored offshore."

"As opposed to . . . ?"

"Having been driven toward land from open water by the storm."

"Okay. Why?"

"Several things, most notably that the anchor was found about a hundred yards south of the ship itself. The anchor is obviously heavier and would sink more quickly than the rest of the boat. But if the anchor hadn't been lowered and therefore wasn't already deep underwater, it probably would have been closer to the wreck, if not within it."

"That makes sense, I guess."

"He also said something about the way the boat was positioned, based on the tide and currents and storm track. Like you said, technical. But from what I could find in these charts and the limited meteorological records, it tracks."

"Okay, so the boat was already here. What does that mean?"

"Well, it certainly gives credence to the theory that the treasure is here in the Keys."

"I didn't see any connection between Brackett and the Keys," Jackson said. "And there's no record of him having a home or a hideout here or anything."

"Maybe they just came ashore to weather the storm."

"And save their loot from a ship that was likely to go down."

Sawyer nodded.

Jackson shook his head. "You're more of a sailor than I am. What's the protocol on weathering a storm? You don't just drop anchor on the ocean side of the island, do you? Especially when the storm's coming from the south and east."

"Who said it was coming from the south and east?"

"Decades of watching The Weather Channel's hurricane coverage."

"Well, not to disparage your years of watching TV, but the precise path of the storm is vital. The wind, rainfall, storm surge can all be drastically different just miles apart based on where the hurricane makes landfall and which quadrant a given location is in."

"So a hurricane could demolish Sugarloaf Key, for example, and leave Key West unscathed?"

"Not unscathed, but significantly less damaged."

He sat back. "Okay, so what's that mean?"

"Do you know where the 1715 hurricane made landfall?"

"There was a book somewhere, *Storms of the Caribbean* or something."

"Yeah, I saw it."

They both looked around, and Jackson spotted it first and thumbed through it until he found the record of the August 1715 storm. "Here we go. Big Pine Key."

"Just this side of Seven Mile Bridge, a little east of here."

"But would they have had any way of knowing where it would hit?"

"No, not by modern standards, but it still might explain why the *Barracuda* sunk here instead of being driven on land. Think about it from Brackett's perspective. He knows a hurricane is coming, knows enough to try to hunker down—and that might explain why he buried the treasure too."

"It might," Jackson said.

"Brackett anchors the ship far enough out to sea that it won't be grounded and hopes it survives," Sawyer continued. "The storm passes east of here, so the worst of the wind and surge would as well, at least assuming it came from the south and east," she said with a twinkle of her eye aimed at Jackson, "but for whatever reason, it still sinks."

"Okay, that makes sense. But why not try to hide the ship a little better, protect it from the storm?"

"The Keys are tricky, even for smaller boats. You take a hundred-foot ship, riding a dozen feet below the surface, sailing, with pre-hurricane winds, maneuvering can be next to impossible. And if his goal was to avoid grounding it . . ."

"Hmm."

"That sounded like a theory-forming 'hmm.'"

"Maybe," he said. "You said one of the theories is that the treasure was stashed in the Keys, but I didn't find anything in my research. You know where in the Keys?"

"Literally a dozen different places. A pawn shop in Key Largo had an Aztec idol, so Brackett must have buried his treasure there. There used to be a clan of Bracketts living on Cudjoe Key. That sort of thing. All are pretty weak."

"Anything relating to Sugarloaf Key?"

"Not that I know."

Jackson sighed. "Okay, what else did you find?"

She picked up another book. "I found quite a bit about *Nuestra Señora de la Granada* and its backdrop. Bear with me if I told you this already." She sat up a little straighter. "The *Granada* was the flagship of the fleet Philip V sent to the Americas, but it wasn't captained by de Castaño."

"Remind me again."

"Gabriel Vicente de Castaño, the Capitán General of the Spanish Navy."

"Quite a title. And he didn't captain the *Granada*?"

"No. It was captained by a Reynaldo Garcia III, a young swashbuckler of a captain."

"Swashbuckler?"

"My words, not the author's," she said with a wink. "He was brash and arrogant and very aggressive. Rumor had it he despised his role captaining a merchant vessel and would have much preferred to be out hunting down pirates like James Brackett."

"So if this RG3 guy was the captain of the *Granada*, why was de Castaño's daughter aboard? It was his daughter, wasn't it?"

"Yes, Liliana," Sawyer said with a smile. "And that's the key question. Because according to this," she said, raising the book, "Liliana and Garcia were lovers."

"So when Brackett kidnapped her, it would have really ticked off Garcia in addition to Capitán de Castaño."

She nodded.

"Assuming Garcia survived the attack."

"He lost a leg, but he survived. The hurricane drove the *Granada* north toward the Emerald Coast and ultimately wrecked it, but a handful of the crew was eventually rescued by another of the fleet. Once Garcia recuperated, he dedicated himself to finding Brackett. So too did de Castaño and the rest of the Spanish Navy. But there's nothing here to indicate they ever found him."

"Where was de Castaño during the attack? Was he on one of the other ships?"

"No. He was waiting in San Juan, which is odd, because in the early eighteenth century, the Spanish headquarters for the region was the Dominican Republic, not Puerto Rico. Puerto Rico was left largely unexplored and undeveloped, and if the *Granada* or any other ships in the fleet were going to stop off on their way back to Spain, the Dominican makes far more sense than San Juan."

"Maybe he wasn't waiting for the fleet."

"Then what was he doing there?"

Jackson shrugged.

"Anyhow, like I said, the entire Spanish Navy searched for Brackett, and rumor has it that even the English were looking for him by the late teens."

"And no one found him or knows where he went?"

"No. There are rumors and theories but no verifiable facts."

"Were there any bodies found with the wreck of the *Barracuda*?"

"A couple. Why?"

"It isn't likely Brackett went down with his ship, then."

"No, he almost certainly survived the wreck. Whether he survived the hurricane is another matter."

Jackson pushed back in the chair. "So where does that leave us?"

"I don't know. We know Brackett and his crew attacked the *Granada* and looted it, and we know the *Barracuda* lies off the coast of Sugarloaf Key and that it's very likely Brackett and most of his crew came ashore before the hurricane. But after that, we know nothing."

"Somehow we have to identify one of these theories that makes the most sense."

"And where do Damon and Louviere and whatever the Missianna is fit in?" she asked.

"Good question. You find anything on either Louviere or the Missianna?"

"No, you?"

"No."

Sawyer stood and stretched. She pulled out her cell phone and looked at it for a moment. "It's getting late. I should get home."

"Tomorrow I'll come back and see if I can get a number off Ben's phone. That, or put my detective skills to serious work and see if I can scare up a number some other way."

"Let me know what you find out."

"I will."

They cleaned up, washing forks by candlelight and stacking Ben's candles on the kitchen counter. They could cool there, and Jackson would return them to the closet when he came in the morning. As they exited the house, they saw lights across the canal on other parts of Raccoon Key. The outage must have been local.

Sawyer drove Jackson back to his hotel and coasted to a stop near the exterior staircase leading to the second floor and thus Jackson's room. She reached down to silence Jason Aldean.

"Thanks for the company," she said.

"Thanks for dinner. And the company."

She smiled. "My pleasure."

"What's tomorrow, Friday?"

"All day and half the night."

He grinned. "You work?"

"No, not officially."

"You maybe want some company tomorrow afternoon?"

"What'd you have in mind?"

"I don't know. Go to the library and research eighteenth-century piracy, hassle any and all of Ben's friends and coworkers I can find, maybe just go fishing."

"Fishing?"

"Not a date, mind you," he added. "Just two people with nothing else to do."

"Well, when you put it like that . . ."

"I'll give you a call."

She nodded, and Jackson got out of the Jeep. He stood and watched her drive off, then headed inside, feeling guilty. Here his friend was missing, likely dead, and he was arranging a social calendar. Even researching an old pirate treasure felt wrong, but it was the only link they had to Ben, at least until Jackson could find Damon's phone number.

He opted not to turn on the TV, instead getting ready for bed and sacking out. Maybe a night's rest would clear his mind.

Chapter Sixteen

Friday, May 17
8:29 a.m.

JACKSON SLEPT FITFULLY as another round of storms rolled through. Thunder wasn't the only culprit. He kept thinking about things he and Sawyer had discussed and researched. He kept thinking about how they still had more questions than answers. He kept thinking about the fun afternoon and evening they'd had, a rare change from recent weeks and months. When he wasn't too busy thinking or awakened by thunder, he dreamt that they had gone on a candlelight dinner cruise in the eye of a hurricane, with New York Yankee great Derek Jeter as the waiter. The end result was that he slept late, having not set an alarm. Who knew, maybe swapping coasts was still messing with him.

The sun was shining again when Jackson peered out of his hotel window, and the palm trees around the parking lot were flapping in a steady breeze. He was filled with hope that maybe today wouldn't be oppressively hot and humid. Fueled by that hope, he showered and dressed quickly and headed down to breakfast. He took it and a cup of coffee to the terrace, where the breeze played with his hair while he ate, drank, and thought some more.

Why would Ben charter a boat? Why would someone attack him on it? Why would he defend himself with a knife (which Jackson doubted he owned) but not survive himself? Why did someone break into his house the other night? Why had he been researching pirate treasure? Who was Damon, why had Ben contacted him, and what did the names Louviere and Missianna mean?

Forget answers, he and Sawyer were even short on theories. Yeah, the Brackett treasure. Based on what had been on his desk, it was clear Ben had been researching it, although not it exclusively. But what about it had led to

Ben allegedly being attacked on his rented boat? Hopefully, Jackson could find contact info for Damon, and he would shed some light on things.

His phone rang as he was finishing his waffle. Waffles were a mess to make, so he took advantage of free ones when he could, even the cheap ones at hotel buffet breakfasts.

The number on his display was Sawyer's, and he flipped the phone open with a smirk. "Wasn't I supposed to call you?"

"What if Ben and Ryker weren't alone?"

"What?"

"I've been thinking this morning. We've been wondering what happened on that boat, why Ryker was dead, who killed him. Remember what I told you in Hawkins' office, that Ben wouldn't kill anybody? Maybe he didn't."

"You think somebody else was out there?"

"It would make sense."

"It would," he said, taking a draw on his coffee. "So where is he?"

"Maybe he had another boat to pick him up, or he drove another boat, or maybe he's an iron man and swam to shore."

"You know this raises another half dozen questions," Jackson said. "Was this guy working with Ryker, independently from him, maybe working with Ben? Did he escape, did he drown, are he and Ben deliriously drifting to Cuba together?"

"Seems we keep having more questions."

"Yeah."

"You been to Ben's yet?"

"No, just finishing breakfast."

"Late mornings a California thing?"

"Should a refined Southern woman like yourself be this much of a tease?"

"Only when the mark is this easy."

"Aha."

"Wanna run over there with me? I've been up since five, I already cleaned my house and washed the Jeep, I really don't have any work today, and I'm restless."

"Sure."

Since his hotel was on her way, she agreed to pick him up. A quarter of an hour later, they were bumming east on the highway, the sun glinting off

Sawyer's sunglasses and her sparkling clean Jeep. Toby Keith and Gretchen Wilson accompanied them this time, and a Florida Keys Electric Cooperative boom truck welcomed them to the end of Angelonia Terrace. A worker in a bright green vest was packing up a trio of orange cones and stacking them on the back of the truck. Jackson motioned for Sawyer to stop and leaned out his window to get the man's attention.

"You fixing an outage here?"

The bearded lineman nodded. "Transformer blew last night with the storm. You folks live around here?"

"Visiting a friend," Jackson said with a nod at Ben's place.

"Yeah, we got no answer there. Wanna let your friend know everything should be back up and running?"

"Yeah," Jackson said. "Thanks."

Sawyer accelerated and turned into Ben's driveway. "What was that about?" she asked.

"Just making sure it was a legitimate outage last night."

"You mean not the work of a treasure-hunting New Orleans syndicate?"

"Something like that."

Sawyer parked under the carport, and they let themselves in again. The phone base in the kitchen displayed a red 0 instead of a flashing 1, as it had the night before. When Jackson picked up the handset and attempted to scroll through recent callers, he found the log empty.

"I was afraid of that," he said to Sawyer. "Power surge wiped the memory."

"So now what?"

"Your phone have data?"

"Yeah."

"Google him or whitepages.com him or something."

"Villars is a kind of common last name in the South," she said. "I want to make sure we have the right one. Besides, he probably called from a cell anyhow."

"Fair point." He checked the time. "I might have an option, but not at this hour."

Sawyer stuck her hands into her pockets. "Okay. Let me call Sheriff Hawkins. Maybe he can get us the number."

"Worth a try."

While she dialed the sheriff, Jackson debated calling Mouse at a little before seven West Coast time. He decided against it. It wasn't like time was of the essence. So he put away the candles, then rejoined Sawyer at the counter.

"I get that," she said into the phone, frustration played on her face. "What if I told you Jackson was a private investigator?" She turned and saw Jackson, her face blanching for a moment. "Yes," she said into the phone. "Well, because he probably didn't see the need. . . . Sheriff—" She sighed. "No, I understand. . . . Yes, I'll tell him. . . . Yes, thank you." She lowered her phone, tapping it to end the call, and sighed again.

"Should I ask?"

"He said he can't give civilians that information. Sorry, I thought telling him you were a private eye might help."

"Never does in my experience," he said with a grin. "Or on TV."

"He also said Ben's uncle is flying in this afternoon from Atlanta to start all the legal processes associated with death."

"That gives it some finality."

"Yeah."

Jackson sighed.

"This option of yours . . . ?"

"I have a guy, an assistant of sorts, but he's not much good before, well, lunch."

She tapped the toe of her shoe on the floor. "Okay. Any other leads we can pursue?"

"Leads, not really."

"But?"

"But, we didn't fully comb through his library last night. He's got charts, maps, more reference books to dig through."

"Looking for what?"

"I don't know. There's a good chance he just has a lot of data."

"But?" she said again.

"But, maybe there's a common thread tying one chart to another map to an obscure book with a dog-eared page. Who knows? But I've already got a tan."

"So do I. Want some help?"

"Two heads are better than one."

"Okay, let's get to it."

They worked together, first studying the maps and photos on the wall and the model ships. They concluded there was no consistent theme, other than a love of the sea and nautical history. Next, they moved to the maps and charts rolled up in a bin in the corner. Three-quarters of them depicted currents, water depths, tides, or just standard topography of the Keys or the northern Caribbean. Even so, there was nothing to indicate a theme. And the remaining maps and charts were even less conclusive.

Sawyer stood back with a sigh as Jackson rerolled the last chart. "So our theory is Ben was looking for Brackett's treasure and somebody else also looking for the treasure—presumably Ryker or his boss—took out the competition? Or tried to, given the fact that Ryker also died?"

"Yeah, that's basically it."

"So two questions. One, how did they find out?"

"I don't know."

"You didn't happen to see a Ryker in Ben's rolodex, did you?"

"No, I thought about that as I flipped through the R's."

"Damon? He's a New Orleans connection."

"Could be. Loose lips sink ships."

Sawyer frowned. "I'm not entirely sure what that even means."

"Me either. But if Ben was doing research, he was probably asking colleagues, old professors, various experts. And if he pulled Damon into the search, he was doing the same. All it took is one of them to ask the wrong person or have the wrong person hear something . . ."

"So unless we know who he talked to or who his resources were, we have no idea who could be responsible."

"Right, and we haven't found anything here to suggest who he's talked to."

"Could your intruder have stolen a contact list, ripped something out of the rolodex, maybe?"

"Sure. I didn't notice anything missing from his desk, but somebody could have easily taken something without me knowing it, especially if it was a slip of paper in a notebook or a card in the rolodex. He could have wiped the hard drive of the computer for all I know." He shrugged. "Or the door might have been swinging in the wind."

She sighed.

"What's question two?"

"Could we be off base thinking this has to do with the treasure?"

"How so?"

"What if Ben *was* looking for the treasure or *was* doing research on Brackett and the *Barracuda* for a book, but he ruffled somebody's feathers by discovering something else, and that something else was what got him killed?"

Jackson looked at her. Then he pointed at her.

"What?"

"That sounds like something a private eye would say."

"So why didn't you?"

"Frankly, because I've been distracted by that thing on your shirt," he said. Sawyer's T-shirt was pale yellow with a brightly outlined, vaguely heart-shaped object covering most of the front.

She looked down. "By the butterfly?"

"Is that what it is? There's so much glitter and sequins."

"There is not that much."

"I didn't take you for the glitter type."

"It was a gift."

"From a guy?"

"Why would that matter?"

"Sounds like a yes. And what's with girls and butterflies anyhow?"

"It was from a female coworker, and I happen to like butterflies. They're amazing creatures."

"So are giraffes, but you don't see women wearing giraffe T-shirts or running around with giraffe tats on their shoulders."

"Are you serious?"

"Little giraffe pendants."

"Are you done?"

"Earrings."

"Do you want me to go home and change?"

"No, I'll manage."

She shook her head. "So back to when this conversation had a point."

"Yeah. No, yeah, that's a good thought. But unfortunately, it doesn't really help because we have even less of a clue what feathers he might have ruffled if it wasn't related to the treasure."

"Well, you picked through his library last night. You feel up to it again?"

"Last night I was looking for info on Brackett and the *Barracuda*, primarily."

"So what do we look for now?"

"Anything on piracy, anything on the Keys, anything on depth and tidal charts or weather patterns—anything having anything to do with what we saw on his desk."

Sawyer looked at the wall of books.

"We're skimming," he said. "Needle and haystack time. But search the tables of contents, search the indexes, search maps and pictures. And figure if he had a book that was relevant, he probably would have it out and on his desk."

"So basically we're wasting our time?"

"As opposed to . . ."

"Going fishing. Snorkeling. Taking a walk along the beach or through a garden, sipping iced tea in the shade."

"Is that how you spend your free time?"

"Some. You?"

"I play a lot of Xbox."

She rolled her eyes.

"And watch the Pacific crash on shore." He checked his phone. "It's almost eleven. Work till one, then I'll call my source in L.A., and then I'll buy you lunch for your efforts."

Sawyer looked at him, perhaps determining if there was anything more behind his lunch offer. There wasn't, and she seemed to sense it. "Deal."

*   *   *

1:03 p.m.

THE NEXT two hours passed both slowly and quickly. Jackson and Sawyer flipped through several dozen books, only finding a few additional factoids tied to Brackett, his ship, his treasure, or any of the legends related to them. None of them came close to cluing them in to what had happened, but they did add to the bank of general knowledge they had amassed. They opted not to delve into general history of the Keys because, for one thing, Sawyer had that front pretty well covered. They also considered knowledge of the Keys to be a far deeper quarry to mine, and any potential clue more like a needle in an entire field of haystacks.

At one, they quit. They tidied up Ben's study, leaving it as much like they'd found it as possible. They got into Sawyer's Jeep and drove, with the top down, into Key West. The day had warmed, but the breeze had, if anything, kicked up, keeping the heat from being unpleasant. Sawyer followed Highway 1 around the north side of the island, then kept going on Truman Avenue until she reached Duval Street. She turned south and parked a few blocks later, on the side of the street.

They got out, and she led them across the street to a small, pale blue bungalow situated a dozen yards off the sidewalk. A cobblestone walk leading to it was surrounded by flowers and shrubs, and larger bushes and palm trees encircled the building itself. A wide porch was supported by white spindles. Spanning two of them on the left was a faded wood sign with "DIXIE'S" painted in cream-colored letters. A similar sign spanned two spindles on the right, albeit with smaller print, reading "Hours: Noon till . . ."

Jackson paused at the bottom of a short set of stairs leading to the porch. "Confederate B&B?" he asked, nodding at a rebel flag hanging over the door.

"That flag represents a lot of things to a lot of people," Sawyer said.

"What's it represent to you?"

"A lot of things. Right now, really good barbecue."

Jackson hesitated.

"What?"

"Are you one of those Southerners who thinks the Confederates actually won the war?"

"I am not."

"But the South will rise again?"

She set her jaw.

"One more. Will you please, just once, in your most natural accent say 'War of Northern Aggression'?"

She raised an eyebrow.

"Okay, I'm done."

They entered a dark, bar-like dining room. There were a couple of booths and tables to the left and right, under windows mostly clouded by external foliage, and a bar that ran the width of the room ahead. Two women worked behind the bar. One was a skinny brunette in a tank top that matched the flag above the door, cut short to reveal her midriff. The other was an extremely heavyset redhead whose tank top revealed doughy arms and was fortunately not cut short to reveal anything else. Jackson pondered which, if either, of them was Dixie while Sawyer ordered two "splattered pigs" with "skins" and two cokes.

Skinny Dixie filled Styrofoam cups with dark-colored soda while Heavy Dixie hollered through a small window, presumably to the kitchen.

Jackson sat on a barstool and looked at Sawyer as Skinny Dixie set the cups in front of them.

"What?" Sawyer asked, taking a sip of hers.

"You come here often?"

"When I need a taste of home."

He nodded.

"You've got a few minutes if you want to give that source of yours a call. He is up by now, isn't he?"

"Fifty-fifty," Jackson said. "But it beats asking what constitutes a splattered pig." He dug out his phone, dialed, and waited six rings for Mouse to pick up. He didn't sound overly groggy.

"Hey, man," Jackson said. "I need a favor."

"Sure, what's up?"

"I need a phone number for a Damon Villars in New Orleans."

"Are you in New Orleans?"

"No."

"Dude, even you can work Google."

"It's a cell, man. At least, we assume. And Villars is a sort of common name."

"So how I am I supposed to get the right one?"

"Do what you do. He placed a call to Ben O'Reilly Wednesday night."

"Are you serious?"

"I am." Jackson gave him Ben's number.

"Is this important?"

"Yeah, it is."

"All right. I'll call you back."

"Thanks." He clapped the phone shut.

Sawyer raised an eyebrow.

"He'll come through."

"Okay."

Heavy Dixie set two plastic baskets in front of them. They were lined with parchment paper and filled with a bed of skin-on, thick-cut French fries on which rested the messiest pulled pork sandwich Jackson had ever seen. Hence the name "splattered."

He paid, and then he and Sawyer took their baskets and drinks outside. "Uh, how exactly does this work?" Jackson asked, looking down at two full hands.

Sawyer answered by nodding and led the way half a block south to a small green space. Tall palms provided ample shade for a meandering sidewalk that cut the corner of Duval and the east-west intersecting street. Several benches were placed along the sidewalk, and Sawyer sat down on an empty one. She set her cup of "coke" on the bench beside her and reached for her sandwich.

"Must we pray over this?" Jackson asked.

"Don't be a stickler."

"Did you at least grab napkins?"

Her eyes widened.

"I'll go grab some," Jackson said.

"Thanks."

He hurried back, hoping Skinny Dixie had put enough ice in his drink that it would still be cool when he returned. He was only gone five minutes, but it was enough time for his phone to vibrate in his pocket as he returned to the park. It was Mouse.

"Yeah?"

"Turns out there are six Damon Villars in New Orleans," Mouse said. "And I'm not hacking four different cell phone carriers to find out which one called your friend."

"That's fair. You wanna give me the numbers? I'll cold-call them."

"You got something to write with?"

"No," he said as he reached the bench. He handed Sawyer a stack of napkins. "Can you take down some numbers on your phone?" he asked her.

She set down her sandwich, wiped her hands, and retrieved her phone. "Shoot."

Mouse relayed six numbers to Jackson, and he passed them on to Sawyer. He thanked Mouse and closed his phone.

"So which one's our Damon?" she asked.

"We can take turns calling them after we eat."

She shrugged in concession and picked up her sandwich so Jackson could sit down.

Albeit messy, the splattered pigs were delicious, with the perfect amount of tang in the barbecue sauce. Same with the fries, which were properly fried and also well-seasoned. Jackson still didn't know if he was drinking Pepsi, Coca-Cola, or something else entirely, but it did its job of washing down lunch. When they had finished eating and had wiped barbecue sauce off their lips, chins (in Jackson's case), and hands, they pulled out their phones.

"Just use mine," she said. "I entered them as contacts, and you can put it on speaker."

"How do I work one of these fancy phones?"

"Are you serious?"

"Have you seen my phone?"

"Aren't Californians supposed to be techy?"

"That's Northern California. Silicon Valley. All the Stanford grads."

"I see. Just press here. The rest is magic."

He winked. "You want to talk or should I?"

"Go for it."

He nodded and tapped the phone to ring the first Damon Villars. He got no answer and only a generic, default voicemail.

The second Damon was a wheezy old man who had no idea what Jackson was talking about.

The third number led to another voicemail, and the Damon who had recorded the greeting didn't sound like the Damon on Ben's machine, either in tone or pacing. Jackson opted not to leave a message, as he had for the first one. Then he dialed the fourth number.

"Hello?"

"Hi, is this Damon?" Jackson asked.

"Who's this?"

"My name's Jackson. I'm a friend of Ben's."

There was a short pause. "Okay. What can I do for you?"

Jackson paused himself, looking at Sawyer before he answered. "I was calling about the message you left Wednesday night."

"What about it?"

"Uh, we actually had a pretty big thunderstorm here," Jackson said. "We didn't get all of it, what with static and stuff on the line. You want to hit the high points again?"

Another pause. "You said you were a friend of Ben's."

"Yeah, Ben Johnson. You called him Wednesday."

"Yeah, right."

Sawyer frowned at Jackson.

"Look," Jackson said, "I don't know who this is, but it isn't Damon."

"No. No, it's not."

"Well, is Damon there?"

"Uh, sort of."

"I forgot to dig the decoder ring out of my cereal this morning. You want to spell it out for me?"

"Yeah, let's start over. I'm Detective Jason Dixon, New Orleans PD."

"Detective. I'm still Jackson Douglas. I'm with Sawyer Collins, which is not a malt liquor."

"Hello," she said, elbowing Jackson in the ribs in the process.

"You all know Damon?" Dixon asked.

"Not really. He called a friend of ours, Ben O'Reilly, last night. Ben's been missing for a few days, and we were hoping Damon knew something."

"Damon Villars?"

"Yeah. At least a Damon Villars. We didn't get the number, so we're trying everyone in the book."

"Well, you won't get much from this one, I'm afraid," Dixon said. "He's dead."

Chapter Seventeen

2:09 p.m.

SAWYER LOOKED UP sharply, her blue eyes wide.

"Dead?" Jackson asked.

"Shot," Detective Dixon answered. "Looks like a home invasion."

"When?"

"Sometime yesterday, probably last night. When did you say he called?"

"About quarter to seven Wednesday," Jackson said, looking at Sawyer. She nodded a confirmation.

"What did he call about?"

"It was kind of cryptic to us," Jackson said, then summed up the basics. Ben appeared to be looking for a treasure and Damon had a few possible leads. Technically, Jackson and Sawyer didn't know if that was what Damon's call had been about, but it was their best guess. "He also mentioned that someone had broken into his house a few nights ago."

Dixon hesitated for just a second. "Yeah, well it looks like they came back. He say anything about who or why?"

"No."

"What about this treasure? Some island rumor?"

"We don't know," Jackson said. "We think he's been researching pirates in and around the Florida Keys."

"And how's that tie to Villars?"

"We don't know. We were hoping Damon could tell us. Like I said, Ben disappeared Sunday." He mentioned the capsized boat, blood, and Ryker's dead body washing ashore.

"You say this Ryker was from New Orleans?" Dixon asked.

"That's right."

"And the cops there are investigating?" Dixon asked.

"Yeah."

"You got a name, someone I can check in with? There may not be a connection, but it's worth checking out."

"Sheriff Hawkins. Monroe County Sheriff's Department in Key West."

Dixon paused again. "This a good number to reach you at if I have any more questions?"

Sawyer nodded.

"Yeah," Jackson said. "You have any idea why Damon was killed?"

"Why and who are the mystery," Dixon said. "But we're working on it."

"All right. Thanks."

"Yeah. This Ben guy turns up, have him give me a call," Dixon said. He gave Jackson his number, thanked him, and ended the call.

"What is going on?" Sawyer asked.

"I don't know, but we're back at square one."

"We should call Sheriff Hawkins," Sawyer said. "If Ben's disappearance is connected to Damon's death, vice versa could be true too."

"Your turn," Jackson said. "He was almost your father-in-law, after all."

Sawyer grabbed her phone. "Father-in-law. Hardly. And decoder rings came in Cracker Jack boxes, by the way."

"I'll remember that."

While Sawyer was on hold, then briefed Sheriff Hawkins, Jackson took their empty baskets and his cup to a nearby trashcan. He returned and paced, trying to think. He was indeed decent at figuring out puzzles and solving mysteries, as he'd told Sawyer the night before, but his brain preferred to mull and ponder at its own pace, not by coercion while Jackson stomped around a park bench. Trouble was, he and Sawyer had spent the previous night and most of the morning soaking up information, and none of it was helping.

"He sounds as confused as we are," Sawyer said when she ended the call.

She stood, and they started walking. They went south, instead of north back to Sawyer's Jeep. The sky was clear and the breeze muffled by the buildings. It was borderline hot.

"So what do we do?" she asked between sips on her straw.

"Google Louviere, I guess. And Missianna. See if that turns up anything."

"That name sounds oddly familiar. I can't place why."

"Which name?"

"Louviere."

"Wasn't there a French guy who helped us in the Revolution?"

"Probably a lot of them."

"I mean with a name like Louviere?"

"I don't recall."

"Hmm."

She took another pull on her straw. "What are the odds that wasn't the right Damon?"

"Slim and none," Jackson said. "Same as Ben's accident being just that, no foul play, despite Ryker's blood being on the boat."

She frowned. "Did we ever hear back from Hawkins definitively that it was Ryker's blood?"

"I don't think so. Just it was AB positive and so was his."

"Negative."

"Whichever."

"But I see your point."

They kept walking.

"So you're the private eye," she said. "What's your gut tell you? What's your theory?"

Jackson took a deep breath. "I think Ben was researching Brackett's treasure. He had the generic research on pirates, including his notes on Brackett personally. He was interested in Caribbean storms, water depths, your photos of the *Barracuda*. Whatever his reason, he was researching it. And I think he had Damon—whatever their connection is, their history—looking into the theory that Brackett showed up in New Orleans looking for another crew. Didn't you say that was part of the legend?"

"It's one of many parts, many rumors."

"I think he had Damon looking into it, and somehow Louviere and Missianna and this logbook are connected. Maybe Louviere's logbook shows Brackett found a ship named the *Missianna*, I don't know. But somewhere along the lines, I think the wrong person found out about the search, and it ended up getting them both killed."

"The wrong person. Ryker?"

"No. I think Ryker's a minnow in a shark pond. He washed up on the beach here before Damon was shot, and I still think your theory that Ryker wasn't alone makes sense. How all that played out, I don't know. And who's behind it, I don't know."

"Louviere, maybe?"

"Maybe, although Damon didn't sound like he thought Louviere was a suspect. But it would make the most sense."

"Let's see what we can find out about him. Damon said he was a New Orleans bigwig, didn't he?"

Jackson nodded.

"Should be easy to at least find the basics."

"You know where there's an internet café around here?"

Sawyer held up her smartphone. She looked down at it. "Although I am low on battery."

"Library?"

"Yeah. I have another idea."

"Okay."

They had reached the last cross street before the beach, which was visible less than a block ahead. Instead of continuing, they turned and walked a block east. Nestled between a small convenience store and a seafood shack was a standalone structure with a low porch featuring a two-sided chalkboard sign that advertised operating hours and daily specials. The smells of freshly ground coffee wafted out the open door beside a wide glass window in which hung a neon sign spelling out "Southernmost Grounds."

"They have public computers?"

"No, but great coffee. And I know the owner."

"There anyone on this island you don't know?"

"A few people, maybe. Come on."

The aromas intensified inside, and Jackson was content to wait while a middle-aged Latina woman served several patrons. She beamed when Sawyer approached the counter. They exchanged greetings in a mixture of English and Spanish, and then Sawyer introduced Jackson to Maria.

"A pleasure to meet you," she said in accented but crisp English.

"Same here," Jackson said.

"What can I get for you?"

"Small caramel iced mocha," Sawyer said. She turned to Jackson. "My treat."

"Medium black coffee."

"Hot or iced?"

"Hot," he said, and they both looked at him as if he were crazy.

"I also wonder if I could borrow a few minutes on your computer," Sawyer said after paying for the drinks. "We need to look something up online, and my phone battery is about tapped."

"Of course," Maria said. "You can use my charger too, if it fits." She nodded to a door marked "Office" on her left. "I'll bring your drinks when they're ready."

"Thanks," Sawyer said. They entered the small office, which contained everything from boxes of extra cups, napkins, and straws to stores of various condiments to a small desk with a laptop on one side, a phone and several loose cables in the middle, and a stuffed file folder rack on the other side. There was one chair, and Jackson nodded to Sawyer. "You drive."

"Okay."

The laptop was powered on, not password protected, and Sawyer quickly opened a web browser and accessed Google's search page. She typed in "Louviere" and waited for the results. The top three were genealogy-based sites, then a combination of news trackers, social media hits, and references to a city in Belgium. The next few pages produced equally fruitless results.

"Here you are," Maria said as she entered with two cups.

"Thank you," Sawyer said.

"Take as long as you need."

"Thank you," Sawyer said again, echoed by Jackson.

Maria left, and Sawyer announced, after a drink of her mocha, that she was going to try adding "New Orleans" to her search. She did, and immediately it generated a result.

"Martin Louviere," Sawyer said, reading a name in the description of the top entry. "Looks like a corporate page for The Louviere Company."

"That's original," Jackson said.

Sawyer clicked the link. The website was generic, showing a panorama of New Orleans' skyline at dusk, embossed with swirling script stating the company's name. Sawyer clicked on an "About Us" link near the top of the screen. Several paragraphs of ambiguous text revealed that The Louviere Company was a prominent Louisiana importer and exporter, specifically of textiles, and featured its own textiles manufacturing division. The company was also heavily vested in real estate and petroleum.

"That doesn't tell much," Sawyer said, sipping from her drink again.

"No. Try that."

He pointed to a hyperlinked reference to the President and CEO of the company, Martin Louviere. Sawyer clicked the link, displaying a photo of a handsome face framed by wavy brown hair tinged with gray around the temples. Age was hard to tell. At least fifty, maybe sixty, possibly close to seventy if he kept in shape and took care of himself. Or was genetically blessed with youthful features. He wore a dark suit, dark tie, and looked at the camera with a smile that exuded warmth and compassion while still being all business.

Beside the photo was a paragraph of text, and Sawyer read aloud. *"'Martin Louviere is a sixth-generation Louisianan. His ancestors ran a prominent shipping company out of the Port of New Orleans. More than two centuries later, that shipping company has blossomed into the multi-faceted Louviere Company and has stayed family-owned and family-run. Herbert Louviere passed the company to his son, Martin, in 2006, and he has served as President and CEO of The Louviere Company since, expanding the company's geographical footprint, influence, and profits by nearly fifty percent.'"*

"No wonder he's smiling," Jackson said, testing his coffee for the first time. It was still scalding hot, and he little more than let it touch the tip of his tongue.

"'A graduate of Louisiana State University's E.J. Ourso College of Business, Martin Louviere earned his M.B.A. at Emory University before joining The Louviere Company as Assistant VP of Marketing. In his thirty-two years with the corporation, Louviere has overseen several departments and has headed The Louviere Company's charitable donations, which are among the highest in the state, since 1996. Louviere is an avid golfer and deep-sea fisherman and is famous in New Orleans as a connoisseur of fine wines. His late wife, Pat, was equally beloved in the city and was a major champion of New Orleans' cultural restoration in the wake of Hurricane Katrina. Louviere has two adult children, Martin, Jr., and Alyssa.'"

Jackson blew into his coffee.

"Doesn't strike me as the type to chase around the Caribbean after pirate treasure," Sawyer said.

"Not particularly. But his family history does reinforce Damon's mention of a logbook. If there are three-hundred-year-old records to be had, a *'prominent shipping company'* CEO would be the ones to have them."

Sawyer spent another fifteen minutes clicking on various links that seemed related to Louviere. The most informative was a Wikipedia page that basically restated what was on The Louviere Company's website. There were a few news articles, mostly about business acquisitions or deals or charitable donations made by Louviere or his company. Nothing that in any way tied to Ben, Damon, Ted Ryker, or the Brackett treasure legend.

After thanking Maria, Jackson and Sawyer took their drinks out to the sidewalk and started back toward where her Jeep was parked on Duval Street.

"Why would Brackett have been looking for another crew anyhow?" Jackson asked as they crossed to the far side of Duval Street and turned north. "That's why he went to New Orleans, isn't it?"

"According to legend." She shrugged. "He and his crew split once. Maybe it happened again. Maybe they took the treasure, and he wanted to get another crew to chase them down. Maybe they were squandering it, and he was sick of them. Who knows?"

"Common refrain."

They walked several blocks. Jackson's coffee was now drinkable, and very tasty. Never mind it was the heat of the day and he was drinking something hot.

"You're quiet," Sawyer said when they were almost back to the Jeep.

"So are you."

"Any particular reason?"

"Just thinking."

"About?"

He turned to her as they stopped at the front of her Jeep. "I should have asked this before, but is there any other reason you can think of—anything at all—why someone might have something out for Ben other than the treasure theory we've latched onto?"

Sawyer thought for a moment, then shook her head. "No."

"Me either. I just wanted to be sure before I go tilting at windmills."

"What do you mean?"

"I mean, I'm going to New Orleans."

Chapter Eighteen

Saturday, May 18
9:54 a.m.

DELTA FLIGHT 1731 was scheduled to depart Key West at 11:15. With a connection in Atlanta and factoring in an hour time change, it would put Jackson in New Orleans a little after three p.m. local time.

After making his case to Sawyer the previous afternoon, he'd had her drop him off at his hotel, where he'd used a lobby computer to price and book flights. Getting to New Orleans from Key West was not easy, with no direct flights and only a handful with one-stop. United wanted to route him through Houston after stops in either Tampa or Miami, and American Airlines wanted to take him to Miami and Atlanta, or Miami and Dallas, or Orlando and Atlanta. Several flights even went through Charlotte. He'd debated driving back to Miami first, or even pulling an all-nighter and making the sixteen-hour drive to New Orleans. Then he'd found the midday flight through Atlanta—and only Atlanta—at a reasonable price and arranged with his rental car company to drop his car off in Key West, for a convenience charge that cancelled the savings from a midday flight. But it was done.

He'd spent the rest of the night watching TV in his hotel and looking somewhat wistfully out his window as darkness fell over Key West. Oddly, he was going to miss the place, at least a little.

Now, as he made the short walk from the rental car office to the terminal, through yet another muggy Florida morning, he again questioned his decision to go to NOLA.

He'd told Sawyer that it was to find answers, because he couldn't let Ben's death rest, because he needed closure. But even as she'd tried to talk him out of it, he'd wondered if his reasons weren't a little more selfish. Was he just avoiding going home? He was due to return to L.A. on Sunday. Changing plans, canceling flights, extending his trip indefinitely—was that all to have a "legitimate" reason to avoid his life back home? And was there any chance the allure of Captain Brackett's treasure was starting to tug at him? Was a lust for gold playing into this? He didn't think so, but it could be hard to tell sometimes.

"What exactly are you going to do there?" Sawyer had asked in the parking lot of his hotel after driving him back.

"I don't know exactly."

"Are you sure about this?"

He sighed. "Ben's disappearance and death are tied to Brackett's treasure somehow. Tied to Martin Louviere's ancestors or this logbook or whatever Missianna is. If I can solve that riddle, maybe it puts me on the trail of whoever did this to him."

"How are you going to solve the riddle?"

"I don't know. I figure I'll start by learning everything I can about Damon and see if I can figure out what he knew. See if Dixon has any clues as to who killed him, or if I can find any of my own clues. I am a P.I., after all, with reciprocity in Louisiana. Plus, this Brackett looking for a crew in New Orleans story had to come from somewhere. Maybe I can find someone who can give me more info on the particulars."

"You know the theory is only that Brackett came to New Orleans looking for a crew? There's no mention of the treasure."

"No, but no one even knows what happened to Brackett after the *Barracuda* sunk. If I can pinpoint his life after that, it's one step closer."

"This sounds like a lot of long shots, grasping at straws," she said.

And she was right. It did. Still. But as Jackson entered the terminal, he remembered the words he'd told her in parting last night, "I've got to do something." He hadn't known then and didn't know now why he had to do something. But here he was, set to board a plane for the Big Easy.

A tall, blond, refined Southern woman in distressed blue jeans and a gray T-shirt with "Key West" printed on the front in teal was waiting for him. She had silver aviator sunglasses pushed up into her hair and a bright blue duffel bag over her shoulder. She smiled when she saw him. "Ten-forty to Miami or eleven-fifteen to Atlanta?"

"Sawyer, what are you doing here?"

"I'm coming with you."

"What?"

"I know I didn't stutter."

"You're serious? You're really coming?"

"If talking you out of it fails, which I reckon it will. Have you thought this through, Jackson? You're talking about trying to solve one or two murders and find clues to a treasure that someone apparently thinks is valuable enough to commit murder over."

"I can deal with danger."

"Well, then so can I. Besides, I can't just sit around here wondering while you're off chasing bad guys through the French Quarter."

A grin tugged at the corners of his mouth. "Have you booked a flight?"

"I was waiting to see what flight you were on. I figured you'd want the quickest flight with the least inconvenience, which means either the ten-forty to Miami or the eleven-fifteen to Atlanta. There's also a three o'clock to Atlanta, but the layover is long and then another whole day is shot. So I'm guessing eleven-fifteen. Am I right?"

"Tell me this isn't the movie where with ten minutes left I find out you're also a P.I.?"

She beamed.

"You know I could have taken the nine-twenty to Tampa and Houston."

"Lot of back and forth and it only gets you to NOLA twenty minutes sooner."

"Why didn't you call?" he asked.

"I thought I'd be harder to refuse in person."

"That's true."

"And it'd be harder for me to chicken out if I was actually here."

"That's also true."

She tapped the toe of her shoe on the floor. "Come on, what do you say? Don't refuse a Southern lady."

"You know you can't play the 'Southern lady' card forever."

"We'll see."

"Don't you have to work?"

"It's the weekend."

"I might be there a few days."

"I've got nothing I can't change."

"And it's okay for a refined Southern woman to travel in the company of an unrelated man?"

"If he's a gentleman."

Jackson nodded.

"Now, are you done trying to talk me out of it?"

"You're a grown woman. I can't stop you from flying to New Orleans on a whim."

"That's right."

"Can you afford it?"

"I have points. Honey of a deal on a credit card a few years back."

"All right, Southern Lady. Let's get you a ticket."

Sawyer beamed again and turned toward the ticket counter.

*   *   *

Three weeks ago . . .
Monday, April 29
8:41 p.m.

SHE WAS waiting for him at a bistro table for two in the back corner. Her blond hair hung on shoulders covered by a leather jacket worn open over a gray T-shirt with an enlarged Tommy Trojan stamped on the front. She flipped through a rolodex of dessert options, looking up as he slowly approached. Her pixie face formed a wide smile, and she slid off the chair to greet him. She stopped just short of giving him a hug, reading the grimace on his face.

"Are you still in pain?" she asked.

"Not too bad." He looked her up and down, which wasn't that far. "You going undercover again?"

Detective Ashley Larson narrowed her bright blue eyes. "No, I am not going undercover."

"Oh. Well, then, you look nice."

"Thanks," she said without any sincerity. They both sat down. "How are you really doing, Jackson?"

He winced as he adjusted his position on the chair. "Doctor cleared me for normal activity, whatever I can do without pain."

"How much is that?"

"Drive myself across town for pie's about it so far. So what's on your mind, Ash?"

140

"You want to order first, get that out of the way?"

He looked at her. "It bad?"

"No."

He slowly nodded. "Okay, let's order."

Big Sky Pie on Montana and 15th purported to have the best pie in Santa Monica, if not all of Los Angeles. Given the prices, they had better. But when Ashley had called that afternoon to see if he was free after her shift, she'd promised to pay. And she had picked the place.

He ordered a slice of cherry à la mode and black coffee. She frowned when the waitress was gone, having opted for something chocolatey that he hadn't understood.

"What?" Jackson asked.

"Cherry pie?"

"It's my favorite."

"And you can get it anywhere."

"I don't go in for frills. Sam . . ." He paused for a moment to shake the thought of her away. "She took me to this cupcake bar once, whatever that is, and the cupcakes cost nine-fifty a pop at minimum and had more frosting and sprinkles and things I couldn't identify. Just give me the cupcake." He looked at her. "But we didn't come here to talk cupcakes."

"No."

"Okay," he said, settling into his chair a little more with another wince. It had been like that for a month, winces and grimaces and outright exclamations of pain at every movement. Thus he'd kept movement to a minimum. "What do you want to talk about?"

She waited as the waitress brought Jackson a steaming mug of coffee. He thanked her, then turned his attention to Ashley.

"So, I have some news," she said.

"What's that?"

"Dylan asked me to marry him."

He stared at her, his mug halfway to his mouth. He eased it back to the table. "Marry him?"

She nodded.

"I didn't know the two of you were even dating."

"We weren't."

He lifted the mug again. "Takes pluck, I'll give him that."

"We were grabbing a bite to eat after a shift last weekend, and he was saying how we've been partners now for three years, and had been through a lot of ups and downs, had become really good friends. And then he said that I was the best thing that had ever happened to him and that . . . he loved me."

"That's a bombshell."

She shook her head. "But the way he said it, it wasn't like he was telling me that he was in love with me, but that he cared for me—like family."

"He say that?"

"Not in those words, but . . . I knew it was what he meant." She sat back, having been leaning forward. "I told him I felt the same way. I hadn't realized it until then, but as he was talking, I found myself agreeing with everything he said. Then he said he didn't want to ever lose what we had and asked if I wanted to make it permanent. I couldn't believe what I was hearing, and then I heard 'Will you marry me, Ashley?'"

"What'd you say?" Jackson said, noting her bare ring finger.

"I asked if he was crazy. And he said, 'Look around us, Ashley. We live in Hollywood, where people fall in and out of love left and right, ruining relationships and marriages and families.' He said maybe we'd be better off with a little less falling in love and a little more genuine love, with relationships based on deep, intimate friendship like we have, two people who know each other, faults and flaws and all, and still care deeply for each other."

"I couldn't agree more."

"Neither could I," Ashley said.

"You say yes?"

"I told him I had to think about it. That's not exactly a decision you want to rush into."

"No."

"He dropped me off at my apartment, and I couldn't sleep. I called him back at two a.m. and said yes."

"You did?"

"I did. Jackson, I'm getting married."

He exhaled, leaned back, and therefore inhaled sharply. When he recovered, he smiled. "Congrats, Ashley."

"You think I'm crazy?"

"No. I think you'd have a hard time pitching it to Hallmark. Although, nobody else ever seems to. No, I don't think you're crazy."

"I've never had romantic feelings for Dylan, and he said he hadn't really either for me. Now, I'm still not sure if I do. But somehow, this seems right. It's been a week now, and I'm more sure of my answer than when I gave it to him."

"That's great, Ash. I'm happy for you."

The waitress brought pie, big slices, but not that big, given the price. And no better than a $2.99 slice at a diner somewhere. But the ice cream was cold, and the coffee was hot, so he wasn't complaining.

"Have you set a date yet?"

"Oh good heavens no," she said after swallowing a bite of her pie. Something about decadent sin or sinful decadence—as if chocolate was evil. At any rate, she wiped a dab of sin off her lip. "We haven't even told our families yet. Kind of big news when they don't even know you're dating."

"I guess."

"And . . ." She looked down. "We want to get settled first."

"Settled?"

"We're moving, Jackson. I put in my transfer this morning. Redding."

"Redding?"

She nodded.

Way north, about as far as you could go from L.A. and still be in the state.

He frowned. "How big is Redding? They have room for two more detectives?"

"Dylan's leaving the force. His dad's been sick for a while, so he's taking over the family lumber store. And I'm going to bust baddies in NorCal," she said with a peppy smile.

"Wow. That's great, Ash."

"I wanted you to be the first to know, Jackson. I know ours has been kind of an odd relationship, pulling levers and calling in favors, but ever since that night eleven months ago when you went to the mat for me and for Dylan, I've known I could always count on you if I needed you. I don't take that for granted."

He nodded. "Has it only been eleven months?"

"Give or take a few weeks."

"Huh. I never would have bet that ditzy Valley Girl in sparkles and sequins would turn out to be my source inside LAPD."

"Like, for sure," she said in her best Valspeak.

"When are you moving?"

"As soon as possible. If I can get out of my lease, possibly as soon as the end of next month."

"A shame I won't be able to help you move, what with my crushed ribs and all."

"Yeah, that is too bad."

He sighed. "I won't lie. I'm going to miss you. But I am genuinely happy for you and Dylan. Thing is, I kind of always suspected it."

"What?"

"That first night, racing across L.A. trying to save both of you . . . I could tell then you two had something special."

"You are quite the detective, apparently. You knew it before we did."

The waitress came back to top off his coffee, and when she left, Ashley regaled Jackson with more plans, expectations, and general effervescence. They finished their pie, then walked out together. The air was cool but comfortable, and they lingered for a moment on the sidewalk.

"Thanks again, Jackson."

"For?"

"Saving my life and always being there."

"After last month, I think we're even on that score."

She gave him a careful, tender hug. He told her to give his congrats to Dylan. She told him to keep his calendar open in the fall. Then they said goodbye, and he watched her walk off into the darkness, thinking about the transitory nature of life.

Chapter Nineteen

Saturday, May 18
10:36 a.m.

IT TURNED OUT there wasn't a mad rush to get out of Key West on a Saturday morning, and Sawyer was able to book a seat next to Jackson for the flight to Atlanta. The connecting flight to New Orleans was a little more crowded, and she had to settle for one several rows in front of him.

They passed through security, and since they had some time before boarding, Jackson made a couple of phone calls.

"Sheriff Hawkins speaking."

"Sheriff, it's Jackson Douglas. I wanted to check in with you. I'm heading to New Orleans."

"New Or-lee-ans?"

"That's right. I think someone there might know what happened to Ben. I'm going to check it out."

"It's a free country," Hawkins said. "Thanks for letting me know."

"I'll let you know if I come across anything pertinent."

"I appreciate it."

Jackson ended the call and then dialed a second number from memory.

"Detective Dixon."

"Detective, it's Jackson Douglas."

"Douglas. I just spoke with your sheriff a short while ago."

He wasn't Jackson's sheriff, but he didn't bother correcting Dixon. "Oh. Learn anything?"

"Not much."

"You got any leads on Damon's death?"

"No, afraid not. Looks like a simple home invasion, but I don't have much else. What can I do for you?"

"Sawyer and I are coming to New Orleans."

"You're coming here? Why's that?"

"We're convinced Ben's death and Damon's death are connected."

"How so? The treasure you mentioned?"

"I know it sounds strange, but yeah. We think Ben was looking for an eighteenth-century pirate treasure and Damon was helping him. Combine that with finding a New Orleans native dead here in the Keys, and, well . . ."

"I don't mean to pull rank, Douglas, but don't you think it'd be better to let the professionals handle this?"

"We have no plans of interfering. I'm a private investigator in California, which grants me reciprocity in Louisiana. But I'm not looking to step on anyone's toes. There's just too much coincidence here to let it go. But, I promise, we'll stay out of your way, and if we crap out, we've only wasted our own time and money. If we find anything, you're our first call."

"I'm not wild about it, but I can't stop you. When's your flight?"

"We get into Louie Armstrong at 3:10."

"You got arrangements on this end?"

"No. Not yet."

"I'll pick you up. I can brief you on what we've got so you don't bother covering the same bases twice, and I'll make sure I know everything you do about Ryker and this treasure business. I can't believe I'm saying this, but people've been killed over less."

"I appreciate it, Detective."

"What's your flight number?"

Jackson gave it to him. The duo exchanged basic descriptions so they could find each other and agreed on a meeting place. Jackson thanked Dixon again, then made one final call. Jackson's grandpa and Reggie were the only two people who knew where he was. After recent events, keeping someone updated seemed like a wise move. So he left Reggie a quick voicemail with the basics, telling him he was headed to New Orleans.

Soon after he closed his phone, the Delta agent announced their flight was boarding, and Jackson and Sawyer joined the small throng of people filing onto the airplane. It was a Boeing 737, and they had the window and middle seat two-thirds of the way back on the right side of the plane.

"Your pick of the litter and you choose the back?" Sawyer asked.

"Didn't feel like looking at a wing all day."

"Aha."

No one came for the aisle seat, so when the flight attendant sealed the hatch, Jackson scooted over to give him and Sawyer a little more elbow room. They taxied for just a minute, paused, and then blasted down the runway. Less than a minute after liftoff, they had cleared Key West and begun to bank north over open water. Jackson looked past Sawyer out the window at the Keys, a majestic sight from the air as they stretched endlessly into the blue. Even from altitude, the water varied in color, reflecting currents, depth, and the reefs beneath the surface.

"Can I ask you something?" Sawyer said when they had leveled off somewhat, although still climbing.

"Sure."

"Where does a private investigator get the money to jet around the country on a whim? I always thought that it was kind of a low-budget, scrape by sort of existence. Or is that different in California?"

"Worse in California," he said. "The cost of living is absurd. But I have very cheap house payments, drive a car that's older than me and is thus insured for about eight dollars, and I bum meals off my best friend."

"I see."

"And I have an emergency stash."

"An emergency stash?"

"Sort of a long story."

Sawyer turned her head out the window, then back at him with a small shrug. The message was conveyed.

"Remember when I told you about the militia group kidnapping my brother's fiancée?"

She nodded.

"It all started when she hired me to find a prostitute who could clear a client she was defending. So we go to Vegas, I find this prostitute, only she's dead."

"Very seamy."

"Kind of what I thought. Well, right after I find her, the cops show up, run me in, and Hillary—my brother's fiancée—has to work her magic to get me off on a murder charge."

"You went to trial?"

"No, she pointed out the various holes in the case before the cops ever went to the D.A. Anyhow, we traced this prostitute's death back to a casino owner, and as cover for getting into his safe in an effort to find proof of his involvement, we conned an invite to an exclusive poker game in his penthouse suite."

"And you won?"

"We cleared close to forty grand."

Sawyer whistled.

"After expenses, we split what was left, and I came out with a nice nest egg."

"An emergency fund."

"Something like that. Then things went south, I shot up a decommissioned Air Force base and took out twenty bad guys, and the rest is history. The short of it is, I can afford to jet around the country on a whim."

"Yours *is* an exotic life."

"That's one word for it."

Sawyer sat back, looking out the window. A flight attendant brought peanuts and offered drinks.

"Can I ask you something else?" Sawyer said when she was gone.

"Ask away."

"When I said this could be dangerous, you said you could deal with danger. What'd you mean?"

"You said the same thing."

"Yeah, but the way you said it. You meant something."

Jackson sighed. "Hillary, my brother's fiancée? She's actually my late brother's fiancée. Two years ago, he and my parents were both killed."

Sawyer's eyes widened, the sorrow evident although she didn't say a word.

"They were at a restaurant and . . . it exploded. My family meant everything to me. It's kind of sucked my will to live."

"I'm sorry," she said quietly. "Is that . . . why you're in a rut with God?"

Jackson nodded slowly. "That, and then my career—the killings, deaths. I had a client commit suicide."

"How awful."

"It's added up. I don't blame God. I know He doesn't owe me a happy, pain-free life. And yet, I guess, it's like I told you on the beach, I kind of do blame Him. I'm struggling through that all."

"Wow. I know you were a little glum the first few days, but you actually seem to be doing pretty well, all things considered."

He shrugged. "All things considered, maybe I am. And it comes and goes. Tuesday was my birthday, the second anniversary of their death. Made it especially hard. Add in Ben's death . . . But, yeah, I can play the superficial dude card pretty well too."

"Doesn't seem superficial. What I mean is—"

"I'm a real dude?"

"You seem to be coping pretty well."

He raised his eyebrows.

"I mean it." She shrugged. "To what I can see, at least."

Jackson stared into her eyes for several seconds. Then he nodded, saved from having to say something by the return of the flight attendant with ginger ale for him and a cranberry juice for her. He took a few sips, then opened his peanuts.

"So how does that all help you deal with danger?" Sawyer asked.

"The Bible says that for a Christian to be absent from the body is to be present with the Lord. I believe that's where my mom, dad, and brother are. Makes me want to be there too. Most people have an aversion to death, even if they believe in God and trust that they'll go to heaven when they die. I don't really have that anymore."

Sawyer nodded.

"I'm not suicidal or anything, but I'm not afraid to die. Danger doesn't scare me."

"I think I understand that," she said. "My daddy would say that's how we should all live our lives."

"Yeah, but more out of faith than a death-doesn't-scare-me, action-hero mentality."

"I'm not sure the latter isn't based on the former, in this case."

Jackson shrugged.

"So do I need to worry?" Sawyer asked.

"How so?"

"Are you going to turn into a cavalier, devil-may-care superman who puts both of our lives in danger?"

"Not without your permission."

She smirked. "Fair enough."

"Besides, I have a feeling you could handle yourself."

Sawyer sat back.

"So can I ask you a personal question?"

She nodded.

"You mentioned your dad several times, but not your mom."

Sawyer rolled her head to look at Jackson. "She died when I was five. A drunk driver."

"I'm sorry."

"I was so young that the full weight of it didn't really hit me then. That happened when I was eight and didn't have anyone go with me to a mother-daughter sleepover or when I became a teenager and didn't have a mom to confide in. Things like that."

"I'm sorry," Jackson said again.

"Daddy was strong," Sawyer said. "And we made it. Harder on him, I'm sure. He loses a wife and has to care for a daughter by himself."

"He seems to have done a good job," Jackson said.

"He absolutely did. The faults that remain are mine."

"He teach you to shoot?"

"He did."

"He share his love of Alabama football with you?"

"He did."

Jackson smiled. "Can I ask you one more thing? It might be a little personal."

She nodded.

"Do you own a hound's tooth dress?"

"That is kind of personal."

"The cute girls at Alabama games are always wearing hound's tooth dresses and hound's tooth skirts and hound's tooth scarves, so I just figured a diehard Bama fan like you must have something hound's tooth in the wardrobe."

"Can't say as that I do."

"You're killing my stereotype, Sawyer."

"Sorry."

They traced the west coast of Florida, catching glimpses of Port Charlotte, Tampa Bay, and what Jackson thought was the giant golf ball dome thingy at Epcot in Orlando but may have just been a distant water tower. Then they passed over solid land, most of it covered in dense foliage. They talked more about their childhoods, with Jackson sharing pleasant memories of his family and Sawyer telling him about her father and growing up with only one parent. The flight breezed by until they made their descent into Hartsfield-Jackson International Airport in Atlanta. They circled the airport several times before finally being cleared for landing. By the time they were on the ground and at their gate, they practically had to race through the concourse to get to their connecting flight. Despite a grumbling stomach, Jackson only had time to purchase a package of M&M's from a vending machine before boarding the plane to New Orleans.

It was nearly full, and Jackson was seated next to a heavyset guy in a suit jacket who immediately put a sleeping mask over his face. With no one to talk to, and with intermittent cloud cover hampering his view of what scenery might have been out the window, Jackson mentally reviewed the detective work that had led them to come to New Orleans that morning, and pondered what Detective Dixon might have for them. Hopefully something. Anything at this point.

The sky was overcast and the pavement wet as they touched down at Louis Armstrong New Orleans International Airport on the west side of the city. The view as they descended had been shrouded in fog, making it hard for Jackson to tell what he was looking at.

They had made good time, arriving at their gate at 3:04 p.m. local time. After reuniting just inside the terminal, Jackson and Sawyer found their way to baggage claim and had no trouble identifying Detective Jason Dixon. He was black, tall and athletic looking, with a gray suit that been through a hectic day of homicide investigation. He had close-cropped black hair, a day's growth of beard, and a tired expression on a handsome face.

"You Douglas?" he asked as Jackson approached him.

"Yeah. This is Sawyer Collins."

"A pleasure," Dixon said, offering his hand. He withdrew a badge from his pocket and showed it to them. "You all have bags?"

They did, one each, and after collecting them, they followed Dixon to a black Ford Taurus parked in the loading and unloading zone. "Cop perks," Dixon said. He opened the back door for Sawyer and helped Jackson lift their luggage into the trunk. Jackson got in beside Sawyer and thought about asking Dixon if they could stop for something to eat as the detective got in. He didn't get the chance.

Dixon cut off a shuttle bus as he whipped the car away from the curb. They took off like a shot, the Taurus's engine whining. Dixon drove like he was headed to a robbery in progress, looking back at his passengers as much as forward as he talked. "You all got a destination?"

"Um, not as of yet," Sawyer said with a look at Jackson.

"I'll run you to Villars' place. Maybe your eyes will see something ours didn't. You mind if we make a quick stop first, while we're out this way?"

"No, that's fine," Sawyer said.

"Good. So you all say this friend of yours, Ben O'Reilly, he was looking for pirate treasure?"

"Yeah," Sawyer answered. "You ever heard of Captain James Brackett?"

"Can't say I have."

Sawyer gave a brief overview of Brackett and the treasure legend, far shorter than the one she had given Jackson a few days prior on the boat. Rain was falling somewhat steadily, casting a gray pall over a warehouse district that didn't need it. They were headed west from the airport and soon took the ramp onto Interstate 310.

"So how's this tie to Damon?" Dixon asked.

Jackson picked up the narrative, explaining about the call from Damon and the believed tie-in to the treasure.

"So you don't know that Villars was calling about the treasure?"

"Not for sure," Jackson said, "but it certainly makes sense, especially when you factor in Ryker."

"The dead guy that washed ashore?"

Jackson nodded.

"So what's your theory?" Dixon asked.

"We're not entirely sure," Sawyer said. "But we're working off the assumption that Ben was looking for the treasure and enlisted Damon's help. Somehow the wrong people found out about it, killed Damon, and came after Ben."

"Ryker?"

Sawyer nodded.

"Ben defended himself," Jackson said, "accounting for Ryker's injuries. But he never showed up either, so we suspect there might have been a third person involved, a partner of Ryker's maybe. We don't know."

"So what are you hoping to find here?"

"Damon's message mentioned a guy named Louviere and some journal, as well as what we're guessing is a boat called the *Missianna*. We're hoping to find out what Damon knew and how it might tie to the treasure or Ben's disappearance."

"You have any idea who Louviere is?"

"We found a sixth- or seventh-generation New Orleans resident by the name of Martin Louviere," Jackson said. "Runs a large business, The Louviere Company."

"Yeah, I've heard of it. You think Villars knew him?"

"We don't know. It's the only connection we could find."

"Well, I've never met Louviere, but I can't imagine a successful businessman like him would be involved in all this."

"Kind of what we thought too," Sawyer said.

Dixon concentrated on traffic for a few minutes. They were crossing the Mississippi River on a rusty old suspension bridge. Far below them, the muddy waters were lined right and left with barges. Jackson thought Key West and its culture was a long ways from California, but he had a feeling it was nothing compared to southern Louisiana.

"What about this logbook?" Dixon asked. "Any idea what's in it?"

"No," Sawyer said. "Nothing more than guesses."

"We're pretty much out of answers," Jackson said. "We're hoping to find more here."

"Well, I'll tell you we haven't found much at Villars' house," Dixon said, merging into the right lane. He put on his blinker. "We checked up on what you mentioned yesterday, that someone broke into his place a few nights ago."

"Yeah?"

"We only found evidence of one break-in, but that doesn't mean the other didn't take place. He say if anything was stolen?"

"No," Jackson said.

They turned onto another four-lane highway, this one leading through a corridor of trees. They continued for several miles, headed farther away from New Orleans, with no signs of civilization on either side or ahead.

They drove for maybe a mile and a half before Dixon slowed and took a left turn onto a narrow two-lane road running through thicker trees. Dixon drove for another mile before taking a gravel road west. He then took the first left, down a rutted road through thick overgrowth and low-hanging trees. Jackson and Sawyer were jostled along as they twisted and turned deeper and deeper into the bayou.

"This stop," Jackson said. "You wrestle gators for spending money or something?"

Dixon grinned. "Retired friend of mine, a mentor really, lives out here. When I'm stuck, I like to bounce ideas off him. And I have to admit," he said, looking back over his shoulder with furrowed brow, "I'm stuck on this one. Factor in the treasure legend you all mentioned and, well, I thought maybe he might be able to give us a clue. Especially if he can hear everything you know. He's a New Orleans lifer, too, so if there's any legend or rumor about this logbook or Missy—what'd you say it was?"

"Missianna," Sawyer said.

"Right. If there's something to the rumors, he'll know it."

Jackson frowned. He bounced theories and problems off Reggie, his grandpa, and anyone who would listen, so an NOPD detective having an old mentor he ran things past was perfectly logical. He just hadn't expected that mentor to be from the cast of *Swamp People*. But hey, he was getting to experience Louisiana in a completely different light.

"Your friend not have a phone?" Sawyer asked.

"No. Duke likes his privacy."

"Duke?"

"Who else would you expect to live out here?" Jackson replied.

After maybe half a mile—and a "No Trespassing" sign—the path ended at a small clearing, surrounded on three sides by trees and on the fourth by murky, languid brown water. It appeared to be the backwater or overflow of a larger body beyond it, separated by a thin isthmus of land in which were rooted a couple of drooping willow trees. On the near side of the isthmus, and connected to it via a suspect footbridge, was a rickety one-story building with a tin pyramid roof. The building was supported by stilts that kept it hovering several feet over the water's surface. The wood siding was faded gray to match the roof, and the windows were dark and shadowy. The whole thing looked ready to collapse at any moment.

Dixon got out and opened Sawyer's door, offering her a hand. Jackson got out and inhaled the torpid air, an improvement over the back of Dixon's

Taurus. The rain had mostly abated, down now to a light drizzle, not much more than the humidity in the air. It was practically visible as it hung over the water, which as far as Jackson could tell was a natural body. Near the middle of the pond was a small island, more of a sandbar than anything. But what caught Jackson's attention was the alligator lounging on the slope, half in and half out of the water.

"Hey!"

Jackson turned to see what had made Sawyer cry out. He found himself looking across the top of the car at the barrel of Dixon's pistol.

Chapter Twenty

WITH HIS OTHER hand, Dixon held Sawyer's arm behind her back.

"What's going on?" Jackson asked.

Dixon pushed Sawyer forward and nodded for her to walk around the front of the car. "Cuff yourself to her," he said, and as Sawyer rounded the front of the car, Jackson saw a handcuff attached to her right wrist. With defiance in her eyes, Sawyer reached her arm out to Jackson. He took the loose cuff and placed it around his left wrist.

"Tight," Dixon said.

Jackson clicked it until the steel pressed against his flesh. "What's going on, Detective?"

Dixon just motioned with his gun toward a path around the edge of the pond, toward the isthmus. On the pond side, the ground fell off in a mixture of dirt, sand, and knee-high grass. On the opposite side of the path, the grass and overgrowth were higher and thicker. The space between was only several feet wide.

"Um, is that safe?" Jackson asked, his eyes drifting to the one gator—he knew about—lounging on the sandbar.

"They're more afraid of you than you are of them."

"Doubtful."

"Move," Dixon said.

Jackson and Sawyer walked close together so as to stay on the path. Several times, Jackson looked toward the sandbar, and he was almost certain the alligator's eyes followed them. He also swept his eyes around the clearing. There were no other vehicles hidden under the trees, no boats or hovercraft on either body of water, no other paths venturing into the woods. The house had no power or phone lines running to it, no antennas, no signs of connection to the outside world. It was less than ten miles from the airport and the New Orleans city limits, but it was totally isolated.

"What's going on?" Sawyer asked quietly.

"I don't know."

"Does he think we—"

"Quiet," Dixon said.

They walked onto the isthmus, ducking under the boughs of a large willow tree. To their left, something of a lake—at least a body of water larger than the pond—stretched out to tree-lined shores a couple hundred feet away. The water was stagnant, the perfect place for alligators, crocodiles, all manner of snakes, probably a few Komodo dragons. Jackson tried not to think about it as he stopped in front of the worn, uneven wooden "dock" leading a dozen feet into the pond to the house.

"Inside," Dixon said. "Now."

"Is that going to support us?" Jackson asked.

"Go."

Jackson didn't argue. Something about Dixon's cool, calculating manner and the smile he plastered on his face made Jackson uneasy. Whether he was a fake cop or a corrupt cop, Jackson doubted he'd have any trouble pulling the trigger on his pistol.

The dock creaked and swayed, but it held. Jackson looked down at the sandy bank of the isthmus. Some rather unusual striations in the mud at the edge of the pond gave him the impression that on a hot sunny day, the shade provided by the willows might have been a welcome respite for some alligators. Awesome.

"Door's open," Dixon said. "Go on in."

Jackson turned the knob and pushed the door open. The interior was dark, but he could make out a few very basic necessities. Two metal-frame bunk beds lined opposite walls on the right side of the room, flanking a dresser beneath a window. On the back wall, beneath another window, a worn couch sagged almost to the floor in the middle. Beside it sat a wooden rocking chair that looked ready to crumble to dust. Against the left wall, an unattached vanity with a sink was situated beneath another window and between a stack of firewood on the right and a rickety panel sticking out from the wall on the left. There was another panel attached to the near wall, cordoning off what Jackson realized was a toilet. More like a chair with a hole over the water. Even more awesome.

"All right, stop right there," Dixon said as Jackson and Sawyer reached a scuffed and dented wood-burning stove. Jackson figured it was even odds it was still functional, although the stack of wood suggested it was.

"What is going on?" Sawyer asked, turning over her shoulder. "Are you even a cop?"

"I doubt it," Jackson said.

"I'm a cop."

"Then you're dirty," Sawyer said.

"Hands up," Dixon said, then frisked Sawyer.

"Careful, Jack," she said as he worked his way up. "I only have one hand, and you have a gun, but so help me I will slap you into next week."

Dixon pocketed her cell phone, then proceeded to pat Jackson down as well.

"Really, my ankles? You think I'm packing a throwaway gun on an airplane?"

Dixon said nothing, lifting Jackson's cell as well. He tossed it on the couch, then did the same with Sawyer's. "Okay, over by the bed."

They obeyed, and Dixon retrieved a second set of cuffs from his waistband. He grabbed Jackson's right wrist and cuffed it to the ladder leading to the top bunk. The ladder, like the frames, was made of cheap metal. Cheap, but strong enough to anchor Jackson and Sawyer in place. The beds were lightweight enough that he could probably drag them across the room, not that doing so would accomplish much. The mattresses were thinner than an Army cot, and he doubted the sagging springs would even support his weight, not that he expected to sleep on the bed.

Dixon made sure the cuff was tight and stepped back.

"What is going on?" Sawyer asked, turning to face Dixon.

"Sit tight," he said. He reached into his pocket for a cell phone of his own and walked out the door.

Sawyer turned to Jackson. Her eyes were wide, but he didn't see panic on her face. That was good.

"Here," Jackson said. "Come over here a second." Sawyer moved beside him so he could raise his left hand. He shook the ladder, but it held tight to the beds. Its poles, although frail looking, were securely welded to each other. He and Sawyer wouldn't be able to break free.

"Who is this guy?" she asked.

"Just what he says, I'm guessing. NOPD detective."

"So he's involved in Damon's death?"

"I'm assuming."

"So why did he . . ."

"Tell us so much," Jackson said. "Yeah, that's the concerning part."

"Okay," Sawyer said, taking a deep breath. She looked around. "How do we get out of here?"

"I don't know. We can't reach our phones," he said, looking at the couch more than a dozen feet away. The ladder was on the end of the bed by the wall, and thus farthest from the couch.

"Maybe if we move the bed?"

"Yeah." He turned to look out the window. Dixon was retracing his steps back to the car, the cell phone to his ear.

"You think he's leaving us here?" Sawyer asked.

"I hope so."

"You hope so?"

"The only thing worse than being stranded in this place is being here with a corrupt cop whose face we've seen. Yeah, I hope so."

"When you put it like that . . ."

"Let's try moving the bed."

They tried several positions, first stretching out so that he could grab one end and she the other, then him using both hands on the end of the frame and ladder and her two hands on the top railing. In neither case were they able to budge it. Jackson peeked around the end and saw why.

"It's bracketed to the wall."

Sawyer huffed.

"Who brackets a bed to the wall?"

"What is this place, anyhow?"

"Hunting cabin."

"Hunting? Hunting what?"

Jackson shrugged. "A place for guys to get away from their wives and girlfriends and chug beer, complain, scratch and belch. I don't know."

"It's certainly no place for a refined Southern woman."

"No place for an Alaska frontierswoman."

"True."

Jackson looked back out the window. Dixon had opened the trunk and appeared to be digging through their luggage. Jackson reported as much to Sawyer.

She processed the info and said, "What about the ladder?"

"What about it?"

"Will it support us, you think? Or can one of us step on it to break it?"

"It's sturdier than it looks, but worth a try."

"You're heavier," she said.

"Yeah."

With Sawyer staying close, Jackson was able to climb to the top rung of the ladder, crouched down because of the cuffs on his wrists. He pushed with his feet, even bouncing a little on the ladder, but it didn't give way. He climbed back down.

"Now what?" Sawyer asked.

"I don't know," Jacksons said, studying the ladder. The rungs were welded to the upright support poles, but the ladder itself was screwed onto both the top and bottom frames.

"Who do you think he was calling?" Sawyer asked.

"His boss."

"Right, but who?"

"I don't know."

"What do you think he's looking for?"

"I don't know that either, but we can't expect him to be gone long. We need to find a way to change . . ."

"What?"

Jackson peeked at the ladder again. He turned back to Sawyer. "Reach into my right front pocket. There should be two quarters there."

"Quarters?"

"Change from an airport vending machine."

She frowned.

"Rudimentary screwdrivers."

Sawyer reached into his pocket with her free hand and withdrew the quarters. She gave one to Jackson and knelt down with the other. It was slow going with their limited reach, but they managed to unscrew all eight screws holding the ladder to the bed.

"Now what?" Sawyer asked as Jackson lifted the ladder free. "Our phones?"

"I don't think there's time," Jackson said as he looked out the window. Dixon was in the process of closing the trunk. As they watched, he turned back to the house. "And we're not going to be able to get this ladder off before he comes back. So we use it as a weapon. Here."

He led Sawyer over to the door and had her stand right beside it, facing the wall. "Let your right arm hang limp," Jackson said. "I'm going to use both hands to swing it as soon as the door opens."

She nodded.

"Then I'm going to pounce. Come along for the ride."

She nodded again.

Footsteps sounded on the dock from the isthmus, and Jackson backed against Sawyer, gripping the ladder like a baseball bat. He tensed, debating whether he should swing the ladder down on Dixon's wrist or wait until the door was wider open, risking detection, but giving him a clear shot at Dixon's head and neck. At the last second, he decided on the latter option due to the fact that his wrist was linked to Sawyer's and the sideways swing motion would be easier to perform.

Jackson heard Dixon's hand on the knob, and the door swung open.

"All right, we—"

Jackson swung, the end of the ladder just clearing the open door. It was a perfect uppercut, a Prince Fielder homerun swing, and the ladder connected with Dixon's chin. It slid down into his neck, knocking him off balance and back onto the dock. Dazed, he fumbled an object in his hands, causing it to fall through the slats and into the muddy water. After a flailed grasp at it, Dixon recovered and started to make a play for his gun. Jackson pounced before Dixon could reach it. Fortunately, Sawyer was ready and came with him.

Dixon reacted quickly, turning his focus from his gun to Jackson. He threw a left-handed punch that connected with Jackson's chin, knocking him back into the doorway. Just that quickly, Dixon went for his gun with his right hand. Before he could raise it, Sawyer jabbed a knee into his hand, pinning it to the dock as Jackson lifted the ladder with his right hand and tried to push it into Dixon's neck.

Dixon responded by grabbing it with his free hand, pulling Jackson toward him. He let go of the ladder and threw a second punch, short and quick but packing plenty of power to Jackson's cheek. It knocked him backward, taking Sawyer with him and off Dixon's hand. He started to reach for the gun, and Jackson flailed with the ladder. He caught Dixon in or near the eye, and the detective instinctively reached his hands for his eye.

Jackson swung the ladder wide, out of his way, and drove his knee toward Dixon's groin. He was unable to get everything into the effort because he was off balance and hindered by Sawyer's weight. Even so, he connected, and the fight went out of Dixon.

While the detective writhed in agony, Jackson pried his right hand away from the vicinity of his gun, and Sawyer quickly drew it from the holster. She tossed it on the floor inside the shack, then looked to Jackson.

"Get up," he said, crawling backward off Dixon. He and Sawyer stood, and he directed her to pick up the gun. She did, checking that it was loaded and turning off the safety.

"Good?" Jackson asked.

She nodded.

He turned to Dixon. "Get up."

Dixon, still in pain, rolled over, then got to his knees, facing away from them on the dock.

"Don't know how much research you've done or how much you know about us, but the lady here's a crack shot," Jackson said. "You try anything, and she puts one in you. And for your sake, I hope you aren't an LSU fan."

Dixon slowly got to his feet, not standing fully erect.

"Hands in the air," Jackson said. "Now lace your fingers on top of your head. Turn around and back toward me."

Wincing, Dixon slowly obeyed.

"You got him?" Jackson asked again as Sawyer held the gun in her left hand.

"I'm good."

"He twitches, shoot him."

She nodded.

Jackson knelt down and carefully frisked Dixon. He found a throwaway weapon in an ankle holster and removed it. There was also a pocketknife, car keys, and a cell phone in his pants pocket. Nothing else that could be considered a weapon. And no handcuff key.

"Where's the key for the cuffs?" Jackson asked, already fearing the answer.

"In with the gators," Dixon answered.

So that was what else he had been holding and had fumbled when Jackson hit him. He sighed and turned to Sawyer. "Shoot him."

"What?" Sawyer asked.

"Just a thought. Okay, slowly get on your knees, then lay down on your stomach. Hands stay on your head."

Once again, Dixon obeyed.

"Now what?" Sawyer asked.

"Player's choice," Jackson said to Dixon. "Either you tell us what's in this place that we can use to restrain you or we take other measures to incapacitate you."

"You're crazy."

Jackson racked the slide on Dixon's throwaway. "I'm lousy at bluffing."

"There's a roll of duct tape in the car."

"Where?"

"Trunk."

Jackson held up the car keys he had taken from Dixon's pocket. "Okay, we do this very slowly. You try anything, she shoots you. She falters, and I peg you. Got it?"

"Yeah."

Slowly and carefully, Jackson and Sawyer marched Dixon down the dock and along the path back to the car, where Dixon retrieved a roll of duct tape. Then they repeated the procedure, marching him back to the cabin. Once inside, Jackson motioned for Dixon to sit down and tape his own ankles. "Tight," he said. "Use more tape."

When he was done, Jackson had him roll over on his stomach and place his hands behind him. Then he had Sawyer bind those, as tightly as possible. Content, he rolled Dixon onto his back. Then Jackson knelt down, gun to Dixon's temple. "Who are you working for?"

"Jackson," Sawyer said.

"Don't look at her," Jackson said. "Who are you working for?"

"We need to get out of here," she said.

"We will, as soon as I get some answers."

She pulled on his arm, leading him to the far corner of the house. "He had the handcuff key out when he came in," she said. "And did you hear what he said before you hit him? 'All right, we—'" Her eyes blazed, not with anger but with intensity. "He was getting ready to move us. Which means someone else knows where we are and is expecting us somewhere else. We need to get out of here."

Jackson thought for a moment. "Yeah, you're right. But we can't go anywhere with this ladder attached to my arm." He turned back to Dixon. "There a hacksaw, anything to cut with? An ax, maybe?"

"No."

"In the car?" Sawyer asked.

"No."

Jackson looked at her. "How good are you really with a gun?"

"Good."

"Left-handed?"

"It's my dominant eye."

"Think you can hit the crossbar of a ladder and not my hand?"

"If the gun's sighted properly."

"Let's test it."

"At what?"

"I don't know. Him? A gator on that sandbar? Anything you want. How about that knot in the wood?"

"I've never shot indoors before."

"I'll keep it out of *Southern Belles Monthly*," Jackson said. "Besides, the door's open."

She shrugged, then took aim and fired. The wood splintered, sending chunks and slivers flying.

"You missed by a foot."

"I hit it dead on."

"The knot's still there."

"I wasn't aiming for that knot."

He looked at her, trying to determine if, despite the circumstances, she was messing with him. She was sober as a judge.

"Okay then."

"How do we do this?"

Jackson held up the ladder, rotating it so that the top rung was extended. He slid his arm as far from the rung as possible. "So this is how DiCaprio felt."

"Ready?" Sawyer asked.

"Did I mention how much I respect Alabama football?"

She smiled, then squeezed the trigger. Her bullet pinged off the ladder, vibrating Jackson's hands before it tore into the wood wall of the cabin. Jackson looked at the ladder. It hadn't been a direct hit but had weakened the rung enough that Jackson was able to break it off. He then slid the cuff off the end of the ladder.

"Want to try with the cuffs too?" Sawyer asked.

"Um, as a last resort. Come on."

"You're going to leave me here?" Dixon asked.

"Would you rather sit outside with the gators?"

Jackson picked up their phones, then turned and led Sawyer down the dock and around the pond. He paused in front of the car, reaching into his pocket for Dixon's cell phone. "They can track this," he said.

"Yeah."

He heaved it into the pond.

"What about the guns?"

"We need this one," he said, taking it from her. He led her to the driver's door and opened the car. Although not a regular black and white, Dixon's Taurus had plenty of police car amenities. That included a GPS system, which Jackson bashed in with the butt of the gun. Then he wiped down the gun and Dixon's throwaway with his shirt and heaved them both into the pond.

"Okay, now what?" Sawyer asked.

He tossed her the keys. "You drive."

Chapter Twenty-One

"WHERE AM I going?" Sawyer asked when she and Jackson had managed to get into the car, still handcuffed to each other. It hadn't been easy.

"Away from here, for starters."

She put the car in gear. "Shouldn't we call the cops or something?"

"With any luck, we'd get Dixon's partner."

"Maybe we can find a farmhouse with a hacksaw."

"A farmhouse? Farming what? Belts, purses, and gentlemen's shoes?"

Sawyer shrugged as she completed a Y-turn and started back down the rutted path toward civilization.

"Besides," Jackson said, "any farmer worth his salt would call the cops if we showed up in cuffs at his door."

"So what then? I'm going to have to go to the bathroom sooner or later and—"

"Refined Southern femininity, yeah, I get it. I'll think of something."

"Maybe we should just go look for the key."

"In muddy, snake- and alligator-infested water. I'd rather have my bladder explode."

"Hmm."

"I'll think of something," he said again.

Sawyer nodded and changed the subject. "You were awful calm back there."

"Like I said, I can deal with danger."

Sawyer turned, now back onto a paved surface. "Can I ask you something?"

"Yeah?"

"Would you have shot him?"

"No."

"Then you lied, about being a lousy bluffer."

"I was bluffing."

Sawyer nodded.

"Something wrong?"

She looked at him. "The look in your eyes made me think you would do whatever you had to."

"I would. But I didn't have to shoot him."

She frowned.

"If your life was in danger, if he knew something that I needed to know to save your life, then yeah, I would shoot him if I had to."

Sawyer nodded again.

"I told you at dinner the other night that if you wanted to run, you could. I'd say the same thing again, except . . ." He held up his left arm, jangling the handcuffs.

"I don't want to run." She stopped at the four-lane highway. "Back to town?"

"I guess. We need to find someplace where we can get our hands on a hacksaw or a set of lock picks or something. Someplace where they won't ask too many questions."

"Okay, so where's that?"

"I don't know. Head back toward the airport. We crossed some railroad tracks. Probably can find a sketchy neighborhood."

"Super."

"We'll need a story, too."

"Not the truth?"

"The truth makes us look like bad guys. Besides, it's too unbelievable."

"Daddy always said to beware of a boy who didn't tell the truth."

"Generally my philosophy as well."

"You got a story in mind?"

"I'm working on it."

Sawyer took the ramp to northbound 310, retracing their path of an hour ago. The skies were still overcast, occasionally spitting some moisture. The warmth and sunshine and relative safety of Key West seemed a lifetime away.

"I assume you're also trying to figure this all out in your head," Sawyer said. "How Dixon ties in, I mean . . ."

Jackson nodded.

"Yeah, me too."

"Homicide detective's probably not the criminal mastermind, just another thug on the payroll. But it strengthens the idea that whoever's behind this originates in New Orleans."

"And enlarges the web."

"Yeah . . . Do you wear makeup?"

"Excuse me?"

"I have a, um . . . a friend back home who doesn't wear makeup. Doesn't need it, just naturally good-looking. And I . . . know another girl, she wears it, but real subtle, you know, like if you're not thinking about it you wouldn't notice. Which is in stark contrast to a lot of the clowns who walk around L.A. with a face full of goop."

"You're kind of babbling."

"Yeah, trying to solve two problems at once."

"I am not wearing makeup."

"You'd never know," he said with a grin, and it earned one in return.

"I do wear it on occasion, however."

"Okay, so that's the real question. Is this trip an occasion? Did you pack any makeup?"

She looked at him. "I did."

He nodded. "Okay." He sat back.

"Why?"

"I was going to ask you the same thing."

"Excuse me?"

"Well, I just have to wonder why a refined Southern woman would pack makeup on a trip like this."

She looked at him out the corner of her eye. "Are you trying to rankle me while we're handcuffed together?"

"Rankle?"

"Because that's probably not a wise idea."

"I wouldn't dream of it, and I'm asking about makeup because we may need it to get these off," he said, lifting his wrist and shaking the cuffs again.

"How?"

"Depends if we can find a place that's open."

"What kind of place?"

"Chop shop, a warehouse, I don't know, where else would you find some bolt cutters?"

"At four-forty on a Saturday?"

"A long shot, I know."

They crossed the Mississippi, any potential views of downtown marred by the low-hanging clouds. Sawyer turned onto Highway 61, which led back to the airport. Jackson started scanning the road for a place that might be able to help free them. With the airport control tower in view, he spotted a couple of dump trucks and a trailer on the opposite side of a chain-link fence half a block down a side street. He instructed Sawyer to turn, and she slowed Detective Dixon's car and made a graceful turn off the main highway.

"Keep driving," Jackson said, and she cruised past a dirty, rundown compound identified as "Leland & Sons" by a metal sign on the half-open gate. In addition to the dump trucks and trailer, there were two large sheds, several rusted out vehicles, several more vehicles somewhere between drivable and rusted out, and piles of everything from tires to scrap metal to what looked like the refuse from a bathroom remodel.

"I'm guessing they have a bolt cutters, and the gate was open, so someone's there."

"Then why are we driving by?"

"That cover story I mentioned."

"You got an idea?"

"I think so. Turn up here."

She made a left onto the next street and, at Jackson's suggestion, made a U-turn and parked on the north side of the street. On their right, an abandoned—by all accounts—warehouse separated them from the fenced-in Leland & Sons property. On the left, another chain-link fence topped with barbed wire protected what looked like overflow parking for a used car lot. Across the street they had just been on, yet another fence cordoned off a self-storage facility.

Jackson shook his finger, then pointed at the self-storage facility in front of them. "That's perfect."

"What is?"

He turned to her. "About the makeup. Do you wear mascara?"

*   *   *

5:03 p.m.

"ARE YOU sure about this?" Sawyer asked. Rain had started to fall again, a heavy mist working toward a light drizzle. The windshield of the car was coated in a sheen, which helped conceal Jackson and Sawyer's presence inside it from anyone who happened along. No one did.

"No," Jackson said. "But the key to selling it is confidence."

"Tell me again why we can't go with the truth?"

"Would you believe two handcuffed people who told you a corrupt cop was responsible?"

"Okay, well, why the double stories?"

"Same reason. We walk in there in handcuffs, they'll be suspicious of whatever we say. So we need a second story ready. Kind of like asking your wife if you can go on a golf trip to Phoenix so she'll let you play one round with your buddy on a Saturday."

"Are you speaking from personal experience?"

"No, but it sounds very stereotypical."

She frowned at him.

"You ready?"

"If you are."

"The key to selling this is confidence. Don't act like a character. Become the character."

"Now are you speaking from experience?"

"A little. And I dabbled in Hollywood."

Sawyer raised her eyebrows.

"Story for another time. Let's go."

They extricated themselves from the car and began walking back toward Leland & Sons, hoping it was still open after five o'clock. Sawyer walked a half step ahead of Jackson, striding tall and confidently. He slouched along with her as they turned and entered the compound through the still half-open gate. They stopped and looked around.

"No guard dogs," Jackson said. "That's good."

"Maybe they're luring us in."

"You'd probably have them licking out of your hands in seconds anyway."

"Shouldn't we be in character?"

"Right."

"Any chance it is abandoned?"

"No. The gate's open, one of the shed doors is open, and that pickup by the trailer looks like it runs. Somebody's here."

"Okay, where—"

"Shout 'Hello.'"

"Are you serious?"

He nodded.

She shouted, "Hello!"

Nothing.

"Try the shed."

They started walking, her again in the lead. "Hello," she called when they were twenty paces from the shed. The ground beneath them was a combination of dirt and gravel, turning to mud, with ruts and potholes everywhere. Weeds grew up intermittently, and heavily around the edge of the shed. It was metal, rusting and graying from its original beige color.

Nobody answered again, and Jackson was starting to wonder if maybe there really wasn't anyone around. That would be okay too. Surely there was something they could use to break the cuffs.

Sawyer had opened her mouth to shout again when a man appeared out of the dark shed opening. He was short, somewhat heavyset, wearing blue coveralls and a greasy purple cap. LSU. Jackson hoped Sawyer could contain herself. A full, thick beard enveloped the man's face. It was lopsided, Jackson realized after a moment, because of the tobacco in his cheek.

"We're closed," he said with a stereotypical Cajun drawl. Then his eyes settled on the handcuffs.

Sawyer took her cue perfectly. "I'm afraid we need some assistance," she said, lifting up her right arm and thus Jackson's left. "I'm Special Agent Cassie Evans, DEA. This is Leon Pinkerton, a.k.a. Leon Pinkers, a.k.a. Leon Pink, a wanted drug trafficker. I just chased him across eight city blocks, and the only way I could restrain him was to cuff him." She squinted at Jackson.

The man looked at them for several long seconds. "What do y'all want me to do?"

"We got tangled up down by the river, and I lost my handcuff key. I'm hoping you can somehow unhook us."

"Y'all want to be unhooked?"

"That's right."

"Aren't y'all afraid he'll run off?"

"Not anymore," Sawyer said. "Not since I wrestled his cell phone from him," she said, holding up and shaking her phone. "He runs, I make one call to his boss on this, and his life isn't worth the rats in the warehouse next door."

The man spat, a juicy stream of brown that disappeared when it hit the wet dirt at his feet. "Y'all got a badge?"

"I'm undercover," Sawyer said.

"There someone I can call to verify y'all is who y'all say y'all is?"

"Busted," Jackson muttered under his breath.

Sawyer elbowed him in the ribs.

"It's true."

"Shut up."

The man shook his head. "I'm calling the police."

"Wait," Sawyer said.

"Told you it wouldn't work," Jackson said, also in a Southern accent.

"Shut. Up." The look in her eyes was so terrifying that Jackson almost smiled.

"I'm not with the DEA," she said as she turned to face the man. He stopped.

"Then who are y'all?"

Jackson sighed.

"Tell him," Sawyer said.

Jackson muttered under his breath.

"How's that?" the man asked.

"I'm Leon the Great."

"How's that?"

"He's a magician," Sawyer said, dripping with disdain.

"I'm an illusionist."

"He conned me into helping him practice for his show tonight, at his 'studio' in one of those garages over there," she said, gesturing across the street at the self-storage facility. "Next thing I know, he's got me handcuffed and can't remember where he put the key."

"I swear it was in my pocket."

"Um-hmm."

"Are y'all for real?" the man asked.

Jackson nodded sullenly.

"Well, why didn't y'all just say so. Come over here."

They trudged after him, feigning disgust. The man introduced himself as Jeb as he led them into the shed. More like a warehouse, with rows and rows of improvised racks containing metal in various forms, shapes, and sizes. Ostensibly organized according to some standard, although Jackson didn't know what. Jeb turned for a workbench on the left wall. It was piled full of all sorts of junk, and behind it was a pegboard that held numerous tools and implements. "Y'all his assistant?" he asked with a look at Sawyer as he searched the pegboard and the workbench.

"I was."

"Oh, cut it out, Sis. Everyone has setbacks."

"Y'all's brother and sister?"

"Afraid so."

Jeb nodded.

"I can probably pick them," Jackson said. "If you've got—"

"I've got a bolt cutters somewheres around here."

Jackson glanced at Sawyer as he masked a sigh.

"Ah, here we are," Jeb said. They held up their arms, and he snapped the cuffs off her right wrist and his left.

"Finally," Sawyer said, rubbing her wrist. She smiled very politely at Jeb. "Thank you." She turned back to Jackson. "I'm out of here."

"Wait."

She didn't look back.

"Sis." He took a step, then turned back to Jeb, extending his right arm with the other cuff. "You, see this hand gets cuffed to—"

Jeb snapped it loose.

"Never mind, I'm going to be late. Thanks, pal." He turned and hurried after Sawyer. "Sis, wait up. Come on. I'm sorry about the rabbit."

Sawyer was almost to the exit and was trying hard not to laugh when he caught up with her. "Keep walking," he whispered, and they hurried along, pretending to argue until the warehouse blocked them from view.

"The rabbit?" she asked.

"Overselling?"

"Maybe a smidge. But, I'm impressed. I didn't think it would work."

He shook his head. "Neither did I. If I'd have known who we'd run into, I'd have gone with the truth."

They got back in the car, Sawyer still behind the wheel. "Where to?" she asked.

"We need to ditch the car," Jackson said.

"Where?"

"Someplace with no traffic camera to spot us. Dixon will get free, and somebody will come after us and we can't leave a trail." He reached into the glove compartment and found a napkin. He wet it by sticking it out the window, then wiped the mascara from his eyes.

"That was a nice touch, by the way, but why was Leon the Great wearing it for a run-through?"

"I said I had a show tonight."

"Whatever."

"Besides, it sells the bit."

"If you say so. Be my navigator."

"Back on the highway."

Sawyer drove past the entrance to Leland & Sons and turned right on Highway 61. The road elevated to cross several railroad tracks, then dropped down again, the airport directly ahead. Instead of continuing on, Jackson directed Sawyer to turn off on a side road that backtracked beside the highway, then underneath it. On the north side of the overpass, parking lots for undefined airport outbuildings were cordoned off by more chain-link fence. On the south side, industrial buildings looked closed for the weekend. Jackson saw no signs of security cameras or any people who might observe them and think their actions out of the ordinary. He said as much to Sawyer.

"Anywhere in particular?" she asked, easing off the gas.

"No, anywhere."

They rolled to a stop on gravel beside the road and next to the concrete columns supporting the overpass. Jackson took several minutes to wipe down everything he and Sawyer had touched in the vehicle, as well as the door handles. Then, carrying their luggage over their shoulders, they set out, walking under the overpass initially to stay out of the rain.

"You think we're going to get in trouble?" Sawyer asked.

"Ehhhh, only if we get caught."

"You think we'll get caught?"

He sighed. "Probably."

"You are not the most encouraging man I've ever met."

"I've never been a fan of false hope."

"Nothing false about hope."

He looked at her.

"Don't get me wrong, Jackson. I'm not one of those people who thinks it doesn't matter what you believe as long as you believe something, at least not when it comes to things that matter. But I also think," she said, stopping, "that sometimes, when the chips are down, all a girl needs is for a guy to tell her everything's going to be all right."

"Even if she knows that he knows it won't be?"

"Even if. Hope gives you a reason to keep going, to keep believing. Sometimes, that's all you need."

Jackson looked straight into her blue eyes, framed by damp strands of light blond hair.

"What?" she asked.

"Why do I get the feeling we're not talking about corrupt NOLA cops anymore?"

She shrugged and started walking.

He caught up with her in a few steps as they walked out from under the overpass and into the drizzle. As he fell in beside her, she smiled, sweetly and simply.

"Sawyer, everything is going to be all right. I'm going to call us an Uber, we'll have a nice dinner of oysters or crawfish étouffée, and then *you* can put on some mascara and we'll go out on the town."

"Don't overdo it or anything."

He shrugged and looked over his shoulder.

"You've been doing a lot of that since we escaped."

He shrugged again. "Past experiences making me paranoid."

"Uh-huh. So lay it out straight for me."

"Give up hope already?"

"Hope doesn't discount reality. Give me the facts, then give me hope."

He nodded. "When Dixon doesn't show up or make contact with whoever he was talking to, they'll get suspicious. Eventually they'll look for him, eventually they'll find him. Probably tonight."

"So why not go to the police ourselves, cut him off at the pass? Surely you don't think the entire department is dirty."

"No, of course not. His boss, however . . ."

"Okay, so no cops. What's our plan?"

"I'm actually not too worried about cops. We didn't do anything wrong—"

"Stole a vehicle. That's grand theft."

"Stole from a corrupt cop who had kidnapped us."

"Escaped custody."

"Of a corrupt cop who had kidnapped us."

"Assaulted a detective."

"A corrupt—"

"Cop who had kidnapped us," she finished. "I get it. But it's his word against ours, isn't it?"

"In theory, but I don't think he wants to pursue this via official channels. He makes accusations, we make accusations, it gets messy, and he has to explain why he picked us up at the airport in the first place, has to explain our phone calls to him." He waved. "I think Dixon—and, more importantly, his boss—will want to settle this . . . unofficially."

"What's that mean?"

"I don't think we have to worry about a city-wide dragnet where every cop in the city's looking for us, hotel clerks and convenience store check-out guys looking at us funny. But it is possible Dixon will use some of his NOPD resources on the sly so he and his boss and his boss's goons can chase us down."

"I think I want some more hope."

"It's a big city. We have a head start. And we'll keep a low profile, especially tonight." He shrugged. "There's no way to avoid that but go home."

"Okay, so what do we do?"

"You think you can find us a place to stay on that fancy little phone of yours?"

"You got a preference?"

"Someplace with or near food."

"That narrows it down."

"Just a hunch, but my take on Dixon is that his sources run more in the vein of former criminals and shady businessmen than they do hotel clerks and maître d's. See if you can find us something downtown or in the French Quarter where we can blend in with the crowds."

"Okay."

"Where'd you say Damon lived?"

"Tremé," Sawyer answered, having done some research while waiting to back away from the gate in Atlanta. "It's one of the oldest neighborhoods in the city, just east of downtown."

"Convenient."

Sawyer tapped away on her phone, all the while trying to shield it from the rain. It was intermittent and still just spitting, just enough to be annoying.

"What about the Hotel Étienne," she asked. "I can get us a suite with separate sleeping quarters for one-seventy-nine or two rooms for one-oh-nine each."

"Where is it?"

"A few blocks from Jackson Square, in the French Quarter. Walking distance from Tremé. Close to the river, downtown."

"That's perfect. But don't book it," he said quickly.

"Why not?"

"One less record to conceivably get traced."

"Can I at least call us a cab?"

"Sure. How much cash you got on you?"

"Couple hundred."

"Okay. Don't give him a real name and tell him we'll pay cash."

"One less record to get traced," she said.

He nodded.

She smirked. "This cloak-and-dagger stuff is sort of fun."

Chapter Twenty-Two

6:18 p.m.

THE CABBIE WHO picked them up was a chatty local with an accent like Justin Wilson. He talked about everything from the Saints to jazz music to Hurricane Katrina while he drove them east on I-10, then south past the Superdome and downtown, and finally through the narrow, cobblestone-lined streets of the French Quarter. He never asked why he had picked them up where he had, along the side of the highway and within sight of the airport. He didn't ask much of anything about "Terry and Nick," the aliases Sawyer had chosen. When asked why by Jackson, as they'd waited for the cab to pick them up, she'd said her inspiration had been Alabama football coach Nick Saban and his wife, "Miss Terry." Jackson had rolled his eyes.

The driver dropped them on Decatur Street, in the figurative shadow of the steps of Washington Artillery Park and only a stone's throw from the Mississippi River. They got out into more light drizzle, to which they had by now become accustomed. The cab pulled away, and they were left with a view across Decatur Street of Jackson Square, named for the hero of the Battle of New Orleans and seventh President of the United States, Andrew Jackson.

Encircled by iron fencing, fronted by rows of horse-drawn covered carriages offering tours of the French Quarter, and featuring Parisian-themed landscaping and walking paths, Jackson Square was one of the icons of New Orleans. The famous statue of Andrew Jackson on bucking horseback in the center of the park was visible from the street. It was framed by the spire-topped, gleaming white-walled St. Louis Cathedral, another New Orleans landmark. It towered over Jackson Square, backlit by the reflection of city lights in the dark evening sky, looking something between regal and haunting in the rain.

Since they had to go that way anyhow, Jackson and Sawyer walked through Jackson Square. She had memorized the directions while in the cab, and Jackson trusted her. Most California girls couldn't find the ocean from the beach without GPS, but Sawyer led them through the narrow streets, beneath centuries-old buildings, like a lifelong resident of the Big Easy. They arrived at the Hotel Étienne, a four-story brick building with wrought-iron balconies overlooking a narrow, busy street that Jackson was sure he had seen on Mardi Gras footage. The entrance was under a canopy, a welcome respite from the rain that had, if anything, intensified.

The lobby was old but well maintained. Marble floors, paneled walls, and plush leather furniture situated around a fireplace gave it a very cozy feel. There was a player piano in the corner, playing jazz of course, and an entrance to a dark lounge beyond it. On the right, next to the check-in and concierge desk, a carpeted winding staircase led to a balcony on the second level. The crown jewel was a magnificent chandelier hanging from the open second floor, its thousands of crystals casting a soft, warm glow over the room.

The desk clerk, a dark-skinned woman with a tan blazer and complementary brown silk scarf, eyed them warily as they approached the front desk. But Sawyer's good-natured smile and charm soothed any suspicions. The Hotel Étienne accepted walk-ins and cash payments but required an ID. Jackson gave his, trusting that such a refined hotel would maintain confidentiality.

A bellhop appeared out of thin air to carry their bags to their third-floor suite. On the walk from Jackson Square, they had debated taking one room or two. For safety and financial reasons, they had agreed on a single suite with separate sleeping quarters. Sawyer trusted Jackson and his motives. He trusted her ability to beat him like a rented mule if he tried anything.

"You know it," she'd said.

Their suite contained a small kitchenette in the front and a spacious living area, featuring a gas fireplace, beyond it. An alcove off the living area contained a pull-out couch and a half bathroom while a separate suite connected on the other side. A small balcony off the living area overlooked the street and provided views of the French Quarter and the downtown skyline in the distance.

"You hungry?" Jackson asked when he had tipped the bellhop. "I'll square with you on fees when this is all said and done."

"I'm not worried and, yes, I'm starved."

"Got a preference?"

"You order a pizza while I take a hot shower?"

They discussed toppings for a moment before Sawyer retreated to the separate bedroom. Jackson phoned in an order to a local pizza place, then used the half bath to change and freshen up. Had flying to New Orleans after being surprised by Sawyer showing up at the airport, being abducted and taken into the bayou, escaping the custody of a corrupt cop only to wander around town handcuffed, conning a junkyard owner to free them, and visiting NOLA landmarks all really happened in one day? No wonder the face in the mirror looked beat.

Jackson splashed some water on his face before pulling on a clean shirt. It wasn't exactly a shower, but he felt better. He brushed his teeth to complete the feeling and headed into the living room to watch the news and see if anyone had found a duct taped detective in a cabin on stilts over a pond southwest of town.

The pizza arrived within twenty minutes, by which time Sawyer had emerged from the bathroom. In the movies, she would have been wearing "something more comfortable," and the combination of her, the popping fireplace, and their recent proximity would have led to something PG-13 at best. In reality, she wore a gray hoodie with a cursive capital A on the front, jeans, and white socks with gray heels and toes; and the fireplace was a little cozy but nothing more. The pizza was piping hot and delicious, and while they ate, they watched a flat-screen TV mounted above the fireplace. Jackson channel-surfed, looking for any mention of what had transpired that afternoon.

"This is so wrong," Sawyer said as Jackson turned the channel again.

"What?"

"A TV above the fireplace. That is not what mantels are for, especially in a place like this."

"Don't stand in the way of progress."

"Hmm."

He flipped off the set. "No news is good news," he said as he reached for another slice of pizza.

"You think Dixon's boss will leave us alone?" Sawyer asked.

"Depends. Assuming this is all tied to the treasure, then the primary goal of whoever's calling the shots is to find the treasure and keep anyone else from doing so. If they think we're in the way, then they'll try to silence us."

"Silence us," she said, tossing a crust into the box. She sat back. "Is that what you think they were going to do?"

"I don't know. I've been wondering that too. Like you said, Dixon was going to move us. If they wanted to get rid of us, he'd have shot us and tossed us in the pond as gator food. He had something else in mind."

"Interrogation?"

"More likely."

"Then gator food."

"That may be."

Sawyer sighed, then rested her elbow on the back of the couch, her head in her palm. "You think Dixon killed Damon?"

"If not, he's clearly covering for whoever did. Either way, it doesn't matter much. He's in on it. And it just confirms our suspicion that Damon's death is tied to the treasure and Ben's disappearance. Why else would Dixon care that we were here?"

"So what's our plan of action with the police out of the equation?"

"I don't know. Damon's clearly not going to give us anything. Dixon didn't reveal much. We can try to find more on Louviere, but without knowing what to try to find, I don't know that we'll get more. Our only other lead is the Missianna, unless by some chance Sheriff Hawkins has heard anything."

Jackson's cell phone rang. Or rather, started playing the James Bond theme song.

"Nice ringtone."

"We play a lot of video games," Jackson said, opening the phone. "Hey, Mouse."

"Hey. How's the Emerald City?"

"That's Oz, Mouse."

"I thought it was New Orleans."

"Crescent City."

"Whatevs. How is it?"

"Rainy. You find anything?"

"Yeah. Detective Jason Marquise Dixon has been on the NOPD for eight years. Worked homicide for the last four. Nothing in his record I could find."

"Partner?"

"William Reagan."

"Anything else?"

"No, man."

"Thanks, Mouse." Jackson closed his phone.

"Who or what is Mouse?" Sawyer asked, a very confused look on her face.

"The source I called the other day, the one who told us about Damon."

"His name's Mouse?"

"A real computer whiz. Anyhow, I called him while you were showering and had him look up Dixon for me," he said, recapping Mouse's brief intelligence report. As he talked, he retrieved the phonebook from an end table next to the couch.

"Now who are you calling?"

"Detective William Reagan."

"Why?"

"Fishing expedition."

He called NOPD and asked to be transferred to Detective Reagan's cell, claiming he had a tip about a case Reagan was working on. He was told Detective Reagan was on vacation through Memorial Day and his partner, Detective Dixon, was fielding all calls. For appearances' sake, Jackson asked for his cell number, then closed the phone and reported to Sawyer.

"Isn't that interesting timing?" she said.

"Very."

"You think he's involved too?"

"Or else with his partner gone, Dixon had a window to make things happen. I'm going to call Hawkins."

"Mmm, let me," Sawyer said, reaching for her phone on the table. Jackson shrugged and sat down, finishing his pizza and turning the TV back on, muted, looking for a weather forecast while she took her phone into the other room. It looked like rain was going to be the story for the rest of the night, but Sunday was promising. Jackson then flipped across all of the major cable news networks one more time. He didn't expect that a New Orleans cop being left trussed up in a shack would make the bottom scrawl, and he didn't see anything. Most of the news was centered on the assassination of some Russian politician, the usual sordid affair.

Sawyer returned and sat down in the chair opposite the couch. "They confirmed the blood found on Ben's boat was Ryker's," she announced. "Otherwise, nothing new."

"What'd he say about Dixon?"

"That he sounded like a hack on the phone. He told us to be careful, unless we wanted to end up like Ben."

"Well, that's encouraging."

"So we're back to square one," she said with a sigh.

Jackson consumed the last bite of his slice of pizza. "Unless we can prove Dixon's part of some massive treasure, murder, whatever-they-did-to-Ben conspiracy."

"Which we can't."

"No."

She sighed again.

"Take a ferry boat ride down the Mighty Mississip?"

Sawyer sent him a glare.

He shrugged.

"You done?" she asked, nodding at the pizza box.

"Mmm-hmm."

She found some cellophane in a drawer in the kitchenette and wrapped up the remaining pieces. She placed them in the mini-fridge and then walked out onto the balcony. Jackson spent a few minutes scanning the ESPNs—a twenty-to-one longshot had taken the Preakness Stakes, and the Dodgers hadn't won in almost a week. He flipped off the set and followed Sawyer.

The drizzle had abated, leaving a gloomy, pre-dusk darkness over the surprisingly quiet streets of New Orleans. Where were the bead-wearing revelers, the drunken tourists, the voodoo magicians?

Jackson dropped into the other chair on the small wrought-iron balcony. At first, Sawyer didn't acknowledge him. Then she turned her head. "We could go to Damon's house."

"And do what?"

"Look around. I don't know, you're the private investigator."

"Are you suggesting we break and enter his house?"

"I thought maybe you could pick the lock or something."

"Like I picked the handcuffs?"

"You didn't have any tools. I thought you could get some."

"It's a Saturday. Private Eyes "Я" Us is probably closed."

Sawyer made a face at him.

"Yes, I could probably scrounge something up to pick the lock on his front door," Jackson said. "If the cops haven't sealed it. If it isn't guarded or watched. If we really want to risk it."

"Do we have another choice?"

"There's always a choice."

Sawyer looked at him. "Not if we want answers."

Jackson stared out at the city, the mist and fog hanging over it like a blanket. It was dark and quiet, not the vibrant, festive place Jackson had envisioned. Maybe it was the time of year, maybe it was the weather. Either way, it gave Jackson hope that they could indeed break into Damon's house undetected. He turned to Sawyer.

"You pack anything black?"

"Does a dress count?"

"You packed a little black dress?"

"Did I say anything about little?"

"I was stereotyping."

"You never know when you might need to attend a dinner party."

"Don't you worry about wrinkles?"

"I carry a bottle of wrinkle-free spray."

Jackson raised his eyebrows. "Unfortunately, I don't think a dress will work."

"This is sort of dark," she said as she flicked the sleeve of her shirt. "I won't stand out."

Jackson eyed her. "That's an entirely different debate." He sighed. "Okay, we'll go check things out. But you've got to listen to me. If I say we abort, we abort."

"You're the private eye."

"I'm going to change."

Jackson donned a long-sleeve black shirt, standard traveling gear, and a darker pair of jeans. "Do Southern women ever use bobby pins?" he asked when he joined Sawyer in the living room. He frowned. "Are they even still called bobby pins?"

"Sometimes, but I don't have any with me."

"Good."

"Good?"

"If you had, and we hadn't used them to pick the cuffs, we'd have looked really stupid."

"Did you think of them to pick the cuffs?"

"Moving on. Point is, bobby pins are still a thing. Where can we get some?"

"Downstairs, I'd imagine. They probably have all sorts of little emergency items for their guests."

"You wanna go ask to borrow a couple?"

She nodded and slipped out of the room. He waited, pacing, wondering how bad of a decision he was making. On one hand, they were already sort of in Dutch with the cops, so why not, right? On the other, they hadn't done anything wrong, he didn't think. Break into a crime scene, that changed. If they got caught. If.

Was this really worth it? They weren't going to bring Ben or Damon back. They probably weren't going to find Captain Brackett's buried treasure. They probably weren't going to catch the men responsible. Was it worth risking his life, so to speak, on a long shot?

He almost laughed aloud. What was there to risk? Besides, long shots apparently ruled the day.

Sawyer returned, smiling, holding up a pair of bobby pins.

"Great. Let's go commit a felony."

Chapter Twenty-Three

8:15 p.m.

THE RAIN HAD morphed into something between a heavy mist and a dense fog as Jackson and Sawyer took a cab from the hotel north into Tremé. One of New Orleans' oldest and most historical neighborhoods, Tremé had been a place where free persons of color and freed slaves could acquire property. It was also known as one of the birthplaces of jazz music, as recognized by the thirty-two-acre Louis Armstrong Park within its boundaries.

But for all its history, the neighborhood had seen better days. The houses were small and rundown, many of them boarded up, and packed like sardines into each block. As he and Sawyer rode north on St. Philip Street, Jackson wondered how much Hurricane Katrina had impacted the condition of Tremé and how much its condition was due to other factors, like time and poverty.

The cab dropped them in front of St. Peter Claver Catholic Church, a towering gothic structure surrounded by an iron fence. It tied an otherwise stately building to a neighborhood in decline.

"You sure 'dis is where you want to be?" the driver asked.

"Yeah," Jackson said.

"All right. Iss' your choice."

Jackson paid him and arranged to be picked up one hour later. He and Sawyer waited until the cab was gone, then started walking. Damon's house was two blocks north, and Jackson felt overly conspicuous walking through an old black neighborhood with a tall white woman beside him. He half expected to encounter a gang roaming the streets or see a jazz band parading down the street on their way to a funeral, both stereotypes from a white boy from California. But all was quiet, the distant sounds of the city muted by the rain and fog.

Damon's shotgun-style house was in the middle of the block under a cluster of power lines. Sixteen feet wide at most, it was separated from similar sized houses by less than three feet. Secluded on a wooded lot would have been preferable. A narrow porch was elevated from the sidewalk by three steps. The paint was chipped and faded, light blue with white trim. The shutters on either side of a wide front window were dark blue, also chipped and faded. The front door was left of the window and wasn't marked by police tape or a CSI seal.

"Sure this is the right house?" Sawyer asked.

"This is the address," Jackson said, verifying gold numbers on the doorpost. He leaned back, looking up and down the block.

"I don't see anyone," she said.

"Yeah, but you know there's an old lady peering out from behind the blinds watching us."

"Try going around back?"

"We'll really look bad if we're spotted creeping between houses. Keep an eye out while I pick the lock."

Sawyer nodded, and Jackson knelt down. It took him two minutes that felt like hours to pick the lock with the bobby pins Sawyer had procured from the Hotel Étienne front desk. With another look up and down the street, he opened the door and stepped in ahead of Sawyer.

"What's that smell?" Sawyer asked as Jackson closed the door behind her.

"Death," he answered.

"It smells like something burned."

Jackson clicked on a small travel flashlight and played it around the room. It was square in shape, with windows on either side, blinds on both of them drawn. Straight ahead was another door, and beside it, a black couch. In the near right corner, a bulky TV sat on a rolling stand. Beside it was a bookshelf containing several dozen books, as well as CDs and DVDs. In the far corner, a small computer desk held an inkjet printer but no computer—laptop or desktop—or monitor.

Jackson turned the flashlight to his immediate right, to a small standalone coatrack beside the front window. A rain jacket hung by its hood on one of the arms. A set of keys rested on a small shelf next to it. A pair of running shoes and a pair of casual loafers sat on the floor beside a welcome mat.

"What are we looking for?" Sawyer asked.

"Anything. Especially anything that looks out of place," Jackson said as he played the light around the hardwood floor.

"Like that?"

His light stopped on a stain in the wood. Blood.

"Must have been where he was shot," Jackson said.

"Coming to the door?"

"Else after he'd answered it, leading someone in."

"Makes sense," she said, then shook her head in disgust.

They worked together, looking over the living room. On the near side of the couch, a basket contained a week's worth of newspapers and a couple old editions of *ESPN The Magazine*. The couch had a sweatshirt draped over one arm and a remote control on the far cushion. No throw pillows. On the stand beneath the TV were a DVD player and an old gaming console. Jackson browsed a few of the book, DVD, and CD spines on the nearby bookshelf, seeing nothing terribly interesting or out of the ordinary.

Sawyer slid a simple office chair away from the sleek computer desk. The printer was on the lower of two shelves, plugged in, but not powered on. A blinking modem and router in one sat beside it, its power cord running to a surge protector on the floor and a coax cable running to a port in the wall. A USB cord connected to the printer fell down to the floor, where it was lost in the dust, presumably having been unhooked from the laptop. It was gone, as was its power cord.

"I suppose the police took the laptop," Sawyer said.

"Probably." Jackson scanned a notepad on the top shelf of the computer desk. Nothing was written on it, and he saw no imprint from the previous sheet when he held the penlight up to it. He looked around the rest of the room, including a nicked wooden coffee table that held nothing but two coasters and a half-burned candle in a mason jar.

"Looks like he kept the place pretty clean," Sawyer said.

"Else it was sanitized," Jackson said, kneeling down by a wire-mesh garbage can beside the computer desk, under the window. It held some torn envelopes, credit card applications, tissues. He looked up at Sawyer. "Might as well," he said, then emptied the can's contents onto the hardwood floor.

Sawyer winced but knelt beside him and began sorting through the trash. Jackson brushed the tissues aside—there were a lot; Damon must have had a cold—and concentrated on potential evidence.

"Wonder why the police didn't do this?" Sawyer said.

"Maybe they did."

"And put it all back?"

He shrugged.

Sawyer straightened up, holding a postcard. "Let me see the light."

He handed it to her, and a moment later she turned the empty side of a cream-colored postcard to him. "See that?"

He leaned in to read a single word scrawled in pencil in the middle of the card: "Missianna." He looked up at her. "Anything on the other side?"

"Yeah," she said, flipping it over and adjusting the light. "'*St. Mark's Evangelical Church Ice Cream Social. Saturday, May 11, 6:00 p.m. St. Mark's Evangelical Fellowship Hall. Twelve-twenty-nine Dumond Street. Various flavors, toppings, miscellaneous desserts.*'"

"Sounds good."

"It was last week. Last Saturday."

"So was this just scratch paper or did he write 'Missianna' on it for a reason?"

Sawyer shrugged. "Dixon didn't seem to react when we mentioned the word Missianna."

"Not that I could tell. But back then, I also thought he was an upstanding if not a little rumpled law enforcement agent."

"Hmm. Why'd he throw it away?"

"Don't know."

"Maybe it's not a ship," she said. "We assumed it was, but maybe it's something else."

"An ice cream flavor?"

Her look indicated she was not amused. And that time was wasting.

"Do we know what Damon did for a living?" Jackson asked.

"No."

"There's nothing else here but dried snot. No bills, none of the worthless info packed into the envelope with bills."

"He probably paid them online."

"Probably. Let's see what else is in the house."

The next room back was the bedroom, smaller than the living room. Another door led to the kitchen and to a stub of a hallway leading to a very cramped bathroom between the bedroom and kitchen. A door off the kitchen opened to a small rear porch and an equally small back "yard."

The kitchen itself wasn't much larger than the kitchenette at the Hotel Étienne. The table in the corner was clear, but a few meals' worth of dirty dishes were stacked on the counter. A pot with residue of something burned on the bottom was still on the stovetop.

"There's your smell," Jackson said, shining the light into the pan. The contents were unidentifiable.

"Hmm," she said. "Nothing else here."

He briefly checked the bathroom—it was a typical bachelor's bathroom—before they returned to the bedroom. They started with Damon's small closet, finding an assortment of suit coats, ties, dress shirts, and pants, along with a few sweaters and pullovers.

"He's a snappy dresser," Jackson said.

"Was."

"Was." He opened a dresser drawer. T-shirts. The next had socks and underwear. Fairly routine.

"Something strike you as odd?" Sawyer asked.

"Such as?"

"This is clearly not the nicest neighborhood in New Orleans. This is an old house squeezed in with other old houses. And while it's clear that a man lived here, it's not falling apart. It actually seems to be in good shape. He doesn't have a lot of fancy possessions, but it's not like he's using cardboard boxes for furniture, either. And now his wardrobe is better than most guys I know."

"Present company included," Jackson said.

"So what gives?"

He shrugged and sat down on the bed. He opened the drawers of a nightstand, finding no will, no hidden packet of confidential papers, no tablet PC. There was an old worn Bible on top of the nightstand. Feeling like a grave robber, Jackson picked it up as he sat down on the bed.

"You really think this is a good time for your devotions?" Sawyer asked.

"I've heard that you can tell a lot about a person by what's in their Bible."

"Hmm. My daddy always said that it's more important to let your Bible mark you than to mark your Bible."

Jackson nodded. "That's very good. I'll remember that. Anyhow, a few months ago I helped track down this ancient Bible that allegedly had CIA codes written in the margins."

"Really?"

"Really. Never confirmed."

"You think Damon was a CIA mole?"

"I think maybe he kept his secrets somewhere." He flipped through the Bible, looking for scribble in the margins, underlined or highlighted text, or a dog-eared page. What he found instead was a small invitation-sized envelope, stuck between Colossians and I Thessalonians.

"What's that?" Sawyer asked.

"Here." Jackson set the Bible on the bed beside him and handed her the flashlight. Then he opened the envelope and withdrew a pair of notecards. The first was almost entirely blank, except for calligraphy scrawl in the middle. Jackson handed it to Sawyer. "You make that out?"

"'M. Damon Villars and Guest.' It's an invitation, but to what?"

Jackson squinted at the second card, still in his hand. One word jumped out at him: "Louviere."

"What is it?" Sawyer asked.

He handed it to her. "A party."

"A gala fundraiser," she said. "Honoring efforts to preserve Louisiana's wetlands, thrown by Martin Louviere at Pontchartrain Manor." She looked up. "That can't be a coincidence."

"How in the Sam Hill is Damon connected to the CEO of a Forbes 500 company?"

"He said he had a line on how to get a look at the logbook. Could this be it?" she asked, holding up the invitation.

"When's it for?"

"Tomorrow evening."

Jackson sat back. "He said he'd call Ben back 'next week.'"

"After the gala."

"What is it, a charity fundraiser?"

"Yeah. Maybe Louviere will be displaying his collection of antiquities?"

"Hmm."

"You think that's why he was killed? Somebody found out about Damon's plans to see the logbook?"

He shrugged.

"You think Louviere is behind this, the one calling the shots?"

"Too early to tell. We should get moving."

"You don't have to ask me twice."

Jackson returned the two cards to the envelope and pocketed it.

"You're taking it?"

He nodded. "It'll be hard to pose as Damon and sneak in without it."

*   *   *

9:31 p.m.

"YOU WANT to walk me through your plan?" Sawyer asked when they were back in their suite at the Hotel Étienne. "You want to go to Louviere's gala?"

"Maybe," Jackson said.

"Posing as Damon?"

"And guest. But first, we have to determine if Louviere knew Damon."

"He invited him."

"Yeah, but remember Damon's voicemail? He referred to him as 'a guy named Louviere.'"

"Implying he didn't really know him?"

"It's not how I'd talk about somebody I knew well enough to be invited to their gala."

"So why was he invited?"

"We need to find that connection."

"You got any ideas?"

"Maybe. Your phone battery any good?"

She checked. "Sixty-five percent."

"Find out what you can about Damon. Check news reports of his death, see if he was on Facebook or Instagram or something, whatever you can."

"Okay. What are you going to do?"

"I've got another lead."

"Okay."

He took his phone out onto the balcony and called Mouse again. Fortunately, his friend wasn't working nor was he too deep in video games to come to the phone.

"What's up?" Mouse asked.

"Remember when you said you didn't want to hack four different cell phone carriers?"

"Yeah," Mouse said warily.

192

"How about one? I need to see who this guy Villars called recently."

"Are you serious?"

"Yeah. Damon had to be getting his intel from somewhere."

Mouse sighed.

"I'll bring you back some beignets."

"Some what?"

"Please, Mouse."

"Yeah, okay."

"Thanks, pal."

Jackson gave him Damon's address so he could identify the correct Damon Villars and asked for a list of all inbound and outbound calls since the beginning of May, and anything Mouse could dig up on the owners of the various numbers.

"Let me guess, you need it yesterday?"

"As soon as you've got it."

"I'll see what I can do."

"Thanks, bud."

"Yeah, yeah."

Jackson closed his phone and headed back inside. Sawyer had her face buried in her phone screen, and he scrounged a leftover piece of pizza. "You want some?" he asked when she looked up at him.

"What? No."

"You find anything yet?"

"Yeah. According to several reports, Damon worked as an aide to Congressman Patterson."

"That explains his nice duds. Who's Congressman Patterson?"

"That's what I'm looking up now."

He ate a few bites of his pizza.

"He's a fourth-term representative from Louisiana's 6th Congressional District. A Republican, married, two grown children. Looks like his focus has been on creating jobs for the lower to middle class, trying to stop the flow of illegal immigrants and drugs into the U.S., and protecting the Second Amendment."

"Any tie to Louviere?"

"Not yet. I'll keep looking."

Jackson sat back, finishing his pizza, wishing he'd brought his laptop along with him. But when he'd packed for Florida, he had planned on unplugging and relaxing for a week, not taking on a case.

"I don't see anything," Sawyer reported. "Let me do a little looking from Louviere's perspective. We didn't exactly do a deep dive on him the other day."

"No."

"So what'd you do, farm out your research to Mouse?"

"I asked him to find out who Damon has called recently."

She looked up.

"We didn't find anything in his apartment to suggest he's an expert on New Orleans history or Brackett or anything. I figure he's tapping some other resource."

"And how is Mouse finding out who Damon called?"

"I don't know."

She raised an eyebrow.

"He does what he does."

She said nothing, turning her attention back to her phone. Jackson turned on the news at ten, flipping between local channels, looking for any mention of the events that had transpired earlier that afternoon. There was none.

"You think he's still tied up in that shack?" Sawyer asked at a commercial break.

"I hope so."

"Well, I can't find much of anything. I did see that Louviere and his company have made campaign contributions to Lucas Patterson over the last couple elections, but that doesn't differentiate Patterson from any other Republican politician in the state. And I'm sure they've rubbed elbows at social gatherings, black tie dinners, charity golf outings. Sounds like that's how Louviere spends a lot of his time."

"Gala fundraisers to save the whales."

"Louisiana wetlands."

"Whatever."

She dropped her phone on the coffee table and sat back. "I still don't get why Damon would be invited."

"If Louviere and Patterson were close . . ."

"Even so, why would a congressman's aide get an invite? To a fundraiser? Aren't they notoriously young and underpaid?"

"Yeah, but Patterson would have the cash. Probably paid for his whole staff to go. A nice tax write-off."

"I suppose."

"Better question, why would the wealthy head of a conglomeration like The Louviere Company be interested in pirate treasure? It can't be that he needs the money."

"Maybe he's not. We don't know that he was after the treasure, just that Damon thought this logbook of his held the key."

"So it could be that Louviere killed Damon before he could ask too many questions, or it could be that Louviere knew nothing of Damon's knowledge and somebody else killed him so they'd have exclusive access to the logbook."

"Meaning Louviere could be behind this all, or he could be the next target."

Jackson nodded.

"Well, that brings me back to my original question. What's your plan for tomorrow?"

He smiled. "We've got the rest of the night and the morning to figure it out."

Sawyer rolled her head to look at him. "I think we should go to church."

"To pray for guidance?"

"To go to church. And to ask about the *Missianna*."

He frowned. "You want to ask about an old ship at church?"

"If it is an old ship. I still think there might be a reason the note at Damon's was written on the invite to the ice cream social."

"You think it was more than the closest piece of scratch paper?"

She nodded. "The gala isn't until late afternoon anyhow, so we have time. Maybe we'll run across some people who knew Damon." She shrugged. "Who knows what they might be able to tell us."

"What time's the service?"

Sawyer checked her phone again. A minute later, she reported that the Sunday worship service at St. Mark's Evangelical Church began at ten.

"Good," Jackson said. "I can sleep in a little. I am, after all, still on vacation."

Chapter Twenty-Four

Sunday, May 19
9:58 a.m.

AN ORGAN AND piano duet prelude rattled the stained glass windows of St. Mark's Evangelical Church as Jackson and Sawyer filed into a pew near the back of a long, narrow sanctuary. The rain of the day before had cleared, and bright sunlight streamed through the windows, filtering their array of colors on the ornate stage, choir loft, and pulpit at the front of the building. A large, wooden cross hung over a baptismal behind it all. It was over a dozen feet tall, and yet it was dwarfed by the massive vaulted ceiling. Old, gothic, beautiful—it was exactly what Jackson had expected in a New Orleans church.

The duet ended with a rousing finish and was cheered by everything from applause to a few shouts of "Amen!" and "Hallelujah!" Almost before the echo had died away, the organ began again. This time, the choir stood behind it. There were about twenty of them, men and women, all dressed in flowing blue robes with yellow trim. They were all black. So was the congregation, but for two.

The members began to sway and clap. Soon they were into a spirited chorus. Jackson looked around, wondering if another white person had meandered into St. Mark's Evangelical. Nope. He shrugged. He'd felt a few eyes on them as he and Sawyer had walked in, but he hadn't seen any offensive or condescending looks. Just curious ones.

He turned to Sawyer. She sat serenely, legs crossed at the knees, perfectly happy to sit and listen to the choir. She wore the black dress she had mentioned the night before, a simple, modest number that worked very well for her. So did the smile that graced her face as she lifted and dipped her chin slightly with the music. She was perfectly comfortable, and Jackson decided he might as well be too. So he sat back, wondering if this choir number was another prelude or the start of the service.

When the chorus was finished, a man in a robe that matched but outdid those worn by the choir assumed the pulpit. While the congregation's response to the song died out, he welcomed his parishioners.

"We have come on this fine morning to worship our Creator!" he called, his voice filling the sanctuary.

"Amen!"

"He is worthy of all of our worship, is He not?"

"He is!"

"Is indeed."

"Amen, brother."

"So let us worship Him!"

The congregation stood. Jackson and Sawyer joined them. The organ and choir got cranked up again, and this time the man in the pulpit led the singing. The entire congregation joined in, and the sound was thunderous. Jackson looked around, trying to spot the projection display showing the words. It wasn't there. No one held a hymnal. But they all sang along, even Sawyer. A church where everyone knew the words to the songs? It was unbelievable.

The song lasted at least five minutes. The next was a hymn, one Jackson recognized, and he added his voice to the others. The third song was unfamiliar again, apparently only to Jackson. He tried to appear soberly focused. It was bad enough being the only white guy in the building, but he didn't want the parishioners thinking he was a godless heathen too.

It helped that he had plenty on which to meditate. Mouse had called just before eleven the night before, likely oblivious to the fact that it was two hours later in New Orleans than Los Angeles. Jackson had been watching TV, waiting for the call, and Sawyer had been curled up in the armchair, drifting in and out of sleep.

Mouse had done his magic, hacking Damon's cell phone and downloading a list of all numbers Damon had called or that had called him from the start of the month up until his death. Then he'd done more magic and matched those numbers with names—all but two. He'd sent the entire list via e-mail, and it was lengthy. Instead of viewing it on Sawyer's phone, Jackson had made use of the Hotel Étienne's business center to print off the list. He and Sawyer had stayed up until after midnight going through the list, doing what research they could and using various methods of deduction to eliminate calls that were likely work-related.

They'd finished up in the morning, before walking sleepy morning streets to St. Mark's Evangelical Church. Six numbers stood out. One was possibly a girlfriend. One was a former high school classmate who was now a public defender in New Orleans. One was a pastor at an area church—not St. Mark's Evangelical. Two more were as of yet unidentified. But the last of the six was a history professor at Tulane, and thus likely their best lead. After church, Jackson and Sawyer planned to call them each and fish for information.

With the song finished and the choir appearing worn out, the man in the pulpit directed everyone to be seated.

"Now, doesn't that make you want to holler?"

"It sure does, Reverend," a female voice from up front answered.

"Amen!"

The reverend mopped his brow and proceeded to make a few announcements. Among them was a statement that Damon Villars had passed away. The reverend didn't say that he'd been murdered, only that the authorities were looking into the matter. Nothing was said about next of kin or extended family, but Jackson gathered from the hush that had fallen over the church that Damon was known and loved by many. He wondered if any of them were on Damon's call list.

The next few announcements were much lighter, and when they were finished, the offering was passed while the choir, their vigor renewed, sang a rousing hymn. The usual chorus of comments followed it.

The reverend returned to the pulpit. Jackson had heard rumors of preachers in black Southern churches preaching all morning and into the afternoon. He was a little worried about it at first, but as the reverend began, Jackson found his preaching easy to listen to. There was a cadence, a rhythm to his message. And yet a flair. It wasn't a style Jackson was used to, but the man knew how to captivate an audience. And he had good material, speaking from Colossians 1 about the supremacy of Christ.

Two more songs followed the sermon, and then the reverend delivered a stirring benediction. The choir and the organ resumed once more, but judging by the movement of the congregation, Jackson determined the service was over.

He nudged Sawyer. "How'd you know all the songs?"

She grinned. "A good Baptist knows her songbook."

"Until somebody rewrites them all at least. You ready to quiz these good folks?"

"If we go up to people like an eager reporter looking to break a story, I don't think we'll get very far."

"So what then?"

"Let the conversation come to us. I have a feeling this congregation is going to be friendly."

"You want lead on this one?"

She didn't get a chance to answer. A middle-aged woman from the row behind them stuck her gloved hand out. "I'm Elise," she said. "Welcome to St. Mark's Evangelical."

Jackson and Sawyer took turns introducing themselves and shaking Elise's hand.

"I haven't seen either of you here before."

"We're from out of town," Sawyer answered.

"Well, we're glad you stopped by." Elise smiled and sidestepped out of her row.

Sawyer and Jackson followed and made it to the back of the sanctuary before an usher stopped them with a handshake and a smile. He introduced himself as Roy and asked if he could help them find anything.

"Actually, we are looking for something," Sawyer said, "but it's kind of an odd request."

"Try me," Roy said.

"Have you ever heard of something called the *Missianna*?"

"Missy Anna? Name doesn't ring a bell. Does she attend St. Mark's Evangelical?"

"It's not a person," Sawyer said. "We think it might be the name of a ship."

"A ship?" Roy's smile waned into a frown. "I don't recognize the name." He turned. "Clarence. Come over here a second." He waved at another, older usher. Clarence patted the hand of a woman and sidled over.

"Clarence, this is Sawyer and Jackson, visiting us from…"

"Key West," Sawyer said.

Clarence grinned a toothy smile and nodded at both of them.

"They're looking for a ship named the *Missianna*."

"*Missianna*," Clarence repeated in a high, scratchy voice. "Can't say as I've heard of it. What kind of ship?"

"We don't know," Sawyer said.

"We're not even sure it is a ship," Jackson offered. "It's just our best guess."

"You come all the way from Key West to look for this ship?" Roy asked.

"Among other things."

"Well, if you don't mind me asking, what in particular brought you here this morning? Other than the Holy Spirit, that is?"

"A friend of a friend," Sawyer said. "Damon Villars."

Roy stiffened at the mention of his name.

"Oh my," Clarence said.

"You knew Damon?" Roy asked.

"Not really," she said. "We knew of him, and had reason to think he knew something about the *Missianna*. But when we learned he had died, we thought someone at his church might know something."

That wasn't a bad summary, all things considered, and not really untruthful. Just without all of the unnecessary facts.

"Saying that now, it sounds a little cold," Sawyer said. "Insensitive, even. We didn't mean to intrude."

Roy shook his head. "No, don't give it a thought. I just wish I knew anything to help you. But I've never heard of your ship. And I knew Damon, but not very well."

"Same here," Clarence added. "He was always smiling, though. That's the memory of him I'll take with me."

"Well, we're sorry for your loss," Sawyer said, then thanked them for their time.

Both men nodded as Jackson and Sawyer stepped into a narrow, crowded foyer. It was less a gathering place and more a wide hallway connecting the front entrance, a coat closet, and the sanctuary with an educational wing that stretched to the left. And Sawyer was right. Despite the confinement and the commotion, several people came up to greet them and make small talk. Jackson and Sawyer played the game and did their best to work in the *Missianna* and subtle questions about Damon, but got nothing in response. The foyer was getting busier, and Jackson reached for Sawyer's hand to lead her toward the door and some fresh air.

A little old lady who made Elise look young and robust stopped them. They exchanged pleasantries, and she welcomed them to St. Mark's Evangelical and immediately began quizzing them. Were they from the area? Did they have a home church? Were they married? Were they courting? She gave up when her equally old husband came along with little more than a nod and escorted her toward the door. The *Missianna* never made it into the conversation.

"Going well," Jackson said.

"Maybe I'm barking up the wrong tree," Sawyer said.

"It was worth a try."

She shrugged. "I'm getting hungry. You ready to go?"

Jackson nodded, and they turned to leave. He stopped when he felt a tug on his sleeve.

"Excuse me," a quiet but gravelly voice said. Jackson turned back to see an older man with a patchy gray beard that was equally wispy as the gray hair atop his head. He was dressed in a brown cardigan that made Jackson start to sweat just thinking about it. He held a Bible in his left hand, a bulletin tucked inside the cover. His eyes were a dark brown as they looked from Jackson to Sawyer. "Did I hear you mention the *Missianna*?"

Sawyer's eyes widened. "Yes. Do you know anything about it?"

"Indeed." He extended a hand. "My name is Grover Charles, one-time deacon, long-time parishioner. Seeing as how you two are visitors at St. Mark's, my bride and I would be delighted if you'd join us for lunch, and I can answer any questions you have."

Jackson looked to Sawyer. This was the point in novels where he always yelled at the idiot protagonist for falling for such an obvious trap. But Grover was a borderline senior citizen, not a slick-talking stiff with a smile or a hottie flirting a little too obviously, and Jackson's initial take was that Grover was sincere. Besides, he was hungry too.

Sawyer apparently shared Jackson's conviction, seeing as how she smiled and nodded. "We'd love to. Thank you."

Chapter Twenty-Five

12:07 p.m.

GROVER'S WIFE SALLY set out quite a Sunday noon spread. Fried chicken, mashed potatoes and gravy, homemade coleslaw, biscuits, and fruit salad, with a promise of apple pie à la mode afterward. Jackson enjoyed every bite.

Sawyer beat him to the punch in complimenting Sally, who beamed like a proud mother as she watched them eat. "When our Ronnie and his wife moved to Memphis a few years ago, we lost our usual Sunday dinner guests," she said. "I'm just happy to have someone to eat my cooking."

Grover cleared his throat. "What am I, chopped liver?"

"Oh hush."

"How long have the two of you been married?" Sawyer asked. She had plied Grover with questions about the photos on the mantle in their living room and a photo album on the coffee table while Sally had prepared dinner (refusing any help). Now she was apparently content to get more of the Charles family history instead of learning about the *Missianna*.

"Nigh upon forty years," Grover said.

"Thirty-eight this June," Sally answered.

"That's wonderful," Sawyer said.

"How long have you two . . . been together?" Sally asked.

"Oh, about a week," Jackson said matter-of-factly.

Sally nearly dropped her fork. Grover crunched on his coleslaw.

"We're not a couple," Sawyer said. "We have a mutual friend who disappeared, and we're looking for him. That's why we're . . . together."

"And this friend, is he why you're interested in the *Missianna*?" Grover asked.

"We think it might be tied to his disappearance." She gave a brief explanation of Ben's absence and presumed death, the call from Damon, and their research into the Brackett treasure. The *Missianna* was a loose end they were trying to track down, hoping for anything that would clue them in as to what was going on.

Grover frowned as she spoke, and when she was finished, he set down his fork and dabbed his mouth with his napkin. "Damon was a good young man. A busy man, working for a congressman, looking to make a difference in the world. He had his head on straight."

"You knew him," Sawyer said.

"I'm the one who told him about the *Missianna*."

Jackson set his fork down as well.

Grover sat back slightly, his chair creaking. "Most young people these days don't give a boll of cotton what old folks like us think."

"Watch yourself, Grover."

He winked at his wife. "Damon was different. He liked to bounce thoughts and ideas off of others, and for whatever reason, I became a sounding board for him. Well, a few weeks back he asked me out of the blue if I'd ever heard anything about a pirate by the name of Brackett and a treasure he'd supposedly hidden somewhere."

Grover cleared his throat while his guests sat with rapt attention. Sally lifted small bites of fruit salad and potatoes and gravy to her mouth. "I didn't know anything about a treasure," Grover said, "but the name Brackett rang a bell. I told him I'd search my memory and see what I could find. Sally will tell you I've got a lot of facts bouncing around up here," he said, tapping his head, "but I don't always have them so well cataloged. Takes me a while sometimes to locate them. So I ruminate."

"Does he ever," Sally said.

Grover paid her no mind. "It hit me about a week ago. My great, great-grandfather, Louis Charles, was the slave of a wealthy Louisiana businessman by the name of Garrison. After emancipation, Mr. Garrison offered Louis a full-time position. He accepted and worked for Mr. Garrison for most of the rest of his life. Many of his experiences, stories he heard, things he learned, were passed down from generation to generation. They're known fondly by my brothers and me as the Charles Legend."

Grover smiled. "Some of them are true, some of them are made-up, a lot of them are half and half. We don't much care, you see, as they're a link to our past. One of those stories that got passed down was about the Devil's Bend."

"The Devil's Bend?" Sawyer asked.

"A switchback a fair piece downriver. It's been known over the years to cause even the best captains some trouble. Not today, mind you, with GPS and all of the modern technology. But back in Great, Great Grandpappy Louis's day, things were different."

Jackson leaned forward, waiting for the connection to the *Missianna*. Had she wrecked at the Devil's Bend? Was the treasure buried in the mud of the Mississippi River? Or halfway to Shreveport thanks to Hurricane Katrina?

"According to legend, Mr. Garrison had lost several ships at the Devil's Bend," Grover said.

"Lost?" Jackson asked.

"Wrecked. But there was a superstition to it as well. According to legend, the Devil's Bend represented a point of no return for outbound ships, almost like the Bermuda Triangle. Once a ship leaving the port reached the Bend, she was 'in the devil's hands.' Same for inbound ships. If they made it past the Bend, they were home free. It came to be back in that day that any ship what left the port of New Orleans and disappeared at sea was considered a victim of the Devil's Bend, whether she was wrecked there or not."

"Sailors and superstition," Sawyer said.

Grover nodded. "Now all that's context for something my father passed down to me. According to Louis, Mr. Garrison didn't believe much in the legend of the Devil's Bend, despite having a few ships wreck there. He chalked it up to chance and circumstance and the danger of the Mighty Mississippi. But at that time, there was plenty of belief that the Devil's Bend was cursed. And apparently, it all stemmed from a fated voyage back in 1718."

"The *Missianna*," Sawyer said quietly.

Grover nodded again. "Legend has it, and bear in mind this is hearsay three or four times over, but legend has it that a ship named the *Missianna* sailed from the fledgling little city of New Orleans in the spring of 1718, never to return."

"What made her so special as to start the legend?"

"Because she was believed to be captained by a ghost."

"A ghost?"

"Now mind, I don't believe such things, but it's the legend. And according to legend, the *Missianna* was captained by the ghost of a man named James Brackett. She was last seen entering the Bend, and when she was never heard from again, well, the worst was assumed. Even three hundred years ago, people knew how to start a good rumor."

"Where was she sailing?" Jackson asked.

"The Bahamas."

"Why?"

Grover held out his palms. "No one knows."

"And she never arrived?" Sawyer asked.

"There's no record of it. The ship sailed and was never heard from again."

"Is there anything more about Brackett's ghost?"

"No. Like I said, it's an old legend that has been passed on time and time again. Fair to say it's changed a few times along the way. As such, I was hesitant to even mention it to Damon. But he'd asked me, so when I remembered where I'd heard the name Brackett, I told him the story."

"When did you tell him?" Jackson asked, already knowing the answer.

"Last Saturday. At a church ice cream social." He looked over at his wife. "When he was found dead the other day, I couldn't but wonder if the two were connected."

"Why?" Sawyer asked.

"Oh, nothing in particular. But people get mighty peculiar when it comes to old legends. Especially when they're tied to a pirate and his alleged buried treasure."

"But you don't have any evidence to suggest that knowledge of the *Missianna* led to Damon's death?" Jackson asked.

"No. If I had anything other than a feeling in my gut, I'd have called the police. I'm sure it's nothing."

Jackson nodded without conviction.

"What about Martin Louviere?" Sawyer asked. "Does his name mean anything to you?"

"Sure," Grover said. "He's well-known in and around New Orleans. A very successful businessman. His family's been here for decades." He glanced at Sally. "Why?"

"He's another loose end," Sawyer said.

"You think he had something to do with Damon's death?" Sally asked.

"We don't know what to think right now," Jackson said.

He and Sawyer asked Grover a few follow-up questions, but he didn't know anything else that shed light on their search. So after slices of pie that Sally insisted they eat, they thanked Grover for his information and he and Sally for their hospitality. Sally made it sound as if they were the ones who had done her a favor, refused help with the dishes, and even offered to pack them some leftovers. They already had dinner plans, Jackson said, but thanked her anyhow.

Grover walked them to the door and onto the front porch. "I get the feeling the two of you know more than you're letting on," he said.

"We're not trying to deceive you," Sawyer said. "It's just that this is very complicated."

Grover shook his head. "Don't worry about me. It's just . . . we never actually heard what happened to Damon. How he was killed, I mean."

"He was shot," Sawyer said quietly.

"Murder?"

Jackson nodded.

"My, my. Well, the two of you be careful. Like I said inside, people get mighty peculiar when it comes to things like old legends and buried treasure."

"We will," Sawyer said. "Thanks again, Grover."

"You're very welcome." He offered each of them a handshake and then a wave as they started down the sidewalk. Having walked to church, they had taken advantage of the beautiful, sunny morning and also walked to Grover and Sally's home in nearby Bywater. Now, under the midday sun, it was hot, and the half-mile walk back to their hotel seemed long. Jackson tried to pass the time with conversation.

"What do you make of that?"

"More rumor, innuendo, speculation . . ."

"Think any of it's true?"

"At the core, yeah, there's probably a nugget. But no, I don't think the undead Brackett captained any ship."

"But assuming the *Missianna* was real and did sail for the Bahamas, it raises an interesting question. Didn't you say another Brackett treasure rumor was tied to the Bahamas?"

"Yeah. It isn't much of one though."

"Hmm."

While they walked, Jackson made a few phone calls, trying to get in touch with some of the owners of the six numbers from the list Mouse had sent. They'd reached a couple on the way to Grover and Sally's house, and Jackson had left a voicemail for the professor from Tulane, the most likely lead. Now, he connected with the potential girlfriend—just a friend and of no help—and the area pastor, who said Damon had called about trying to form a network of political aides and assistants who could start a bipartisan Bible study. It hadn't gotten off the ground.

He was about to try the professor again when his phone vibrated between calls. The number was familiar, a 310 area code. Reggie.

"Hey, Hoss. What's up?"

"Hoss?" Sawyer mouthed beside him.

"Just calling to see if you're ever coming back, J."

"It's been a week, dude."

"How you doing?"

"Swimmingly. I'm strolling the French Quarter with a beautiful woman on my arm, the sun on my face, and fried chicken and apple pie in my stomach."

"Found a beautiful woman, did you?"

"And a pretty good cook. You should be nervous."

"Uh-huh. You sure you all right, man?"

"I'm good, Reg. Honest."

"All right. Keep a brother posted, will you?"

"I will."

They said goodbye, and he closed the phone.

"Who is Hoss?"

"My homeboy back in L.A."

She raised an eyebrow. "You have odd nicknames for all your friends?"

"That's pretty much the list."

They walked a few steps.

"Sorry if that all sounded sexist or misogynistic or whatever we're calling it these days."

"The beautiful woman on your arm crack? I took it as a compliment."

"I really like Southern women."

She smiled.

"Back home, that'd have gotten me a lawsuit or a court order or something."

"Why do you live in California if you seem to hate it so much?"

"It's home. And I don't hate it."

"Odd, the order of those two statements."

"I don't hate it. Scenery's as beautiful as anywhere in the world, and the girls are, for all their flaws, pretty cute."

Sawyer nodded.

"And I don't have a lot of friends, but the ones I have are there."

"That's a good answer."

His turn to nod.

His phone rang again.

She looked at him as he looked at the display. "Professor King." He tapped a button and put the phone to his ear. "Jackson Douglas."

"Mr. Douglas, Eldon King. You called me earlier."

Jackson noted that the professor didn't refer to himself as such, nor use any titles.

"Yes, thank you for returning my call, Professor. I'm inquiring about Damon Villars. I understand he was an associate of yours?"

"Damon and I attended LSU together. Mr. Douglas, I don't mean to be rude, but what is this about?"

Jackson explained, as briefly and as truthfully as he could. King listened quietly, then remained silent for a few seconds longer. "Damon asked me about the Brackett treasure a few weeks ago," he said at last. "He knew I was a history buff with a focus on pre-Revolutionary America, and wondered if I could tell him anything. I said not really but put him in touch with a colleague of mine who teaches at LSU. Also a history professor, but with more letters after his name than I have, and he specializes in Louisiana history. I figured if anybody could help Damon, it was him."

Sawyer tapped Jackson's arm, motioning that they needed to turn left. He followed her across the street, and they continued down the sidewalk.

"Would you mind giving me his name? I'd like to follow up."

"Raul López, but it won't do you much good, I'm afraid."

"Why's that?"

"He's spending the summer in France researching a book. Graded his last final and caught a plane for Paris."

"Do you know if Damon reached him before that?"

"I don't. There would have been a window of a few days, factoring in when Damon died. Do you think this had something to do with it?"

"We don't know."

"Well, I'm sorry I can't be of more help."

"Nothing to apologize for, Professor. If you don't mind, one more question."

"Certainly."

"Did Damon tell you why he was interested in the Brackett treasure?"

"No, and I thought it a little odd. He'd never shown much of an interest in chasing treasure legends. But if he was working at the behest of your friend in Key West, that would explain it."

"It would. Oh, Professor, one more question."

"Go ahead."

"Does the name Martin Louviere mean anything to you?"

"Martin Louviere? The local businessman?"

"The one and same."

"I've never met him," King said, "but I know the name, same as a dozen other area CEOs and executives. Their names are in the papers or on the news for this or that. Why?"

"His name has come up several times, and we're wondering if there's any connection."

"Well, I don't see how there could be. I'm sure Damon wouldn't have interacted with him socially."

"Probably nothing," Jackson agreed. He thanked King for his time, then reported to Sawyer. By now they were only a few blocks from their hotel.

She sighed. "Is this what being a P.I. is like, never-ending clue trails that only lead to more questions?"

"Usually by now I've hacked somebody off by asking the wrong person the right question. But yeah."

They strolled a few paces.

"Hmm," Jackson said.

"Hmm what?"

"Just thinking. There seems to be a lot of LSU going around. Louviere went there, Damon went there, the professor he contacted went there, the professor he told Damon about teaches there."

"Is that why you asked Professor King about him?"

He nodded. "What was your take on Grover's summary of Louviere?"

"Same as everybody's, which is to say, not much."

"Yeah, that's what I thought. No strong feelings either way."

"I've been thinking about Garrison," she said, "Grover's great, great-grandfather's master."

"How so?"

"It's another old Louisiana family, like Louviere."

"You think there's a connection?"

"I think it's yet another loose end," Sawyer said. "There's too much not knowing what we don't know. Makes me nervous about sneaking into Louviere's party this afternoon."

"Yeah," Jackson said. "Me too."

Chapter Twenty-Six

4:48 p.m.

"MAYBE WE SHOULD have just rented a car," Sawyer said.

Jackson looked across the backseat of the Uber that had picked them up outside the Hotel Étienne thirty minutes ago. "Wouldn't have saved us much money," he said, "and would have left a bigger paper trail." He glanced at the driver, a young black man with dreadlocks who, if he was paying any attention to them, was doing a masterful job of hiding it. He played contemporary jazz on the stereo, drove quickly but safely, and minded his own business. Earning himself a nice tip.

"Still, now we're at the mercy of someone else. If we have to leave quickly . . ."

Jackson pursed his lips, watching the scenery out his window. Lake Pontchartrain stretched as far as the eye could see, as did a row of towers supporting power lines that conceivably ran twenty-four miles to the estuary's opposite shore. The interstate turned slightly, veering inland through a thick overgrowth of trees and bushes. They likely stretched to the Texas border.

He turned to Sawyer. "I didn't think of that."

"And you're the famous private investigator."

"I never claimed to be famous. Besides, you're the refined, composed Southern belle."

And she was. They'd had time for some quick shopping in the French Quarter, and she had purchased a floral sundress, a pair of heels, and a small clutch purse. No dignified Southern woman would show up at a gala without a purse that matched her outfit, Sawyer claimed. Jackson had found a discount gentlemen's haberdashery where he had purchased a three-piece suit. He'd left the coat in the hotel, wearing the pants and the vest, his sleeves rolled to his elbow, his tie loose. He was going for an ambitious, slightly cocky, brownnosing intern. Sawyer said he looked the part, which he wasn't sure was a compliment.

The car exited the interstate and headed north on Old U.S. 51, parallel to Interstate 55 along the western shore of Lake Pontchartrain. The terrain was a mixture of swamp and woods, similar to the path they had traversed with Dixon the day before. But today, the sun was shining brightly, its heat penetrating the back of the car despite the air conditioning.

"Are you sure about this plan of yours?" Sawyer asked.

Jackson loosened his tie a little more, given the heat. "Why, are you not?"

"It's just that it's . . ."

"Dangerous?"

"How do I put this delicately . . . ? Half-baked."

He closed one eye. "Just out of curiosity, how would you have put that indelicately?"

"I just mean after everything we've learned, I'd feel more comfortable with, well, more of a plan."

What they'd learned was that Raul López, the colleague whose name Professor King said he'd given Damon, not only taught at LSU but had attended LSU, back in the day, back when Martin Louviere had been earning his business degree there. A few phone calls and a little hacking by Mouse had revealed they'd had several classes together and thus likely knew each other. It didn't mean López was complicit or had given up Damon to Louviere, or that Louviere was in any way involved in Damon's death. Lots of people had gone to LSU. Lots of colleagues and friends and acquaintances had connections that could be linked six ways to Sunday. But both Jackson and Sawyer had agreed there was too much smoke for there not to be a fire. And now they were heading straight into the flames.

"Look, Sawyer, if you want out . . ."

"I don't want out. I want answers. And if this is how we have to get them, okay. I just want to make sure we're playing our best hand."

"Given our cards, I think so."

Sawyer nodded. "Then I'm all in."

"You're sure?"

"I'm positive."

"Because there's a chance, if Louviere's dirty, that he and Dixon are in communication and he knows our names and our faces, and we'll be blown two minutes after we walk past a hidden camera."

"That might have been worth mentioning a few hours ago."

"Better late than never."

She looked at him. "You think he has our names and faces?"

"Names, yes. Descriptions, probably. Faces, I doubt."

"What's the term, acceptable risk?"

"Something like that."

She nodded. "I'm still positive. Let's do this."

Jackson nodded and sat back. Between stores, Sawyer had placed a call to Sheriff Hawkins, just checking in, seeing if there was any news. He'd told her Ben's Uncle Malcolm was proceeding with funeral plans. In the absence of a body, there would be no burial, but a marker would be placed by his parents' headstones at the family plot in Atlanta. Just a graveside service. Tuesday. Jackson and Sawyer had briefly discussed aborting plans in New Orleans to attend but had decided to press on.

Hawkins had also told her that his department had still uncovered no signs of foul play, nothing to indicate Ben had been killed. Against Hawkins' recommendation, Ben's death had officially been ruled an accident. Ted Ryker's death had also been ruled an accident, based on the coroner's ruling that he had drowned. There was clearly more to the story, but that investigation had stalled out too. Whatever had happened had happened at sea, it appeared, and there was no record of him in Key West—no hotel bills, boat rentals, restaurant receipts. He was a mystery man who had turned up dead, and while Hawkins was still suspicious, he had nothing actionable.

That all meant that as far as finding what had happened to Ben, Jackson and Sawyer's only lead was Ben's research into the Brackett treasure. With him dead, with his contact in New Orleans (Damon) dead also, their only potential source of information was Martin Louviere and the logbook he owned. If they weren't able to glean anything from him, or if what they learned wasn't significant, they were back at square one.

Thus their determination to find out everything they could at the gala at Pontchartrain Manor.

To that end, their plan was not only to look for the logbook Damon had referenced but also to surreptitiously question Martin Louviere. They would get a feel for him, whether he was a potential ally with whom they could have a frank discussion or an enemy to be circumvented. It was something of a desperate plan, and a dangerous one. One might even say half-baked.

Thus Sawyer's wariness and Jackson's desire to make sure she was good to go. The look in her eyes confirmed she was.

Several miles north of I-10, the car turned onto a two-lane road heading east through the trees. They drove less than a mile before crossing a set of railroad tracks. Shortly after that, the road curved northward. Intersecting with the curve was a blacktopped driveway that led through a canopy of trees. The driver slowed and read the address on a simple but elegant sign sticking out of the undergrowth, looking back to confirm it was the right place.

Jackson nodded, and they proceeded down the driveway.

The canopy of trees parted and the driveway formed a circle. Several dozen vehicles, ranging from fancy sports cars to governmental SUVs, were parked in the grass beside the driveway, around the circle, and in front of a large garage left of the circle. The driver stopped at the top of the circle and looked back. "Here you folks go. Looks like a hot party."

"We'll see," Jackson said, looking at Sawyer. "You ready?"

"As I'll ever be."

"You've got it easy. You're playing yourself."

Sawyer looked at him with a grin tugging at her mouth. "So are you."

They got out and, as the car drove away, looked up at Pontchartrain Manor.

It was impressive. Just in sheer size, it was one of the most remarkable buildings Jackson had ever seen, towering three stories tall and stretching close to one hundred fifty feet wide. It looked even bigger with its numerous recessed sections and projections, all surrounded by perfectly manicured bushes, shrubs, and flowers, and all perfectly symmetrical. By far the dominant feature was a wide front porch, spanning nearly fifty feet and elevated from the surrounding lawn by flights of stairs in the middle and on either end. Four massive granite columns towered over the porch and supported the roof, which was covered in green shingles. They matched shutters on numerous windows and the stately double front doors. Everything else was white. Pure white. Marvelous white that seemed to glow. Pontchartrain Manor was picture perfect, like something out of a storybook.

The grounds were immaculate too, the grass like lush fairways. Giant weeping willows drank in the sunlight on the northwest corner of the house, between the garage and maintenance shed, both of which were gleaming white with dark green shingles like the house. To the right, south of the driveway circle, a couple dozen palm trees shaded a fenced-in tennis court. And this was just the front lawn. Pontchartrain Manor was situated on a clearing as wide as a football field—with both end zones and maybe a little more—bordered by woods on either side. It stretched as far as Jackson could see, which wasn't very far, thanks to the size of the house in front of him. He guessed, given the name and a quick look at a map on Sawyer's phone, that the lawn stretched all the way to the lake.

"I don't think we belong here," Sawyer said, lightly touching Jackson's arm as they walked past two red-vested valets waiting at the top of the driveway.

"Yeah, but we're the only ones who know it. Come on."

He led her up the steps and clanged the brass knocker on the front doors. They both swept open a moment later, and a man dressed in a white dinner jacket smiled at them. "Welcome to Pontchartrain Manor."

"Thank you," Jackson said, handing the man the invitation he'd found in Damon's Bible.

"Mr. Villars, Ma'am, welcome."

"Thank you," Jackson said again, echoed by Sawyer. They entered a wide hall, open to the third-floor ceiling, lit by a resplendent chandelier. Ornate, curving staircases ran up either side of the hall, which opened into a spacious room beyond them.

"There are powder rooms left and right off the main hall," the man said, gesturing with his hands, like a flight attendant signaling the location of a plane's emergency doors. "There's a full bar in the ballroom ahead, as well as on the back patio. And you are just in time. Hors d'oeuvres will be served shortly. If I can be of any service to you, please let me know."

They thanked him again and walked forward. Inside, Pontchartrain Manor was as magnificent as out. Marble floors, gently textured walls painted in warm colors, crown molding everywhere—all bathed in soft lighting.

Once they passed the stairs, the hall widened, with narrower hallways branching off left and right. Directly ahead was a gymnasium.

Nope, just a ballroom. It was as wide as the porch, close to fifty feet, two-thirds that deep, with a pitched ceiling that was three stories high. A giant fireplace drew attention on the right, even though unlit. Above the mantel hung a portrait of several dozen people, likely generations old, judging by their apparel. The Louviere clan, Jackson surmised. A twelve-foot-long bar fronted by wood stools and backed by an assortment of bottles and decanters was the focal point on the left. Giant floor-to-ceiling windows on the far wall let in a day's worth of natural sunlight while providing views of a deck, patio, swimming pool, and back lawn. And, way off in the distance, the sparkling blue waters of Lake Pontchartrain.

"Must be rough, being rich," Jackson said as he and Sawyer stopped just into the ballroom. Fifteen to twenty people mingled at several seating areas arranged by the fireplace, at bistro tables in the middle of the room on what could also serve as a dance floor, or around the bar. None of them paid more than a passing glance at the two newcomers.

"Mm, I don't know. I'll take my two hundred-square-foot house and a life of simplicity," Sawyer said.

"Simplicity. These guys probably have guys who bring lemonade to the guys who bring it to them."

She looked at him with a thin smile. "Did we ever establish my name?"

"What's wrong with Sawyer?"

"An operation like this, I'd rather use an alias."

"What's your middle name?"

"Rae."

"That works."

"It's a little short."

"What about Savannah?"

"A little stereotypical, don't you think?"

"Okay, well how about I just call you 'Peaches' or something."

She glared at him. "And what do I call myself?"

He sighed. "Who was your best friend growing up?"

"Ricky."

"A guy?"

She shrugged.

He sighed. "Trust me, you smile and call yourself Savannah with a little Southern twang, no red-blooded American man will think twice about it being stereotypical."

"What about the women? They're the ones who can sniff out a fake."

"You leave the women to me."

She rolled her eyes.

"I meant—"

"I know what you meant."

He sighed. "Are you ready . . . Peaches?"

She raised an eyebrow.

"You look nice, by the way."

"Are you coming onto me?"

"I'm trying to instill confidence in you."

"We're about to approach a wealthy businessman, with you posing as a dead man that he might have had killed, in an effort to determine if he might also want to kill us, all while also sneaking around trying to get a look at a logbook that will tell us where a buried treasure he might be looking for is hidden, and you think telling me I look cute in my sundress is going to give me confidence?"

"I'm used to Southern California girls, remember? They don't have the stock of Southern women."

"Stock?"

He grinned. "Come on."

Chapter Twenty-Seven

5:11 p.m.

JACKSON AND SAWYER crossed the ballroom and exited through French doors. The deck was made of wood, painted green to match the roof and shutters. It was about ten feet wide, running the length of the back of the house, with a buildout in the center providing a vantage point overlooking the grounds. Since no one else was there, Jackson and Sawyer walked up to the railing to survey the scene.

On either side of the buildout were staircases leading down to a patio that was wide and broad and covered with small tables under white umbrellas. Several more bistro tables spaced around the patio and on the lawn provided places to congregate. So did a large tent on the lawn to the right, in front of a trio of oak trees. The tent housed a string quartet, the soft strains of their music wafting across the patio and deck. The tent also provided a respite from the unrelenting sun, as did an enormous live oak to the left of the patio. While no horticulturist, Jackson guessed it dated back to the antebellum period, its thick, long branches providing a canopy over the lawn.

He scanned the grounds, estimating there were close to two hundred people present. The women all wore sundresses or cocktail dresses, the men some variation of a suit. A few still wore the jackets, and Jackson had to give it to them. It was at least ninety degrees, and the humidity and dew point weren't much below that number.

"You see Louviere?" Jackson asked.

"Over there," Sawyer said with a slight nod. Jackson followed it to the corner of the patio where a small group had formed a circle around a man in a tuxedo with a white dinner jacket. Like the man who'd opened the door for them, and like the waiters circulating around the patio, and yet very, very different.

"All right," Jackson said. "Mingle, see if you can get a feel for who's here, what the conversations are about, etcetera. See if there's anything planned— dinner at a certain time, a speech, something like that. And keep an eye on traffic patterns. How often are people going in or coming out? Is it just through the doors in the ballroom or are there other entrances? Maybe step inside to use the powder room and see who's moving about inside too."

"Do I find you or will you find me?"

"If not the latter then the former."

"Okay."

"Wish me luck."

"You look nice," she said with a smirk as she turned to leave. Jackson grinned. The insincere comment didn't do anything for him, but the fact that she was relaxed enough to joke did. Smirking himself, he swung by the exterior bar to pick up a prop drink, then made his way toward Louviere.

The man cut an impressive figure. He was tall, a few inches over six feet, and well built without looking like a bodybuilder. His face was as handsome as the picture Jackson and Sawyer had found online. His wavy brown hair was slicked in place, perhaps containing a dash more white around the temples. He smiled, same as he had in the photo, as he spoke with the group around him, and he seemed impervious to sweat. In his hand was a drink, a martini by the look of it, and Jackson edged toward him.

". . . so I told him, follow the market."

Everyone chuckled at what must have been a punch line. Jackson feigned a sip. He'd never touched alcohol, even undercover, and just the sting of the whiskey on his lips made him want to hack.

Switching the glass to his left hand, he inched through the group and took advantage of a lull in conversation. He extended his hand. "Mr. Louviere, a pleasure to meet you."

Louviere's eyes showed confusion but also warmth. He returned the handshake.

"Jack Goldman," Jackson said, using a common alias and working on a bit he'd rehearsed mentally all afternoon. "Wonder if I could have a moment of your time."

"Of course, Mr. Goldman. Excuse me, gentlemen." Louviere gestured toward the stairs that led down a few feet to pool level. It was empty, save for a few floatable flower arrangements drifting across the serene surface. The patio that ringed it was wide enough for the two men to walk side-by-side comfortably. "What's on your mind, Mr. Goldman?"

"I appreciate you're a busy man and I have nothing but respect for your charitable efforts today, so I'll get to the point. Have you ever heard of a man named Ben O'Reilly?"

He watched Louviere's eyes closely. They were brown to match the hair, and they maybe clouded for half a second. Louviere pursed his lips and then shook his head slightly. "No, it doesn't ring a bell."

"Well, I didn't expect it to. Mr. O'Reilly's a small catfish in a big lake, to put it in Louisiana terms," Jackson said with a grin. "However, certain . . . behavior exhibited by Mr. O'Reilly put him on our radar screen a few years ago."

"Our?"

Jackson nodded. "I work for a private company based out of Los Angeles. We specialize in, among other things, recovery options."

Louviere pursed his lips again as they stopped walking at the end of the pool. "I'm not sure I follow."

"Well, it's purposefully vague. We have a number of specialists—experts, really—who find missing persons, missing funds, long-lost heirlooms, and so forth. Just last month a Silicon Valley company that lost six figures to embezzlement hired us to find it. Complicated scheme—you won't believe what they're doing with electronic fraud, by the way. But I digress. We also have a branch that specializes in finding antiquities, and I don't mean Grandma's rocking chair. Mayan idols, artifacts from the Pharaohs, etcetera. You hire us, we'll find it. And that's where this all comes back to Mr. O'Reilly. Let me ask you one more question. You ever hear of an old buccaneer by the name of James Brackett?"

This time Louviere's eyes actually narrowed, but just for a second before he shook his head. "No, can't say that I have."

Jackson nodded and followed Louviere as he stepped off the patio and began walking across the lawn. It rolled gently toward several strands of willows fifty yards away, on the shore of the lake. Several boats skimmed its surface in the distance, locals drinking in the last moments of their weekend.

"Long story short," Jackson said, "there's quite a legend about his missing treasure. Tons of Spanish gold. We were hired about eighteen months ago by a young woman from Miami who claims she's some descendent of this guy Brackett. Since no one knows where this gold originally came from, she figures she has as much stake to it as anyone."

"She claims she's a descendant of a pirate?"

"That's right."

"Have you been able to validate her claims?"

"No, but they didn't exactly keep detailed records back then."

"I'd be wary of such a claim," Louviere said with some measure of sternness. He took a sip of his martini, and they continued to stroll leisurely across the grass. "But I'm sure I don't need to tell you how to do your job."

Jackson waved it off, as if he would never consider that was what the mogul had been doing.

"So would this woman have a right to the treasure? Not the Spanish government?"

"No more than the Incas who probably owned it in the first place. At this point, it's basically finders, keepers."

Louviere nodded and had another drink.

"Anyhow, we started researching and realized this O'Reilly was doing quite a bit of research too. At first, we considered him a rival, if you will, but our investigation led us to believe he was only interested in this treasure academically. We were about to contact him for information when he disappeared."

"Disappeared?"

"Yes, sir. Just a few days ago. Official word is a boating accident, and he's presumed dead."

"I'm sorry to hear that."

They'd reached the beach—patchy grass mixed with dirt, then a thin strip of sand, then the lapping water. They stood in sunlight, just outside the shade of willows on their right. To the left, a boardwalk made of grayed, weathered planks wound through several more willows to a small dock that extended into the water beside a two-story boathouse. It was bigger than any boathouses Jackson had seen down Florida way, but pedestrian considering the property.

"It gets complicated," Jackson said after faking a sip of his drink. "There's evidence to suggest foul play. But again, that's getting off topic. The reason I'm here to see you is that Mr. O'Reilly had a journal of sorts that we gained access to. In it he had hundreds of names written down, one of which was yours."

"Mine?"

Jackson nodded. "Your name, your company's name, city of New Orleans."

Louviere shook his head. "I don't know why. Like I said, I've never met the man. I suppose it's possible our paths have crossed and I simply don't recall it."

"That's what I figured. Maybe he worked with a charity to which you donated or has some ties to one of your companies and thought he could ask you to fund his research."

Another shake of the head. "Sorry I can't be of more help, Mr. Goldman."

"One last question, if you don't mind?"

"Please."

"This journal . . . it also referenced a logbook. From what we could tell, he had reason to believe you might know something about it."

"A logbook?"

Jackson nodded.

"What sort of logbook? Logging what?"

"We don't know. All we have is the word logbook and a question mark written after your name. We have no idea what it means, but I thought I'd ask."

"No, I'm sorry. I'm afraid I don't know anything about it."

"I understand," Jackson said. "You're one of many names on our list, and well, you being who you are and with the logbook reference, it seemed like a good place to start."

"And you came all the way from Los Angeles to ask me these questions?" he asked. They turned and started walking back up toward the patio.

Jackson grinned. "No, there are a few other folks in the area I need to speak with. And like I said, you're the top of the list. Recent intelligence suggests this treasure might be bigger than we originally thought and, given Mr. O'Reilly's somewhat suspicious disappearance, more treacherous to locate. So it's all hands on deck."

"Well, I wish you the best," Louviere said.

"Thank you, sir."

"I trust we can count on your company for a contribution to our preservation efforts?"

Jackson shook the hand Louviere had offered. "You can count on it, Mr. Louviere. Myself as well. I think you are doing great work here. I really mean that."

"Thank you, Mr. Goldman. I hope your schedule permits you some time to enjoy the food and music for a little while."

"I think I could squeeze that in," Jackson said. "Thank you very much for your time."

They split at the patio, with Louviere heading for the tent and Jackson walking the other way, toward the giant live oak. He stopped at the northeast corner of the patio, taking a moment to admire the largely glass east walls of the house, then surveying the crowd on the patio for signs of Sawyer. Her floral sundress wasn't anything that would easily stand out, but she would. She was taller than most of the women, better looking than most of them— which was saying something—and she carried herself with confidence, with a natural poise. He didn't spot her.

A waiter offered him a crawfish salad puff, and it was delicious. He trusted Sawyer was mingling inside, or constructing a mental blueprint of the house, or powdering her nose. So he weaved through the crowd for a few minutes, enjoying a few more hors d'oeuvres. He thought he recognized a few faces, one on a middle-aged woman in a shimmering dress and one belonging to a tall black guy who may or may not have played basketball for the Hornets—now Pelicans. He didn't really know and didn't really care. He'd learned what he could from Louviere. Now it was time to find Sawyer and see if, by chance, they could find the logbook Damon had mentioned.

He grabbed one more crawfish salad puff and placed his drink on an empties tray. As he turned for the deck, he saw Sawyer emerge from the ballroom. It took her just a moment to spot him. He gave a subtle nod toward her, and she nodded too. He climbed to the deck, and she met him at the top of the stairs.

"Did you talk to him?" she asked.

He nodded.

"What'd you find?"

"Depends."

"On?"

Jackson looked back down at the patio, looking for Louviere in the crowd. He turned back to her. "Whether he knew I was blowing smoke."

"You think he did?"

"I don't think he did, but he might have been conning me better than I was conning him. Game knows game, you know."

Sawyer raised an eyebrow.

They walked to the north end of the deck, and Jackson rehashed the conversation, pointing out his references to Ben and the treasure and the logbook, as well as Louviere's responses. "He claimed to know nothing about any of it, nor to having a logbook."

"So he was lying."

"That, or Damon's intel was off. But that was my read on him. Question is, was he lying because he's a criminal mastermind or because he saw through my cover story?"

She shrugged. "You were the one talking with him."

"I was. And I've got nothing concrete, just intimations and observances of mannerisms and facial expressions."

"But . . ."

"But, my take is that Martin Louviere is dirty as a coal miner's pants."

Chapter Twenty-Eight

AFTER PICKING UP small plates of hors d'oeuvres, Jackson and Sawyer left the hubbub of the patio and strolled around the side of the house and under the large live oak tree. When he was sure they were alone, Jackson asked, "What'd you find?"

"This is a real who's who," Sawyer answered. "Politicians, the mayor, actors and actresses."

Jackson nodded, not bothering to ask how she knew the New Orleans mayor.

"From what I overheard, about half of them are here because they legitimately believe in Louviere's cause and half of them just want to be seen and recognized. But aside from the names and faces I recognize, the jewelry, clothes, and conversation made it quite clear these people have money and clout."

"You spot Congressman Patterson?"

"No."

"Anyone else pertinent?"

"Not really. But I didn't see everybody."

Jackson nodded and had a cracker with a small piece of shrimp and cocktail sauce on it. A little cheese, too. Delicious.

"As for the schedule, I don't think there is one," Sawyer said. "No formal dinner, no planned entertainment or anything like that."

Jackson tried a little caviar because he'd always wanted to. He made a face and looked for something else on his plate. "What about traffic?"

"Mostly outside. The ballroom has thinned a little. Still a handful at the bar, a couple of ladies chatting up a guy around the fireplace."

"Anything restricted?"

"Not that I saw. But I didn't try bedroom doors or anything."

"You learn the lay of the land, beyond what Jeeves told us?"

"That wasn't an objective."

"A good operative would have—"

"Kitchen and dining room are to the north down the main hall," Sawyer said with a smile, "along with a lounge and a small art gallery. There are also a pair of parlors or sitting rooms in this corner, off the ballroom. On the far side, there's another sitting room along with a library. Up front, there's a den and a billiards room, and on the south end of the hallway, a two-story solarium."

"A what?"

"Glorified sunroom."

"Everything but a bowling alley."

"I didn't check the basement," she said with a grin. "Second story has bedrooms, I presume, but also a large loft-slash-sitting area-slash-gallery that wraps around the staircases. And there's a third floor too. I didn't go up there."

"Still, you made the rounds."

"It's what you told me to do. There's a patio here, you can see," she said, pointing to one on the north side of the house. Wings on either end were only two stories tall. "Those doors lead to a small nook or informal dining room. Similar doors on the far side lead to the solarium."

"Those the only other entrances?"

"Front and three on the back, to the deck."

Jackson frowned. "One to the ballroom, one to the sitting rooms on the corner. What's the other one to?"

"I don't know. There are double doors leading in from the deck, double doors from the ballroom, and double doors from the library, but I have no idea what it is."

"Hmm. You didn't see an office anywhere, did you?"

"Not that I noticed."

"That could be it. Else it's attached to the master suite."

"So what's the plan?" Sawyer asked. They had stopped amid a trio of willow trees near the maintenance shed. Jackson took a long look back toward the party. Louviere was again holding court, this time at the top of the stairs at the other end of the pool. It was hard to tell from the distance, but Louviere's body language didn't look stressed.

"You learn anything else?" Jackson asked.

"I made a friend," she said, turning her shoulders so that the flared hem of her sundress swished back and forth.

He looked at her for more.

"Martin Junior. Louviere's son."

"How'd you meet him?"

"By chance," she said with a shrug. "Or because he thought I looked nice in my sundress. I don't know, he came up to me."

Jackson frowned. "How so?"

"The way guys come up to girls at parties. Smiling, making small talk, flirting a little."

"What'd you talk about?"

"Well, I figured I might make use of him and mentioned that I'd heard his father had a collection of historical artifacts and sold that I was intrigued. I thought maybe he'd take me on a private tour and show me a logbook."

"Did he?"

"Got interrupted by a state senator and he begged off to talk about bayou conservation efforts."

Jackson frowned again. "You believe him?"

"I do. I'm not incapable of being bluffed, but I think his interest in me was genuine, and so was his reason for leaving."

"I'll take your word for it. How'd you know Martin Louviere had a collection?"

"I saw half of it in the gallery and the loft. Old guns, swords, paintings, antique commemorative plates. And Damon's rumors about the logbook. I figured it wasn't a stretch." She shrugged. "Plus, I was vague and said I'd heard rumors."

"Smart."

"He didn't show any signs of being suspicious."

"Okay. Any other secrets? You didn't discover a secret passageway to the boathouse or actually find the logbook sitting on a shelf, did you?"

"No."

He sighed. "Best guess is it's in his office. That or a secret lair. Any rooms somewhere you didn't identify?"

"Yeah, there were a few. One off the billiards room, but it's small. And I didn't explore much upstairs."

"Could also be in the master suite, tucked away in a private safe or under his pillow, for that matter."

"So where do we start?"

"The office. I'm guessing it's the room on the southeast corner."

"Isn't that dangerous?"

"It is. We talked about that."

"I mean, the office is right off the deck. Somebody could see us."

"Not likely. It's very bright out here. Look in any of the windows. You can't see anything. All the light reflects. That said, if you want to call this off, we call it off."

"No. We've come this far. Besides, we can always rely on the local authorities to have our backs." She forced a smile. "What do we do?"

"You introduce yourself to anyone besides Marty Junior yet?"

"Just my alias to a few people. Even Junior doesn't know more than 'I'm Savannah.'"

"He goes by Junior?"

She nodded.

"And he doesn't know why you were here or who you were with?"

"No."

Jackson nodded. "Then our relationship isn't defined."

"Why does that matter?"

"We talked about Louviere having our names but probably not faces. And he's probably got someone checking my story, but it will be hard for him to prove I'm not who I said. However, if things do go south, there's nothing to tie you to me."

"Unless we're caught together."

"In that case, be prepared. I'm going to plant one on you and act like we were looking for privacy."

"Really? You've got nothing better than that old fallback?"

"Sorry, my creativity's burning a little low. And there's a reason it's an old fallback."

"Yeah, because guys always come up with the plans for covert ops."

He shrugged.

"Whatever, just lay off the seafood if you might kiss me." She made a bit of a show of eating a parmesan garlic crab cake, and Jackson didn't know quite how to read the move. "So that's the contingency," she said. "What's the actual plan?"

"Was there anybody in the library when you were in there?"

"No."

"Okay. That's our best point of entry. Ballroom has too much traffic, and the deck's obviously out."

"And if we get caught having broken into Louviere's office, do you think your 'we're just an amorous couple' idea will hold water?"

"Probably not. That's where we wing it."

Sawyer sighed. "I guess you'll lead."

"Ready?"

"As I'll ever be."

"Then let's roll."

They wandered back to the patio, where the party was still in full swing, the quartet still playing soft classical music, and groups of well-dressed people still talking and eating and drinking, oblivious to Jackson and Sawyer's machinations. Jackson scanned the crowd, looking to see if Louviere or his spitting image or guys who looked like retired linebackers with earpieces happened to be watching them. He saw nothing but people having a good time, and he and Sawyer entered the ballroom.

There were a dozen people in the room. Two men in adjacent chairs by the fireplace. Two couples around a bistro table, laughing and smiling. A group at the bar. Nobody stood out except for a dark-haired lady in a red dress. She was facing away from him, so he couldn't see much of her face, and figured the only reason she stood out was the color of her dress. He didn't dwell on her, instead being glad there were no familiar faces or obvious security personnel in the room.

Without dawdling, he and Sawyer walked across the ballroom, veering to their left and to a doorway a dozen feet beside the fireplace. Pocket doors were open, permitting entrance to a sitting room. It was twenty feet by twelve, with several seating alcoves in the corners, a writing desk against the left wall beside a doorway and under a portrait of an austere woman. It was vacant.

"What are you looking at?" Sawyer asked.

"The room."

"Any particular reason?"

"Trying to figure out what differentiates a sitting room from a parlor."

Sawyer sighed.

"Or from a den. Or a living room."

"I think it's a wealth exclusivity thing," Sawyer said. "If you don't know, you don't know."

"Mm-hmm."

"Should we get moving?"

"Yeah."

Open pocket doors connected the sitting room to the library, a room twice its size. There was a fireplace on the left, opposite the one in the ballroom. A loveseat faced it, backed by a pair of desks facing each other, with green-shaded banker's lamps like in old, academic libraries. Bookshelves lined the walls, floor to ceiling, each full of books. The only exception was on the right wall, which was shorter than the left wall thanks to buildouts in each flanking wall. The result was a room shaped like an elongated half rest. Instead of a bookshelf on the short wall, a pair of cushy armchairs flanked an end table with a built-in lamp. Above them, an oil painting depicted the New Orleans skyline at dusk.

Jackson peeked back into the sitting room, then eased the pocket doors shut. He turned to Sawyer, who was scanning the shelves. "Any logbooks?" he asked.

"No, but a pretty good collection."

"Did you check for the logbook before?"

"Spent two minutes."

"Let's spend five more. We haven't done anything wrong yet."

"'*As he thinketh in his heart, so is he.*'"

They looked for five minutes but didn't see any logbooks or anything else that appeared to precede the American Revolution. It wasn't a surprise. Hiding a book in plain sight was a decent strategy, but not one Jackson expected Louviere had employed with the logbook.

They convened in front of French doors in the east wall. Sheer curtains on the inside blocked any view of what lay beyond.

"Last chance?" Jackson said.

"That's like the fourth time you've said that."

"Then you'd really better not turn it down."

"Let's do it."

"And hope it's not the security control center on the other side of the door." He nodded at Sawyer's clutch purse. She unsnapped it and handed him two bobby pins. "I half expected the door to have keycard access."

"Dollars to donuts he's got the logbook in a safe. You ever crack a safe?" she asked as Jackson knelt down in front of the door handle on the right French door, the one with a keyhole.

"Once. And never again."

She nodded.

He inserted the bobby pins into the keyhole in the handle. On TV, private investigators picked a lock with the same ease with which regular people unlocked them with a key. It wasn't quite that simple, but if you knew the drill, it wasn't that hard. At least not on most locks, and this one wasn't anything special. He could feel he was close when Sawyer tapped his shoulder.

"Yeah?"

"Uh, I think you'd better kiss me now."

Jackson turned his head and saw the woman who'd caught his eye by the bar. She was tall, attractive, more so because of her red halter-top dress. Unlike most of the women at the party, her black hair was down, wavy as it dangled in front of her shoulders. In a different moment, she would have been beautiful. Now she was just stern.

"Who are you?" she asked, her mouth forming a snarl. "And what are you doing in here?"

Chapter Twenty-Nine

6:00 p.m.

IN AN INSTANT, in the time it took him to stand, Jackson decided his best bet was to go on the offensive. Especially since the woman wasn't noticeably armed, or built like Serena Williams. And he figured dropping a name might help.

"I'm looking for Congressman Patterson."

Her eyebrow shot up for only a moment. "In there?"

"I've checked everywhere else."

"So you thought you'd pick the lock on your host's office door?"

"I'm afraid it's urgent that I find him."

"Who's she, your guardian angel?"

"Excuse me?" Sawyer said.

"Well, according to the newspapers," the woman said, taking a few steps closer, "you're dead. But then, I know that you're not Damon Villars, either. So I'll ask you again, what are you doing in here?"

Jackson returned her gaze, nearly melting under the glare from her blue eyes. For a second, he thought about rushing her. Even if she was a fighter, he thought he could take her, given the restrictions of an evening gown. But rushing her in an attempt to make a break for it meant giving up on finding the logbook, and he still held out hope that he could talk his way out of things. So he took another tack.

"I'm Special Agent Goldman. This is Special Agent Brown. FBI."

The woman actually smiled. "Let me guess, you're undercover and don't have a badge with you."

Jackson raised his eyebrows. "All right, Sassafras, what do you want?"

"The truth."

He frowned and looked at Sawyer. Then nodded. "On one condition. First you tell me who you are."

"I'm Ruby Mae Patterson. Congressman Patterson's daughter."

"Of all the people at the party."

"Right?" she said with a fake smile. Then she continued in a rich, soft voice, tinged with a Southern accent. Almost as if she was trying to sound like a Southern belle. "I saw you talking with Martin Louviere earlier, saw you whispering as you sneaked in here. So I asked the gentleman at the front door who you were, and he remembered you as Mr. Villars and guest. Since I know Damon was killed Thursday night, I was more than a little suspicious. So I thought I'd investigate and see who was pretending to be my dead friend, and that's when I found you breaking and entering."

"You were friends with Damon?" Sawyer asked.

Ruby Mae nodded. "We weren't terribly close, but yes, I considered him a friend. Did you kill him?"

"No," Jackson said. "We're here to find out who did."

She looked back over her shoulder, through the pocket doors, then stepped around the loveseat in front of the fireplace. "Why does that bring you here?"

"Long story. Short of it is, our friend was also friends with Damon. He disappeared under suspicious circumstances last weekend. Wednesday night, Damon left him a voicemail mentioning Louviere's name and some logbook. Friday afternoon, we heard that Damon was dead. We came here to find out what exactly is going on."

"So who are you?"

"Sawyer," he said with a nod at her, "and Jack."

Ruby Mae waited a beat, then said, "The cops think Damon was killed during a random break-in."

"The cops are crooked as the Mississippi," Jackson replied. "At least the one we know."

Ruby Mae shook her head. "I don't buy it either. Damon has been . . . distracted lately. I think he had found something—I don't know what—but I think it got him killed."

Jackson looked at Sawyer. She nodded.

"You ever heard of the Brackett treasure?" he asked Ruby Mae.

"Yeah, I think so. Another rumor about a buried treasure?"

"Another long story," Jackson said. "But the short version is we think our friend was looking for it, he had recruited Damon to help, and Damon learned that a logbook held by Louviere contained a clue."

"What kind of clue?"

"No idea."

"Damon said something about it being a log of inbound and outbound ships in the 1700s," Sawyer said.

"What specifically we're supposed to find in it, we don't know," Jackson said. "But that logbook is the only clue we have to follow, and this treasure hunt, oddly enough, is our only link to maybe finding out what happened to Ben."

"You think the same person killed him as killed Damon?"

"Good chance."

"And you think the answers are in a logbook owned by one of New Orleans' preeminent citizens?"

"Conceivably."

"And why does Martin Louviere own this logbook?"

"We don't know. What can you tell us about him?"

"Not much. I know he and my father have a professional relationship, but I've never liked him."

"Why not?"

She shrugged. "He comes off like the proverbial snake-oil salesman."

"You think he could have killed Damon?" Sawyer asked.

"Never. He didn't know Damon existed."

"He had an invitation to the party tonight."

"My father's doing, I'm sure. He was fond of taking one or two of his aides to these sorts of events. This must have been Damon's turn. But I meant that Louviere, for all of his charity work, wouldn't dirty his hands with someone as 'lowly' as Damon."

"Okay, do you think he would have had Damon killed?" Jackson asked. "If he thought maybe Damon was getting too close to a treasure Louviere was also after?"

Ruby Mae shook her head. "I don't know."

Jackson nodded at the door. "So what do you say, you want to blow the whistle or walk away?"

"Neither," she said. "I want to join you. I don't care much about a treasure, but I want to know who killed Damon. If the logbook might have a clue to who did it or why, then how can I help?"

"For starters, figure out an excuse for what in the Sam Hill we're doing if somebody else finds us in here." He knelt back down, and in less than a minute had picked the lock. He looked up at Sawyer. "No alarm."

"No audible alarm."

"She's a real downer," he said over his shoulder to Ruby Mae. He stood. "Okay, if this goes south, one of you start making out with me, and the other one hit me with your purse."

"Is he for real?" Ruby Mae asked.

"I think he is."

"Come on," Jackson said, opening the door.

It was quite an office. Except for sheer-covered French doors in the middle, the far wall was a bank of windows that curved up at the top, turning into skylights for several feet as the ground level of the house extended several feet farther than the second story. Maybe because they would have let in so much light otherwise, or maybe for privacy, the windows were tinted, confirming Jackson's belief that, given the brightness outside, the trio would be almost invisible to anyone on the deck or patio.

The office was essentially split in two. On the right, an L-shaped desk faced the windows, giving Louviere a marvelous view of the lake as he sat in a deluxe-model office chair behind it. The desk was sleek and modern, with a glass surface that was clear of clutter. A trio of cushy armchairs faced the desk. Behind it, the wall projected out, same as in the library, with a narrow door in the near side. A closet?

The left half of the room contained a small conference table with seating for six in front of a bookshelf and display panel that housed a flat-screen TV. There was also a small couch by the windows, for mid-afternoon naps in the sun or frank conversations with Junior. Or whatever.

"Okay," Sawyer said, "so where do we find a logbook?"

"Probably a safe," Ruby Mae said, turning toward a series of photos on the wall behind the desk. They showed famous par-three golf holes around the world—Augusta National, Pebble Beach, Royal Troon.

"You ever been in here before?" Jackson asked.

She huffed a laugh, an incredulous look on her face. There was nothing behind the photos but painted sheetrock, and she turned to the bookcase. Sawyer joined her, while Jackson checked the desk. There was a closed laptop on its surface, along with a leather pen stand, a small notepad, a desk lamp, and two photo frames—one of a woman and one of the woman along with Louviere and two adults half their age. The desk had one shallow slide-out drawer with the usual assortment of office items—pens and pencils, sticky notes, paper clips, rubber bands, breath mints. No side drawers or hidden compartments.

He turned to a filing cabinet in the corner. It was locked. Lousy location anyhow.

"Over here," Sawyer said.

Jackson joined her and Ruby Mae by the bookshelf. It was a large, beautifully crafted piece, the wood a dark cherry, rich and varnished to a shine. It was broken into three sections—left, middle, and right. The middle section contained a TV, about a thirty-six-inch model, if Jackson's estimate was right, big enough that anyone at the conference table could see all they needed to. Below it were a pair of push-open doors, likely leading to various components—a DVD player, perhaps, or remote control storage. Below it were two rows of books, reference volumes, it seemed. Above the TV was a narrow shelf with a few knickknacks, what appeared to be souvenirs from various locales. The left and right sections of the bookshelf were identical, featuring several shelves of books both top and bottom, and two display shelves in the middle. The books were a wide variety, everything from novels to old history textbooks. The shelves on the left contained framed photos of Louviere with New Orleans Saints quarterback Drew Brees, Louviere with a well-endowed actress Jackson recognized but couldn't place, and Louviere with a man in a suit—a man who bore a strong resemblance to Ruby Mae Patterson. The congressman. The middle shelves on the right contained an odder assortment of items. There was a model ship. Jackson didn't know whether it was a galleon or a schooner or a clipper—just that it was old. There was a row of what he first thought were candles, but then realized were open jars. Each was a different height, arranged from tallest to shortest. They contained sand. There was a brass spyglass, a genuine article, it appeared, and a flintlock pistol, also very real.

And then there was an old book, bound in cracked, coppery leather. It was long, eighteen inches or so, twice as long as high, and maybe three-quarters of an inch thick. It was propped on a stand, its gold clasp scuffed and tarnished but still sparkling as it caught the evening light.

Jackson looked to Sawyer, who stood in the corner, to the right of the bookshelf. She looked across him to Ruby Mae, who in turn looked to Jackson. He started to reach for the book.

"Tell me you brought gloves," Ruby Mae said.

"Oops," Sawyer said.

"We're kind of flying by the seat of our pants," Jackson said. "Besides, nobody will ever know we were here."

He lifted the book off its stand and carefully turned, setting it down on the conference table. Sawyer and Ruby Mae crowded in, close enough that he could smell Sawyer's perfume and Ruby Mae's shampoo. Or the other way around. He tried not to dwell on either as he unsnapped the clasp. Fearing it might crumble, he opened the cover and stared down at the book. The pages were old and worn, yellowed, and the print was hardly legible. And it was in French.

"Oh, awesome."

"What?" Ruby Mae asked.

"*Parlez-vous Français?*"

"*Oui.*"

"Really?"

"I took several semesters in college. I'm not fluent, but I can find my way around Paris."

"This isn't backpacking with your boyfriend. This looks like eighteenth-century scribble."

"Let me take a look."

He turned the book to her and looked at Sawyer. She shrugged.

Ruby Mae tucked her hair behind her ears and stood up. "This isn't a logbook."

"It's not?"

"No. It's the personal diary of Captaine Eamon Toussaint," she said.

"Who is . . . ?"

"The captain of an eighteenth-century French merchant ship named the *Majesté Royale.*"

"When in the eighteenth-century?" Sawyer asked.

"Looks like 1712."

"Anybody else perpetually confused by centuries not corresponding with the dates?" Jackson asked. "You know, eighteenth century is seventeen hundreds?"

"No," Sawyer said. She looked at Ruby Mae. "See if there's anything about 1715. That's when Brackett and his crew robbed the *Nuestra Señora de la Granada* and when the hurricane sunk the *Barracuda*."

Ruby Mae nodded and began flipping through the diary.

"You come to these sorts of parties often?" Jackson asked her after several minutes.

She looked up. "What?"

"Tell me you're not hitting on her now," Sawyer said.

"No. I'm not."

Ruby Mae raised an eyebrow. "Yeah, too often."

"How long till someone notices we're missing?"

"Depends how drunk they are."

He paced around the room, then back. Had Damon simply mixed up words when he'd left Ben a voicemail about a logbook? Had he been given bad intel? Was this not the clue he'd expected to find—was there an actual logbook somewhere else in Louviere's possession?

"Here we go," Ruby Mae said. "In August of 1715, the *Majesté Royale* sailed from Marseille. It arrived in Port Bayou St. Jean on September 27, via Haiti and the Bahamas."

"The Bahamas," Jackson said to Sawyer.

"That mean something?" Ruby Mae asked.

"Maybe. Where's Port Bayou St. Jean?"

"New Orleans."

He and Sawyer exchanged a glance. "What else?" he asked, leaning over Ruby Mae's shoulder even though he couldn't read a lick of French. It didn't matter. A moment later, his eyes picked out a word that didn't need translation. Brackett.

"There," he said. "What's going on here?"

"It says . . . they picked up a delirious man named Brackett off a small island in the southern Bahamas. He kept claiming he was a captain and mumbling something about 'rich man's bones.'"

"Rich man's bones?" Jackson asked. "You sure?"

"Yeah."

"Not conjugating anything wrong. You're sure of the French?"

"I'm sure," Ruby Mae said.

"Anything else?" Sawyer asked.

"They dropped him off in Bayou Port St. Jean. After picking up their cargo, the crew of the *Majesté Royale* set sail for France on September 29, hoping to make it back before winter."

"What was the cargo?" Jackson asked.

"Furs."

"Hmm," Sawyer said.

Ruby Mae's phone vibrated from within her purse. She took it out and looked at it, but didn't answer it. Sawyer, meanwhile, snapped several pictures of the diary with her phone. Jackson stood back, thinking, trying to tie the pieces together.

On July 31, 1715, *Nuestra Señora de la Granada* sailed from Veracruz bound for Spain. Two or three days later, it was attacked by Brackett and his crew aboard the *Barracuda*, who stole its treasure and captured the daughter of the Capitán General of the Spanish Navy. Three days later, a hurricane slammed into the keys and sunk the *Barracuda* a mile and a half off Sugarloaf Key. Brackett, his crew, and the treasure disappeared into the world of legend and rumor.

Meanwhile, across the Atlantic, the *Majesté Royale*, under the command of Eamon Toussaint, departed for the New World on a fur run and swung by the Bahamas to pick up a delirious Brackett, who they dumped in modern-day New Orleans. Assuming it was Captain James Brackett the *Majesté Royale* picked up, and never minding for the moment what he had been doing in the Bahamas, did this new piece of information do anything but kick the can down the road, delaying Brackett's departure from the history books several weeks?

Ruby Mae's phone vibrated again. She took it out and looked at it again, this time sighing. "My brother, Bobby."

"He here at the party too?" Sawyer asked.

"So to speak. He works for Louviere," she said, texting a response.

"He works for Louviere?" Jackson asked.

"He's a courier or something. Very low on the totem pole. Appropriate for Bobby." She returned the phone to her purse. "I put him off for a little while, but we shouldn't linger."

"Are we missing anything else in here about Brackett?" Jackson asked. "Any mention of the *Barracuda* or a treasure?"

"No."

He nodded. "I guess we might as well get going." He closed the diary, clasped it, then wiped his sleeve over the gold to remove fingerprints. Sawyer sighed, and he handed the diary to her to place back on the shelf. He let go a second too soon, and it fell to the corner of the table, then tipped and plummeted all the way to the floor.

"Smooth move, ex-lax," Ruby Mae said.

"I got it," Sawyer said, beating him to crouch down and pick up the diary.

"Yeah, than—"

"What?" Ruby Mae asked, hearing the catch in his voice.

Jackson didn't answer, instead staring out the office window at a man in a dark suit jacket and dark pants. He had an earpiece with a cord running from under the collar and around his ear. Security. For whatever reason, he had approached the window, close enough that his considerable body mass blocked enough light that he could see inside. That was evident by the scowl on his face as he stared straight at Jackson.

He hesitated only a moment, turning and pushing Ruby Mae toward the door to the library. "Go!" he said. Before following her, he took one glance back at the window, just long enough to see the man turn toward the French doors leading into the office from the deck.

Chapter Thirty

6:23 p.m.

THE DUAL FRENCH doors shook but did not open. It made sense. Louviere would have them locked. Ostensibly his security personnel would have a key or a code, however, so Jackson wasn't greatly encouraged. He could see the form of the man through the sheer curtains on the doors, even if the man couldn't see in because of them. That too would change in a moment.

Jackson turned back to Sawyer, who was still kneeling on the floor behind the table. He pulled her up and ushered her past him, after Ruby Mae into the library. He then followed, turning over his shoulder to see the French doors fly open and a security "guard" barrel into the office. Only it didn't happen. Maybe he didn't have the key after all.

"What do we do?" Ruby Mae asked breathlessly when they had entered the library.

"I don't know," Sawyer said, "but I don't think we're kissing our way out of this one."

"You know that guy?" Jackson asked, closing the French doors behind them.

"No. I didn't even see him."

"How'd he see us?" Sawyer asked.

"No idea," Jackson said as he stepped around her and skirted the table. "Tipped off, dumb luck, she's a mole," he said, tossing his thumb at Ruby Mae.

"I'm not a mo—"

"Just joking."

"Now?"

He flicked his eyebrows up and peeked into the sitting room. Empty. He motioned over his shoulder for them to follow. He then signaled they should stop while he approached the pocket doors to the ballroom. He peeked his head around the corner, then immediately withdrew it.

"What?" Sawyer hissed.

He didn't answer, instead motioning them back toward the library.

"What?" Ruby Mae asked.

He took her arm and gave it a gentle shove, herding her first, then Sawyer, into the library. He followed, closing the pocket doors behind them, momentarily sealing off the sitting room.

"What are we doing?" Ruby Mae asked.

"Guy One has a twin, big shoulders, buzz cut, former military, in a dark jacket, hand to his ear."

"Security?" Sawyer asked.

Jackson nodded. "We burst out of there, he's onto us immediately."

"So what do we do?" Ruby Mae asked.

"This way," Jackson said, taking the lead, around the table again, back to the French doors leading into the office. The picked door had not relocked, and Jackson inched it open. The doors on the opposite wall, leading to the deck, were still closed. So were those leading to the ballroom. A quick glance out the windows showed no lurking security guards, just the milling crowd and the property sloping down toward the lake.

"Wait here," Jackson whispered. He slipped into the office and turned to his right, to the narrow door built into the built-out wall. Same as in the library. He played a hunch and tried the knob. It was locked.

He looked at the windows again. Nothing. Guy One had seen him, tried the doors, found them locked. He'd radioed Guy Two in the ballroom. Maybe radioed for a key. Guy One was not peering in the windows to keep tabs on the intruders he'd spotted, meaning he was either procuring a key, marshaling forces, or headed for another means of entrance—the library via the sitting room.

"Ruby," Jackson hissed, since she had been closest to the doors. At the same time, he reached into his pocket for the bobby pins.

Ruby Mae eased the door open. "What?"

"Both of you come in here, but stay low," Jackson said. He began working his picks into the lock. He thought about how on *Magnum, P.I.*, Tom Selleck's character always found himself trying to pick a lock under pressure, like while a pair of Dobermans was bounding across the lawn toward him.

Magnum's advice—focus on the lock—worked. He always got it open just in time.

"What are you doing?" Ruby Mae asked as she and Sawyer knelt behind him.

He didn't answer, following Magnum's advice.

"Jackson," Sawyer said. "A guy in a dark coat just entered the library."

"Lock the door."

He heard it click as she turned the lock. A second later, he heard another click. He turned the knob, and the door opened. Just like Magnum, just in time.

He scooted to the side, drawing the door open. "Go."

"Into a closet?" Ruby Mae asked.

"No," Jackson said, having peeked ever so briefly inside to confirm his hunch. A narrow staircase led up, and he unceremoniously hurried both women up it with pushes on the backside. They could sue him for sexual harassment later. He followed on their heels, pulling the door shut behind him and making sure to lock it.

The staircase was pitch black, and they stumbled for a moment until Ruby Mae pulled out her cell phone. The screen lit the passageway enough for them to make out the succeeding steps. It was bare and musty, just wood stairs and unfinished drywall on the sides. The staircase reversed halfway up, turning and ascending through room borrowed from the library. And it dead-ended at a wood panel, as evidenced by the now stronger beam from Ruby Mae's flashlight app.

"'*Hast thou taken us away to die in the wilderness?*'" Sawyer asked.

"You guys ever see that *Sesame Street* where Grover climbs 'The 39 Stairs' only to get to a brick wall?"

In the semi-darkness, Ruby Mae and Sawyer looked at each other. Then at him.

"Monsterpiece Theater?"

They said nothing, just stared at him, Ruby Mae with her mouth open.

He pressed between them, which wasn't easy on the tight staircase. He pushed both hands against the panel, felt it give ever so slightly. Still applying pressure, he slid his hands right. The panel moved. Another pocket door.

"You mind?" Jackson asked, reaching for Ruby Mae's phone. She gave it to him, and he shone the light ahead of them.

The room was dark, but not compared to the staircase. It was, as he'd expected, the master bedroom. A king-size, if not bigger, four-post bed was on the right, between two windows covered by more sheer curtains. They let in enough light that the phone flashlight wasn't necessary, and he handed it back to Ruby Mae as she and Sawyer followed him out of the doorway.

There was a fireplace directly ahead, above the one in the ballroom. A low credenza on one wall, nightstands built into the wall under the windows beside the bed, some simple décor. A lot of doors. Sliders to the right, letting in more light despite their sheer curtains, likely leading to a balcony. One on the immediate left, beside the pocket door to the secret stairs. A closet, maybe? Double French doors in the wall on the left, leading out.

"How d—How did you know this was here?" Sawyer asked.

"I didn't, for sure. But the projection into the library and into the office—Something had to be behind those walls."

"And you assumed it was a staircase?"

"Right size."

"Leading to the master bedroom?"

"Well, I didn't know where it would lead, but this makes sense for a secret passageway."

"We should keep moving," Ruby Mae said. "They'll be right behind us."

"Not necessarily. I'm guessing this is the last place they'd look because they wouldn't expect us to try to hide in what looks like a closet. I'm guessing they'll surmise we escaped out one or the other door when they weren't looking, meaning we bought some time. Still, probably best not to linger."

"So where do we go?" Sawyer asked. "How do we get out of here? Louviere will have people looking everywhere."

"You have a car?" Ruby Mae asked.

"Took an Uber," Jackson said with a wince. "Didn't know we'd be making a mad dash escape."

"That's going to take half an hour, at least, to get someone here."

"You know how to hotwire a car?" Jackson asked Sawyer.

"I am not stealing someone's car."

"We can take mine," Ruby Mae said.

"You drove separately?"

"I came with a date, of sorts, but he dumped me for a slinky blonde two minutes after we got here. He can walk home."

"Or take an Uber," Jackson said.

She grinned and reached into her purse. "Valet has the keys, but I have a spare."

"That still doesn't help us get to the car," Sawyer said. "Louviere's sure to have the front door covered."

Jackson looked to Ruby Mae. "How many people on his security staff, any idea?"

"With an event like this, probably five to six. Plus my father has people here. And I'm sure Louviere has others who aren't security who would help conduct a manhunt. Like my brother."

"Great," Sawyer muttered.

Jackson snapped his fingers. "Manhunt."

They both looked at him.

"That guy looked in the window and saw me. He never saw you," he said to Sawyer, "because you were kneeling down behind the table. I'm not even sure he got a look at Rubes here, because she was turned the other way."

"So?" Sawyer asked.

"So, they're looking for me and a possibly unidentified woman. They aren't looking for you."

"Meaning?"

"You can take the key, sneak down and get the car, and we'll rendezvous with you later."

"Haven't you been seen with her?" Ruby Mae asked.

"Maybe by a few people, but we've kept a low profile as a couple." He made eye contact with Sawyer. "Honestly, they may be to the stage of known associates and be on the lookout for you too, but our best chance is that they're not looking for a single woman but for a couple."

"So I just waltz out of the bedroom and go get the car?"

"Yeah. As long as no one sees you coming out of the bedroom, you should be fine. Walk out to the car like you're going to get a sweater or a wrap or something, and then leave."

"And where and how do we rendezvous?"

"We'll find another way out," Jackson said. "Call you when we're clear and tell you were to pick us up. If all goes well, at the bottom of the porch. Otherwise, maybe we hike to the end of the driveway."

"You make it sound so easy."

He shrugged.

"And what happens if you can't find another way out, if you get caught?"

"I have some pull," Ruby Mae said. "If he and I are caught together, I can talk us out of it. Not if there's three of us, though."

Sawyer hesitated.

"It's the best way," Jackson said.

She sighed, then took the key Ruby Mae extended.

"It's a black Jetta, and I'm pretty sure there's only one of them here. Plate starts with DDA if not."

"Are you sure about this?" Sawyer asked Jackson.

"Yeah. Keep your phone close, and we'll call you the second we're clear."

She nodded, reaching for and squeezing his hand. Then the trio exited through the French doors, which led into a parlor, a room the size of the bedroom, with a couch, a couple of armchairs, and a TV. Three more sets of doors led out of the room, including a double set down a very short hallway. Based on the room design and the layout of the house, Jackson assumed it led to the loft at the top of the main hall staircase. He crept to the door first, eased it open a crack, and peeked out.

"Coast's clear," he said to Sawyer. "Remember, act like you belong."

"Be careful," she said to him and Ruby Mae.

He winked, and she slipped through the door. Jackson closed it behind her and turned to Ruby Mae. "You think there's another secret passage in here?"

Chapter Thirty-One

6:30 p.m.

THERE WERE NO more passageways, but the master suite at Pontchartrain Manor was practically a labyrinth. In addition to the bedchamber and the parlor, there were spacious his and hers closets, a bathroom fit for a palace, and a second parlor done up in feminine décor—a drawing room, by antebellum parlance. Jackson's whole house was a cracker box by comparison.

He and Ruby Mae, having split up to search, met in the bathroom. Along with a rain shower, a whirlpool tub, his and hers vanities, and a cordoned off water closet, it had its own fireplace. It likely existed to combat the draftiness from all the wide open space, and from three doors—one to her closet (empty, since Louviere was a widower), one to his closet, and one to the drawing room. There was also a window above the whirlpool tub, but instead of opening to the outside, it opened to the solarium on the first floor.

"There's a window in the drawing room," Ruby Mae said, "but it's second story."

"Balcony in the main bedroom, but same problem."

"Maybe we can sneak down the stairs like Sawyer did. She your girlfriend, by the way?"

"No."

"To which part?"

"Both. She's not my girlfriend, and I'd be shocked if we make it to the bottom of the stairs. It's fifty-fifty she does."

"Yet you sent her out there?"

"It was our best play. And like you said, if two of us get caught, we can talk our way out of it, maybe. Three . . ."

"Well, we're going to get caught if we don't find a way out of here. Unless you want to hide in the closet until Louviere goes to bed."

Jackson stepped up onto the sides of the whirlpool tub, enabling him to look through the window down to the solarium. It was empty. A couple of seating areas, a small bookcase, a wet bar. A lot of plants, some even growing two stories tall. They gave him an idea.

"We can get out through the solarium."

"What?"

"There's nobody in there," he said, stepping down from the tub. "And why would there be? If you want to hang out in the sun, hang out in the sun. Nobody comes out of the heat into the air-conditioning to go sit in a sunroom. It's for cool November mornings and too-short February afternoons."

"Okay, so it's empty. But it's on the first floor."

"Go tear the sheets off the bed."

"Are you serious?"

"We'll make a rope and let ourselves down. There's a couch right under the window, which saves us a couple feet of drop, and even though there are a lot of windows, there are also a lot of plants. Plus there's nobody on this side of the house, whereas if we go out the drawing room window or the balcony, we're probably doing so to an audience."

"You're crazy," Ruby Mae said.

"They said that about Tesla too."

"And he kind of was."

"You got a better idea?"

She sighed and turned for the closet, which would lead to the parlor, which would lead to the bedchamber. Jackson, meanwhile, looked for something around which to anchor a bedsheet rope. He was still looking when Ruby Mae returned with two sheets.

"Okay, problem," he said.

"What?"

"There's nothing to attach it to. Nothing that will hold our weight, anyhow."

"So I'm playing maid service for nothing?"

"Maybe." He looked her up and down.

"What?"

"You look like you're in pretty good shape. Are you athletic?"

"Enough."

"If we tie the sheet around the bathtub faucet, and one of us holds it, I think the combined anchoring force will enable the other one to get down."

"Anchoring force? That a scientific term?"

"I'm thinking you lower me, and then I can be down there to catch you."

"Catch me?"

"Even if we hang onto the window sill, I think it's a little too far to free fall without turning an ankle at best. But if you can hold the rope and ease me down, I'll catch you when you fall."

Ruby Mae studied him for a few seconds. He was expecting a snarky reply, but instead she nodded. "That could work."

"Great. Twist this into a rope."

She started to do so, and he took one end and tied it around the faucet of the bathtub. "Place like this really ought to have an old, cast-iron, claw-foot tub, shouldn't it?"

She ignored him. "You got a plan once we get down to the solarium?"

"There's a patio off the back, pretty well concealed by foliage, if my view from the patio was right. We sneak out, sneak around to the front of the house, and then play it by ear."

"Play it by ear?"

"If the coast is clear, have Sawyer pick us up at the driveway. If not, sneak to the trees and head for the road."

"Sure, I'll just pull my safari jacket and hiking boots out of my purse."

"This date of yours, the one who left you for the slinky blonde . . ."

"Yeah?"

"He mean you don't have a boyfriend."

She narrowed her eyes. "Why?"

"I kind of like you, Ruby Mae." He grinned as he stood. He opened the window, which was big enough for a person to squeeze through, albeit not with a lot of margin. He peeked down into the solarium again. Still vacant.

Ruby Mae handed him the end of the sheets not attached to the faucet. They had been twisted and knotted in the middle, and were long enough to reach almost to the top of the couch beneath the window.

"You ready?" he asked.

"Let's do this."

He climbed up onto the tub and sat on the window sill, ducking his head to extend it out. One leg followed. Meanwhile, Ruby Mae kicked off her high-heeled sandals and climbed into the tub. She took hold of the sheet with both hands, ready to brace herself and anchor him.

One more peek down, then he swung his other leg through, so he was dangling out over a dozen feet of empty space, the couch beneath him. It was not a La-Z-Boy man-cave lounger. More of a grandma's antique heirloom. But it was better than nothing.

"Ready?"

She nodded.

Jackson grabbed the sheet rope with one hand, winding it around his arm and clutching it tightly. With the other, he reached for the window sill, then dropped himself. Even with Ruby Mae and the faucet anchoring him, his dead weight created quite a jolt when his other arm caught on the sill. He winced to avoid crying out. Both arms quaked as they tried to support him, but he managed to lift his head. "You good?" he exhaled.

"Yeah, but don't dawdle."

He took his hand from the sill and grabbed the sheet. He slipped, and heard a cry from Ruby Mae. Freeing his left arm from the sheet, he rappelled as quickly as he could until his feet hit the back of the couch. He scrambled to find footing on the cushion, then released the sheet. His arms throbbed, but he had made it.

He quickly looked around. No one had decided on a stroll into the solarium. Outside the windows, shrubs and bushes provided some concealment, and the lawn beyond them appeared vacant.

"Okay, pull it up," he said to Ruby Mae. The bedsheet rope disappeared and was replaced by her head sticking out the window.

"Wait one," Jackson said, then hurried to the door leading out of the solarium, presumably to a hallway. It did not have a lock. He walked back to the couch. "Untie the rope," he said.

"And do what with it?"

"Toss it in a hamper? I don't want them knowing what we did if they should trace us to the bathroom."

Ruby Mae's head withdrew from the window, and Jackson busied himself moving the couch to an opening on the west wall, beside a potted fern that threatened to overtake the entire room. He then stood beneath the window, waiting for Ruby Mae's head to reappear.

"Any suggestions on how I do this?" she asked.

"As ladylike as possible?" he said with a smirk.

"Helpful, thanks."

"If you can, climb out so you're hanging down from the sill. Then let yourself go, and I'll catch you."

"Just like that," she said, pulling her head back. It was replaced by her hand, which dropped her sandals and purse. Jackson caught one sandal and the purse. The other sandal clattered to the marble floor. He kicked it aside and tossed the other sandal and purse after it. When he looked back up, Ruby Mae already had one leg out the window.

He gave her credit. She was performing a difficult move, and doing so in an evening gown. It took her just over a minute to let herself down so that she was hanging onto the window sill, and doing so without apparent strain on her arms. She was more than in shape.

"Whenever you're ready," Jackson said, positioning himself beneath her.

"One, two, three," she said. She pushed off with her feet and hands, launching herself away from the wall. She wasn't able to generate much separation, but enough that Jackson had to reposition himself on the fly. Spreading his arms, he cradled one around her shoulders and the other under her knees. Her weight caused him to lose his balance, and he braced himself on one knee, nearly dropping her in the process. Fortunately, she was ready and braced herself with her arm.

Breathing heavily, Jackson set Ruby Mae down. When she had her feet on the floor, he felt his way back to the couch, sitting on the edge of it.

The next thing he knew, Ruby Mae had practically jumped on him, knocking him onto his back. She fell on top of him and proceeded to kiss him like he was a returning war hero.

Chapter Thirty-Two

6:42 p.m.

JACKSON'S FIRST THOUGHT was that Ruby Mae was really a very nice kisser. His second was that she was one of those people who became overjoyed and responded spontaneously. His third was that he maybe shouldn't have asked about a boyfriend and mentioned liking her quite so cavalierly.

Then she stopped kissing him and sort of sat up. He turned his head, following her gaze, to where a trio of people stood just inside the doorway. Two women and a man. The man and one woman were young, Jackson's age or so. Good-looking, very well dressed, probably had a solarium in their house. The other woman was older, brown hair starting to gray, maybe sharing some physical characteristics of the man. It was hard to tell, what with their mouths agape.

Jackson winked at them, then pulled Ruby Mae back down. He kissed her and she kissed back, and two seconds later, he heard the door close with some authority. He turned his eyes to see the trio had disappeared, and he pulled back from kissing Ruby Mae. "They're gone."

She sat up all the way. "Thank goodness," she said, pushing off the back of the couch to stand up. "You taste like Lieutenant Dan."

"Maybe if you hadn't given me a full dental examination."

"Please." She extended a hand and pulled him up, reminding him his arm still was sore. "We should get moving," she said.

"You mean since you caused a scene?"

"And what was with winking?"

"I was playing a part."

She shook her head, then retrieved her sandals and purse while Jackson returned the couch to its place under the window. The open window. So much for not leaving a trail.

He guided Ruby Mae by the elbow, the way Rockford always did, toward the east end of the solarium. Sliding glass doors opened with a hiss, like an airlock, into a smaller room that was hot and steamy. A sauna, complete with a hot tub, and a miniature water feature on the wall. It too was vacant.

They skirted the hot tub and pushed through another set of French doors, out onto a patio. The air was much like that in the sauna, still warm and humid. The patio was mostly in the shade from the building and protected by a head-high row of hedges on the east side. The hedges created privacy for a second hot tub, this one covered. For when you wanted to soak under the stars with a glass of wine, presumably.

Jackson led Ruby Mae around the corner of the solarium and through something of a flower garden. The abundant foliage shielded them from view of anyone on the south lawn. But there was no one. The south lawn was half open space, covering some fifty yards to the tree line, and half a grove of palm trees around the tennis court. Louviere's party had apparently not spilled out in that direction, and Jackson and Ruby Mae reached the front corner of the house undetected.

"I should call Sawyer," Jackson said. "We might make a clean break of it."

He whipped out his phone and quickly punched in her number. Her phone rang six times, then went to voicemail. "Sawyer, Jack. You got this, hit me back." He clapped his phone shut.

"Why isn't she answering?"

"I don't know."

"Now what?"

Jackson scanned the grounds. "We've got a lot of open terrain to cover on this side," he said, noting the tree line. "Let's cross over, then we can sneak around behind the garage. Limits our exposure from the house."

"Sneak over? The valet will spot us for sure."

"Then let's not sneak. Just act like we're a couple out for a stroll around the grounds."

"And if he's been told to watch for us too?"

"Then we resort to Plan B?"

"Which is?"

"To be determined." He didn't give her any more time to think about it, instead taking hold of her hand and pulling her around the corner of the house. He forced himself to walk leisurely. To her credit, Ruby Mae again got into character, holding his hand and arm and cozying up to his shoulder.

Their movement attracted the valet's attention, and he turned their way briefly. He didn't startle or double-take. He didn't make a run for the front door, blow a whistle, or reach for a radio. He just continued to stand in place, very proper.

"We're good," Jackson whispered. They kept strolling, and he smiled and nodded and offered an "Evening" to the valet as they passed. He returned it with a smile.

They continued around the front of the porch. The garage was a hundred feet ahead and to their left, beside a pair of willow trees glowing green in the evening sunlight. Still in front of the house, Jackson angled them to the right a little, so the columns of the porch would block them from the valet. His plan was to continue strolling leisurely, assuming no one from out back saw them around the corner of the house, and then dart under the shade of the willows to the rear of the garage.

Ruby Mae spoiled his plan. "We've got a problem," she said.

"What?"

She stopped and turned, pointing to her left, to the edge of the driveway. Jackson followed her gaze and saw a black Jetta parked between an Audi and a Hummer.

"That's my car. So where is Sawyer?"

Jackson tried to quell the panic rising up in him. There were numerous reasons why she hadn't reached the car yet and wasn't answering her phone. She could have taken an alternate route to the front door to avoid security. She could have stopped off for some Muffuletta pinwheels. She could have been grabbed by Louviere's goons and was now tied to a chair in the wine cellar being interrogated.

"Where is she?" Ruby Mae asked.

"I don't know," Jackson said, studying the Jetta. The sun was from the opposite side, enabling him to clearly see into the front seat. No driver, no passenger.

He reached for his phone again, but Ruby Mae stopped him with a hand on his elbow.

"What?"

She pointed in the other direction, around the corner of the house, under the shade of the giant live oak, down to the willows on the edge of Lake Pontchartrain. Two people were walking slowly, side by side, on the path leading between the willows toward the boathouse. One was a man in a bright white shirt and maroon pants. The other was a woman in a floral sundress, her blond hair glistening in the sunlight.

"Isn't that Sawyer?" she asked.

Jackson frowned. "Yeah. Any idea who that is with her?"

"Actually, yeah. That's Martin Louviere Jr."

"That's Junior?"

She nodded. "He was wearing a maroon suit, like he's Samuel L. Jackson or somebody. Must have shed the coat."

"What is he doing with Sawyer? Why are they going to the boathouse?"

"Doesn't look like she's under duress."

He looked at her. "What do you know about Junior Louviere?"

"He's the grown son of a wealthy businessman. Draw your stereotypes and he fits every one."

"So if he was headed to the boathouse with a woman . . ."

Ruby Mae nodded.

"Not Sawyer," Jackson said.

"And not now."

"So what's going on?"

"How do you want to play this?" she asked.

He thought for a moment. "How many other women have you seen with a red dress?"

"Here? One or two."

"Doesn't seem like Louviere's turned this into a police state, but it won't be forever before they start piecing this together and figure out you're with me."

"I never saw the guard's face, meaning he never saw mine."

"No, but he might have seen a woman in a red dress, and the valet saw our faces."

"Circumstantial."

"In a courtroom, sure."

"Plus my father, who will vouch for me no matter what. I'm not worried about me."

"Okay. Then lay low while I go get Sawyer."

"Wait, lay low? And what do you mean, 'get' Sawyer?"

"I mean whatever I have to do."

"I can help."

"You're right, your exposure is minimal right now. Let's keep it that way, to make sure Daddy's vouching for you is good enough."

"So, what, just hide in the trees?"

"Maybe not in that get-up, but maybe hang out in the dining room. And stay by a window or door and keep an eye out for us."

"I've got a better idea," she said.

"I'm listening."

"What if I go on offense?"

"Offense?"

"Go back to the party, act as if nothing happened. If they're looking for me, I'll cut them off at the pass."

He thought for a moment. "Could work. But the exit strategy's not good. How do we get back to you?"

"You don't. Sawyer has the key. So when you 'get' her, hit the road."

"And call you an Uber?"

"I'll ride home with my father."

"Won't that leave the somewhat awkward matter of explaining what happened to your car?"

"Dad only knows I rode with my date. He doesn't know we took my car." She shrugged. "I'll tell him the chump left without me."

"How are we supposed to get your car back to you?"

Ruby Mae reached into her purse and came out with a business card for a New Orleans bank. She was an assistant manager. "Call me and tell me where you put it. We can work out all the details on the phone, but right now, time's wasting."

"You sure about this?"

"I'm positive. Go."

He raised his eyebrows and handed the business card back to her. "Won't look good if I get caught with this. Besides, I memorized your cell."

"Already?"

"Yeah. Thanks for everything, Ruby Mae."

She leaned forward and gave him a very quick kiss, so impassionate it was practically biblical. But still with a little spark. Then she turned back toward the stairs on the end of the porch, theoretically circumventing the valet. Jackson, meanwhile, rolled down the sleeves of his dress shirt and unbuttoned his vest. He tossed it behind a bush on the north side of the house, then cinched his tie a little tighter. It was as much as he could alter his appearance on short notice.

He had the length of a football field to get to the boathouse. For most of that distance, once he came around the northeast corner of the house, he would be visible to anyone on the patio or deck. Working in his favor was the shade of the live oak he could walk in for a while and the fact that he doubted Louviere's people were waiting in sniper's nests for him to show his face. Still, his odds weren't great.

He walked with purpose as if he had nothing to hide. He stole several fleeting glances toward the patio, seeing that not much had changed since he'd last been outside forty-five minutes to an hour ago. Maybe it had thinned a little. His furtive peeks did not reveal the location of Louviere or any of his henchmen.

Exiting from under the live oak, Jackson turned his attention toward the lake ahead of him. He saw two people standing at the water's edge, actually on the beach. Other than them, the lawn was empty. Long shadows of grayish green stretched across it, knifing into otherwise orange-tinged grass. The willows ahead of him, around the boathouse, were imbued with light, whereas the ground beneath them was murky with shadow. What had Sawyer and Junior Louviere been doing? Was she his prisoner? Had he been holding an unseen weapon? What part of the equation was Jackson missing?

He was halfway between the patio and the boathouse when Junior Louviere appeared from out of the willows. He walked purposefully up the boardwalk and then across the lawn, toward the patio, passing within a few yards. He never slowed, offering a quick head nod at Jackson.

Now he was really confused. He thought about stopping Junior, about confronting him. But Junior had shown no signs of recognizing Jackson, and if he had done something sinister to Sawyer, he had the best poker face Jackson had ever seen. Sensing it prudent, Jackson kept going.

He reached the planks leading through the trees and chanced a quick look back. Junior was almost to the patio. Nothing indicated Jackson had been spotted by anyone else or that Louviere's security forces had been alerted. He stepped into the shade of the trees and hurried down the boardwalk to the boathouse.

It was big. Jackson guessed almost a thousand square feet per level. There were two, and a cupola, like on the main house. About a quarter of the boathouse rested on dry land. The rest extended over the lake, which was calm as it shone in the setting sun. The boardwalk through the trees transitioned into a small deck, and then to a dock running parallel to the shore for twenty-five to thirty feet. It then jutted out into the water as far as the boathouse did. A trio of old-fashioned lampposts were spaced equally along it, their lamps providing soft light over the otherwise mostly shaded dock.

Jackson stepped gingerly onto the deck, stopping at the door. It was recessed under a small awning, lit by lamps similar to those on the dock. Four windows, two on each level, were all dark.

Jackson turned the knob, and the door opened. He stepped carefully into the boathouse. There were stairs immediately to his right. A closet to the left. Lockers beyond the stairs and a workbench on the left. Beyond the lockers and workbench, the wood floor formed a U-shaped platform around a yacht that barely fit inside the boathouse. Its gleaming white hull, darkly tinted windows, and chrome railings all gave it a sleek, speedy appearance. Even its position, situated with the long bow pressed right against the large overhead door, gave the impression it was ready to race across the lake.

The yacht creaked once, then twice, floating on the water with no margin on either side. Jackson saw no signs that anyone was on or had been on the yacht, and he turned for the stairs.

Like those in Louviere's secret passageway, they reversed on themselves halfway up, opening to a narrow corridor running perpendicular to shore. A small bathroom was across the corridor from the stairs. Bedrooms, as evidenced by the open doors, were next down the corridor, which then opened to a room spanning the full width of the boathouse and covering the back half of the second level. The wood floor was covered in a large throw rug, which provided space for a loveseat and two chairs. They were oriented around an unlit fireplace, the stone façade of which caught the glow of the setting sun through windows on the opposite side. So did the blond hair of a woman in a floral sundress.

Sawyer.

"Decided you were just having too much fun to leave?" Jackson asked.

She startled briefly, and her shoulders noticeably slumped when she saw Jackson. "What are you doing here?"

"I was going to ask you the same thing."

"I asked—"

"First, yeah. I'm looking for my getaway driver."

"Sorry, I was interrupted by Junior."

"Interrupted?"

"As I was headed for the front door, he stopped me."

"Smiling, making small talk, flirting a little?"

"I tried to brush him off, but he mentioned my interest in historical artifacts and he said there was something he wanted to show me."

"You're not serious?"

"I knew it was possible he was just feeding me a line, but he seemed genuine, then and now. He said it was in the boathouse. I figured it was worth a shot, that maybe he'd show me something that would help us, and I could always grab Ruby Mae's car and pick you guys up a little ways down the driveway. Where is she by the way?"

"Providing cover. So where's Junior? What'd he want to show you?"

"This," she said, nodding at the painting over the fireplace. Set in an ornamented frame was a large oil painting depicting a ship sailing through rough seas. To Jackson's eye, the ship looked an awful lot like the model on Louviere's office bookshelf. But what really drew his attention was the small gold plate on the bottom of the frame. Etched into its surface were two words: *Majesté Royale*.

Jackson looked at Sawyer. "Toussaint's ship?"

"Uh-huh. The one that picked up Brackett."

"Did Junior say anything about it?"

"No. He didn't even get to say anything. He suggested I make myself comfortable while he went to get a bottle of wine." She shrugged. "I figured it was a decent idea because it would give me a few minutes to look around on my own before I slipped away."

"You find anything?"

"Just the painting. There's other nautical décor, but nothing that seems relevant or to be anything more than a decoration."

"Okay. Then let's get going. Unless you want to stay behind and have a glass of Chardonnay with Junior."

"Come on, tell me if it was you and a beautiful woman in a shimmering red dress, you wouldn't have tried the same thing."

"That's different."

"How so?"

"I'm a sucker for a pretty face, and you're a refined Southern woman."

She grinned.

"You did good, Sawyer. Now let's get out of here before Romeo gets back."

"Yeah, sure."

Jackson let her go down the corridor first. He paused at the top of the steps to look out the window. Then he put out a hand. "Wait, wait, wait."

"What?"

"Either I wasn't as sneaky as I thought, or Loverboy set you up."

She stood beside him and peeked her head around the side of the window. Like Jackson, she was now looking at four men in dark jackets and dark pants approaching the boathouse.

Chapter Thirty-Three

7:04 p.m.

"WHAT DO WE do?" Sawyer asked.

"Make yourself comfortable on the couch and play dumb," he said, reaching into his pockets. He lifted out his wallet and his phone.

"What?"

"Nowhere to run, nowhere to hide. Where's your purse? And Junior had no reason to set you up, so they're here for me."

"What are you going to do?" she asked, holding out her purse to him.

He put his wallet and phone in the purse and handed it back. "Nothing, because I was never here." He hurried down the steps.

"Jackson."

"Trust me."

He hit the bottom of the stairs and fired a glance out the window. The four men were a dozen paces from the door. Praying he was right and they wouldn't harm Sawyer, he ran along the platform to the bow of the yacht, to the one place where he could enter the water. Taking a deep breath, he dropped into the water, finding it cooler than he had expected.

He stroked toward shore, following the yacht's hull as a guide. He hoped that he could find a pocket of air when he reached the shore, beneath the part of the boathouse that was over dry land. If not, he was sunk. Literally.

In books and movies, people could hold their breath interminably. Jackson's supply was running short, and he considered turning back and trying to come up under the bow. Then he felt solid ground beneath him and crawled and clambered forward. When his torso was out of the water, he turned over and breathed deeply, staring up at the floor joists.

He could hear the platform creaking above him as the four men searched the boathouse. He heard voices, but couldn't interpret them. More creaking.

They were moving about. Then less. And more distant. They had gone upstairs.

Jackson exhaled, praying that Sawyer could keep cool. He smiled mid-prayer. Of course she would keep cool. She was a poised, confident, refined Southern woman. So he prayed instead that the goon squad would buy whatever she told them and leave her alone.

A minute passed. Maybe two. Then the creaking got louder. Ripples of water washed against Jackson's body. At first, he feared they were onto him and one of the men had entered the water. Then he realized they were aboard the yacht.

More creaking, now of different tones and pitches. More ripples too. A few hard to interpret voices. They talked for maybe thirty seconds, mostly garbled, but Jackson did pick up a few words: shore, trees, party, lying. He had no way to piece them together, and no time. Loud creaking followed by a slamming door was followed by silence, and he expertly deduced the men had moved on.

Taking a couple deep breaths, Jackson eased back into the water and managed to turn around without concussing himself on the yacht's hull or the underside of the platform. He crawled and swam back toward the bow, and as soon as he had clearance, poked his head up above the surface. It was possible one man had stayed behind, but he had to risk it. The alternative was blacking out.

The coast was clear, and Jackson hauled himself onto the platform. As he did, Sawyer descended from the second story. "Are you okay?" she asked.

"I'll dry. They believe you?"

"Seemed to. I went out onto the balcony and told them I'd been there for several minutes, waiting for Junior. I figured they might have followed you, and that would give me plausible deniability."

"That's good thinking."

"So now what? Junior will be back any minute." She turned and looked out the window. "In fact, he's coming now."

"How far?"

"End of the patio."

"See any of the guards?"

"No."

Jackson thought for a second about making a break for it. Even though she could see Junior, he would be looking into the shade, and might not see them. They could scurry to the tree line and . . .

One of the four men had said "tree" or "trees." They would be looking there. Besides, Sawyer was in a dress and heels. Not exactly make-a-break-for-it apparel.

"Jackson?"

He tipped his head. "Make yourself comfortable again."

"Seriously?"

"When he comes up, take his hand and lead him to the balcony."

"And then what?"

"I'll think of something. Go."

She didn't hesitate but turned and climbed the stairs. Jackson sat back on the platform and eased back into the water. He didn't submerge, instead hovering under the bow, out of sight from the entry. He put himself in Junior's shoes. He had a bottle of wine, a pretty girl waiting for him by the fireplace upstairs. He wasn't going to dawdle. Hopefully, he wouldn't notice all the water on the platform either.

Jackson heard Junior enter, and heard his footfalls on the stairs as the door closed behind him. He chanced a peek around the yacht, saw nothing, and quietly climbed back onto the platform.

He was dripping audibly and did his best to wring out his clothes. He removed his shoes, setting them by the lockers and padding toward the stairs. He was still dripping, but short of undressing, couldn't do much about it. He listened for a moment, then climbed the stairs.

He paused at the next to last step, listening again. Quiet. He took a step and extended his head. The living room, as far as he could see, was empty. A bottle of wine sat on a small coffee table, unopened, next to a pair of wine glasses.

Jackson stepped into the hallway and inched forward, leaving wet, smudgy footprints. He stopped again at the entrance to the living room, seeing nothing. At the end of the room, French doors—with all too familiar sheer curtains—opened to the balcony. One door was half ajar. Jackson crept forward, around the loveseat, pausing within reach of the ajar door. He again listened.

Sawyer giggled.

Sawyer did not, in his experience, giggle.

He used his finger to edge one of the sheer curtains aside an inch, just enough to see through the glass.

Junior stood with his back to Jackson, a foot beyond the closed door, and angled slightly to his left. Sawyer stood facing him on the opposite side, her back to the railing. As Jackson watched, Junior reached up and moved a strand of hair off the side of Sawyer's forehead. Judging by the few romantic movies Jackson had been coerced into watching over the years, he guessed he had at best fifteen seconds before Junior made his move.

So Jackson made his.

He stepped to his left, giving him line of sight through the ajar door out to the lake. He gripped the handle of the left door with his left hand, silently twisting it. Then he yanked it open, taking a half step forward with his left foot.

Junior spun around at the sound, spinning into a right-fisted haymaker Jackson threw with all his weight. Full Joe Frazier, practically jumping out of his shoes to kayo Muhammad Ali. His momentum carried him forward, and he would have fallen into Junior if Junior had still been there to fall into. But the punch had caught him flush, spinning his jaw, and turning out his lights. He fell half against Sawyer and half against the railing, then slumped to the balcony deck like an invertebrate.

Jackson managed to keep from falling on top of him, taking a few hop steps and reaching for the railing for balance. He looked up at Sawyer, who had recoiled back and out of the way, and also emitted a soft cry of alarm.

"You wanna maybe shout 'Intruder!' while you're at it?" Jackson asked.

"I'm sorry. You surprised me."

"Him too. Let's get him inside."

Junior was out cold, and Jackson and Sawyer dragged and carried him into the living room and onto the loveseat. Sawyer looked down at him. "He was a nice guy."

"He still is. He's not dead."

"You sure?"

"Chest's rising and falling." He looked at her. "You okay?"

"I got out of the way."

"No, I mean being bait. I thought he might pour a glass of wine before going in for the kill."

She raised an eyebrow. "I was wondering how far I'd have to carry the charade."

"I had to let Ruby Mae kiss me."

"Had to?"

"Semantics. What do you say we get out of here?"

"Love to."

They walked to the top of the stairs, and Jackson again peeked out the window. Darkness was falling fast, with almost the entire property in shadow. That was good and bad. It made it hard for anyone to spot them, but also made it hard for Jackson to see if any of Louviere's people were lurking about.

"I've got an idea," he said.

"Why is my stomach falling already?"

"We've got a lot of ground to cover, you're in heels, and I stand out like a sore thumb being half drowned." He started down the steps.

"Are you just trying to cheer me up?"

He stopped at the landing and looked at the yacht.

"You're not thinking of stealing Louviere's boat, are you?"

"Not me," he said with a grin at her. He winked and started back up the stairs.

*   *   *

7:26 p.m.

FROM THE helm of Louviere's yacht, Jackson looked at Sawyer. "You ready?" he asked.

"Ready."

He turned the ignition, and the yacht's diesel engines grumbled to life. More like purred. He pushed a button on a small remote control attached to the console, and the overhead door of the boathouse began to open. Thankfully it was well maintained, lubricated, and probably new, and it was as quiet as the yacht's engines.

Jackson looked back at Sawyer. She nodded again. He turned his focus to the door. As soon as it was higher than the bow, Jackson eased the throttle ahead. Instantly, he turned and scrambled down from the helm to the stern platform. It was already several feet from the boathouse platform, and he jumped. His penny loafers were still wet and provided very little traction, so it was closer than it should have been, but he made it. He took one last look at the yacht as it edged out into the lake before he joined Sawyer at the boathouse door.

"All clear," she said, opening it.

"Let's go."

He led the way out into the gloom. Sunset wasn't for another half hour or so, but the trees around Pontchartrain Manor were tall enough that sunset had effectively occurred. It was especially dark in the shade created by the willow trees that surrounded the boathouse. Jackson and Sawyer used them to slink quickly toward the thicker trees on the property's northern edge. They did so without spotting any dark-jacketed security personnel and without, presumably, being spotted by any of them.

The foliage was thick, and Jackson had second thoughts about entering it. But they were committed now. Pushing aside twigs and branches, he led them several yards into the overgrowth, far enough that they would be hidden from the sight of anyone at the party.

He led, keeping his eyes peeled. He doubted alligators invaded the trees, but more varieties of snakes than he cared to imagine surely did. Water moccasins and cottonmouths and bayou boa constrictors. Not to mention poisonous tree frogs, probably a number of deadly insects, maybe a few panthers or badgers or ROUS. Sawyer followed with a hand on his shoulder, keeping whatever fears she had to herself.

The foliage thinned a little, and Jackson caught a glimpse of the house up ahead. They were halfway there, he figured. He heard the sounds of the party—the din of multiple conversations, the strains of the string quartet, an occasional clink of a glass or silverware on a plate. No shouts or cries of alarm, no panicked voices. That was good.

Sawyer squeezed his shoulder, and he stopped. She let go of him and reached down to undo her sandals.

"I can't walk in these things in here."

"Want me to carry you?"

She laughed softly.

"What?"

"Jackson, I grew up running around barefoot through the swamp."

"Step on a black widow spider, don't say I didn't offer."

"Let's keep moving."

They did, avoiding detection or wild animal encounters until they reached the maintenance shed. They emerged from the trees on its far side, using it and several willow trees to conceal them as they crept toward the near corner of the garage. They stopped again, less than forty feet from Ruby Mae's black Jetta.

Sawyer looked at Jackson, waiting.

He tore his eyes away from the lake a hundred or so yards to his left, and from the white yacht gleaming in the sunlight as it puttered slowly away from shore.

"You still have the key?" he asked.

"Yeah, but what about her?"

"New plan. She said we could take it and rendezvous later."

"Are you serious?"

"I am. And if you don't mind, I'll explain the fine print on the road."

Sawyer opened her purse, which she had hung onto the entire walk, and withdrew a key. "Why don't you drive this time?"

He nodded, took the key, and looked for people. There were two valets now, but currently no partiers ready to leave. The valets were talking to each other, one leaning against the column at the base of the porch stairs and one shuffling from foot to foot. Neither was looking toward the garage.

"Okay," Jackson said. "Walk quietly but naturally, not like you're slinking. If they do see us, good chance they'll think we just walked around the house, and it's too dark for them to see that I'm still soaked or to ID us."

"Okay," she said.

"If something does happen, watch my cue."

She nodded.

"Let's go."

They walked quickly but naturally. Jackson kept his eyes roving between the valets, Ruby Mae's car, and the rest of the grounds. They reached the car unobserved, and he quickly unlocked his door, opened it, and let Sawyer in.

Before buckling in, before she was almost seated, he had the car started and in gear. He backed out, forcing himself to follow his earlier advice and behave naturally. No careening wildly as he backed up or tearing down the driveway. He drove like an aristocrat leaving a gala. His few glances in his mirrors indicated nothing out of the usual.

"Is it that easy?" Sawyer asked, turning around to face forward as they made their way down the driveway.

"Maybe."

"Maybe?"

He briefly explained Ruby Mae's deal with him, how she would go on offense and cover for them, and they would return her car later. By the time he was finished, they were on the two-lane road, headed west. "If Louviere or Ruby Mae's dad get suspicious," he said, "they could figure out pretty quickly we're in her car, report it as stolen, put out an APB . . ." He looked at Sawyer. "I'll rest easy when we've dumped the car and are tucked away safely in our hotel."

Sawyer sighed and sat back. She was silent until Jackson turned onto Old U.S. 51. Then she turned his way. "What do you think will happen to Junior?"

"He'll wake up with a very sore jaw, wondering why he's the only one on the yacht and if he actually drank that whole bottle of wine himself."

"You don't think spilling it all over him was a little much?"

"He did try to get fresh with you."

Sawyer narrowed her eyes slightly.

"What?"

"Is that why you coldcocked him?"

"Why?"

"Some combination of chivalry and protectiveness."

"No. I coldcocked him because it was the quickest way I could think of to eliminate an obstacle in the way of our escape."

"I see."

"Chivalry is why I enjoyed it."

"I see," she said again, this time with a budding grin.

Chapter Thirty-Four

9:18 p.m.

"MMM," SAWYER SAID, closing her eyes. "Sometimes you just need a big, greasy hamburger."

Jackson nodded and chomped on his po'boy, a disastrously messy combination of shrimp, buffalo sauce, some sort of Cajun slaw mixture, and tomatoes that hit the spot.

They had parked Ruby Mae's Jetta in a safe-looking free lot not far from the Superdome and taken a cab back to the Hotel Étienne. Sawyer had let him shower first, under the provision that he procure dinner afterward while she did. He'd found a sandwich and burger joint a few doors down that satisfied their cravings, and had returned to their suite just as she'd been exiting the bathroom. That had been five minutes and half of two sandwiches ago.

"Although, there's something to be said for fine French dining," Sawyer added. "And we are in New Orleans."

"Yeah, well, you're not exactly dressed for it."

She looked down at the gray sweats and maroon and white raglan shirt she had changed into. "True."

Jackson took another massive bite of his po'boy and crammed a few fries into his mouth after it. They took a little of the bite out of the buffalo sauce, which was otherwise clearing his sinuses. He looked down at Sawyer's phone, which was between them on the couch, and on which she had done some brief research while he'd been in the shower. For starters, she had plugged various phrases from Toussaint's journal into online translators. Free internet software was never foolproof, and they were working off her interpretation of handwritten French via photos on a smartphone, but she had concluded Ruby Mae's initial translation had been accurate.

"So to recap," Jackson said. "On July 31ˢᵗ, 1715, Brackett and his crew hit the *Nuestra Señora de la Granada* under the command of Reynaldo Garcia III. A few days later, a hurricane slams the keys, sinks the *Barracuda*, and seemingly wipes Brackett and his treasure into the history books. Except a month and a half later, a French merchant ship picks a delirious Brackett up off a small island in the Bahamas. He's cuckoo for Cocoa Puffs, and all he says is something about rich man's bones. The *Majesté Royale* drops him off in soon to be New Orleans, where he again disappears for three years until his ghost curses the *Missianna* as it sails for the Bahamas. Does that about sum things up?"

Sawyer nodded and munched on a few fries before returning to her burger like a starving man attacking a turkey leg.

"And somehow," Jackson continued, "Martin Louviere—whose ancestors were big in the shipping industry in the fledgling city of New Orleans—has Toussaint's journal, a journal that Damon knew about and told Ben about. Now Damon's dead, Ben's dead, and Louviere denies it all. Factor in a dead Louisianan named Ryker, and a corrupt NOLA cop who is covering up the truth about Damon's death, and did I miss anything?"

"You forgot that Louviere has a painting of Toussaint's ship and a pretty close replica of it in his office, by the journal," she paused from eating long enough to say.

"So either the Toussaints changed their name to Louviere somewhere along the way or Marty developed some sort of a fixation."

"Or the Bracketts changed their name," she said.

He snapped his fingers. "Didn't you say there was a rumor that Brackett had a wife and kids?"

"Yeah. Just a rumor."

"Maybe when he arrived in Would-be New Orleans, crazy as a loon, some pretty little local girl nursed him back to health and won his heart."

"Could be."

"Then he and she set sail, perhaps still pale from the sickness and looking ghostlike, to find a buried treasure that would serve as their nest egg."

"Good as any rumor," she said before biting down into her burger.

He leaned back. "What if the local nurse just happened to be the daughter of a shipping magnate?"

Sawyer swallowed. "What, Louviere?"

"It would explain his fixation with the treasure."

"So would gleaming, glittery piles of gold."

"True."

He took a long slurp on his milkshake. Sawyer cast him a disapproving glare, but he silenced it by reminding her that she was ranch-dipping French fries while dressed like a Crimson Tide defensive lineman.

"So you think the treasure's buried in the Bahamas then?" she asked.

"Only reason I can think of for him wanting to go back there."

"Which you're assuming because Grover's 'great, great grandpappy' referenced a legend that said the *Missianna* was headed there, without any evidence or reason why."

"You disagree?"

"I just think there's not more there than rumor." She took a drink of her milkshake with dignity.

"There's also the question of why he was in the Bahamas in the first place."

"You think he was hiding the treasure?"

"Maybe."

"After surviving the hurricane?"

"It would explain why there isn't any gold down on the wreck of the *Barracuda*."

She furrowed her chin. "It would. Still a lot of missing pieces, though."

"Admittedly. But it's a theory." He exhaled and sat back. "Rich man's bones. You happen to run that through the online translator?"

"Um-hmm."

"Same thing?"

"Yep. Ruby Mae nailed it."

"Rich man's bones," he repeated.

"You ever call her yet?" Sawyer asked.

"No, I was letting the heat die down a little."

"Maybe you should. In the rush, we didn't ask if the journal gave any more details about which island it was or where in the Bahamas."

"Southern was all she said," Jackson answered. "But I'll call her."

He did, pacing out onto the balcony after punching in her cell number from memory. The air was still warm, but pleasant compared to the heat of the day. And somehow, being surrounded by the hubbub of the French

Quarter made what had taken place a few hours earlier seem a lot more distant.

"This is Ruby Mae."

"Ruby, the hay is in the barn."

"Jackson?"

"Safe and sound in New Orleans."

"I was starting to wonder. Louviere turned this place upside down."

"You're still there?"

"He and my father are meeting, and someone took my car."

"Are you okay? They don't suspect anything?"

"No. The guard who saw you is colorblind. They've been looking for a brunette in a pink gown."

"Huh. By coincidence, so was I."

"Funny."

Jackson smiled himself for a second. "So why's he tearing the place upside down?"

"Looking for the guy who assaulted his son," she said, an accusatory question hanging in the air.

"Somebody assaulted Junior?"

"Out on the lake, on Martin's yacht. It was spotted half a mile from shore, didn't respond to any calls, and finally had to be chased down by a neighbor's fishing boat. Junior was just coming to, sloppy drunk, claiming he wasn't, and asking about Savannah."

"Never heard of her."

"Uh-huh. Long story short, Junior finally convinced everyone he wasn't drunk and had been walloped in the jaw by some unseen guy."

"Didn't get a look at him, huh?"

Ruby Mae's smile almost came through the phone. "No. Louviere figured it was the same guy who broke into his office, and he started a property-wide manhunt. Just short of bringing in dogs, I think."

"Any sign of actual law enforcement?"

"None. Sounds like he wants to handle this in-house."

"Hmm."

"Kind of killed the party. Now I'm sitting here alone at the bar while he and Dad talk about who knows what."

"Well, that's a sad picture, you alone at the bar."

"Tell me about it."

"Where's the chump who brought you to the party?"

"He went home in my car, remember?"

"For real?"

"Went home with the slinky blonde, I'm guessing."

"Sorry."

"Yeah, well, win some, lose some."

Jackson segued into a thank you and explained where they had left her car, key under the visor. He then asked if there was anything else she had gleaned from the brief look at Captain Eamon Toussaint's journal, particularly as it related to a location in the Bahamas.

"No," she said. "It wasn't specific. Just 'southern Bahamas.' It was probably all they knew. Most of the islands didn't have names back then, I'm guessing."

"Anything else you saw that happened to trigger a thought, you know, while you're sitting alone at the bar?"

"You're a real smart-aleck, you know that?"

"So I've been told."

"No, nothing else. Sorry, looks like you went through all that for nothing."

"Not nothing," he said. "I got to kiss a pretty Louisiana girl."

"And don't you forget it."

"I doubt I will. Thanks, Ruby Mae."

"Anytime," she said with just a touch more of that rich, soft Southern accent. He closed his phone with his chin and held it there for a moment, thinking. He'd thanked her for her help. The way she'd said "anytime" made him wonder if she had been thinking about that or about the kiss. More likely just messing with him.

He turned to go back inside, but Sawyer met him at the door.

"Hey."

"Hey," she said. "Any luck?"

"No."

She nodded, held up her phone, and then sat in one of the two chairs on the balcony. "So I've been doing some research. Seven hundred islands in the Bahamas."

His eyebrows went up.

"Seven hundred. Not to mention what three hundred years' of tides and hurricanes might have done to little cays and spits of land."

Jackson too sat down. "Any of them happen to be called Rich Man's Island?"

She shook her head, looking back down at her phone. She scooted her chair closer, and so did he. "This is an alphabetical list of every island with a name in the Bahamas. There's no Rich Man's Island."

"He never said it was an island. Just that he wanted to find the rich man's bones."

"I know, and for all we know it could be actual bones. But I thought maybe it was some geographical feature or something. Besides, I Googled it and got nothing. So I'm thinking it has to be some sort of ancient colloquialism."

"Makes sense." He shrugged. "Let's look through the list."

Sawyer jumped to the top of the list and slowly scrolled down. They made it to the L's before one of the names practically jumped off the screen.

"There!" Jackson said.

Sawyer saw it too. "Lazarus Island."

"That cannot be coincidence," Jackson said.

She handed him the phone and got up. She ducked back inside and returned less than a minute later, carrying a hotel Bible. "Not King James," she said, "but it will have to do."

"One gets by when one travels."

She flipped it open and in seconds was reading aloud.

"There was a rich man who was dressed in purple and fine linen and lived in luxury every day. At his gate was laid a beggar named Lazarus, covered with sores and longing to eat what fell from the rich man's table. Even the dogs came and licked his sores.

"The time came when the beggar died and the angels carried him to Abraham's side. The rich man also died and was buried. In Hades, where he was in torment, he looked up and saw Abraham far away, with Lazarus by his side. So he called to him, 'Father Abraham, have pity on me and send Lazarus to dip the tip of his finger in water and cool my tongue, because I am in agony in this fire.'

"But Abraham replied, 'Son, remember that in your lifetime you received your good things, while Lazarus received bad things, but now he is comforted here and you are in agony. And besides all this, between us and you a great chasm has been set in place, so that those who want to go from here to you cannot, nor can anyone cross over from there to us.'

"*He answered, 'Then I beg you, father, send Lazarus to my family, for I have five brothers. Let him warn them, so that they will not also come to this place of torment.'*

"*Abraham replied, 'They have Moses and the Prophets; let them listen to them.'*

"*No, father Abraham,' he said, 'but if someone from the dead goes to them, they will repent.*

"*He said to him, 'If they do not listen to Moses and the Prophets, they will not be convinced even if someone rises from the dead.'"*

She looked up at him, slowly closing the Bible. For several minutes, neither of them spoke. Then she said, "So if the island is Lazarus, who is the rich man and what are his bones?"

"Is there another island nearby? Maybe a bigger one?"

Sawyer pulled up a satellite map and zoomed in on the Bahamas until she found Lazarus Island. Located in the southwestern corner of the chain, it was fairly isolated from the rest, twenty to twenty-five miles away from any other major islands. The island ran northwest to southeast, less than three miles in length.

"No," she said. "Nothing."

"Wait, what's that?"

He pointed, and she zoomed in on a small speck of white about ten miles southeast of Lazarus Island. It was shaped like a mitten, and was, according to the key, only a few hundred feet in length. "Not a rich man," Jackson said with a sigh. "It's barely more than a sandbar."

"But look at this." She pointed to the name that had appeared on the screen. "Little Lazarus Island."

Without him having to suggest it, Sawyer entered both Lazarus Island and Little Lazarus Island into a search engine. Lazarus Island had a few hits, including a Visit Lazarus Island tourist page. But nothing in its history that hinted at rich man's bones or Captain Brackett or anything of the like. Little Lazarus Island had nothing but a Wikipedia page that identified its coordinates in the ocean. And searches of Lazarus Island or Little Lazarus Island combined with 'rich man's bones' brought up nothing but the Bible passage from Luke and random nonsense.

Jackson sighed. "We're still nowhere."

Sawyer sat back in her chair.

"What's the main island like?" he asked after a minute. "Maybe there's a rock formation or some geographic feature that resembles a skull or a skeleton."

Sawyer returned to the satellite image on her phone, and they examined the island together. There were no small number of cays and reefs forming the edges of the island, which save for a long, crescent beach on its western shore, was mostly jagged. However, nothing along the shore—none of the visible reefs or outlying spits of land—resembled anything even remotely skeletal.

"What are we missing?" Sawyer asked.

"I don't know. But I'll bet you that fine French dinner you were talking about the answer's on one of those two islands."

Chapter Thirty-Five

10:03 p.m.

HIS BACK STIFF, Jackson stood and walked to the balcony railing. Contrasted with the night before, the New Orleans streets below were filled with cars and pedestrians. Music wafted out of bars and restaurants, and the smells of food and liquor and who knew what else fueled the ambiance. Jackson and Sawyer, on their balcony, were immune to it all, lost in a world of Bahamian islands, Bible verses, and Brackett legends.

Sawyer joined him at the railing. She turned his way, blond hair hanging at her cheek. "What are you thinking?" she asked.

"About flying to Lazarus Island to look for pirate treasure." He made eye contact with her. "And about why I'm thinking about doing it. About why I'm doing anything."

"About Ben?"

"Him too." He turned to face her. "I won't lie to you Sawyer, I've got the jazz."

"The jazz?"

"Something Hannibal used to say, on *The A-Team*."

"I never saw it."

"Too much time running around barefoot in the swamp?"

"The jazz?" she asked, a hint of bemusement in her eyes.

"I'm excited about the hunt. Grover's stories and crashing the party and making a mad getaway, and now having a clue, another lead to pursue, nebulous as it may be."

"It brings out the investigator in you."

"It does. But it's more than that. It's the pot of gold at the end of the rainbow. I can't deny that's appealing."

She nodded slowly. "To me too."

"Really?"

Sawyer tucked hair behind her ear. "I've lived my whole life simply, from growing up in a small country cottage, making do with garage sale toys and clothes passed down from my cousin. I live in a house smaller than Martin Louviere's bathroom, for crying out loud. And I'm happy. I'm content. And yet . . ." She shook her head. "I can't lie to you either. The treasure—even the possibility of treasure—calls to me. Like sirens beckoning to Odysseus."

"Wow, now you're sailing references over my head. Touché."

"What do we do, Jackson?"

"I don't know."

A few minutes of silence passed.

"It's not just the treasure," he said. "It's like we've been saying, I want the truth. I want to know what happened to Ben, and why. I want the people responsible to pay for what they did. And I don't want them getting their hands on the treasure."

"Me either."

"Part of me thinks maybe we should go after it to keep them from getting it and to—I don't know, this sounds dumb . . ."

"Honor him by finishing what he started?"

He looked at her. "Yeah. How'd you know?"

"I've had the same thought."

"Thing is, I can't tell if that's a legit thought or just an effort to satisfy my conscience that I'm not going full Gordon Gecko." He waved her off before she could ask.

"What do we do, Jackson?" she asked again. She looked straight at him, waiting on his decision.

He took a long look out at the city, to the sky beyond, in the direction of Key West, where this had all started. Slowly, he drew his eyes back to Sawyer. Hers hadn't left him.

"We finish what we started," he said. "We set out to get to the bottom of this, find out what happened to Ben, find out who's behind it. We have no proof that Louviere's done anything, no way to evidentially tie him to Ben or Damon. So we either quit or play this out. And like I said, we finish what we started."

"By pursuing the treasure."

"It's the only lead we have. And the further we follow it, and the closer we get, the more likely I think we are of drawing out Louviere and whoever else is involved."

She looked at him.

"Could be dangerous. More dangerous than it's been so far."

"Could be."

"And the jazz and sirens, they're going to get stronger and louder."

"Probably."

"Sawyer, I . . . I don't want to be responsible if something happens to you. I can't guarantee I'll be able to protect you from Louviere or his goons or from turning into a gold-crazed forty-niner."

"I'm not asking you to, Jackson. I'm a grown woman, responsible for my own choices."

He nodded.

"And who knows that I won't be the one that ends up protecting you."

He smiled.

She placed her hand on his, on top of the railing, and squeezed. She took it back. "We should look into flights. I don't suppose it's easy to get to Lazarus Island."

"Yeah. Give me a minute?"

"Okay," she said, turning with a thin smile and heading inside.

Jackson leaned on the railing, breathing deeply, thinking about the last two days. Dixon and his alligator lair. Breaking into Damon's house. Masquerading as Damon at Pontchartrain Manor, picking his way into Louviere's office, escaping by the skin of his teeth. He was like Hannibal, on the jazz again.

He'd been on the jazz for the better part of a year, dueling with gangs in L.A., shooting up militia members in Nevada, busting out of a crooked businessman's hacienda in Mexico, eluding killers in the Middle East, and surviving terrorists in his own backyard. How much longer could this go on? How long until the jazz stopped playing?

He thought of Sawyer, sticking up for him with Sheriff Hawkins, pulling him out of the doldrums on the beach in Key West, bravely sojourning with him to New Orleans, and gamely matching him stride for stride when things got crazy. He still couldn't put his finger on it, but there was something about her. Something that made him pray, asking God for wisdom and strength to see this through—to see her through it safely. He couldn't afford to let anything happen to her, to lose her.

He'd lost too much already.

*   *   *

Two weeks ago . . .
Saturday, May 4
12:16 p.m.

"YOU LOOK good."

"So do you."

Tori Walker smiled. "I meant it."

"So did I," Jackson said.

They sat across plates of burgers and onion rings at Burger Lounge, off Arizona in Santa Monica. The last time they'd seen each other, she had been nursing a dislocated shoulder and some cuts and bruises, and Jackson had been hopped up on painkillers after Russian terrorists had used him for a punching bag. A memory Jackson was trying hard to forget. Sitting across from Tori made it fairly easy. She had a pixie face, intense green-brown eyes, and auburn hair that curled in just below her chin. Very professional but with just a hint of sass, which fit her perfectly.

"So you never said, how long have you been back in L.A.?" he asked.

"Beginning of December."

"Getting settled?"

"Now that a psycho isn't hunting me, yeah."

Five years ago when they had both lived in San Diego and worked as "grunts" at a now-defunct P.I. firm, Jackson and Tori had conspired to take down a crooked computer salesman named Skyler. They'd scammed a scammer and gotten away with it until he'd shown up in L.A. and started harassing Tori, now a self-employed private investigator just like Jackson. She'd come to him for help, at the same time as Jackson had been protecting a dying World War II vet from bomb-hunting Russians. Jackson had nearly been tortured to death by them, and Tori had escaped Skyler's attempt at retribution with help from, of all people, Maggie and her new boyfriend.

"I still can't believe he had the guts to come after you," Jackson said.

"I wish I'd had the guts to punch him in the neck."

280

"I'd pay to see that."

They each ate for a minute.

"You enjoying life as a P.I.?" he asked.

"Yes and no. I like being my own boss, but chasing claims is pretty monotonous."

"I kind of miss the insurance gig," Jackson said. "I was a claims adjustor for two years."

"And you miss that?"

"I like the freedom, like you said, but not getting your ribs ground to powder by old Soviets or blowing up old Air Force bases and killing mercenaries by the dozens has its appeals."

"Yeah, I guess. You've had quite a year."

"Has it only been that long?"

She frowned.

"Sorry, didn't mean to be a downer. So how else is life in L.A.? You settling in?"

Tori kept frowning. "What are you driving at?"

"Not driving," he said, reaching for an onion ring.

"No, you're dancing around something. Which isn't like you, Douglas."

He shrugged, finished the onion ring.

Tori leaned forward, causing her hair to flutter in front of her cheek. "Why'd you ask me to lunch, anyhow?"

"I told you, I wanted to catch up."

"M'kay. We caught up?"

"You got a hot date or something?"

She looked at him. "Is that what this is?"

"What?"

"Are you hitting on me, Douglas?"

"What?"

"You are." She sat back. "I don't believe it."

"I'm not hitting on you, Walker."

She raised an eyebrow.

"Not exactly."

"You're hitting on me," she said with incredulity both in her voice and in the furrows in her brow.

"Will you calm down?" He said. "Good grief, announce it to the whole restaurant and see if I can't end up on TMZ for sexual harassment or something."

"What?"

"Look," he said, "we're friends, right? We get along, work together well, have a secret we're both keeping. You're cute, I'm reasonably decent looking when I take care of myself. I thought, maybe, you and I could see if there's a spark there."

"You wouldn't be asking if you didn't think there was a spark."

He shrugged.

She reached over and whacked his arm. "Come on, Douglas, I've never seen you like this. You're all nervous and hesitant."

"I'm sorry. This is awkward."

"No duh."

"Look, Walker—"

"If you're going to ask me out, use my first name."

"Fair enough. Tori, would you go out with me?"

"Where?"

"I don't know."

"You really planned this well."

"I'm not looking to take you to the prom. We don't have to go on a date. I just want to know if you think there might be a spark too and want to explore the possibility."

She sat back.

He reached for a much-needed drink.

"I thought you were dating that brunette that helped me out."

"Maggie? Not so much."

"But you liked her?"

"Never met a person who didn't."

"I don't mean like that."

"Come on, Walker, I don't think it's any secret that I've liked other girls before. You're dodging the question."

"I am."

He sat back.

"Douglas, you're right. We are friends. And I like you. Just . . . this is going to sound so cold."

He made a come-here motion with his fingers.

"I like you, but not like—"

"—like that," he finished along with her.

She winced. "I'm sorry."

"Don't be sorry."

She opened her mouth, then shut it.

"It's okay, Walker. Say it."

"It's not you, it's me."

He rolled his eyes.

"I mean it. It's not that you aren't boyfriend material. I just don't see us that way. And . . . I kind of don't want to. I like us the way we are."

"'Worst she can say is no.'"

"What's that?"

He shrugged. "What I told a buddy back in college when he had his sights set on a classmate but couldn't screw up the courage to ask her out."

Elbow on the table, she coyly placed her chin her palm. "What happened?"

"She laughed at him and he overdosed a few weeks later."

"Are you serious?"

"Almost died." He shrugged. "To be fair, he did have some other issues."

She huffed. "Yikes, you throw a guilt trip."

"Relax, Walker, I'm not guilting you. And I'm not going to kill myself."

"That's good to know."

"I may, you know, take a few more reckless risks as a P.I. now . . ."

She kicked him under the table, the way Maggie always used to. Then she smiled. "We still up for hitting Venice Beach?"

"Of course." Before he could stop himself, he said the same absurd words Maggie had said to him five weeks ago. "We'll still be friends."

He hadn't believed it then, either.

Chapter Thirty-Six

Monday, May 20
3:25 p.m.

THE SUN WAS high and hot as Jackson and Sawyer's small turboprop touched down on the three-quarter-mile-long airstrip at Lazarus Island Airfield. Already, Jackson was in awe.

They had flown from New Orleans to Miami, then to Nassau where they'd had lunch during an hour-long layover. From there, they had flown almost straight south for some hundred miles over open ocean with hardly any islands even visible on the horizon. The water had been beautiful, varying shades of blue, dotted here and there with little spits of land, sandbars, or underwater rises. Sawyer had napped most of the flight, but Jackson had been unable to pull his eyes from the window.

They'd landed from the west, over the northern promontory of the island. Jackson had studied while on the flight to Miami and recognized the geographic features of Lazarus Island—North Point, East Bay, Lake Donovan, and finally the jumble of trees, brush, and ramshackle huts that made up the northeast portion of the island, next to the airfield. Woodes Town, a small fishing and tourist community that surrounded Lazarus Bight, had been on the other side of the plane, but Jackson had been able to steal a few glimpses of brightly colored buildings and teal water as they had come down.

Sawyer yawned as they walked across the apron to the small, single building beside the runway. Window air conditioners rattled beneath the windows, and the peeling shingles seemed to bake in the sun. Trees and low scrub blocked the view from ground level in all directions, and from where he stood, Jackson couldn't tell the Bahamas from Georgia.

"Did we settle on a hotel?" Jackson asked.

"Sir Donovan. We have reservations."

"Donovan. I wonder how much on this island is named for him."

"Well, you settle an island . . ."

"I suppose."

He knew, from his research, that the island had originally been settled as a British colony by Donovan Lazarus in the early 1700s, and much on the island had been named for him.

Geographically, the island ran from North Point to an unnamed spit of land three miles to the southeast. It flexed and bulged in the center, with a mass of tamarind trees covering everything south of the airport and east of Lake Donovan. West of the lake, stretching from North Point some mile and a quarter, was the crescent-shaped beachhead, a pristine run of white sand caressed by turquoise water. Along its length were several blocks of buildings—a mix of hotels, restaurants, bars and nightclubs, tourist shops, and homes—that made up Woodes Town. Situated roughly in the middle of the beach was the Hotel Sir Donovan, Jackson and Sawyer's home for the next two days, at least.

Baggage Claim at Lazarus Island Airfield was a corner of the terminal where all the bags were stowed in a pile. Both Jackson and Sawyer were traveling light, having picked up a few necessities on their way to the airport early that morning. Grabbing their luggage, they headed toward the exit where a couple of old-model taxicabs were parked, their drivers leaning on the hoods chatting, smoking, or playing on their smartphones. At least Lazarus Island had cell service.

"Preference?" Jackson asked.

"Not the smoker."

"Right." He approached the guy on his phone. He was in his thirties or forties, tanned, aloof. "Hotel Sir Donovan," Jackson said as the guy pocketed his phone.

"Five U.S."

"Here's ten," Jackson said. "Help the lady with her bag."

"The lady?" Sawyer asked when they were seated in back.

"It's how Jim Rockford talks."

"Who?"

"I'm insulted."

She shrugged. "But I guess it sort of counts as more chivalry."

They turned out of the airport driveway and, a few hundred feet later, turned right onto a main highway. Main in that it was paved. It ran along the edge of a green, stagnant puddle of water known as Lake Donovan. Originally connected to the sea, in all likelihood, some or other storm or hurricane or act of God had closed it off. Jackson couldn't imagine it was good for much.

"First time to Lazarus Island?" the driver asked.

"Yeah," Jackson answered.

"Honeymoon?"

"No."

The driver met Jackson's eyes in the mirror. "Hey, I don't judge."

"What do you know about the history of the island?" Sawyer asked.

"It was first settled in the early 1700s," the driver answered. "I think. Before that, it was just a stopover for pirates."

"Pirates?" Jackson asked.

"Yeah. Same for all the islands down here. They were always looking for a safe place to drop anchor."

"What about Little Lazarus Island?" Sawyer asked.

The driver chuckled. "It's just a sandbar. Never been anything there."

"Who's the town named after?" Jackson asked, even though he already knew. The last thing he wanted was for a cabby with a smartphone to Tweet out that a nice-looking couple was on the island and interested in pirate treasure. Better to play generally curious.

"Woodes Rogers, the first governor of the Bahamas. He was famous for driving pirates out of the islands. He also rescued a real-life Robinson Crusoe."

"You don't say."

"He circled the globe as a privateer and spent time in prison in England between his terms as governor. They've got a little museum on 3rd Street. Interesting guy."

They had entered town, driving past single-family homes with bright stucco exteriors, clay shingled roofs, no lawns, and plenty of palm trees. Numbered streets ran approximately north-south, at least to Jackson's eye— what he was considering north-south. (Technically, they ran almost due northeast-southwest, but on a map, they looked north-south.) They passed

4th, 3rd, and 2nd Streets, but no 1st Street. The houses gave way to commercial buildings, an odd and cluttered assortment of structures.

They stopped at a light. The current road ended, with a parking lot directly ahead, and then the beach and the ocean.

"Atlantic Drive," the cabby said as he turned south. "Main drive in town. Plenty of restaurants, shops, nightlife to the south. Mostly homes north."

"Where's a good place for dinner?" Sawyer asked.

"Can't beat the West End Grille for a sunset," he answered as he made another quick turn, this time into the circular driveway of a three-story turquoise building, The Hotel Sir Donovan. He pulled under a carport and was out of the cab almost before it stopped. He quickly opened Sawyer's door and offered her a hand. By the time Jackson got out, his and Sawyer's bags were on the curb.

Having already tipped the guy one hundred percent, Jackson simply offered a, "Thanks," as he picked up both of their bags. Ocean breezes awaited them inside the open-air lobby, stirred by ceiling fans two stories above them. It didn't have the marble floors and elegant décor of the Hotel Étienne, but the Hotel Sir Donovan was inviting and cozy in its own way. Jackson wished he was there to relax, having never really gotten his Caribbean vacation.

A friendly woman with caramel skin to contrast her bright floral shirt welcomed them and provided them directions to the various hotel amenities. "We have you in rooms 1215 and 1216," she said. "Here are your keys. You can take the staircase to the second floor, make a right, then all the way down on your left."

Jackson followed her gaze to a curving, open staircase in the middle of the lobby. Catwalks led to northern and southern wings of the hotel. It looked like a treehouse.

Sawyer swiped her key off the counter and started for the stairs, so Jackson followed her. The catwalk to the southern wing formed a T, leading either to ocean view or island view rooms. Following the desk clerk's directions, Sawyer turned right. They walked through a doorway—no door— and Sawyer stopped, leaning on a railing that was wobbly but anchored. Jackson stopped beside her and admired the view. Beneath them, the beach stretched for about fifty feet before giving way to the Atlantic Ocean. Left and right, the beach made a sweeping curve so that they could see all the buildings along it, from a marina and short pier at North Point to a rocky outcropping Jackson assumed was West End. In between, nothing but beautiful azure water under a sky spotted with tall cumulous clouds.

Sawyer looked at him, then trudged to the end of the corridor. Rooms 1215 and 1216 were the last two. Beyond them, the corridor wrapped around the building, joining with the one servicing the island view rooms. A staircase in the middle led up to the third floor or down to the beach.

The rooms weren't anything fancy, but they were clean. They had TVs, all the right fixtures in the bathroom, running water that was colorless and odorless. They would do.

They each took a minute to drop their bags, then met back on the walkway, leaning on the railing.

"So what's next?" Jackson asked.

"You're the P.I."

"So you keep saying."

She shrugged. "We need to figure out who the rich man is."

"First guess," Jackson said. "Lazarus."

"Donovan Lazarus?"

Jackson nodded.

Sawyer stood up. "Rich man's bones. We need to find a cemetery."

Jackson nodded again. "If that fails, we hit up locals, check out the Woodes Rogers Museum, or walk along the beach looking for an X."

"There has to be a hall of records or something like that. Maybe that'd have some information."

"Worth a check."

"Okay, so give me a few minutes to freshen up, and we'll get moving."

Jackson nodded. "Sounds good."

They entered their respective rooms, which were adjoining. Jackson opened his door and crashed onto the bed, feeling as if he'd been awake for forty-eight hours straight. Then again, in the course of the last week he had flown across the country, flown a third of the way back again, been taken captive by a corrupt cop, turned the tables on said cop, broken into a dead man's house, infiltrated a prominent businessman's office to snoop at a three-hundred-year-old journal, and then flown to the Bahamas. He had a right to be tired.

Sawyer's knock on the door startled him. She had changed into a tank top and shorts, her hair pulled back in a stub of a ponytail. "You fall asleep or something?" she asked.

"Just resting my eyes."

"Um-hmm. Are you ready?"

"Yeah, let's roll."

Their cabby this time was an old black man with a gray tuft under his jaw. He looked like Danny Glover. His cab smelled of incense, and his dash was lined with an assortment of religious symbols and figures. "What does you fine folks want at da cemetery?" he asked.

"We're looking for an old friend," Jackson said.

The man nodded. His name was Willie, he said. Jackson introduced them as Jack and Savannah.

The Lazarus Island Cemetery was on the far end of the island, beyond the airstrip, on a bump of land that stuck out into the ocean. The road there led through the trees and emptied into a green field. It was lined with crude grave markers for a few hundred feet, then seemed to drop off into the water some dozen feet below. Clouds had mushroomed quickly over the Atlantic, bringing the threat of an afternoon storm. But it was still a ways off.

The cemetery had maybe five hundred headstones, and there was a clear progression from old to new. Jackson had expected to find generations of several prominent families buried together, but as he and Sawyer wandered the rows and looked at names, it wasn't the case.

"You know, it could be another rich man," she said.

"Not Lazarus?"

She nodded. "But if that's the case, we have no idea what we're looking for. We could see it and not even know it." She sighed. "I suppose it would be too much to see the name Brackett."

"I was hoping for an epitaph about a 'rich man' in quotes."

"Good luck on that." Sawyer stopped. "Where would they bury rich people?"

"Same as all the rest."

"Would they? Or would they have a place of honor?"

"Heads of family or prominent citizens, maybe. But just a rich man . . ."

"I suppo—Jackson."

He joined her in front of an old, listing slab of granite. "Sir Donovan Lazarus," Jackson read. "Born 1705, London, England. Died, July 4, 1775, Lazarus Island." He looked up. "Hmm."

"So he was a teenager when Brackett and crew attacked the *Granada* and just sixteen when the *Missianna* sailed for the Bahamas."

"I doubt they were looking for him."

"Certainly not his bones." She looked around. "So where does that leave us?"

"Some of these headstones clearly were here before Brackett's time. So it's possible he was referring to someone here."

"But who?"

Jackson nodded. "You were right, we need to check if there is a hall of records that would list any wealthy citizens from the late seventeenth or early eighteenth centuries, and then we can cross-match those names with people buried here."

"Maybe they even have a register of who's buried where."

"Yeah, could be." He looked at her. "You know, a good P.I. would have thought of that first."

"You're jetlagged."

"Yeah. You hungry?"

"Getting there."

He looked up to the sky as a distant rumble of thunder sounded. "That storm's moving faster than I thought. Let's get back."

Willie had waited for them and, as they got back in the cab, he asked if they had found their friend.

"Not really," Sawyer said.

"Dat is too bad. Are you sure your friend is buried on de island?"

"We're not sure where our friend is," Sawyer said. She raised an eyebrow as she looked at Jackson, recognizing the double meaning in her statement.

"Does the phrase 'rich man' mean anything to you?" Jackson asked.

"Rich man? Your friend, he is rich?"

"No. But this rich man could lead us to him."

"Rich man," Willie repeated. "A lot of rich men on de island. Some live here. Some, dey just come to play."

"More specifically, we're looking for his bones," Jackson said.

"A rich man's bones?"

"Yes."

"Dat is why you come to de cemetery?"

"Yes."

"Is there any legend about a rich man?" Sawyer asked. "Centuries old, probably."

Willie stroked his chin as raindrops splattered against the windshield. He turned on wipers that turned the rain into a streaky mess. "Dere is one, sort of."

Sawyer leaned forward.

"About ten miles south of here is a little spit of an island. Little Lazarus Island, it's called. Well, de word is that many, many years ago, it was known as Rich Man's Island."

"Rich Man's Island?" Jackson asked.

"Yes."

"Do you know who the rich man was?"

"Yes, de rich man from de Bible. You have perhaps heard de story, from de book of Luke. Lazarus was a beggar who sat outside de gate of de rich man, but de rich man paid him no mind. When dey bot' died, de rich man was in torment looking at Lazarus. De story goes dat castaways and criminals were left stranded on de island, close enough to see Lazarus Island, but too far to swim dere or seen to be rescued." He looked over his shoulder. "It was also a cruel joke, you see, in dat de person on de island was probably very poor, not rich."

Jackson and Sawyer looked at each other. "What about pirates?" she asked. "Did they ever use Rich Man's Island?"

"Oh, I'm sure dey did. Pirates was all over dese islands before Mr. Woodes cleared dem out."

The rain was heavier now, a sudden downpour that made conversation almost impossible. It continued drumming on the roof of the taxi until Willie pulled under the carport of the Hotel Sir Donovan. "I hope dat you find your friend," Willie said as Jackson paid him through the driver's window. "But I must warn you. Dey also say dat Little Lazarus Island is cursed."

"Cursed?" Sawyer asked from behind Jackson.

Willie nodded. "Be very careful."

Chapter Thirty-Seven

6:19 p.m.

WHILE THE THUNDERSHOWER pounded Lazarus Island, Jackson had a shower of his own in his hotel room. By the time he emerged to see if Sawyer was ready for dinner, the clouds had cleared, leaving bright evening sunshine playing across the Atlantic.

Sawyer had swapped her shorts for jeans and now wore her hair down. "Dinner preference?" he asked.

"Seems we're in the business of relying on cabbies. Let's try the West End Grille."

He looked to the horizon. "Walk?"

She nodded, and they headed down to the beach.

Woodes Town stretched along the crescent-shaped beach for about half a mile, ending at West Street. Atlantic drive continued a little farther west, curving with the beach onto a promontory of land that was half sand, half surf-pounded rock. It and the few buildings on its side of West Street were known as West End. Jackson had learned this from the guidebook in the hotel room, which also offered a detailed map.

With the Hotel Sir Donovan located in the middle of town, the walk to West End wasn't long, and the post-storm air was warm but accompanied by a tropical breeze. From just south of the hotel, a concrete and wooden boardwalk ran between the beach and the buildings lining Atlantic Drive, offering access to many of them from the beach or the street. Hotels and condominiums gave way to restaurants, bars, and the usual assortment of beachy souvenir shops. Everything was a little older, in a little worse state of repair than back in the States, but a tourist boom in the 1990s had helped modernize Lazarus Island. So Jackson had also read in the guidebook.

West End tapered at the end of Atlantic Drive, such that the small peninsula was no more than a hundred fifty feet wide, with the open ocean on one side and the cay- and reef-lined shore on the other. The spit of land widened a little at its very tip, where it was almost exclusively rock. The West End Grille was built as far out as was tenable, consisting of a square building surrounded on three sides by a fenced-in patio. A few palms provided a little shade for the patio, but most of it came from large white and red umbrellas that flapped in the breeze.

There was no parking lot for the West End Grille, just dirt and gravel shoulders of the road where a dozen cars haphazardly sat. A large banner over a door in the main entrance proclaimed "Welcome!" in English, the official language of the Bahamas, stemming from its two and a half centuries as a British colony. Jackson and Sawyer entered and were promptly greeted by a woman with pasty white skin and a European accent. She led them out onto the cobblestone patio, navigating around puddles. Maybe a third of the tables were occupied, mostly with white people, meaning tourists. The population of Lazarus Island reflected the Bahamas in general, being ninety-percent black.

The woman seated them in the corner, under an umbrella and near a palm tree that also blocked the setting sun. It was potted, as were all of the plants on or around the patio, likely because nothing grew on the rocks of West End. She placed menus on either side of a flickering white candle and left them. Jackson had no idea what to expect with Bahamian cuisine but was delighted to see it offered plenty of "American" options.

"Is this normal for you?" Sawyer asked, lowering her menu after a young man with skin the exact opposite of the hostess's had come to take drink orders and tell them about the specials.

"Is what normal?"

"Exotic locations, big adventures, quirky women sidekicks."

"Quirky?"

"To your palate, I assume, what with normally being surrounded by California women."

Jackson thought over some of his recent clients and contacts— Shay/Ashley, Ryan, Stephanie, Marissa, Hillary, Maggie, Noelle, Abby, Robyn, Aliana. Yeah, quirky was a good word for it.

"More than I expected," he answered. "I worked for a few years as a gofer at an investigative firm, and it was ninety percent paperwork."

"Do you like it?" Sawyer asked. "I mean, this life? For the long term?"

He met her dark blue eyes. "I like this part of it. The exotic locations and quirky women sidekicks. The death-defying adventures I could do with less of."

"What happened to the jazz?"

"The jazz is like adrenaline. It wears off. Usually about the time all the shooting starts."

She nodded but didn't say anything.

Jackson looked back at his menu. "How about you?"

"How about me what?"

"Painting and taking pictures and singing and waiting odd tables." He looked back up. "Do you like that life, long term?"

Sawyer shrugged. "I don't know. I like it now, but . . ."

He waited.

"I'd say I want to settle down, but that makes it sound like I'm in a band touring around the country or something." She looked up at him. "I don't know. I want to get married someday, have kids, a family. But I also have trouble seeing myself as a stay-at-home mom—I'd go stir-crazy."

"You don't have to stay at home."

"Somebody has to raise the kids. I'm not going to bring children into the world only to pawn them off on somebody else while I chase a career or my dreams or something."

"So much for feminist empowerment."

"I just feel like if I'm going to have a family, my family should be my dream, should be the thing I'm chasing."

"Not both?"

"Maybe. But too many women—and men—I see are neglecting families for other aspirations. I don't think that's right. I'm not going to let that be me."

"You've thought a lot about this, apparently."

"When you grow up without a mom, you spend a lot of time thinking about what you want your family to be someday."

"I guess."

They returned to their menus and eventually ordered. Jackson found a surf 'n turf plate that was right up his alley, and Sawyer opted for steamed conch and rice. When their waiter had taken their orders, she leaned forward.

"How about you?"

He looked at her.

"Wife and kids someday?"

"Someday, maybe."

"Just not anytime soon?"

"I'm not sure I'm very good husband material," he said, looking out at the ocean, toward home, thinking of the last time he'd seen Sam.

"Why do you say that?"

"Different things." He looked back at her. "I wouldn't provide a very stable home life. No fixed income, odd hours, quirky female clients might be off-putting to a wife, and so would the occasional getting shot or half killed by Russian terrorists."

Sawyer said nothing.

"Plus, I just have a hard time seeing myself as a dad. I'm thirty yea—thirty-one—and I still see myself as the kid half the time."

Sawyer leaned in a little more. "How so?"

"I spend my free time playing Xbox and watching reruns of old TV shows. My dates were pizza and pinball with Maggie or tennis and grilled steaks with Sam, not candlelight dinners or putting on a jacket and tie to go hear the symphony. I once prayed that the Rams would move back to L.A.—and I don't mean once when I was six but once like two years ago. Maybe Hillary was right, maybe I'm refusing to grow up."

To her credit, Sawyer didn't ask who Maggie and Sam were. Then again, maybe she didn't care. "I don't know Hillary—"

"Count your blessings."

She raised an eyebrow. "And I don't know what she said about you, but from the little bit I've seen and from what I've gotten to know, you seem plenty mature."

"Don't confuse scars for maturity."

"I'm not. So you play video games. You also seem more than happy hanging out at the beach all day, so it's not like you're some *Dungeons and Dragons* fanatic who never leaves the basement."

"Did you just make a pop-culture reference?"

She grinned. "And nobody says you have to put on a jacket and tie and go to the symphony. I'd rather be barefoot on the beach than all dolled up. Does that make me immature?"

"No."

"And the way you've handled yourself the last couple of days, while we were traveling alone and could have found ourselves in compromising situations . . . That tells me all I need to know."

"You know, I've been meaning to ask you about that."

She squeezed some more lemon into her tea. "Oh?"

"Back at the airport, I asked you if it was okay for a refined Southern woman to travel alone with a man, and you said if he was a gentleman."

She listened.

"We barely knew each other then. We barely do now. How'd you know you could trust me?"

She sipped her tea through a straw before answering. "Remember when we went fishing and got caught in the rain?"

"Sounds familiar."

"And I was afraid the rain was going to make my shirt see-through? Most guys I've known would have at least taken a glance. Your eyes never dropped below mine. I figured then I could trust you, that it was safe to be alone with you. If you were the type of guy who'd try something, you'd also be the type to sneak a peek."

He nodded. Then shrugged. "I thought it was because, in addition to owning a Ruger rifle, you also knew Krav Maga and Kung fu or something and knew you could kick my butt if push came to shove."

Sawyer leaned in with a crooked smirk. "That too."

Jackson chuckled and sat back. Sawyer continued to smile, her hair caressing her chin as it was lifted by the breeze. In that moment, Jackson felt a pang like he hadn't felt in a long time, if ever. The pang of being alone. Maybe it was still the loss of his family two years ago and the heightened awareness of it that his birthday brought on. Maybe it was the talk of marriage and kids serving as a reminder that his life's trajectory didn't seem to include either. Or maybe it was the exotic location and the quirky woman across the table from him messing with his emotions.

Their waiter returned, announcing that their entrées would be up shortly. They waited quietly, watching the waves, the residual clouds on the horizon, or the simple fluttering of palm fronds. The aromatic scent of fresh seafood preceded the waiter, who delivered sizzling plates. The food looked delicious, and as soon as the waiter left, Jackson was about to dig in when Sawyer extended a hand to him.

He looked down at it. "We didn't pray in the Nassau food court."

"There's no need to be legalistic."

He placed his hand in hers.

"Do the honors?" she asked.

He nodded, closed his eyes, and said a simple prayer of thanks for safe travels, good company, and appetizing food. He asked for wisdom and prudence, and closed with a customary "Amen."

Sawyer echoed it, and they opened their eyes and unclenched hands. Then they dug into their dinners. The smell was only half as good as the taste, and they swapped a few bites and compared flavors for several minutes. Then they were quiet, enjoying the food and the trade winds. The West End Grille's business had picked up marginally, with now about half the tables full. Even so, Jackson and Sawyer's table seemed isolated, as if they were the only two people having dinner on West End.

Sawyer finally broke the silence. "What do you make of Willie?"

"Wasn't his accent Jamaican?"

She tilted her head at him.

"I thought he was a great source until he went all '*Black Pearl*' on us. The island is cursed?"

"We seem to be running into that a lot. Ships captained by ghosts, islands cursed." She took a drink. "You think Little Lazarus Island is what Brackett meant?"

"It's plausible. Worth a check, at least."

She sat forward. "So then what are the bones? If the rich man is the island itself, what would be its bones?"

"Could be anything from a geographical feature to actual human bones."

"What are the exact dimensions, do you know?"

"Under half an acre. It's tiny."

"Geography?"

"Mostly trees and scrub."

"The question is, how old is the scrub? Three hundred years ago, it could have looked a lot different."

"I still think we need to find some form of records department," Jackson said. "See if there's any mention of Brackett or his ship here, see if the *Missianna* ever sailed here, and learn what we can about Little Lazarus Island.

Who knows, maybe the locals refer to Little Lazarus' bones, and no one's ever heard of rich man's bones."

She looked around, then leaned forward. "What if the treasure is here?" Sawyer said. "How do we ever recover it?"

"I suppose we should look into the Bahamas' rules on that. It's different for every country, state, territory, and cranky old man's property."

"And then what," she said. "What if we do find a stash of gold? How does that help us bring down whoever's behind Ben and Damon's death? I know that's our end goal, but how does it all work out?"

"We're a few bridges away from that one," Jackson said as the waiter stopped by to check on their dinners and bring tea refills. When he was gone, Jackson said, "Besides, I think we should just enjoy a nice romantic dinner."

Sawyer cast him a sideways glance. He reached across the table to take her hand, leaning in over his salad and slightly to the right. He let a beatific smile play across his face. "There's a guy at eleven o'clock in a bad Hawaiian shirt, surly disposition. Eating alone and he hasn't taken his eyes off of us. Either he's checking you out, or he's watching us."

"Maybe he's just a creep."

"I also saw him as we were leaving the hotel. He fell in a few hundred feet behind us."

"He's following us?"

Jackson nodded.

"What do we do?"

"For now, enjoy your conch and the sunset. We'll act like we haven't a care—or a line on a treasure—in the world."

"I think I can do that," Sawyer said.

Jackson smiled as he sat back. The smile was purely external. Either Louviere's people had somehow followed them to the Bahamas, or someone local didn't like the questions they were asking of cab drivers. Whatever the case, spotting a tail spoiled the notion that they were safe and secluded on an island paradise.

Chapter Thirty-Eight

7:27 p.m.

BOTH OF THEIR meals were delicious, and Jackson and Sawyer lingered over a pineapple tart for dessert. They made small talk and watched the sunset, a dazzling display with the sun peeking in and out from behind the last traces of the afternoon storm. It rivaled anything in Key West. Meanwhile, the guy in the bad Hawaiian shirt nursed a couple of beers and an appetizer. At one point, he made a short phone call, and he didn't seem to notice that Jackson had noticed him.

"We're running up quite an expense tab," Sawyer said as Jackson reached for his credit card to pay for dinner.

"Only a problem if we don't find the treasure."

"Are you planning on keeping it?"

"Honestly, I haven't even thought about it. But if money becomes a problem, we can tap out."

"I'm okay."

Jackson knew where his stash had come from—the poker game in Vegas the year before and a lucrative stint as a Middle East treasure hunter—but he wasn't sure how a jack-of-all-trades had saved as much as Sawyer had. He certainly wasn't going to worry about it now.

"So how do we play this?" she asked after the waiter took his credit card.

"He doesn't know we're onto him, so if we bolt or try to lose him, we lose that advantage. Plus he knows where we're staying; he picked us up right after we left the hotel. So it doesn't do much good to lose him."

"So what then?"

"We'll take a walk back through town. I want to get the lay of the land anyhow. Somewhere along the way, I'll take a picture of you with your phone and try to get his face. Mouse might be able to find out who he is. Other than that, we lay low for the night."

The waiter returned, Jackson signed the check, and he and Sawyer got up to leave. They watched the end of the sunset from a vantage point on the rocks, and when the color drained from the sky, they headed back toward the hotel. They took their time, following Atlantic Drive, which was evidently the hub of tourist activity in town. At West Street, they cut over. They looked left down 1st Street, which ran several blocks before dead-ending in the park across the street from the hotel. That explained why Jackson hadn't seen a 1st Street on their initial drive into town.

Since 1st Street appeared to house more local shops and bars, and since more lights beckoned from 2nd Street, they continued another block. They found a gas station, a Burger King, a local grocery store, and, a half block north on 2nd Street, a building identified as "City Hall & Lazarus Island Department of Records." Jackson didn't slow.

"Don't you want to check the hours?" Sawyer asked with a hand on his arm.

"Our friend's still behind us," Jackson said. "I don't want him to know we're interested."

To her credit, Sawyer didn't look back.

"Besides, I glanced at them as we went by. Tomorrow it's open from noon till four."

They passed more local shops and started to get into homes, so they cut back over to Atlantic Drive.

"He still there?" Sawyer asked.

"Like a bad habit."

"Following your lead."

They browsed a few souvenir shops, and at a postcard rack next to $5 T-shirts, Jackson was able to furtively observe their tail for several seconds. He had stopped outside a fish and chips restaurant, pretending to read the menu. The guy was a hack, and Jackson thought about confronting him. Had he been alone, he might have. Instead, he moved over to a bin selling cowboy hats, fake Rastafarian dreadlocks, fishing company ball caps, and a few other types of headwear.

He lifted a cowboy hat onto his head and checked himself in the mirror. Hawaiian Shirt was now lingering at a small stand with pamphlets for area attractions. He'd closed the gap from earlier, now within forty feet of them. Jackson again thought about approaching him, but didn't.

He removed the cap and looked at Sawyer. "Okay, Playful Southern Belle, try on a hat, smile and sway your hips, and I'll take a picture."

Sawyer reached into the bin for a somewhat floppy straw hat and placed it over her hair. Then she pulled on Jackson's sleeve. "Come on, selfie."

"Adlibbing, are we?"

"It's my phone, so it doesn't make sense for me to have you take a picture of me. It does make sense for me to want a picture of us."

"I suppose."

She tapped the screen a dozen times, orienting the camera slightly to take pictures. Then she actually bought the hat.

"Way to sell it."

She beamed.

They continued on, the lively island music streaming from bars and restaurants. The street wasn't packed, but there were still plenty of people milling about. Jackson guessed it was about half and half between tourists and locals, plus or minus a few stalkers.

When they returned to the hotel, Jackson suggested they enter through the lobby. "Just in case he didn't see which room we came from," he added. "I don't want him to be able to follow us back to the door quite as easily."

"Makes sense."

They took the lobby stairs and the catwalk to the second story and followed the exterior corridor to their rooms. As they ducked inside, Jackson swept his eyes over the beach and up and down the corridor. He saw no one.

The doors had deadbolts, and Jackson turned his before knocking on the adjoining door to Sawyer's room. She opened right away.

"You bolt your door?" he asked.

"I did."

"Good."

"You can come in."

He did. She sat on the corner of her bed and called up the pictures on her phone. "There," she said, turning it so Jackson could see. "That him?"

"That's him. Mind if I send these to Mouse?"

"What's his number? I'll text him."

"Uh, he doesn't have a cell."

"Do you all live in a time warp in Southern California?"

"Says the girl who runs barefoot in a swamp instead of watching '80s reruns."

"Not sure you didn't make my point there. E-mail?"

He gave her Mouse's address, then called him on his phone. It was three hours earlier in L.A., so unless Mouse was working, he'd be home gaming. He answered on the fourth ring.

"Yeah?"

"Mouse, it's Jackson."

"Dude, what's up? You need me to hack more numbers?"

"No. We're in the Bahamas now."

"What?"

"I need an ID on a face. My friend just e-mailed the image to you. Anything you can do with that?"

"I'll try."

Jackson listened to Mouse's fingers on the keyboard for a few seconds. Then a couple clicks. "Get it?" Jackson asked.

"Yeah. Wow, dude, that's the girl you're with?"

"That's her."

"She is hot."

"I'll tell her you said so."

"Dude, what are you doing in the Bahamas?"

"Eloping. It's a long story, Mouse. Give me a call on my cell when you know something."

"Will do. Have fun, man."

Jackson ended the call. "Mouse thinks you're cute," he said.

"I am flattered." She pulled her legs under her. "So what's our plan for tomorrow?"

"I think Willie's intel would suggest we should check out Little Lazarus Island."

"Agreed."

"But I'm hesitant to chase over there with a bunch of shovels and start digging for treasure until we know more. I think we spend the day tomorrow learning everything we can about these islands. Talk to locals, visit any tourist info hotspots, chamber of commerce if there is one, a library, and then the department of records."

"Sounds like a busy day."

"And depending on what Mouse turns up on the guy in the Hawaiian shirt, play hide-and-seek with him."

"How's he going to identify his face, anyhow?"

"Best if we don't know."

"I see."

"What are you doing?" he asked.

Sawyer held her phone in her lap, looking at the screen. "I'm seeing what I can find on Little Lazarus Island."

Jackson pulled up a chair, and for the next half hour they researched the geography of Little Lazarus Island, looking for any online mention of it as Rich Man's Island (finding none), and checked on treasure recovery laws in the Bahamas. They were about to price boat rentals when Jackson's phone emitted the James Bond theme.

He flipped it open. "Yeah, Mouse?"

"You're lucky. Or unlucky. The guy's got a record."

"I'm putting you on speaker, Mouse."

"With the hot girl?"

"Hi, Mouse," Sawyer said.

Jackson smirked as Mouse took a few moments to gather himself. "Um, yeah, hi."

"Who is he?"

"His, uh . . . his name's Frank Baldwin. Local Bahamian originally from Freeport. Small-time criminal. A couple of B&E's and petty theft. He's been clean for the last few years."

"Any idea what he does for a living?"

"Works at a dive shop in Nassau."

"Nassau. Not Lazarus Island?"

"Where?"

"Nothing. You sure?"

"Uh, yeah, pretty."

"You find out anything else about him?"

"Hey, man, I didn't know you needed a full bio."

"The name's great, Mouse. Thanks."

"Sure."

"Hey, Mouse. Do me one more favor, will you?"

"Why not?"

"Check into a guy named Martin Louviere. He's a big businessman in New Orleans, and we think he's tied to this."

"How do you spell it?"

Jackson spelled out the name.

"What do you want me to find?"

"I don't know. Any skeletons in his closet, criminal connections, family bribes of cops."

"I'll see what I can find."

"Thanks." Jackson closed the phone. "Forgive him, he's socially awkward."

Sawyer grinned. "So why is Frank Baldwin following us?"

"I don't know."

"You think he picked us up in Nassau?"

"I didn't see him on the plane, but I guess he could have. Thing is, why? If he's not working for Louviere, he'd have no reason to follow us here. And if he is, why is a guy like Baldwin on Louviere's payroll?"

"Maybe he's not," she said. "Maybe he needed some local muscle to keep an eye on us."

Jackson shrugged.

"He knew we were looking at the journal, deduced we were coming to the Bahamas, and figured picking us up in Nassau would be the easiest. If he's as dirty as we think, I'm sure he'd have the criminal contacts to arrange it."

"I suppose. He hires Baldwin to follow us, see if we find anything, and let him know if so."

She nodded.

"Which means, Louviere has no idea what is or isn't supposed to be in the Bahamas or where. He hasn't figured out the 'rich man's bones' clue."

"Except now we've led him here."

"Yeah, but he doesn't know about Little Lazarus Island. He doesn't know we've found anything. And we have to make sure it stays that way tomorrow."

She yawned, which prompted him to look at the clock. It was just after nine-thirty, which meant only eight-thirty in New Orleans. Even so, Jackson and Sawyer had been up early after a long, hectic Sunday, and were both ready to call it a night.

She followed him to the doors between their rooms. "How early do you want to get cracking tomorrow?"

"Grab some breakfast around eight?"

She nodded.

"Good night, Sawyer."

"Good night, Jackson."

They closed their doors.

Jackson was exhausted and got ready for bed quickly. Then he lay in his bed unable to fall asleep, his mind equally focused on trying to figure out the riddle of 'rich man's bones' and mulling his and Sawyer's discussions about marriage and family. The latter wasn't something he'd thought too much about, until lately. Did the fact that it was on his mind more now mean anything?

And if so, what?

Chapter Thirty-Nine

Tuesday, May 21
6:18 a.m.

TUESDAY'S SUNRISE WAS breathtaking. It took place behind the hotel, on the other side of the island, but the reflection off a low bank of clouds turned both them and the glassy calm waters of Lazarus Bight vibrant shades of lavender, then pink, then fiery orange. The beach was dead calm, the town was utterly quiet, and Jackson felt as if he was alone in the world, watching its Creator and Sustainer show off.

Several days of jet-setting and adventure had thrown off his sleep cycle, and he'd awakened at six with a realization that he wasn't going to sleep any longer. So he'd brewed some coffee in his in-room coffeemaker and taken a steaming mug out onto the balcony. He leaned against the railing until it left indentations in his arms and the colors in the sky and on the sea had diminished to standard brilliance. Woodes Town was coming to life, evident by the sounds of traffic. The beach was now home to a handful of shell-seekers strolling barefoot at the water's edge or joggers pounding down the beach in tennis shoes. Gulls circled overhead, cawing and bleating. Jackson wished he could just sit back and relax for a day in the Caribbean, as had been his original plan before Ben disappeared.

He thought about Ben as he went back inside, showered, and dressed. People always talked about doing things to honor dead loved ones—playing in the big game after a parent's passing, completing a business venture after a friend died, going on with life as usual in the wake of tragedy. They always said it was what the departed would have wanted. So Jackson wondered, would Ben have wanted him and Sawyer to chase down Brackett's treasure? Was that even what Ben had been doing? Had his interest in Brackett been more academic in nature?

Or what about their grand idea of taking down Martin Louviere—somehow—if he was indeed behind Ben's death? Would Ben even care? Would Damon? Were Jackson and Sawyer deluding themselves? Was justice merely an excuse for making a gold rush? Was that old sin of greed rearing its ugly head? If there was one person Jackson could believe would have no interest in the treasure, it was Sawyer, and she'd admitted the allure and the pull it had on her. Was there any hope for him?

At a quarter after seven, he opened his door leading to Sawyer's room to find hers already open. She sat cross-legged on her bed, head down with hair blocking her face. A Bible was open on her lap. Jackson began to back away, but she looked up.

"Sorry, didn't mean to interrupt."

"It's okay," she said, tucking hair behind her ear. "I was just finishing up."

"In that case, you ready to grab some breakfast early?"

"More than." She closed her Bible and stood. "You have a place in mind?"

"First place that's open."

"Okay then."

She stepped into a pair of white flip-flops to compliment white Bermuda shorts and the crimson V-neck with "Bama" scrawled on the front in white she had worn that first day in Sheriff Hawkins' office. She grabbed her sunglasses, and they set out.

The air was already warm, but mitigated by a pleasant breeze. They walked north this time, for something different, and Jackson kept an eye out for Frank Baldwin. He didn't spot him, which was at the same time comforting and disconcerting. Better to know where he was.

They found a small café a block and a half north, just past where the main road intersected with Atlantic Drive. The café sold coffees, pastries, and a few breakfast sandwiches, and offered outdoor seating on a patio with a view of the beach and the street. Not a bad surveillance point.

While they ate, Jackson and Sawyer made a list of things to do and objectives to meet. First objective, confirm Willie's story that Little Lazarus Island was also known as Rich Man's Island. Second objective, determine what the 'rich man's bones' were and if any local lore or legend made reference to them. Third, see if that same local lore had any reference to

James Brackett, the *Missianna*, or the *Majesté Royale*. Fourth, pick up any additional knowledge of the islands that may become pertinent. Last, do all of the above without tipping off Baldwin, should he be watching them. Without knowing who he was working for or what his purposes were, there was no way of knowing if pretending to be tourists would throw him off their trail or not, but it was worth a try.

After eating, they backtracked south, since the town thinned farther north. At the north end of Atlantic Drive were the marina and several bait and tackle stores and dive shops. A sixth objective, pending success on some of the earlier ones, was to plan a trip to Little Lazarus Island, likely the next day, possibly with digging tools. But for now, everything they wanted lay to the south.

They stopped at an unmanned tourist stand and picked up several brochures and maps, which they took to the park across the street from the Hotel Sir Donovan. The park covered a couple square blocks and was filled with palm trees, fragrant hibiscuses and lilies, and winding walkways around a central fountain with a statue of island founder Donovan Lazarus in the center. They found a bench and sat down to plan their morning.

The town's library was in the same building as the school, which was just on the other side of the park on 2nd Street. However, the library didn't open until ten. The Woodes Rogers Museum on 3rd Street opened at nine. So they wandered leisurely toward the museum, browsing at a few shops on Atlantic Drive and chatting up store owners to no avail before cutting over to 3rd Street. Still no sign of Baldwin. Maybe, Jackson speculated, he'd been on a one-day retainer. Or maybe, Sawyer countered, he had a partner they'd yet to spot.

The museum opened just as they arrived, and Jackson and Sawyer were the first customers of the day. That earned them something of a private tour from the proprietor, a thin black man with a thick crop of graying black hair. He guided them through the small museum, highlighting Woodes Rogers' early life as a privateer in the British war with Spain, his journeys around the world—including his rescue of fellow privateer Alexander Selkirk that inspired Daniel Defoe's famous novel, *Robinson Crusoe*—and his two terms as governor of the Bahamas, in between which he had been imprisoned back in Britain for debt incurred during his first term. Rogers had also famously rid the Bahamas of pirates, a fact that gave Jackson and Sawyer an opening to question the proprietor about the Brackett treasure. He was familiar with the legend but could add nothing to it. Nor was he familiar with any legends of "rich man's bones" or relating to pirates and Little Lazarus Island. Historically informative, their time at the museum gained them nothing.

The day had warmed, and the humidity increased under a hot sun. The Lazarus Island school encompassed all grades, and classes were in full swing when Jackson and Sawyer arrived. They entered through the main door and spoke to an administrator who guided them to the library, a large room with no air-conditioning. Windows on opposite sides were open, allowing the island breeze to provide some measure of relief. Ten minutes were spent gaining permission to use the library, and it took them another half hour to search the small collection of reference materials to find relevant books. They met up at a table near the window and got to work.

Jackson skimmed two histories of the island while Sawyer dug through an island reference book. They didn't find much. Jackson did corroborate what Willie had told them the day before, that Little Lazarus Island had at one time, at least to some, been known as Rich Man's Island. There was no reference to Brackett or his ship, but it confirmed they were barking up the right tree.

Just before noon, as they were wrapping up, Sawyer spun a second book she'd been working through to Jackson. "Take a look at this."

"What?" he asked.

She jabbed a finger at a paragraph in the middle of a page. Jackson read a historical account of the murder of two sailors by a Spanish captain by the name of Garcia. He'd been arrested and sentenced to death, only to be mysteriously pardoned by Woodes Rogers the day before he was to be hanged. He was released and never seen again.

"When is this?" Jackson asked, studying the page.

"If this is chronological, which it seems to be, early 1719."

"Four years after the *Barracuda* was sunk and a year after Brackett allegedly sailed for the Bahamas."

"It doesn't say, but this has to be Reynaldo Garcia III, right?"

"You did say he dedicated his life to finding the people who attacked the *Nuestra Señora de la Granada* and kidnapped his girl, didn't you?"

"That's the legend."

"You find anything else?"

"No."

"Let's walk and talk," Jackson said, noting that the library was filling up. Mostly with schoolkids, but also a few adults. All listening ears, and he'd rather avoid them. They returned their books, thanked the librarian for her assistance, and exited the school. They cut through the park back toward Atlantic Drive, thankful for the shade of palm trees and building clouds.

"Toussaint's journal said they picked up a delirious Brackett from an island in the southern Bahamas in 1715," Jackson said as they walked. "Four years later, Garcia murders two men on the island. And in between, Brackett sailed for the Bahamas, per Grover's account."

"So what's the connection?"

Jackson shrugged. "Maybe after leaving the Keys, Brackett and his crew sailed to Lazarus Island, discovered a useless spit of land ten miles south, and buried the treasure there. Something happened to the crew, leaving only Brackett half out of his mind to be picked up by Toussaint."

"What's Garcia's tie-in?"

"Maybe he got wind of Brackett's plans to sail to the Bahamas and tracked his new crew down here. Or maybe some of the original crew also survived, made Lazarus Island their home as a way to stay close to the treasure, and he tracked them down."

"We're still missing a few pieces," she said.

"At least." He sighed. "It's after noon. Grab a bite to eat, then hit the department of records?"

"Sure."

They found a cantina on 1st Street that sold cheap fish tacos, and ate as they walked. The sky above was now half blue, half gray and white clouds. Jackson wondered if the Bahamas were the same as every other tropical locale, where you could pretty much set your clock by an afternoon rainstorm.

They stopped while Sawyer admired some blown-glass artwork on display in a window front. She still had a few bites left in her taco. Jackson's was gone, and he held just a paper cup of weak lemonade. The sculptures were impressive, but she took a greater interest in them than he did. So his eyes wandered and, as they often did, picked out a pretty female who was eating an ice cream cone a hundred feet down the sidewalk. She wore a lime green sundress, offsetting her mocha skin. Most striking was her jet black hair, which cascaded in waves down her shoulders. She was indeed attractive, but no more so than a hundred women Jackson had seen in the Keys, at Louviere's party, or since arriving on Lazarus Island. There was nothing about her to stand out.

Except that he had seen her in the park before they grabbed lunch. She'd been casually drinking a coffee, just hanging around, like she was doing now.

"Hey, Sawyer."

"Yeah," she said, without looking.

"I think you should buy another hat."

She turned his way. "We have a tail?"

"Maybe. Green sundress, eating ice cream, a hundred feet north."

Sawyer didn't turn.

"Also saw her in the park."

"Could be coincidence."

"Could be."

"What do you want to do?"

"I'm not much in the mood for playing cat-and-mouse through town. Too hot. And you're not in running shoes."

She waited.

"Besides, the fact that they're following us means they probably won't buy we're honeymooners just enjoying the local sites."

"Probably not."

"So let's do what we came to do."

She winked. "Let's do it."

Chapter Forty

JACKSON AND SAWYER headed for the department of records via Atlantic Drive and West Street. A block away, Sawyer stopped, presumably to remove a pebble from her flip-flop. It gave her a chance to sneak a peek back and confirm that the woman in the green dress was still on their tail. Undaunted, they entered the City Hall & Lazarus Island Department of Records. It was a tiny building without air conditioning, and the most ancient records were stored in a musty basement. No computer, no microfiche, just stacks of boxes and books and documents. At least they were categorized—sort of.

A few minutes into their search, Jackson's phone buzzed in his pocket. He fished it out and flipped it open, glancing at the display in the process.

"Yeah, Mouse."

"Hey, dude. Am I on speaker?"

"You want to be?"

"Not really."

"What you got?"

"I looked into this Louviere guy last night. I found a lot, but not much suspicious."

"But some?"

"You said something about bribing cops. For whatever reason, that stuck in my head, and so when I found this, it stuck out."

"Found what, Mouse?" Jackson asked with a glance at Sawyer.

"One of Louviere's charitable contributions, way back, was to sponsor a kid from the inner city in some junior police academy or something. Turns out it was your cop friend, Dixon."

"Jason Dixon?"

"Yep."

"That's good, Mouse. Real good. Anything else?"

"Nothing of interest. He's kind of boring."

"All right. Thanks, bud."

"Sure."

Jackson closed his phone and reported to Sawyer.

"So Louviere is behind all this?"

"I'm convinced. There's no way his sponsoring Dixon is a coincidence."

"He figures he bought him, so he uses Dixon to cover up his indiscretions."

Jackson nodded.

"Baldwin too, you think?"

"If I were a betting man . . ."

"Yeah."

They got down to work and spent the better part of three hours sorting and digging through the records, looking for births or deaths, marriages, immigrations, arrests—anything that might be on file and show the presence of Brackett, the *Missianna*, or anyone associated with him. They came up mostly empty. Sawyer did find a list of pirates who accepted the "King's Pardon," an offer of clemency from the British Crown to all pirates who surrendered. Woodes Rogers, as Captain General and Governor in Chief of the Bahamas, was assigned with executing the pardon, and he documented the names. Among them was Calvin McNair, whose name also appeared on a Lazarus Island death register in 1723. McNair, Sawyer said, was the same name of Brackett's long-time first mate, according to legend.

"So Brackett's first mate quit the life of piracy and lived on Lazarus Island for five years until he died."

She nodded.

"There's a lot of smoke here for no fire."

"Yeah, but where's it blowing from?"

"Good question."

"We still don't know what the bones are. Are they on Rich Man's island? Are they on Lazarus Island? Are they where the treasure's buried, or where some other clue is located?"

Jackson shook his head.

Having found all they could, they exited the department of records and walked back to Atlantic Drive. They saw no signs of Green Dress or Baldwin. Since they had already walked Atlantic Drive several times, they cut over to the beach and headed north, dodging sunbathers. There weren't many, as clouds had mostly filled the sky, and Jackson expected rain to suddenly start pouring at any second.

"Grover said the story is that Brackett and the *Missianna* sailed from New Orleans for the Bahamas, right?" Jackson asked.

"Right."

"But there's no record anywhere of him arriving. There is record of his former first mate living here, of Garcia—who was hunting Brackett and his crew—killing two people here, and of Toussaint stopping here on his way to the States."

"They weren't the States in 1715."

He narrowed his gaze at her.

"But yeah, go on."

"My theory is Brackett, some of his crew, and the treasure survived the hurricane. For whatever reason, they brought it to Little Lazarus Island and hid it. Something happened to Brackett to make him crazy, and when Toussaint rescued him, he took him to New Orleans where, once he came to his senses, he attempted to come back here and find the treasure. Meanwhile, various old crew members had the same idea and made Lazarus Island their base of operations. Whether any of them found it . . ."

"Why would Toussaint's crew take him all the way to New Orleans instead of leaving him here?"

"Maybe . . ."

"What? I can see your brain spinning."

A raindrop fell. Jackson ignored it.

"Maybe they didn't rescue him from Lazarus Island."

She frowned.

"Remember what Willie said, that Little Lazarus Island was used as a place to maroon castaways and criminals. Maybe it was a place where mutineers would strand pirate captains too."

"Okay, but why would Brackett's crew mutiny?"

"Because he failed to pull off the raid of the *Nuestra Señora de la Granada*."

"That wasn't exactly his fault."

"Nobody said pirates were reasonable."

"Okay," she said, disregarding a drop of water that pelted her shoulder, "so then the treasure isn't buried there?"

"No."

"Then why was Brackett coming back to the Bahamas? What was McNair doing here, or the people Garcia killed?"

"Garcia, I don't know. They could have been anybody. But McNair, and especially Brackett, were looking for a map."

"A map?"

"Think about it. There are only two reasons for Brackett to want to come to the Bahamas, either because the treasure was buried here or something that would tell him where the treasure was buried was here."

"A map?" she asked again.

"Yep."

"Why would Brackett need a map? Shouldn't he know where his treasure was?"

"Unless his delirium caused him to forget. We don't know how bad he was, but if he was marooned and thought his life was over, maybe he made a map so that someone could find the treasure. Then he's rescued, having gone full *Looney Tunes*, and when it passes, maybe he can't remember where the treasure is, but he does remember where his map is. With the 'rich man's bones.'"

Sawyer thought about it for a few paces. The raindrops were growing more frequent.

"A map," she said again.

"Yeah. Somewhere on Little Lazarus Island."

The heavens opened, and they took off sprinting the last hundred yards to their hotel.

*　　　*　　　*

7:05 p.m.

JACKSON AND SAWYER dined on sautéed grouper, baked macaroni and cheese, coleslaw, and johnnycakes at Victoria's, a moderately upscale restaurant overlooking the marina at North Point. They'd discovered it when shopping for supplies—a case of bottled water, some energy and granola bars, fruit, and a shovel—after the storm rolled through. It had been followed by another, which had stranded them at Lazarus Island's small hardware store. That was okay; it gave them time to call the marina and charter a boat for early Wednesday morning.

Following their hastily ended discussion on the beach, Jackson and Sawyer had met in his room while the thunderstorm raged. They'd rehashed all their evidence, weighed various theories, and concluded their best course of action was to investigate Little Lazarus Island in person. Small as it was, and even though half covered in scrub, it had far too much beach surface for them to dig up in the hopes of finding a buried map. But they still hadn't solved the "bones" component of Brackett's delirious clues and hoped that, in person, they might find something that would enable them to hone in on Brackett's meaning and thus the map. It was at least worth a try.

They had taken a cab to Victoria's because of the rain, but by the time they finished a guava-filled dessert called duff, the sun was out, as was a rainbow in front of rapidly diminishing dark gray clouds. "Walk back?" Sawyer asked, nodding at the beach.

Jackson patted his amply full stomach. "Sure."

She still wore the V-neck "Bama" shirt, now with jeans. She rolled up her pant legs and carried her flip-flops in her hand. Jackson trudged along in his shoes, as he always did. Very un-California-like.

"You want to hear something corny?" Sawyer asked as they walked.

"No. Not really."

She backhanded him in the arm.

"I mean, I would love to."

They took a few steps, then she said, "The fall after my mom died, my dad and I were both having a rough time. My dad being who he was, he kept his pain pretty well hidden at the time. He was more focused on making sure his little girl was okay. Somehow, he scored tickets to an Alabama game. I don't even remember who they were playing, some no-name non-conference team. For three and a half hours that Saturday afternoon, I sat enthralled as he explained the game to me. I was captivated by the sights and sounds of the crowd, the pop of the pads, the flow of the game. And I fell in love with Alabama football."

They were walking slowly, alone for all intents and purposes on the beach, the scent of rain and the tang of salt mixing in the air.

"After that," Sawyer said, "Daddy and I watched football together every Saturday. We didn't have cable, so we'd go to my uncle's house or one of his friends for the ESPN games. But we never missed a game. Haven't missed a game together since 1991."

"Wow."

"That day didn't make everything better. We still both missed Mom terribly—he the wife he'd known and I the mom I hadn't. There were days I had to be strong for him, and days—and years—he had to be strong for me. But we made it. And we're still making it. But no matter what, we always had each other, and we always had Alabama football as a three-and-a-half-hour escape each Saturday. And so as much as I love Alabama football because they eat everybody else's lunch and because ever since that day as a six-year-old kid I've been in love with the game itself, I also love Alabama football because of what it means and has meant to Daddy and me."

They had almost stopped walking. Jackson studied Sawyer, the breeze swirling her blond hair, and the sun peeking around storm clouds accentuating her hair and tanned skin. She was beautiful—radiant, in fact—and not just physically. There was a beauty in her vulnerability, a sweetness in her sentimentality, a peace despite her pain.

"You look like you want to say something," she said after nearly a minute of silence.

"I do, but . . . I don't know what."

"The rainbow," she said, nodding at its fading colors. "It rained during the fourth quarter of that game Daddy and I went to. He wanted to leave; he was afraid I'd get sick. I begged him to stay. I loved the new game so much, loved being there with him. Without knowing it, I probably loved the fact that I'd found a respite from my sadness for a little while."

She tucked hair behind her ear, and they trekked on.

"As we were leaving the game, the sun came out, like this," she said, gesturing with her hand, "and then a rainbow." She smiled placidly. "I've never seen one since without thinking about that day . . . about him."

Jackson offered her his sincerest smile. "I still don't know what to say, except that's not corny."

Her smile back was as bright as the setting sun.

They kept walking. She told him more about her childhood, about her love for the outdoors, about learning to hunt and fish, about navigating her first school dance without a mom.

"I didn't think Baptists from Alabama were allowed to dance."

Sawyer narrowed her left eye at him.

"Sorry, I'm a lousy person to get sentimental with. All I can do is crack wise in return."

"I don't mind. And it was card-playing and movie-watching that were really frowned upon."

They walked some more.

"What were your parents like?" she asked.

"They were perfect," Jackson said. "I mean, they had faults of course, like everybody. Mom could fuss over me a little too much, and Dad could turn everything into a Naval analogy. But as far as I can tell, they did everything right. You know, I've always heard other people talk about some precious moment with their mom when they were little that shaped them, or a really special talk with their dad where he imparted some piece of wisdom." He shrugged. "I don't have one thing or one moment I can point to. I can't pick out one or the other attribute that made them great parents. I just have twenty-nine years of consistent, godly, wise parenting."

"That's beautiful."

He looked at her. "I never appreciated it. I mean, I did, but the same way I appreciate pizza and USC being in the Rose Bowl and breathing. Then, in one moment, it was snuffed out. And all I can think about is how much I had and how much I don't."

Sawyer touched his arm, stopping him. He turned her way, and she embraced him in a tight, warm hug. Right there on the beach, in front of everybody but nobody. He felt the softness of her hair as the breeze carried it into his face, smelled the subtle citrus fragrance of her perfume.

"I am so sorry," she said, still holding him tight. Without realizing what he was doing, he held her back. "For everything—your loss, your pain, your struggle." She backed away, far enough to make eye contact with him. For a few seconds, she just looked into his soul, then she let go of him and stepped back. She picked up her flip-flops, which she had apparently dropped before hugging him, then stuck her free hand in her pocket and resumed walking. Jackson waited a second and followed.

A few paces after he caught up, she looked his way. She swiped hair back behind her ear and returned her hand to her pocket. "I think you do remarkably well."

He raised an eyebrow.

"Losing both parents at once, and a brother. And when they clearly meant so much to you . . ."

"I don't feel remarkable," Jackson said.

"Being in a rut with God, you mean?"

"Yeah."

"But you haven't quit. Haven't bailed, walked away. Haven't done what Job's wife said, 'curse God, and die.'"

He said nothing.

"God knows your pain. He experienced your pain. He understands your struggle, and your struggle with Him. He is patient and long-suffering, however long it takes you to struggle through this."

He said nothing.

"You may feel like you've wronged Him, and maybe you have in all this. You probably have, because we all do. But He's forgiven that too."

Jackson nodded.

"One more thing, and then I'll stop preaching."

He grinned.

"I don't mean to sound like I'm minimizing what you're going through, and can't begin to know what you are, but it's like I told you before, Jackson, from where I stand . . ." She shook her head. "I think . . . I think you're doing better than you give yourself credit for."

Jackson swallowed hard. Twice. He nodded, finding his voice. "Thanks, Sawyer. That means a lot."

She smiled, and they walked for a while. They were past the hotel. Jackson had a feeling Sawyer knew too and, like him, didn't care.

"How early do we have to leave tomorrow?" she asked.

"Early."

"How do we do it without being tailed?"

"Don't know."

He thought about that for a while. They hadn't spotted either Baldwin or Green Dress since arriving at the department of records that afternoon. That didn't mean they weren't there, or that there weren't others in the ring who were taking a turn tailing them.

They walked all the way to West End, by which time the sun had set and left the western sky a fresco too amazing to be replicated. They turned around, trudging slowly in the dark. Sawyer's free hand was still in her pocket. Jackson's eyes were on the shops and stores and the people along Atlantic Drive. He saw nothing out of the ordinary.

Back at the hotel, they set alarms for five a.m. They said goodnight and closed doors.

Then Jackson did some math and called Reggie and his grandpa before sacking out.

Chapter Forty-One

JACKSON'S ALARM WOKE him from a dream in which he had been fighting over treasure on a beach with Captain Redbeard from his old LEGO sets. It took him a moment to come to and to realize why in the Sam Hill he was awake at five in the morning.

He sighed and threw off the sheet he'd slept under. He set coffee brewing and hopped in the shower. As he went through the motions, he thought through his and Sawyer's plans for the day and pondered their talk on the beach the night before. She had made good sense, as she always did, and he was starting to figure out just what it was about her that made her special, that made her so likable. And yet, he couldn't help but feel there was more of a wedge between him and God than a reassurance from a relative stranger could break apart. Question was, was that wedge real or the product of Jackson's imagination?

He also thought about Frank Baldwin and Green Dress, who they were working for, how they knew to follow Jackson and Sawyer, and what else they knew. Was it possible Martin Louviere had had Ben and Damon killed because they got too close to the treasure, but now was letting Jackson and Sawyer find the next clue? Or were their assassins merely waiting for the opportune moment? In which case, getting alone on a boat away from civilization probably wasn't the keenest of plans.

Or was it possible that Baldwin and Green Dress weren't working for Louviere after all, that they were actually with a third party that held an interest in the treasure? If so, who were they? Did Ryker, Ben, and/or Damon's deaths tie to them instead of to Louviere? There were too many pieces on the board, and they weren't wearing clearly defined colors.

At five-thirty, a showered, dressed, and caffeinated Jackson peered out the curtains on his window. Sunrise on Lazarus Island was set for 6:38, but already the sky was showing hints of light. With the lights in his room off, Jackson was able to make out the waves breaking gently on the beach, and as he let his eyes grow accustomed to the darkness, see enough of the beach to conclude it was empty. Empty, that was, except for an abundance of shadows where Baldwin or anyone else could hide.

He knocked on Sawyer's door a few minutes later, and she opened it dressed and ready to go. Jackson had always sort of shared the Beach Boys' thoughts on California girls, but Sawyer was making him rethink that. Who got showered, dressed, did whatever it was she had to do with her hair each morning, and apparently ate half a banana in thirty minutes? Make it three-quarters of a banana.

"You cub up wib a pan . . ." She swallowed. "To make sure we aren't followed?"

"That wasn't very refined."

"It's early."

"Circumspection," he answered.

"I tried prayer."

"That assumes God wants us to find the treasure."

"I'm thinking more of justice for Ben and Damon. He would want that."

"Then it's assuming He wants us to be the ministers of justice."

"It's too early for all this thinking."

"Yeah."

"You ready?" she asked.

"Just gotta grab our gear."

"You call for a cab?"

"And that."

"I'll call. You grab the gear."

"Fair enough."

He grabbed the shovel and the backpack they'd bought at the hardware store the night before. The backpack contained eight bottles of water, more fruit, some granola and energy bars. He hefted it onto his shoulder as Sawyer put her room phone back on the cradle. She turned toward the door between their rooms. "Five minutes."

"Great."

"All you're missing is the metal detector."

"Should have checked on rentals."

"I did, at the hardware store. No dice."

He nodded. "What time'd you get up?"

"Pardon?"

"I got up at five. You?"

"Quarter till. Why?"

Forty-five minutes. Still put California girls to shame. And not one of them could hold a candle to her. Well, one. But he didn't want to think about her.

"No reason. Let's go."

They headed down through the lobby, spotting no one, not even a desk clerk. They waited by the curb of the hotel's semicircle driveway for two minutes until a pink cab pulled up. The driver was young, wide-eyed, and drove like a Cat 5 was bearing down on the island. But he got them to the marina safely, and Jackson would have paid to watch Baldwin or Green Dress try to keep up with them.

The proprietor at North Point Charters was a graying old man with a faded Lazarus Island cap on his head. His long and gnarled hands jotted down their names, checked IDs, and processed payment. The afternoon before, Jackson had been pleasantly surprised that the marina and the charter company opened at five a.m., catering to fishermen according to the younger man—possibly this guy's kid—on duty then. It worked for them.

In addition to a twenty-four-foot powerboat, they also rented a small cooler in which Jackson stashed their bottled water and snacks. Shortly after six, they cast off from the dock, and Sawyer steered the boat through the buoy-lined channel to deeper water, then curved around to the west and south.

The sun peeked over the horizon, illuminating Sawyer in the same orangey-gold hue as the night before. Her hair and the ties of a swimsuit under a loose teal tank top flapped in the breeze as she studied the horizon from behind her silver aviator sunglasses. Jackson scanned the shoreline to their left, the lights of Woodes Town going dark as the sun quickly warmed the day. Then he scanned the water all around them, spotting four other vessels. Three were fishing trawlers headed into deeper waters, and the other was a sailboat more or less following the coastline south. None of them concerned him.

"I didn't see a tail," Sawyer said.

Jackson shook his head. "Me either. And we should be able to spot anyone following us out on the open sea."

Ten miles due south of Lazarus Island, Little Lazarus Island sat on the surface of the water, looking like a mitten from above. The palm and part of the thumb were covered in foliage except for a thin line of sand that ringed them. The tip of the thumb and the four fingers were open beach, with a very shallow inlet between them. Instead of steering the boat into the inlet, Sawyer ran it onto a shallow underwater bank extending like a point from the fingers of the mitten.

Kicking off her flip-flops, she jumped overboard, slogging through shin-deep water to dry land.

"Don't we need to anchor this to something?" Jackson asked from the bow.

"You see anything around?"

He shook his head. The tallest "tree" on the island was a five- or six-foot palm stub, and the nearest was fifty or sixty feet inland. "What about the tide?" he asked.

"We're just past high tide," she answered. "If anything, we'll have to push it out to deeper water when we leave."

He nodded.

"If you're worried, keep an eye on it. It won't go far, and we can swim to it."

"Super." He kicked off his shoes and vaulted over the bow, joining her on dry land. She stood with hands on her hips, waiting for instructions.

"Rich man's bones," Jackson said. "Let's circle the island. See if we see any grave markers, odd geographical features, or human markings of any kind. Or a path through the bramble in the middle."

"Want to split up and go opposite ways?"

"I'd rather have two sets of eyes on everything."

She nodded, and they started walking. There was nothing of interest as they circled the west and south sides of the island, just a thin strip of beach separating the ocean from thick ground cover. On the east, the coast was more jagged, and they had to pick their way carefully along the shore. At the point of the thumb of the mitten, they stopped.

"Rich man's bones," Jackson said again. "I'm pretty sure they didn't have mittens in 1715, but they had hands. When you think of a hand, where do you think of bones?"

"Everywhere. Fingers, especially. Knuckles."

Jackson nodded.

"But I don't know that the island has that much definition."

They kept moving around the thumb, a twenty-foot-wide peninsula. It was a beautiful scene, with transparent turquoise water in every direction. Jackson squinted to see Lazarus Island in the distance. The curvature of the earth limited ocean vision to thirteen or so miles unless either the viewer or the object in question towered over the surface. The third story of the Hotel Sir Donovan was probably the highest point on Lazarus Island, and it was just barely visible over the ocean swells.

"Kind of eerie, isn't it?" Sawyer said, stopping beside Jackson.

"Yeah, I can see why they'd compare being marooned here to the rich man's plight."

"A ten-mile swim, probably worth a try, but given the current we came through, unless you're Michael Phelps, you'd likely be carried wide of the island."

"If the sharks didn't get you first." He turned over his shoulder. "You see any freighters as we were coming down this way?"

Sawyer shook her head.

"I'm guessing we're just far enough north, far enough up into the islands, to be too far away from shipping channels, then or now. Unless you pull a Keira Knightley and light . . ."

"What?"

"You ever see *Pirates of the Caribbean*?"

"Is that the movie with Johnny Depp?"

He nodded.

"I saw half of it once. Looked pretty dumb."

"Agree to disagree. Did you see the scene where they were marooned on the island?"

"No."

"He wanted to drink all the rum because he was a pirate, and she used it to light palm trees on fire and signal a passing ship."

"You think Brackett did the same?"

"It would explain how Toussaint spotted him out here in the middle of nowhere."

"Assuming Brackett was marooned on the island."

"Correct."

"And that Toussaint didn't sail to Lazarus Island for some reason, thus bringing him within eyesight of Little Lazarus Island."

"Assuming that too."

She shrugged. "Viable theory."

"That's all it is. It doesn't do us any good."

She dragged her toe through the sand absentmindedly. "We're working on the theory that Willie was right about castaways and criminals being stranded here, and maybe mutinied pirate captains too, right?"

He nodded.

"And the theory would suggest most of them didn't light a signal fire like in the movies, right?"

He nodded again.

"So what happened to the people who died?"

"Probably nothing. Nobody would have cared about a criminal's body, or that of their mutinied captain, for that matter."

Her turn to nod. "So what happened to the bodies?"

Jackson shrugged. "They rotted."

"Except their bones."

His eyes widened.

"Presumably, Brackett wasn't the first person marooned here. Maybe he wasn't even marooned, but used the island because he knew it was so desolate."

"So we're looking for real bones of some poor slob marooned here?"

"Maybe."

"That Brackett used to mark the location of the treasure or give some clue about the treasure?"

She shrugged.

He sighed. "Okay, let's check the beach," he said with a nod at the fingers of the mitten. He trudged around the space between the thumb and forefinger of the mitten. Sawyer waded through knee-deep water in the inlet. Jackson couldn't blame her. It was already getting hot.

They took their time covering the few thousand square feet of open sand, looking for anything out of place. They found nothing and were about to give up when Sawyer stopped suddenly.

"What is it?" Jackson asked.

"I don't know. Something hard." She swept the sand back and forth with her foot and then dropped to her knees as Jackson approached. Brushing sand away with her fingers, she unearthed a long, white object. She tugged it out of the sand and extended it to Jackson.

A human bone.

They looked at each other for a moment. Then they began clawing at the ground, stopping a minute later when Jackson's fingers rubbed across something hard. Another bone.

"This is it," Sawyer said. "I don't believe it."

Jackson stood and surveyed the ocean. Not a vessel to be seen. He hurried back to the boat and retrieved the shovel. He also brought back a cool bottle of water and a granola bar for each of them. After quickly replenishing their strength, they resumed digging, he carefully with the shovel and Sawyer more delicately with her hands. An hour after she found the first, they had close to a dozen human bones, mostly arms, legs, and ribs. Jackson hadn't studied anatomy recently enough to know their technical terms, and at the moment, he didn't care.

"There's no way this is coincidence," Sawyer said as they sat back and looked at the pit they had dug, three feet in diameter and about half that deep.

"No," Jackson said, turning one of the bones in his hand.

"So we found the rich man's bones," she said. "Now what?"

"The answer is probably on the next page of the journal." He tossed the bone onto the pile. "I'm not a forensics expert. You have any idea if we're looking at more than one body?"

"Unless this poor guy had some serious mutation. We have four femurs."

"All right then. We have at least two bodies, and they're not lying naturally. And there aren't enough bones for two whole bodies to have been dumped here in a heap."

"Meaning?"

"We've got mostly long bones. No skulls. I think they were purposefully stacked here as some sort of a marker, before centuries of wind and storms and erosion."

"I'd agree. But marking what?"

Jackson looked around again, making sure no one was sneaking up on them. "I guess we keep digging."

While Sawyer took a turn with the shovel, widening the hole, Jackson went deeper, scooping handfuls at a time. They found two more ribs and a humerus, according to Sawyer. Then Jackson's hand brushed over a wide, circular bone. "Uh, Sawyer."

She stopped and turned his way.

"I think we found Hamlet."

"You mean Yorick?" she asked.

"Whomever. But this is a skull."

She bent forward to help him exhume the skull, and he let her gently lift it from the sand.

It rattled.

Sawyer stopped. She slowly rotated the skull. Jackson nearly did a double take when his eyes rested on a stubby brown bottle jammed inside it. Sawyer's eyes indicated similar disbelief.

"Great," Jackson said at length. "Captain Brackett gets rescued and all his delirious mind can think of is where he hid his last bottle of rum."

Sawyer lifted the bottle out and set the skull aside. "It's corked," she said as she handed it to Jackson. "But it's empty."

He took it and tried to peer through the glass. It wasn't very translucent, but Jackson thought he saw a shape inside. So he popped the cork, sending it flying into the sand. "Whoo," he said, pulling back his head from the opening.

"A little aged?"

Jackson tipped the bottle up to his eye.

"There something in there?"

"Yeah. Looks like a piece of cloth or a scrap of paper or something."

"Can you get it out?"

Jackson nodded and stood. He walked a few paces over to a small piece of driftwood and banged the bottle on it. Glass cracked and splintered, and he tapped the bottle against the wood a few more times. A folded and rolled piece of paper fell out. The corked bottle had preserved it well, and he carried it back to Sawyer.

"You have a gentle touch."

"Yeah, well." Jackson unrolled and unfolded the paper and immediately knew he had something. It was a little larger than a standard sheet of copy paper, yellowed and worn, but in good shape. Black ink, faded in places, was largely legible.

"What is it?" Sawyer asked anxiously.

"Oh, nothing. Just a treasure map signed by James Brackett."

Chapter Forty-Two

SAWYER SCRAMBLED OVER beside Jackson to view the map. She immediately frowned. "It's pretty vague."

It was indeed. It depicted a large, bulbous circle, a line going to the right from the circle, then a line going down from the end of the first line to an X. Two squiggly, roughly parallel lines ran from the top right to the bottom left. The upper line bowed around the circle, intersecting the line that ran right from the circle. The lower squiggly line bisected the X. There were no other lines, no geographical references, no north arrow.

"There are directions up here," Jackson said, pointing to a pair of lines of print just below the map. "'*From the large oak at Rum Runner's Pointe, bear fifteen paces east and twenty paces south.*'"

"That's it?"

"Also pretty vague. And somewhat dependent on finding Rum Runner's Pointe."

"Well it's not on this island," she said, looking around. "No oak tree."

"Not now, but in 1715?"

"I still doubt it. This doesn't strike me as the place for an oak tree." She pointed to a paragraph at the top of the paper. "What's this?"

"I don't know. I'm reading it now." He tipped the paper so she could see it a little better.

September 5/6, 1715

I have lost track of the days, but I am confident I shall not find rescue. Perhaps it is the fate I deserve. A fortnight ago, I and my crew set upon the Spanish ship Nuestra Senora de la Granada, relieving her of her cargo. We were hired by Capitan de Castano of the Spanish

Armada, with the promise that the Granada's treasure would be ours if we also liberated his daughter, Liliana, from the hand of the Granada's captain. We succeeded and left the Granada adrift in the ocean. We sailed for San Juan, where we were to meet with Capitan de Castano. However, Fate, or perhaps Providence, intervened. A hurricane forced us to seek solace in the islands off Florida. By the time the storm had passed, our ship was sunk and our number depleted. Most tragic of all, the sweet, innocent Liliana was dead by the storm.

I take the blame for her death, and for that of my crew. We commandeered a passing fishing ship and sailed for the Bahamas in the hope of finding a new ship or a vessel bound for England. However, my crew had other plans. Blaming me for the events that had transpired, they marooned me on this island, where it appears I shall meet my Maker.

I have no expectations of seeing another human soul again. Below are instructions for finding the Granada's treasure. May God be Judge and determine its rightful owner now, and may He hold me responsible for dear Liliana's death.

Signed,
Captain James L. Brackett

Jackson and Sawyer looked up at the same time. She then lowered her eyes and read it again. When she was finished, all she uttered was a quiet, "Wow."

"I don't know where to start," Jackson said, skimming the letter again himself.

"So the Spanish hired an English pirate to hit their own ship?"

Jackson nodded. "Meaning he was on the run from both the Spanish and the English."

"How do you figure?"

"He hit a Spanish ship, and probably the only two people who knew why were Brackett and de Castaño. The rest of the Spanish Armada would have been after him and his crew. And when Brackett didn't show in San Juan, de Castaño had to assume the worst about his daughter."

"Meaning he'd be after Brackett too."

"Right. And if these guys had any smarts at all, they put out an 18th century BOLO on Brackett."

"BOLO?" Sawyer asked.

"Be on the lookout. An APB. And if it was me, I'd have used whatever back channels existed in the day to let the English know that their native son was consorting with the Spanish, making him guilty of treason in their minds. So now everybody but the French would be after Brackett, and let's face it, the French are the French. Their national anthem is 'I Surrender All.'"

Sawyer raised an eyebrow at him before continuing. "Brackett probably knew all this going in. So when Liliana died in the storm, he knew he was sunk."

"Very good," he said with a mock clap.

"No pun intended. Brackett couldn't deliver Liliana to de Castaño, meaning he would want his treasure back—"

"Which wouldn't have played well with Brackett's crew."

"And de Castaño would also want Brackett's hide for losing his daughter."

"Which couldn't have played too well with the crew either."

"So after they escape from the Keys, they maroon him on Rich Man's Island and . . . what?"

"Again, if it's me, try to find the treasure."

"Wouldn't they know where it was?"

"Depends when and where they ditched it. If Brackett was smart, he didn't let his crew know exactly where he buried it."

"How would they not know?"

"If it's me, I take four grunts and my boatswain ashore. Have the grunts bury it, and then I and the boatswain shoot them all on the way back to the ship. Then I shoot the boatswain, leaving no one alive who knows the location of the treasure."

"You sound as if you've thought about this."

He shrugged. "Even if it's buried on an island this small, it would take an awful long time to find it if you didn't know where to dig. Make it an island the size of Lazarus Island, which is pretty small compared to some, and we're to needle in a haystack territory without a map."

"So why maroon your captain? Why not . . . persuade him to tell you where it is?"

"Maybe they thought they did know." He shrugged. "Or underestimated how hard it would be to find it."

"And why did they hide it in the first place? Did he have a change of heart after falling for Liliana?"

"You think he fell for Liliana?"

"It's in between all the lines."

"If he fell for her before the hurricane killed her, he might not have wanted to go back to de Castaño anyhow. I doubt the Capitán General of the Spanish Navy would have okayed his daughter marrying a pirate if he didn't approve of her relationship with one of his own captains."

"Right. So why not sail away with the treasure? Why hide it somewhere?"

"Maybe he thought he'd never escape the Spanish dragnet, so he hid it, planning to come back for it later. Then the crew mutinied, and he was marooned here. Or maybe he hid it so the storm wouldn't send it to Davey Jones' locker."

Sawyer sighed. "That brings up another question: Why did Brackett seem to know where he'd hidden the treasure when he wrote this note, but when the French found him a week or two later, all he could do was babble about some bones? Didn't Ruby Mae say the *Majesté Royale* arrived in New Orleans on September twenty-seventh?"

Jackson nodded.

"And this was written on the fifth or sixth. I don't know how fast the *Royale* would have sailed, but I'm guessing they picked him up around the twentieth. That's two weeks."

"Two weeks alone on an island, no food, maybe some dysentery, a failed attempt to swim to Lazarus Island . . . your faculties could go."

"So why not just take the bottle when he was rescued?"

"The journal just said that Toussaint's crew picked up a delirious man. It doesn't say what shape he was in or how long it was before he identified himself and started mumbling. Maybe they revived him with some whiskey first, by which time they were already on their way again."

"I suppose. There are just a lot of unanswered questions."

"I agree. But we have the important facts. Brackett buried the treasure, and we have his personal instructions where to find it."

Sawyer frowned. "Where do you suppose he got the ink and paper?"

"Pricked himself with a stick?"

She looked at him out the top of her eyes.

"I don't know. Maybe it was standard rations for a marooned man so he could write a proper suicide note."

"I guess it doesn't matter. We have the note."

He nodded and, as they stood up, he again surveyed the horizon. A pleasure yacht drifted several miles to the northwest. Maybe it was sport fishermen. Otherwise, the sea was as empty as the sky above it.

"Makes you wonder whatever happened to the *Missianna*," Sawyer said. "Assuming that it was actually Brackett's voyage to find his map and thus the treasure."

"You know, we're forgetting another possibility. Maybe the delirious Brackett kept mumbling about the rich man's bones because he knew it was where he'd left the map. It doesn't mean three years later when his brain cleared that he still needed his map. Maybe he remembered where his treasure was buried and was sailing there."

"So it could be anywhere in the Bahamas?"

"Or anywhere at all," Jackson said. "Remember, the same legend that holds the *Missianna* was sailing for the Bahamas also claimed it was captained by Brackett's ghost."

Sawyer sighed. "So basically, we need to figure out where Rum Runner's Pointe is."

"Yeah. And wherever it is, hope it's home to the world's oldest oak tree."

"Is there anything else we can do here?"

"I don't think so. Except bury these bones again."

"Why?"

"I'd hate for Louviere to stumble upon the island this afternoon and realize we found something."

"Might want to clean up your glass shards then too."

"Good point."

Jackson carefully placed Brackett's map in a glove box aboard the boat before returning to help Sawyer bury all of the bones and cover them with sand. It was slow going, taking almost an hour to fill in all the sand, then doing their best to sweep sand across the filled in hole. When they were finished and had trampled around the general area, only the faint indentations of footprints remained.

Hot and sweating, Jackson felt like taking a dip in the inlet. Instead, he merely suggested they get back to Lazarus Island. Sawyer concurred (she didn't concur with his idea of digging another hole and not covering it up so well as a decoy) and they returned to the boat. She had been right earlier, as the tides had stranded the powerboat on the shore. With both of them pushing, they dislodged it. Two minutes later, Sawyer had eased away from Little Lazarus Island and taken aim at Lazarus Bight.

"So how do we play this?" she asked.

"How's your poker face?"

"Fair to middlin'."

"We go back to the hotel and figure out our next steps, but assume we're being watched all . . . the . . ."

"What is it?"

Jackson had let his eyes roam the seas yet again, and the pleasure yacht/sport fisher had turned back toward Lazarus Island. It was following them, sort of, at about eight o'clock.

"Maybe nothing," he said. "You notice when that yacht over there showed up?"

Sawyer turned her head. "First time I've seen it."

Jackson nodded. "Like I said, poker face."

"Okay, so now to the real question. What about lunch?"

"What sounds good?"

"You ever had a really good Cuban sandwich?"

"Can't say as I have."

"I saw a place the other night that looked like fun. On South Atlantic."

"Works for me. We can stash the map back at the hotel, clean up, then have a late lunch and figure out what's next."

They returned to the marina, and while Jackson squared with the proprietor for gas money, Sawyer called another cab. As it drove them back along the beach, Jackson looked out at the bight and saw the yacht a half mile out, headed for the marina. Could still be just a coincidence.

Upon returning to the hotel, they were both hungry but agreed to shower and change before meeting up for lunch. Jackson closed his door behind him and exhaled. Could it really be? Were they deciphering one phrase away from finding a three-hundred-year-old pirate treasure? And could doing so somehow lead them to finding out what had happened to Ben and who was behind it?

Jackson removed the map from his pocket and studied it for a moment before placing it on the table. He kicked off his shoes and stepped into the bathroom, turning on the water before starting to undress.

A scream interrupted him.

Jackson poked his head back through his shirt and listened. He heard a thud and a muffled second scream and hurried to the doors between his and Sawyer's room. "Sawyer!" he yelled, jerking open his door.

The response was another muffled scream, and Jackson twisted open her unlocked door. He burst into her room just in time to see her leg pulled out the front door before it slammed shut.

Chapter Forty-Three

12:19 p.m.

JACKSON TRIPPED AS he plunged into Sawyer's room. As he got to his feet, he had the presence of mind to take one second to look around the room. No one was there. No clues jumped out at him. No issues were apparent other than Sawyer's absence.

Jackson hurried to the door. He yanked it open and burst through, catching himself on the railing. The corridor was empty to his right, and there was no way anyone could have made it out of the room and all the way to the lobby entrance in the few seconds since Jackson had seen Sawyer dragged from the room. So he turned left, stopping to look over the railing of the stairs. A hulking black guy had Sawyer over his shoulder in a fireman's carry as he hurried south away from the hotel. Another man who might have been Frank Baldwin ran beside him.

Jackson gave just a moment's consideration to vaulting over the railing as his eyes simultaneously searched the beach to see who might stop an obvious kidnapping. There were several sunbathers a few hundred feet up the beach, a small group playing in the shallow water, and a handful of people walking at various points along the shore. Everyone else was at lunch or avoiding the heat of the day. Nobody gave more than a passing glance as Sawyer was carried away. Wondering why she wasn't screaming, Jackson resumed his pursuit.

In a flash, he was around the side of the hotel and down the steps. He sprinted across the beach, maybe fifty feet behind the man carrying Sawyer. Sixty max. The guy was moving, but Jackson had no doubt he could catch him, even in just socks. Taking him down and rescuing Sawyer, plus dealing with the other guy, would be a different matter.

Before Jackson could formulate a plan, they turned, veering across the beachside pathway and into a narrow alley between establishments on

Atlantic Drive. Jackson followed them around the corner and was broadsided by a punch. He fell backward, nearly slamming his head on the alley pavement.

Jackson's assailant followed his punch by lunging at Jackson as he tried to get back up. The guy was sturdy but slow, and Jackson was fueled by urgency and adrenaline. Not in a position to throw a punch, Jackson kicked at the man's groin. It wasn't a direct hit, but it slowed the guy and knocked him off balance. Jackson scrambled to his feet as the guy charged again. He attacked like a bull, lowering his shoulder in an effort to drive Jackson back into the wall of a building. Jackson was off balance for a moment but managed to slow the guy's momentum. He then brought his knee up, this time not missing the groin.

The man staggered back, wincing in pain. Jackson stepped forward and drilled him in the chin with a downward right cross. Landing with a thud, the man hesitated for a moment before slowly rolling and pushing to his hands and knees. If Jackson had been interested, he could have finished the guy off, but he took the opening to run toward the street in pursuit of Sawyer and her kidnapper.

Foot traffic along Atlantic Drive was sparse. Most of it revolved around a few eateries, and Jackson quickly spotted Sawyer and her kidnapper a hundred feet ahead. They weaved around the few people on the sidewalk, none of whom made an effort to intervene. Jackson didn't know why, unless it was that they were scared off by the size of the man carrying her. Instead of yelling for help, Jackson used all his energy to run, dodging pedestrians and a rickshaw. He had closed the gap in half by the time the man turned into another alley. Jackson slipped as he reached and turned the corner, but he righted himself in time to see the man dump Sawyer unceremoniously beside a dumpster and take off up the beach.

Sawyer was already on her feet when Jackson reached her, and he grabbed her shoulders to steady her. "Are you okay?" he asked, eyes darting from her to either end of the alley.

"I'm fine," she panted. "He . . . He's getting away."

"Let him go. He didn't hurt you?"

"Just knocked the wind out of me. And a few bumps and bruises. I'll be fine. Where's the other one?"

"I left him in the first alley. Let's get you back."

"I'm fine, Jackson. Really," she said, checking a scrape on her arm. "A little rumpled for a refined Southern woman, but I'm okay. I took more punishment playing Powder Puff football."

"Even so, we should get back," Jackson said, a pit forming in his stomach. He doubted it had been his tireless pursuit or intimidating physique that had caused Sawyer's kidnapper to drop her. Thoughts of the yacht that had followed them back to shore and of the Brackett map he had left in his room filled his head. "You want me to carry you to the beach?" he asked, looking down at her bare feet and the rough alley pavement.

"Else lend me your socks," she said, reminding Jackson that he had chased her for several blocks without shoes. Suddenly he felt the scrapes and scratches caused by the sidewalk and alley. Not exactly *Die Hard*, but painful nonetheless.

"I'll be fine," she added once again. "Let's go."

Jackson thought that maybe the chase had drawn a crowd that he had failed to notice while running, but no one paid them any attention as they walked along the beach. Maybe women were dragged from their hotels frequently on Lazarus Island.

"What happened?" Jackson asked.

"I was about to hop in the shower when I heard a noise at the door. I thought it was you, and all I could wonder was why you didn't use the door between the rooms. Then my door flew open, and those two guys walked in. They grabbed me and dragged me out. I thought maybe I could fight them off until you got there, but that guy had hands like a vice. When he threw me onto his shoulder, the wind went out of me, and I didn't get it back until just before he threw me down."

"Had you deadbolted your door?"

Sawyer shrugged sheepishly. "I didn't."

Jackson nodded and tensed as they approached the alley where he'd scuffled with the man. But he was long gone, adding to Jackson's growing fear that Sawyer's kidnapping had been nothing more than a diversion. He quickened their pace and took the steps to the Hotel Sir Donovan's second story two at a time.

"Hang back a sec," Jackson said to Sawyer as he approached her door. He peeked in and saw that it was vacant but in disarray. Most of the contents of her suitcase had been strewn on the floor. The bed had been ripped apart, the sheets and comforter piled in the corner. Several dresser drawers were open, as were both of the nightstand drawers.

Jackson ducked into his room and saw that it was as he'd left it. Running water sounded from the bathroom where he'd left the shower on. He took a step toward the bathroom and stopped.

The table was empty.

"How's your room?" Sawyer asked from the doorway. "Oh, that's nice. They . . . What is it?"

"The map," Jackson said. "It was on the table."

She looked at him. "Smash and grab."

"More like misdirection. That's why they gave up, why he dumped you. They just needed a few minutes' distraction."

"And we fell for it. Well, I feel like a fool."

"They duped us both," Jackson said. "And now they have the map."

*   *   *

2:34 p.m.

CLOUDS HAD formed in a low bank to the east, forerunners of a storm, according to Sawyer. For now, the only other indication of a change in the weather was a steady breeze blowing offshore as she and Jackson walked along the beach north of the Hotel Sir Donovan. First, they had walked to South Atlantic Drive to the Cuban sandwich shop Sawyer had spotted, where they had both enjoyed roast pork, glazed ham, and Swiss cheese sandwiches. Now they were walking with the general goal of reaching the old fishing pier near the marina, some half mile from the hotel. Walking helped her think, Sawyer had said, and Jackson hadn't objected.

They had notified the hotel staff of the break-in, not mentioning what had been stolen or giving any indication that they knew why they had been targeted. They had accepted the hotel's apology and the comping of their third night's stay, and left their rooms behind. Whoever had broken in had gotten the object they wanted, so there was no reason to believe they would be back. If they had wanted to harm Jackson or Sawyer, they'd had their chance. Jackson surmised the map was all they were after.

He'd also surmised it had been Baldwin or Green Dress who had taken the map while the other two characters, neither of whom had they seen before, had carried out the abduction to lure Jackson from his room. He'd also concluded the yacht he'd seen trailing them back from Little Lazarus Island had been involved. The timeline was tight, but anyone aboard the yacht could have made it back to land and to the Hotel Sir Donovan in time to be part of the abduction/theft. How they knew Jackson and Sawyer had found something and why they hadn't simply waited for them to go to lunch were questions that would go unanswered.

"Okay, I think I've sulked long enough," Sawyer said as they padded along a barren stretch of beach. "You want to tell me why you've been hiding a smirk for the last two hours."

Jackson glanced around to make sure they were alone. Just up the shore to their right, Atlantic Drive followed the slow curve of the shoreline. Across the road, the terrain was thick with trees, and except for a few private residences beside the road, it appeared they were in the middle of nowhere instead of a quarter mile from Woodes Town.

"They have the map," he said. "But that doesn't mean we don't."

"Come again?"

"I've got a pretty good memory," he said. "Almost photographic. I memorized every word on that paper."

"When?"

"On the boat on the way back."

"So you can re-create the map and instructions, everything?"

He tapped the side of his head with his finger. "All up here."

Sawyer walked, head down, for a few paces. "Okay, so what does that mean?"

"It means, if we can solve the riddle before they do, we can still find the treasure."

"So why didn't you say so right away? Why have you let me pout for two hours?"

"Because they might still be watching us. If we act glum and confused, they'll think that we've lost hope."

"You really think they're watching us?"

He shrugged. "Who knows? But the last thing we want to do is tip them off."

"Okay, so what do we do?"

"Figure out if the treasure is on the island or not. My guess is not, but if it is, we need an excuse as to why we're staying here after losing the map. If not, then we leave with our tails tucked between our legs."

Sawyer kicked at the sand and trudged on a few paces. "Okay, tell it to me again."

"*From the large oak at Rum Runner's Pointe, bear fifteen paces east and twenty paces south.*"

She mulled for a dozen steps. "Rum Runner's Pointe. That's the key, right?"

"I would think so."

"Okay, let's walk through this again," she said. "Brackett and the crew of the *Barracuda* attack the *Granada* in the Gulf of Mexico in early August of 1715. They take a load of gold bound for Spain and also kidnap Liliana de Castaño, daughter of the Capitán General of the Spanish Navy. According to Brackett's confession, they did so at the behest of Capitán de Castaño, who didn't approve of her relationship with Reynaldo Garcia III, Captain of the *Granada*."

"Sounds a little like an eighteenth-century soap opera."

"A few days later, a hurricane slams the keys and sinks the *Barracuda*, depleting Brackett's crew and killing Liliana. Brackett and his surviving crew commandeer a passing fishing ship and head for the Bahamas, which were under British control in the 1700s, hoping to find another ship or gain passage back to England. Do I have that right so far?"

"Almost verbatim."

A gust of wind took Sawyer's hair and strung it across her face, and she paused to redirect it before continuing. "Okay, so doesn't that mean they had the treasure with them? They wouldn't consider going all the way back to England without it, would they?"

"Maybe, if they were afraid of taking it with them on a defenseless fishing ship. Maybe they intended to come back and get it once they had a reliable ship, and he left that part out."

"Yeah, maybe," she said. "Or maybe it wouldn't have fit on the fishing ship. Depends how big it was, how many of the crew survived, etcetera."

"So they could have left it behind, but let's work on the theory they took it with them for now."

"Okay," she said. "They sail for the Bahamas with the treasure, and somewhere in there, they decide they've had enough of their captain and maroon him on Rich Man's Island. Why?"

"He wouldn't share the treasure?"

"That's not typical. Most pirates operated by a pretty strict code that dictated who aboard the crew got what."

"Okay, so maybe he didn't stick to the code."

"Maybe . . ."

"Or they realized that because of Brackett's dealings, the entire European Union was after them. Or maybe it was as simple as finding out their English captain had consorted with the Spanish. There's any number of reasons."

"So they maroon him," she said. "Where was the treasure at the time? It would seem to me from what we know that it was already hidden near Rum Runner's Pointe."

"Unless by the time he made the map, Brackett was already daffy."

"If that's the case, we're nowhere."

"Okay, so assume he was of sound mind. Why bury a treasure?"

They had reached the pier, a somewhat dilapidated wooden structure that rose from the beach and extended a few hundred feet into the water. There were no warning signs posted, and an old, hunched over fisherman was coming their way off the pier. Though old, it still looked structurally sound, so Jackson had no qualms following Sawyer onto the pier. Once the old fisherman was out of earshot, they continued talking.

"I've always wondered why pirates buried treasure," Jackson said. "My only guess, it was the best way to keep it safe while they pillaged some more."

"Or until they could find a better ship to transport it."

"So Brackett buried his treasure somewhere between raiding the *Granada* and getting dumped on Little Lazarus Island. Could be in the Keys, the east coast of Florida, the Bahamas, or maybe he made a quick run down to Cuba for some cigars and buried it on the beach outside Havana. And he may or may not have known where he put it when he sailed from New Orleans, and his crew may or may not have found it while he was writing his memoirs in a bottle. That about where we are?"

Sawyer nodded with a frown and leaned on the railing. Jackson joined her, watching the waves crash against the pier pylons. The sky to the north and west was still bright blue but muted by the clouds moving in from the south and east and quickly overtaking the island. The breeze had intensified, and Jackson wondered if the storm would be on them sooner than he'd thought.

"So how do we find Rum Runner's Pointe?" she asked after a while. The waves crashing against the pier pilings were rhythmic and soothing. Jackson was reminded of the Santa Monica Pier back home. For some reason, home wasn't soothing.

"That is our next move, right?" she asked.

He nodded.

"Back to the internet?"

"That or the local cabbie force. Maybe somebody older and more native than Willie knows someplace on the island that used to be called Rum Runner's Pointe."

"I'm really starting to dislike this private investigator business," she said. "Too much research."

"Yeah. But it beats bullets flying at your head."

"Or goons snatching you from your hotel room?"

"That too."

Sawyer sighed and looked wistfully out at the ocean, its beautiful aqua and teal being turned to shades of darker blue and gray. "All right, let's get to it."

The beach around the Hotel Sir Donovan had cleared since their departure an hour earlier, as had the sun's rays. Jackson and Sawyer approached their rooms somewhat tentatively, but found nothing out of place other than an invoice on each of their floors, showing the hotel credit for their third night.

"I still feel a little guilty about this," Sawyer said. "It's not like it was the hotel's fault."

"Your room wasn't broken into," Jackson said. "That means somebody had a skeleton key card, which they likely stole from the hotel."

"Still . . ."

He shrugged as he flipped on the TV, looking for a weather report. The nearest station was out of Nassau, but they had a radar that showed a weakening thundershower moving their way. It wasn't going to be a soaker, it didn't appear.

Sawyer retrieved the rest of her lunch sandwich and sat down next to Jackson. Since she was eating, she handed him her phone, and he began searching for Rum Runner's Pointe, at first just by itself, then in combination with Lazarus Island, the Bahamas, the Florida Keys, James Brackett, and any other phrases he could think of. None panned out.

Sawyer sighed.

"You don't recall coming across any Rum Runner's Pointes in Ben's writing, do you?" he asked.

"You're the one with the photographic memory," she said. She followed up by shaking her head. "No."

"Me either. Although . . ."

She looked at him, just waiting.

"The Point," he said. "Any idea where it got the name?"

"It's a point of land," she said with a shrug.

"Three hundred years ago . . ."

"I suppose it could have been Rum Runner's Pointe. But there's nothing I know that suggests that."

"You know any historians in Key West?"

"I did, until he went missing at sea."

It was Jackson's turn to sigh.

"You know," Sawyer said, "I've been thinking about the location of the treasure. Remember Ben's theory that the *Barracuda* was anchored off Sugarloaf Key when the hurricane hit?"

"Yeah."

"So, Brackett wrote that he and his crew sought relief from the oncoming hurricane in the Keys. If you're them, you take the treasure ashore, right?"

"Yeah."

"If they hadn't, divers would have found parts of it all around the wreck of the *Barracuda*. So they take the treasure ashore and what? Leave it on the beach? Or stash it somewhere to make sure the hurricane doesn't get it?"

Jackson leaned forward. "Stash it someplace safe."

Sawyer nodded. "Right. So now you've buried your treasure, you've survived the hurricane, and you commandeer a fishing ship to sail to the Bahamas to find a bigger boat to take you back to England. So do you bring the treasure along, subjecting it to the rigors of the sea, the possible attack of other pirates, and who knows what in the Bahamas while you're looking for a larger ship? Or do you leave it buried, leave it safe, with a plan to come back to it someday?"

"After stuffing gold down my pocket like the Fresh Prince, I probably leave it hidden until I can transport it securely."

"Fresh Prince?"

"You never watched *The Fresh Prince of Bel-Air*?"

She shook her head.

"Will Smith?"

"I know Will Smith, but I've never seen any show about a prince."

Jackson grinned. "Never mind. Anyhow, your theory would make sense when wondering why they marooned Brackett instead of beating the location of the treasure out of him. Maybe they knew and planned to come for it later."

"Which begs the question, whatever happened to the crew?"

"Didn't you say there were rumors of them showing up in various places?"

"Primarily the Lesser Antilles, yeah."

"Maybe they came back and found it."

"And so now it's gone?"

"But Brackett had reason to believe or hope they hadn't. Else why did he set out for the Bahamas to find his map? Or was he going to find the treasure? Or hunt down his old crew to pay them for marooning him? Or for the fishing?"

Sawyer raked her hand through her hair. "Every question raises ten more."

"Yeah," Jackson said. He grabbed the paper wrapper from her sandwich, balled it, and threw it toward the garbage can. He missed, and it bounced off the wall and the side of the dresser, clipping the corner of the garbage can before rolling halfway back to him on the floor.

"Nice shot," Sawyer teased.

Jackson ignored her, his eyes suddenly focused on the paper. It was balled in such a way that the restaurant's logo was facing him. It displayed the name of the restaurant in the rough shape of a sub sandwich, behind which stood a solitary palm tree. The wheels in Jackson's mind began spinning, and Sawyer noticed.

"What is it?"

"The Point restaurant. What's their logo?"

"A big oak . . . tree," she said, her eyes brightening. "You think?"

He nodded. "Somehow, that piece of land became known as The Point, and for some reason, it's associated with a big old oak tree." He shook his head. "I can't believe that's a coincidence. Someone somewhere has to know if they used to call it Rum Runner's Pointe, and whoever they are, we have to find them."

Chapter Forty-Four

Two weeks ago . . .
Tuesday, May 7
11:30 a.m.

"YOU DON'T LOOK so hot," Dr. Zachary said as Jackson trudged into his office and dropped onto the couch. For no other reason than that laying down beat sitting up, Jackson prostrated himself on the psychiatrist's couch.

"A sentiment shared by the majority of women in Greater L.A., coincidentally."

Zachary raised his eyebrow. "Something you want to talk about?"

"Not especially."

Taller than his clothes, which had been out of style as long as Jackson had been alive, Furman T. Zachary, Ph.D., was a hippie misplaced. His graying black hair was in a short ponytail. His long face, pointed nose, and trimmed goatee gave him an almost cartoonish appearance. Jackson thought he looked like a white Snoop Dogg. Or was he Snoop Lion now?

A Native American hide vest, complete with beads, killed the rapper resemblance, as did the pipe in Zachary's right hand. He smoked from time to time, but it was more a prop than anything. A yellow legal pad sat on his legs, ready to take notes on Jackson's tortured soul.

"How are you holding up physically?" Zachary asked.

"I'm alive."

"Are you in pain?"

"I'm sore. But only when I move."

"You've certainly had quite a year—your ordeal with the Russians, which I read about in all the papers, traveling the world in search of crusader treasure, getting shot."

"And let's not forget all the fun of last year."

"Sounds like it's taking a toll on you."

Jackson narrowed his eyes. "You reading from a script?"

"Excuse me?"

"Nothing," Jackson said.

Zachary was quiet for a minute. "Next week is your birthday, is it not?"

"It is."

"How do you feel about that?"

Jackson shrugged.

"Do you have any plans?"

"Just finalized it last night, I'm going to see an old pal in Florida."

"Really?"

"I need a vacation, Zach."

"Sounds like fun."

"Yeah, it does."

"You don't seem convinced."

"Fun's kind of an abstract concept, lately, Doc. Remember what we said a while back, about how I was just coping, just surviving?"

"I do."

"Seems like we're back there. All the progress I thought we'd been making in life, all the steps forward I was taking—well, they've kind of unraveled."

Zachary crossed his legs. His already short pant legs rode up, revealing some kind of marking on his calf. A tattoo, Jackson assumed.

"How so?" the doctor asked.

"I don't know. Life's just . . . I feel like I'm getting a raw deal."

Zachary traced his eyebrow with his finger. "Let's explore this raw deal."

"You know what I've been through. You know about my family. You know the things I've had to do as a P.I."

"I do. You've experienced a lot of suffering that many people will never know. But, you've also experienced a lot of joys many people will never know."

Jackson looked at him.

"You had a loving family for nearly thirty years, Jackson. You still have your grandfather, good friends who are like family, still have a Heavenly Father."

Jackson said nothing.

Zachary switched gears. "How's Reggie?"

Jackson was distracted for a moment by the tattoo. It looked like a . . . flaming sun?

"I don't know. He seems a little out of sorts."

"Out of sorts?"

"When he was looking for me, he met this exotic, sexy German secret agent."

"German?"

"I know, right, a sexy German? She was originally from the Caribbean. Anyhow, he liked her. But she played him. He's seemed a little off ever since."

"That would be understandable."

"I'm a drain on him, and then I'm the reason it doesn't work out with his new lady friend. In fact, I seem to be the reason nothing works out with lady friends."

Zachary again traced his eyebrow. "Let's explore that idea for a moment."

"Which one?"

"Things not working out with lady friends."

Jackson dropped his head back and looked at the ceiling. "Maggie dumped me on Easter."

"Ouch."

"For the pastor's kid."

"Double ouch."

"Only, thing is, she didn't really dump me because we weren't really dating. Except she had offered we could, and I suggested we wait, and then she jumps ship."

Zachary didn't need to say, "Triple ouch."

"She wants to stay friends," Jackson said with derision in his voice. "You know how that goes."

Zachary was single, but he'd been in the business long enough. Surely he'd run across that old line before.

"Then a couple of weeks ago, Sam stops by and gives me the same song, different tune. She's ready to move into a Norman Rockwell print, and I don't fit in. And she's got some guy too." He lowered his eyes to meet the doctor's. "Zach, I nearly tried to find the guy. That's how pathetic I am."

"Not an unnatural response."

"I wasn't going to beat him up or even confront him. I just wanted to know who had replaced me."

Zachary said nothing.

"Actually, that's not the most pathetic thing. Saturday, I hit on my old friend—just a friend. I mean, what is this, *The O.C.*?"

"That's a lot to deal with in the last month, on top of everything else."

"And Ashley's moving to Redding, getting married."

"Ashley?"

"Cute lady detective I met last year. I've told you about her."

"Did you have feelings for her?"

"Not in any serious way. But that's kind of the story of my life, it seems."

Zachary licked his lips.

"You can say it, Zach. We're at that stage."

"You said life had given you a raw deal. Perhaps . . . you're returning the favor."

Jackson frowned.

Zachary lit his pipe. That meant things were getting serious. "Maggie was ready for a serious relationship," Zachary said, "but you declined. Sam wants to move forward with a husband and family, I gather, and you don't. You admitted not having 'serious' feelings for a 'cute lady detective' and are upset that she's leaving. Is it possible you are holding back?"

"Fear of commitment? Really, Zach, you're going with that old fallback?"

"It's an 'old fallback' for a reason, Jackson."

"Why would I be afraid of commitment?"

"I don't know. Why would you?"

"Let me guess, I'm afraid if I give my heart away it will get smashed again like it did with my family."

"That's a possibility."

"Or I'm afraid to make a life with Sam 'cause I'll miss Maggie, or vice versa."

"Also possible."

"Or could be I'm really cut out for this sort of life, chasing 'bangers and thwarting terrorists, and it's best not to get tied down with a wife and family because I'll just end up breaking their hearts by not coming home someday. Maybe there's a reason there's never been a Mrs. James Bond."

"There are a lot of cops and soldiers and special agents with families."

"But?"

"But, that's also a legitimate reason you might be holding back."

Jackson sighed. "So what's your professional opinion, Doc?"

"That you have some soul searching to do."

"Funny, I thought that's what you were for."

"I can only help if you're willing to be helped."

"You think I'm not?"

Zachary just stared at him as he took a puff on his pipe and exhaled smoke toward the ceiling. "I think you're holding back for a reason. And I think you know what it is."

"I don't."

"I think you do, deep down inside."

Jackson sighed again. "Soul searching."

Zachary nodded.

"Well, it will have to wait."

"Florida?"

"Uh-huh. I'm not spending my vacation analyzing my thoughts and feelings and figuring out where I've gone wrong in life. I'm going to lounge in the shade of some sultry palm trees with a cold drink and do everything I can to avoid adventures and danger and navel-gazing and serious relationships with women."

Zachary looked long and hard at Jackson. "You are coming back, aren't you?"

"That's the plan."

*   *   *

Thursday, May 23
4:29 p.m.

JACKSON AND Sawyer practically staggered off the Boeing 737. They had left Lazarus Island at 8:30 that morning on one of only two outbound commercial flights. After a two-hour layover in Nassau, they had flown to Miami, where they'd grabbed lunch and waited for a flight to Key West. It had been delayed almost an hour because of heavy thunderstorms that had peppered the East Coast of Florida all day. The same weather system had caused for a bumpy landing in Nassau and nearly grounded their initial flight from Lazarus Island. So by the time their feet touched on solid ground for good, Jackson and Sawyer were both worn out.

The night before, after spinning every possible scenario in their heads and scouring the internet for any possible clues, they had enjoyed a relaxing dinner at a seafood place on the east side of Woodes Town. By the time they had realized the Keys were their next destination, the last flight of the day had already departed Lazarus Island. Since the weather had cleared and since they wanted any possible observers to think they had given up pursuit of the treasure, they had done their best to enjoy a relaxed meal without any treasure conversation. The evening and night had passed uneventfully, with no signs that anyone was watching them.

In Nassau, Jackson thought he had spied a tail, but he had been unable to confirm that it was anything more than another traveler, and the guy hadn't resembled Baldwin or either of the two yahoos who had grabbed Sawyer. After boarding the flight to Miami, he had seen nothing more to trigger his suspicions and had figured their days of being tailed were over. After all, since the map had been stolen, there was no reason for anyone to follow them.

After collecting their luggage, which surprisingly had island hopped along with them, they proceeded to where Sawyer's Jeep was waiting for them in the parking lot. The rain had abated for the time being, leaving low, dark clouds scuttling below a gray sheet. Even so, the seats of the Jeep were speckled with raindrops.

"You left the top down?" Jackson said as he stowed their bags behind the front seats.

"I was in a hurry," Sawyer said as she pulled herself by the roll bar into the driver's seat. "Toughen up, surfer boy."

"Yes'm."

They swung by the Sheriff's Department to update Sheriff Hawkins and see if he had any updates of his own. He was amused with their account, which left out some of the quasi-legal stunts in Louisiana, but didn't see how any of it was relevant to him. He'd heard nothing more from Dixon, had no further contact with any authorities in New Orleans, and didn't know anything about a Bahamian hood named Baldwin. Not a surprise.

Their first order of business after leaving Hawkins was dinner, and they swung by a McDonald's on North Roosevelt Boulevard. "Let's say we find it," Sawyer said as they ate. There were others in the vicinity, which explained why she hadn't used the word "treasure."

"Okay, we find it."

"We've danced around this a little, but how specifically do we use it to identify and catch Ben's killers?"

Hawkins had reported that Ben's Uncle Malcolm had come and gone and that the department had moved on. It had been over a week since Ben had been declared missing at sea and presumed dead. That wasn't changing. Hawkins hadn't come right out and said it, but Jackson and Sawyer had both agreed he'd seemed to be questioning what they were doing chasing down a treasure legend. That had gotten Jackson thinking introspectively too, as it apparently had Sawyer.

"We use it as bait," he said.

"Okay." She ate a bite of her chicken sandwich. "Okay, but how do we use it as bait?"

"Trade it for the truth."

She shook her head. "Even if we could arrange that, why would Louviere tell us anything? He'd have to believe we're wired or would go straight to the cops."

"Depends on how we play it and on how greedy he really is. Admittedly, the strategy would work better if Ben was still alive and we could propose a trade."

They finished eating and, since the sky promised more rain, they put the top up on Sawyer's now dry Jeep. Then they headed for the Monroe County Public Library. Known for its extensive reference and Florida history sections, the library was Jackson and Sawyer's best hope for finding facts about Rum Runner's Pointe. Neither of them recalled anything in Ben's studies, and since he'd written "The Point" on a notepad, they theorized that he had planned to research it. What had led him to The Point was a mystery, but one they could leave unsolved for now.

"This bait idea," Sawyer said as she drove west along the northern coast of Key West. "How do we arrange something? How do we notify Louviere if we do find the treasure?"

"Assuming he doesn't know . . . there are ways."

"You know of any?"

"I'm kind of a kick-down-the-door sort."

"I see."

"But I presume there are discreet ways too. But we're getting the cart a little before the horse."

"True."

She turned onto Southard Street and, a few blocks later, north on Elizabeth Street, then back east on Fleming. It was a one-way thoroughfare, with parking on either side of the street. Sawyer found a spot under a palm almost directly in front of the Monroe County Public Library.

Surrounded by a variety of trees and shrubs, the pink stucco building featured an Alamo-style arch over the front entrance. A light drizzle had resumed, and as they climbed the steps in front of the library, the rain began to come down harder. Jackson held the door for Sawyer and followed her inside.

On a rainy weeknight, the library was empty and, of course, quiet. Jackson and Sawyer spent half an hour in the stacks, looking for books they hoped would give them a clue about Rum Runner's Pointe. Then they met at a corner table away from anyone to pore over a dozen different volumes.

"You know, the internet kind of makes indexes obsolete," Jackson said after thumbing through the first few books.

"Yeah, well, until somebody turns the world's supply of reference materials into e-books, it is what it is."

Jackson grabbed the next volume from the stack, a thick tome that was more or less a complete history of the Keys. The index was exhaustive but contained no entry for either Rum Runner's Pointe or The Point. There were, however, some references to Sugarloaf Key, so he began skimming them one by one.

"Here's something," Sawyer said. She held up a much thinner book than Jackson's. "It doesn't mention any place in particular, but it says that the Keys were used by rum runners and pirates as early as the mid-1600s. Razorback Key was even called Drunken Key until 1755."

"No mention of Sugarloaf Key or Brackett or anything?"

"No. But it suggests we're on the right track."

"Well, that's something." He glanced at the clock and resumed reading. The library was open till eight, and at the rate they were going, they wouldn't be close to done by then.

A crack of thunder shook the building, and almost immediately a steady din of rain began to drum against the roof and windows. Jackson flipped to the last Sugarloaf Key reference in his current book and had just started reading when Sawyer called his name.

He finished a sentence before looking up. Her eyes were wide.

"This book is titled *Legends, Rumors, and Myths of Old Florida*," she said, "so take this with a grain of salt, but listen to this. *'Known as a haven for pirates, the Lower Keys have long been rumored to contain multiple hidden treasures. The coves and cays and coral reefs, along with the dozens of shipwrecks that inhabit the shallow waterways, have since been searched by professional recovery specialists and amateur treasure hunters alike.'*"

She looked up. "It goes on to list a handful of smaller finds and a few of the legends associated with them." Lowering her head, she continued to read aloud. *"'Perhaps the most famous pirate rumored to have buried his treasure somewhere in the Keys is Captain James Brackett.'* Jabber, jabber, jabber about the attack on the *Granada* and the wreck of the *Barracuda*. *'No one has ever found the Brackett treasure, and there are dozens of theories as to its ultimate whereabouts. However, the most prominent of those holds that it is somewhere in the Florida Keys. It's not just a recent development, either. Even as early as the 1720s, Captain Roland Robitaille made Sugarloaf Key his favored haunt, establishing a small community there. Robitaille, a Frenchman, was rumored to have ties to Brackett, and historians theorize that he spent so much time on Sugarloaf Key because he was looking for the legendary pirate's buried treasure.'"*

She sat back as Jackson pondered her words. "This is the first time we've heard the name Robitaille," he said.

"He could have been a fellow pirate, a crew member aboard the *Barracuda* who became a captain of his own ship, or maybe he had ties to Captaine Toussaint of the *Majesté Royale*."

"Or another pirate who heard a rumor about a treasure."

"Whatever the reason, he apparently believed Brackett's treasure was here. This says he had ties to Brackett. Maybe they even talked."

"In a book of legends, it adds to the legend," Jackson said. "It say anything more about Robitaille, like if he found the treasure?"

"It doesn't say. Just that he was killed while raiding a Spanish ship in 1730."

Jackson stroked his chin and looked at the clock again. They had half an hour. "Let's keep digging."

She nodded, and they both returned to their books. His described the history of the Keys, from their earliest inhabitants to the days when Flagler's railroad crossed them in the early 1900s. He skimmed the eight or nine pages about Sugarloaf Key, then flipped back through them. Not reading, he ran his eyes up and down the pages, looking for words that might jump out at him. He was about to quit when a pair of capital R's near the bottom of a page caught his eye. He found Sawyer's leg under the table and kicked it softly.

"Ow. What?"

"'*Sugarloaf Key's numerous inlets and coves provided a perfect hiding spot for pirates, smugglers, criminals, and castaways. In the late seventeenth century and early half of the eighteenth century, the southeastern cape was used prevalently by rum smugglers as a haven from the authorities and pirates alike. It also became a trading post of sorts, earning the name Rum Runner's Pointe.*'"

"That must be it," Sawyer said, her voice a few decibels loud for the location, and she quickly covered her mouth. "The Point is Rum Runner's Pointe."

"And somehow, Ben suspected it was where Brackett buried his treasure without chasing to New Orleans, the Bahamas, and back."

"I wonder if that's what got him killed."

Jackson shook his head. "I don't think so. I don't think Louviere and Baldwin and whoever else is after us have a clue where to look. Else they wouldn't be chasing us across the Caribbean. Right now, we've got intel they don't."

"Then why did they kill Damon and maybe Ben?"

"Because they learned something that Louviere already knew, or were close to finding it."

"The journal?"

Jackson nodded. "The whole New Orleans angle."

"So why haven't they killed us?"

"I don't know. Maybe they want to let us do the dirty work since we've come this far. Whatever the case," he said, lowering his voice, leaning forward, and looking around to make sure no one was eavesdropping, "we've learned something Louviere hasn't. That gives him reason to keep us alive."

"At least until we find the treasure," she said.

A flash of lightning was followed by another crack of thunder, the sudden intrusion to their discussion serving as an eerie reminder of what was at stake. Since it was almost closing time, Jackson and Sawyer returned their books to the shelves. Most libraries preferred patrons didn't re-shelve their books and risk putting them out of order, but Jackson didn't want someone to come along and find out which history and reference books had recently been viewed.

The rain was still falling steadily, and Jackson and Sawyer hurried to her Jeep. As they drove, they rehashed what they had discovered.

"So Brackett buries his treasure somewhere on Rum Runner's Pointe, modern-day Sugarloaf Key," Sawyer said. "And somehow Roland Robitaille has reason to believe the treasure is there five to ten years later. But he never finds it."

"Likely because he didn't know where to look."

"But now we do, assuming we can find the location of an old oak tree."

"We'll have to check satellite footage for any large oak trees on The Point," Jackson said. "It's a longshot, but I've heard of trees that old."

"Oak trees?"

"I think so."

"They'd probably be on an historic register by now," she said. "And huge. I'm sure I'd know where it was if it was big enough to be three hundred years old. I've been all over the Keys."

"Well, if it's not still there, maybe we can find out where it was. Old photos, history books, the founder of The Point restaurant who put the tree in the logo."

"More research," Sawyer mumbled.

"The name of the game."

The rain had slackened to a slight drizzle by the time Sawyer dropped Jackson at the same hotel he'd stayed at before heading to New Orleans. They had vacancy, and he booked a room for two nights while Sawyer waited in the Jeep to make sure he didn't need a ride to another establishment. He took his key out to the Jeep and grabbed his bag. After agreeing to meet in the morning, he and Sawyer said goodbye, and she drove off.

Jackson started some laundry, then crashed in front of the TV. He surfed channels for ten minutes before settling on the Stanley Cup Playoffs. The New York Rangers staved off elimination with an overtime win against the

Boston Bruins, and Jackson thought of Maggie throughout. She was an avid Rangers fan, and probably celebrated by playing a little tonsil hockey with her new boyfriend.

Jackson canned the TV, retrieved his laundry, and went to bed to the sound of more rain and thunder.

Chapter Forty-Five

Friday, May 24
9:01 a.m.

JACKSON WAS EATING a waffle and some thin, greasy bacon on the hotel terrace when his phone rang, playing the "Sweet Home Alabama" ringtone he'd chosen for Sawyer. A bit on the nose, perhaps, but it was catchy. He swallowed, then flipped open his phone. Before he could say anything, Sawyer started talking.

"I found the oak tree."

Alone on the terrace, he stood and paced away from the table. "Where?"

"In a photo of The Point from 1905."

"Why was there a photo of The Point in 1905?"

"Because Henry Flagler was preparing to build the Overseas Railroad across southern Sugarloaf Key."

Jackson stood. "Where's the tree?"

"Quarter mile up the coast from the restaurant, around the . . . point, I guess you'd call it, that sticks out into the water."

"I'm finishing breakfast," he said. "I can pick you up in fifteen minutes."

"I'm already out. I'll come get you."

"Okay."

He closed the phone and quickly gulped down the rest of his breakfast. He had his phone and wallet, so he didn't bother going back to the room, instead hanging out under the hotel's carport to wait for Sawyer. The morning was bright and sunny, the storms of the night long gone, and the top was down on Sawyer's Jeep as it careened into the parking lot.

She flung her seatbelt off and jumped down. She wore a loose Alabama tank top—what else—tucked into the front of denim shorts and left to flow out the sides and back. She also wore an ear-to-ear smile and reached into her back pocket as she walked to Jackson. She withdrew a folded sheet of paper and thrust it at him, interrupting his, "Morning."

"What's this?" he asked.

"Look at it."

He unfolded the paper to see a photocopy of a black and white photo with a sepia tint, depicting a beachhead, a lot of trees, and a fair amount of underbrush. What stood out a quarter of the way in from the right was a massive live oak, towering at least a hundred feet into the air and spreading easily that far in diameter. It was a magnificent tree, the type of thing that might get emblazoned on a restaurant sign.

"Where did you get this?" Jackson asked.

"A friend of mine who collects old photos. She has a number of books full of old, historical pictures and portraits of everything. I got to thinking last night that maybe one of them might have old photos of the Keys, and one did. This is from a book written in 1936 just after the Overseas Railroad ceased operation. It documented Flagler's quest to build the railroad and had hundreds of photos."

"And you're sure this is Rum Runner's Pointe?"

"Read the caption."

Jackson looked down at the photocopy again. "'*Southeastern Sugarloaf Key, also known as "The Point," initially proposed as the path of the Overseas Railroad.*'"

"If you look at the map, it sort of makes sense for the railroad to jog south and follow the southern edge of the Keys. At least for a while." She jabbed a finger at the paper. "But this has to be the tree."

"You think we can find this?" he asked.

"As far as I know, it's public land. There isn't as much beach now as on the photo, and most of the shoreline is mangroves in that area. So there won't be much land to cover."

"Worth checking," Jackson said. "You happen to a have a laptop in your tiny house?"

"An old one. Why?"

"Before we drive out there, I'd like to check out some satellite photos. We could go to the library otherwise."

"Doesn't your hotel have a business center?"

"You're right. Come on in?"

She followed him inside, where he quickly acquired permission to use a lobby computer. "You have breakfast?" he asked as he accessed Google Maps.

"At Jackie's."

"Your friend?"

She nodded.

"She keeps early hours," he said.

"She does. What exactly are we looking for on satellite views? You won't see the tree."

"No, but I want to get an idea of where it was. I also want to see how we can get there without using the restaurant parking lot. Especially if we're going to be hauling digging tools."

Sawyer nodded.

It took a few minutes to zoom in on Sugarloaf Key, but when Jackson did, he and Sawyer quickly identified the restaurant as the only building in the area. Just across the languid water behind the restaurant was an indefinite coastline, a combination of shallow water, sand, and mangroves. Southeast of the restaurant some two hundred yards, the coast jutted maybe a hundred yards out into the sea before turning and heading northeast for several hundred yards before a rounded "point" of land marked a more northward turn in Sugarloaf Key's coastline. In the middle of that stretch was a swath of beach, maybe thirty to forty feet at its widest and running for several hundred feet, separating the foliage from the shallow waters of the Straits of Florida.

Holding the photo side-by-side with the monitor, they tried to compare geography. None of the trees from 1905 were likely to be visible as none of the trees in that area now were near large enough to be over a hundred years old. And the ground cover was too thick and the image too grainy to make out details such as a huge stump. So they resorted to trying to gauge the shape of the beach. But given a number of hurricanes, tidal erosion, and advancement of the trees onto the beach, it was a losing battle too.

"Super," Sawyer said. "We find the place and find the tree, and we still don't know where to dig." She sat back in her chair. "We need some sort of GPS system that can pinpoint a location based on 3D imaging or something."

"That or a machete."

She frowned.

"You know, to cut our way to the stump."

"You think it's still there?"

"Depends on why the tree came down. I'm guessing a storm took it down, which means the remnants of it are probably still there. And even if humans felled it, rooting out a stump that size wouldn't have been easy, especially back in the early 1900s."

"So we could stomp around looking for it."

"And if we both survive the gators and cottonmouths and quicksand, we'll be in business."

"What were the directions again? Fifteen paces east and twenty paces south?"

Jackson nodded.

"Well, that eliminates any of the beach left of the tree. And look here. The oak is on the edge of the tree line—out a ways from it, actually. So even with the overgrowth, it shouldn't be too hard to find a stump in the underbrush."

Jackson nodded again.

"You zoning out on me?"

"No. Look at this photo," he said as he pointed with his finger. "See that?"

Sawyer leaned in. "No. What is it?"

"I think it's a rock."

"A rock."

"A big one. Mostly buried. Meaning it could still be there."

Sawyer's eyes flashed with excitement. "That would pinpoint it pretty well."

Jackson nodded as her phone rang. She quickly checked the caller ID and stood. "Hi, Jackie."

Instead of listening to half of a conversation, Jackson did some online research on Florida's treasure recovery laws. With a little ambiguity, they basically boiled down to finders, keepers. He also confirmed that the beach in question was public land, and therefore no permit was required to dig. He had expected reels and reels of red tape, and the surprising lack of it was almost unsettling.

"I think we have confirmation," Sawyer said when she'd finished the call. "Jackie has several old, unique Keys history books, and I asked her to look for any reference to Rum Runner's Pointe or the old oak tree. She found a reference to a two hundred fifty-year-old oak tree that was felled by a hurricane that hit the Keys in 1910. If my math is right, that puts it at 1660. So by 1715, it could have already been pretty big."

Jackson agreed and reported his findings on recovering the treasure.

"So does that mean we can go get our hands dirty?"

"Yeah. You got any digging equipment at your house?"

"A small gardening trowel. I pot a few plants."

After a few more minutes of miscellaneous research, they left the hotel and headed for an Ace Hardware near the marina. Already the air was hot and thick, and Jackson didn't relish the idea of physical labor in this climate.

They purchased a pair of shovels, two five-gallon buckets, a small cooler, a bag of ice, and several bottles of water. "Doing some yard work?" the lady at the counter asked. She had thin black glasses and curly brown hair pulled into a ponytail. Her name tag identified her as Serena.

"Something like that," Jackson answered.

She nodded with a frown, and Jackson began to wonder if buying digging implements could get you on the terrorist watch list. But she let them go with a friendly smile, and, shortly before eleven, Jackson and Sawyer arrived on Sugarloaf Key.

Sawyer followed the same roads they had taken to get to The Point for dinner the previous week. But instead of turning on the gravel drive to the restaurant, she continued on the unpaved road, which became a rutted dirt path, encroached on more and more by trees and underbrush. She nearly scraped her mirrors on a pair of trees with branches hanging above her windshield and coasted to a stop just beyond them. Whatever road had at one time traversed the hundred yards of brush and trees ahead of them had long since been consumed. This was the end of the line.

Sawyer stood up, looking over the windshield. Hers was not the first vehicle to come and stop this far. A crude, overgrown turnaround apparently saw just enough traffic to keep from being consumed by the surrounding foliage. With a little imagination, it was also possible to discern a narrow footpath through the brush and trees, leading toward the ocean. It had been fifty-fifty if the narrow, winding line they'd observed on satellite photos was indeed a path or the result of the random nature of plant growth. Now, Jackson still wasn't sure.

"Not exactly the I-5. I take it this isn't a path worn by lovers strolling to a secluded moonlit beach."

"More like key deer, probably." She jumped down to the ground.

"Or alligators," he said, still in his seat.

"Relax. Alligators prefer freshwater."

"For real?"

Sawyer nodded, and Jackson finally unbuckled his seatbelt.

"American crocodiles are what you have to worry about. They're actually drawn to the salinity of the ocean."

"Awesome."

She smiled, and he forced himself to be a man and get out of the Jeep. She tossed him a bottle of water. "Good to stay ahead of dehydration."

"Right. Let's leave the tools and check it out first."

"Okay."

Keeping an eye out for various members of the reptile family, Jackson led the way through the brush and trees. He wasn't sure if he was on the path or not, more focused on walking where there weren't plants, but knew he was headed generally south.

"I think we could go for that machete about now," Sawyer said.

"Or some steel-toed boots," Jackson said, noting her flip-flops.

"Mmm."

After a hundred feet, any semblance of a path disappeared, and they had to hack through branches and bushes by hand for about ten feet. Then they broke through onto a beautiful but small beach. It ran maybe a hundred feet to their left, and twice that to the right, on a southwest to northeast line. A couple of miles out to the left was Lois Key. Somewhere to the right of that, the wreck of the *Barracuda*. In between them, a channel for boats heading up the eastern shore of Sugarloaf Key.

"You see the rock from the photo?" Sawyer asked.

"No."

"Could have been covered by sand from a hurricane."

"I thought the beaches were being eroded. Global warming and all that nonsense."

She just shrugged, and they fanned out to look for a rock outcropping on the beach. After fifteen minutes, they gave up, concluding that it was either buried under the sands of time or had been driftwood instead of a rock. So they resorted to looking for the oak tree stump.

According to the photo, the tree was approximately a quarter of the way from the eastern end of the beach, not too far from where they'd exited the trees. Again fanning out, they searched the overgrowth of trees, bushes, shrubs, and grasses that encroached on the beach. Jackson nearly stepped on a lizard, and it was hard to tell who was scared more by the encounter. With Sawyer some twenty-five feet away, he stifled a girlish scream and moved on. It was hard work, hacking through thick foliage, and they really could have used a machete. Or a backhoe.

"Jackson!"

He hurried over to where Sawyer had partially disappeared behind a couple of sand pines. She gently pushed a bush aside so Jackson could see the cracked, rotting remnants of what had been a huge tree. Nearly six feet in diameter, the tree had been broken off just a few feet up from the ground. After a hundred years, it had been completely enshrouded by overgrown brush and trees that probably hadn't even been seeded at the time of the storm that wrecked it. It was far enough into the woods that a casual passerby on the beach would never spot it.

"This has to be it," Sawyer said, excitement in her breath.

"Yeah."

"My paces or yours?"

"Thirty-five total, if we're off by two inches each, we'll dig forever."

"How tall was Brackett?"

"He looked tall in the book illustrations."

"We both pace and split the difference?"

"Yeah. Only I didn't bring a compass."

Sawyer reached into her pocket for her phone. "Just a sec."

"And here I thought we'd have to wait for the North Star."

Sawyer had a compass app on her phone, and standing at the base of the oak, she divined east. "Go for it," she said, and Jackson marched off fifteen paces, counting aloud, doing his best to walk in a straight line through thick brush and around a sand pine. Sawyer kept him in line, and confirmed it again when he stopped. He could barely make out her crimson tank top.

Making his best guess at a ninety-degree angle, he turned right and started counting. At three paces, he stepped onto the beach. At fifteen, he stopped.

"Uh, Sawyer," he said, turning over his shoulder.

"What?"

"I think we may have a problem."

"Fourteen, fifteen . . ." She stopped behind him and peeked her head around him. "Oh."

A very gentle, very shallow wave rolled onto the shore, the foamy edge of inch-deep water brushing against Jackson's shoes. It quickly receded, leaving wet, mud-like sand in its wake. Jackson took two more paces before the water began to rush back at him, and he retreated to dry ground.

"He buried it at sea," Sawyer said.

Chapter Forty-Six

11:27 a.m.

"THAT'S DIRTY POOL," Jackson said, staring five yards out into shallow water. Sawyer did him one better, kicking off her flip-flops and wading five paces into the ocean. She stopped with water swirling around her ankles, rising halfway to the knee when the next wave rolled ashore.

"It's warm," she said.

"Super. Let's go for a swim."

She made a face at him. "Tide should be going out." She waited until the next wave ebbed, and dug her heel into the mucky sand, making a primitive X. "There. X marks the spot."

"Ish."

She slogged back to dry land and reached for her phone. In a minute, she had called up a tide table on the screen. "According to this, low tide is around three-thirty this afternoon," she said. Handing the phone to Jackson, she got up and walked back into the water. He checked the next high tide, not until almost midnight.

"It's so shallow, it should recede quite a ways," Sawyer called. She had waded out to her knees, some fifty feet out.

"The variance from high to low tide is only about a foot. Maybe fourteen inches."

"So it should come back to at least here," she said, coming back and stopping where the water rose about a foot up her leg. She slogged a few more paces. "It'll be a couple of hours yet before we can dig."

Jackson nodded. "You want to grab some lunch?"

"Might as well."

They retraced their steps through the woods and back to the Jeep. They considered going to The Point, but Jackson suggested they not be spotted in the area if possible. So Sawyer picked a deli back on the main highway, and they ordered sandwiches to go.

They ate as they drove back to Key West, where Sawyer wanted to change into better digging clothes. She dropped Jackson at a local hardware store where he bought string, several small stakes, a tape measure, and more ice. He also picked up some jerky, energy bars, and fruit so that he and Sawyer could work through dinner. They would only have so much time before the tide came back in.

Now wearing jeans and athletic shoes, Sawyer also had a dew rag tied around her head, Willie Robertson-style, holding her blond hair back behind her ears. The bandanna was crimson to match her tank top, and Jackson couldn't decide if she looked like a World War II propaganda poster child, a railroad worker of yesteryear, or just a tough Southern woman ready to do some work.

It was still early afternoon, but with nothing else to do, they drove back to Sugarloaf Key and the assumed Rum Runner's Pointe. They parked in the same place and followed the same trail back to the beach. It was still deserted, as expected, and the only boat on the horizon was a cruise ship steaming toward Key West.

"I've been wondering something," Sawyer said as they began pacing off the distances from the stump. They used Jackson's stride, Sawyer's stride, and a tape measure, counting three feet as one pace. Jackson's stride proved almost exactly three feet; Sawyer's a few inches under.

"What's that?" he asked, tying a length of string around a stake marking fifteen paces. The other end of the string was tied around the stump.

"If Brackett knew a hurricane was coming," Sawyer said, "why would he bury the treasure underwater?"

"Maybe he thought it would be safer. Hadn't heard from Jim Cantore about undertows and beach degradation and all that."

She shrugged.

"Or maybe this wasn't underwater then. Maybe the beachhead has moved."

She shrugged again.

"Maybe it's moved a lot. What if a dozen hurricanes since eroded the beach and the treasure floated out to sea?"

"It would have sunk," she said. "And somebody would have found it, I'm sure."

"And we're still left to wonder why the crew never came back for it. Unless . . ."

"They did, and we'll find nothing."

He nodded.

"One way to find out."

They started measuring twenty paces south, but the tide had not quite receded far enough. So they sat down and did some math. "The hypotenuse of any triangle is the square of the other two sides squared, right?" Jackson asked.

"Yeah."

"So what's twenty squared plus fifteen squared?"

Instead of digging out her phone, Sawyer closed her eyes for a minute. "Six and a quarter."

"Sure?"

"Fifteen times fifteen is two-twenty-five. Twenty times twenty is four hundred. Add them up, it's six-twenty-five."

"Okay. What's the square root of that?"

"Twenty-five."

"Duh, you're right."

Jackson stretched out the tape measure and cut a string that was twenty-five yards long. When the water had receded a little farther, they were able to drive a stake into the soft sand twenty paces south of the first one. With Sawyer holding one end of the string at the stake, he took the other directly to the stump.

"How is it?" she asked.

"About a foot short, but we're bending around a pine. Close enough." He rejoined Sawyer as an oncoming wave stopped a foot shy of the stake in the wet sand.

"Well . . . ?"

"Here goes nothing," he said as he grabbed a shovel. He jabbed it into the sand with a thwap, lifted the muck and tossed it to the side, then turned back and thrust the spade into the soft earth again. He lifted another pile, dumped it, and swung his shovel back around again.

"Hey, John Henry, want to think this through before attacking the beach," Sawyer asked, still leaning on her shovel.

Jackson chucked his third shovel of earth. "What do you mean?"

"I mean, we could be digging deep. And we don't know if we're in exactly the right spot. So it could be wide before we're done."

"Yeah, so?"

"So maybe we ought to pile it a little further away so we don't end up moving it twice."

"I was just being energetic to set the tempo."

"Uh-huh."

He grinned and scooped his first few piles of sand, tossing them as far up the beach as he could.

"We might also want to start our pile on the ocean side," she said. "You know, so when the tide comes back in, we have a natural dam."

Jackson tipped the handle of his shovel in her direction. "That," he said, "is using your head for more than a bandanna rack."

With Jackson making several cracks about Sawyer's future as an engineer, they excavated a ten-foot diameter circle of sand that was a foot deep. Using the sand, they constructed a semicircle earthen barrier around the perimeter of the hole. Given the receding waves that exposed more and more of the beach, it seemed unnecessary.

"You're a scraggly-bearded buccaneer, how deep do you bury your treasure?" Jackson asked as they paused for drinks. The sun was still high in the sky, unblocked by clouds, and he gulped the cold water while waiting for her answer.

"Since I've got expendable crewmen to do my dirty work," she answered, "deep. Especially if I'm burying it offshore."

"You think maybe he did it so that he could tell his nonexpendable crewmen which beach it was buried on and still not have them find it?"

"You mean if he was ever marooned and threatened with torture?"

Jackson nodded.

"Plausible."

They resumed digging, removing another foot of dirt from half the hole. Sawyer retrieved snacks, and they sat on the edge of the hole. "Quarter to four," she announced, pocketing her phone. "We're looking at low tide."

Jackson bit off a hunk of jerky and turned to watch the waves. They came to within fifteen feet of their makeshift dam. "How long till they get back here?"

"High tide's not until eleven-fifty-something."

"But how far up the beach is high tide? There isn't a line of shells or seaweed to mark it."

She shrugged and bit off the end of a banana.

They washed down the jerky and fruit with more water and resumed working. After a while, they took turns filling the five-gallon buckets with sand and dumping them at the end of the dam. It now resembled a U, stretching a dozen feet up the beach at least a foot high all around and twice that at the bottom. Jackson hoped it would ensure dryness if the tide returned.

At five feet deep, the work slowed. Their hole had turned into a cone, and after another break, they worked to widen the bottom of the hole. Hours of digging and lifting and carrying had both of them complaining about the pain in their arms, shoulders, backs, and everywhere else. It was just after six o'clock, and as they broke to eat again, they considered their strategy.

"How deep do we go?" Sawyer asked.

"Until we hear a thunk."

"And what if it's eighteen inches deep a foot outside our perimeter?"

"At high tide, we go get some Aleve and 5-hour Energy and get back at it."

She nodded.

"Seriously, I say we go down till sundown. We don't have any lights, and as authentic as digging by torchlight would be, it's not very practical. If we don't have anything by the time it gets dark, I say we call it a day and tomorrow go wider."

"I wonder if we could get a backhoe through the trees."

"Yeah, we'll consider that too."

Sawyer drained the last quarter of a bottle of water and tossed it up the beach toward their cooler. Then she stood and climbed back into the hole. Jackson had to admire her. She was far from the dainty, delicate, fainting Southern belle stereotype, but she *was* a member of the weaker sex. And she had been shoveling right along with him all afternoon.

Jackson downed one more gulp of water and joined her in the hole. They resumed their bucket brigade, moving slower than before, but still steadily. The sun was nearing the tree line by the time they had leveled out the bottom of the hole. The sun's orange rays bathed the sand in a warm, peaceful glow.

They took one more water break, not bothering to wipe the sweat off their foreheads and faces since there was no part of their body or piece of clothing that was dry enough to make a difference.

"You holding up?" Jackson asked.

"I'm good," Sawyer said.

"I never asked. What's your dad do for a living?"

She furrowed her brow—confused, not taking offense, Jackson thought. "He's a Baptist preacher. Why?"

"I thought maybe you grew up on a farm or hoeing cotton or something."

"That a crack on the South?"

"Compliment. You dig like Mary Anne."

"From *Gilligan's Island?*"

"From *Mike Mulligan and His Steam Shovel.* Children's book. Loved it as a kid."

She raised her eyebrows.

"It was a compliment. I'd say you work like a man, but that would be sexist."

"I'm too tired to care. Let's get back in there."

"Whip cracked."

They trudged back down into the hole and Jackson took the first shift carrying buckets that Sawyer filled. After ten, they switched positions. Jackson's second jab of his shovel into the sand resulted in a thud. He stuck the shovel again, getting another thud. He moved the shovel over a foot. Thud again.

"What is it?" Sawyer asked from "stairs" Jackson had carved out of the side of the hole.

"Treasure or the Great Wall of China."

She joined him with her shovel, and in five minutes they had shoved enough earth aside to reveal the top of a wooden chest. Jackson fell back against the damp sand wall of the hole. Sawyer leaned on her shovel handle. Neither of them spoke for a moment, too exhausted and too expectant.

"Well, I suppose we ought to open it," Sawyer said at last.

"Yeah."

They had to dig for another ten minutes to unearth a lock and hinges on the chest. "I can't believe it," Jackson said, kneeling in the cool sand. "This is just like the movies and books I read as a kid. It's a real treasure chest."

It was nearly three feet long, close to two feet wide, and the lid was curved, rising about nine inches in the center. The wood was clearly old and worn, yet preserved by the sand. Brass straps held the wood together, and an old, rusted lock kept the chest sealed.

"I wonder who has the key," Sawyer said.

"Me," Jackson said, raising his shovel. He looked at her, then jammed the spade down on the hasp. It broke, most of the lock thudding into the sand as a small piece of shrapnel flew back at Jackson's leg. Jamming the shovel into the sand, he again dropped to his knees. His hands on the lid, he looked back at Sawyer.

"Go for it."

The hinges on the old chest creaked as Jackson pried his fingers under the lid and began to raise it. It lifted freely but reluctantly, and Jackson put enough muscle into his effort to throw the lid wide open. Then he very slowly exhaled.

Even in the waning light, the gold glittered. The chest was full of hundreds and hundreds of loose coins, jewel encrusted gold goblets and plates, a few small idols, and an assortment of other gold objects. Jackson reached a hand into the coins, lifting several of them up and letting them fall with a clank. They were real.

He turned back to Sawyer, who stood motionless, her eyes fixated on the treasure. Finally, she let her shovel fall and squatted beside Jackson. He let out a small sigh of relief.

"What?" she asked.

"Oh, nothing. I was just sort of half-expecting you to whack me in the back of the head with your shovel."

"What?"

"Well, if this was a novel or something, this would be the place where your hair and countenance darkened, you got a Grinch-like smile on your face, and whistled to your shady partners in the trees."

"You have quite an imagination."

"I watch too much TV."

"That too."

He reached into the chest again and withdrew a coin. "Flip you for it?"

Sawyer grinned. "I think there's more than enough to go around," she said, picking up a gold plate and fingering it. "This is priceless," she said as she grabbed a gold cross inlaid with rubies and emeralds.

"Millions," Jackson said. "It has to be worth millions."

Sawyer replaced the plate and cross, took a deep breath, and faced Jackson. "What do we do now?"

"Find out if we can lift it."

"I mean, where do we go with it?"

"Banks aren't open, and I don't know if we can just cart a chest of gold into the First National Bank of Key West anyhow. We should probably get a lawyer or a notary or something so my soon-to-be minions can't accuse your soon-to-be minions of taking one too many doubloons. And then we have to—"

Sawyer stuck her hand at Jackson.

"What's that?"

"In place of a notary or a lawyer."

"Southern honor and your word is your bond and that sort of a thing?"

"Something like that."

Jackson smiled as he shook her hand. He liked a woman who, with millions at stake, would put her trust in something as simple as a man's honor. With this kind of money on the line, the legalities and paperwork could become a mess in a heartbeat. Or, if both parties were reasonable, it could all be handled quite simply.

"There, that settles that," she said.

"First thing first, I think we need to get this someplace safe," he said. "Then we can figure out what to do and how to do it. But right now, we need to make sure it doesn't fall into the wrong hands."

Sawyer nodded. "My house?"

"No. Louviere knows you, knows your name by now. It's too dangerous. In fact, I don't think you should go back there until this money is secured."

"Where then?"

"A hotel. Find some dive off the beaten path, park in the rear, and stash it. We can sleep, eat, and clear our heads to make a good decision."

Sawyer nodded. "That makes sense."

"Which brings us back to finding out if we can lift it."

They dug some more dirt and found a pair of brass handles on either end of the chest. Again setting their shovels aside, they tried to lift the chest with no luck. With it buried below the ground they were standing on, they were unable to budge it.

"Any idea how much gold weighs?" Jackson asked.

"More than the two of us can bench."

"You happen to have a collection of handbags at home?"

She shook her head.

"What about rope in your Jeep? Or chains? Jumper cables?"

"You think we can pull it out?"

"Maybe. We can use the shovels as rollers. It's how they built the pyramids."

"Great. That worked out so well for the Hebrew slaves." She wearily climbed out of the hole. "I'll check the Jeep."

"I'll make a ramp."

Exhausted to the point of never wanting to turn a spade in the ground again, Jackson remodeled his rudimentary staircase into a ramp. Sawyer returned with her jumper cables and a pair of bungee cords, saying they were all she had to offer. She pitched in with the digging, and by the time they had a workable ramp, darkness had fallen over the Florida Keys.

Panting for breath, they stood side by side and looked down into the hole at the chest containing untold riches. Busy with work and trying to plot their next steps, Jackson's mind had been too busy to consider all the ramifications of what they'd found. But already dreams of what he could do with the money, how he could be set for life, and how he wouldn't have to work another day if he so chose all filled his mind. He felt guilty. Their purpose in looking for the treasure had been to catch Ben's killers, not to become filthy rich. And yet, the allure of wealth had bled into their motives, and now he was borderline giddy at his newfound fortune. Deciding to sort out his greedy emotions later, he forced himself to concentrate on how to get the chest to Sawyer's Jeep.

Looping Sawyer's jumper cables inside the brass handle on the near end, Jackson handed her two of the terminals and took the other two. Pulling them over their shoulders for leverage, they took positions and began tugging. They had excavated the near end of the chest, and it moved a few inches.

"Again," Jackson said, and they strained against the jumper cables. The chest moved a few more inches. "Again." A few more inches. They stopped.

"We're never going to get it up the ramp," Sawyer said.

"Yeah, and the cables or the handle are going to break." He dropped the cables and wiped his forehead on his arm. Both were equally wet. "Any chance we get your Jeep through the woods?"

"I don't think so. More likely we get it stuck."

Jackson sat back on the chest. "Other than put the gold in something else, what other options do we have?"

"Bring in help."

"What else?"

She thought for a moment and shook her head.

"Okay, where's the nearest place to buy luggage?"

"There's a Sears or Kmart in Key West. Or probably something on Big Pine Key."

"You want to go or guard the gold?"

"I'll go," she said.

"I'll sit here and smack anyone who comes along in the face with a shovel."

"Sounds like a solid plan."

Jackson tapped the chest. "You want to take some collateral?"

"What, in case you turn into Samson and carry it off on your back?"

"Something like that."

"I trust you."

"Take a few doubloons for payment."

Sawyer smiled. "I'll go with the Visa. You can pay me back in emeralds."

"Deal."

Chapter Forty-Seven

8:13 p.m.

SAWYER HURRIED OFF, and Jackson plopped down on the side of the hole. The odds of someone stumbling upon their dig after dark were between slim and none, but just sitting there with all the gold exposed made him nervous. Then again, so did sending Sawyer off on her own now, given recent events.

She disappeared into the trees, and Jackson said a prayer for her safety. Then he prostrated himself in the sand. If memory served, Big Pine Key was near the western terminus of Seven Mile Bridge. Jackson guessed it to be about a half hour drive each way, plus shopping time and explanation to the clerk as to why Sawyer looked like she'd just swam in from Havana. It gave him time to kill.

His muscles protesting, Jackson decided to work. He began filling in the hole around the chest, leaving them room to get in and load up the luggage. For no reason other than it gave his mind something to do besides complain about the work, he counted shovels of earth. At one hundred, he took a break to check the tide. It hadn't reached their dam yet, and Jackson was whittling away at the dual prongs of the U. They were safe for a few more hours.

After another hundred shovelfuls, Jackson stopped to watch a full moon rising over Lois Key. It was big and orange and beautiful. It also illuminated a key deer that poked its head onto the beach, looked at Jackson for a moment, then darted furtively back into the cover of the trees.

Jackson refilled some more of the hole, stopping when it would have meant throwing dirt on the chest. He sat in the cool sand and waited, watching the moon some more, musing over the events of the last week. He wondered what had happened to Ben, why, how specifically Louviere was involved, what had come of Frank Baldwin's gang and the map they now possessed, and how in the world he was going to get half of a chest of gold through airport security.

"You're keeping a real sharp watch, I see," Sawyer said, thumping a set of luggage in the sand beside Jackson.

He turned and looked at her. She carried a package of bottled water in one hand, and withdrew a bottle and tossed it to Jackson.

"Get a good deal?" he asked.

"Relatively speaking, a steal. But you should have seen the looks they gave me."

"I don't know, I think the sandy, sweaty, and pooped look works for you," he said, then took a gulp of water, half of it entering his mouth.

"Yeah, well, there's another set of luggage in the Jeep."

"I'll get it."

He trekked back through the woods to the same parking spot and carried the second set of luggage back to the beach.

At Jackson's suggestion, Sawyer snapped a few photos of the stash with her phone before they began the process of loading the suitcases with gold. They didn't take time to examine the various pieces but still couldn't help marveling as they filled the new luggage. With gold piled into seven of the eight suitcases, they stopped with one doubloon remaining in the bottom of the chest.

"I say we leave it there for whoever comes along next."

"That's cruel," Sawyer said.

"It might be Louviere."

"I'm too tired to argue."

Jackson nodded and closed the lid.

"So, you want to haul gold to the Jeep or start filling in the hole."

She lifted her head. "We do need to fill it, don't we?"

He nodded. If for no other reason than not leaving public land a mess. But it would also be a good idea not to leave evidence that they had found the treasure. It wouldn't be long before a biplane or an ultralight or a curious pleasure cruiser spotted the dig. It would still take some work to trace it back to Jackson and Sawyer, and by then they would hopefully be in the clear. But Jackson didn't want to take chances.

"I'll carry suitcases," she said.

"Fair enough. But if I hear tires peeling out, I'm going to be miffed."

Sawyer offered a thin smile and lifted the first suitcase. Jackson grabbed a shovel and began heaving dirt back into the hole. He made good progress during Sawyer's seven trips to the Jeep. Halfway through her transportation, he thought better of packing the Jeep full of gold while they were on the beach. But he wasn't about to suggest she haul several suitcases back to the beach. It spurred him to shovel faster.

Sawyer eventually joined him, and by the time they had scooped the majority of their dam back into the hole, the moon was high in the sky, and the waves had reached them.

"I say good enough," Sawyer said as water sloshed around her ankles. "The waves will take care of the rest."

Jackson nodded. There was still a foot or two indentation where the hole had been, and a small mound still formed a slight breakwater. But he agreed with her assessment. After a few tide cycles, it would be back to normal.

Completely exhausted, they trudged back to the Jeep, bringing their shovels, buckets, cooler, and one empty suitcase with them. They collapsed into the front seat of the Jeep. Sawyer removed her phone and set it in the center console. The time showed 11:34.

"Okay, where to?" Sawyer asked.

"Priority one right now, secure the gold. Find an out of the way motel, get a room, and lock the door, slide the deadbolt, and move the dresser in front of the door."

"I was hoping you were going to say Denny's."

"That's next."

"Okay. Do you care where this hotel is?"

"Out of the way but not so isolated that we'll stand out."

"I think I know the place."

Sawyer started the Jeep and turned it around, heading back to U.S. 1.

"How's she ride?" Jackson asked.

"Low," Sawyer said with a small grin. She turned west on U.S. 1 toward Key West. The night air had finally cooled, rushing over their sweat-covered bodies as they journeyed across the Saddlebunch Keys. Too tired to speak, they rode in silence. Jackson pondered scenarios in his head, trying to come up with the best plan for the next bunch of hours. Food and sleep factored in heavily.

Sawyer drove all the way to Key West before venturing off U.S. 1. She took South Roosevelt Boulevard around the airport and along the coast. They came to a small collection of cheap but new motels that looked across the road at the open ocean. Adjoined to the parking lots of a Mom & Pop restaurant and a souvenir shop, they were backed by swampland and backwater.

"Good?" Sawyer asked.

"Yeah," Jackson said looking around. "Perfect."

"Care which?"

"No."

Sawyer turned the Jeep into the first motel, the Sunrise Inn. It was shaped like an L, with all the rooms facing the road and thus the ocean. Shaking off a sense of déjà vu from his last case, Jackson got out as soon as she parked. "Wait here. I'll be right back."

She nodded, and he headed to the motel office at the foot of the L. The desk clerk was a heavyset woman in an orange Gators T-shirt. She looked gruffly at Jackson. "Yeah?"

"I need a room, please."

She ran her eyes from his sweaty, tousled hair to the sand caking his arms to his dirty and damp pant legs. "Cash or credit."

"Cash," Jackson said.

"Still going to need to see an ID."

Jackson had no choice but to plop his driver's license on the table, along with forty-five dollars for the room and taxes. "You know what," he said, reaching back for his wallet. "Make it two nights."

She grunted something and handed him a key on a dongle. An actual key. "Room 8," she said, counting the cash with a suspicious eye.

Jackson took the key and returned to the parking lot. Sawyer had not driven off into the mythical sunset with the gold.

"Let's get these suitcases inside," Jackson said, glancing around the lot. There were a few other cars, but no people. Same was true of the Mom & Pop next door. Taillights in the distance marked the only traffic on the highway, and the beach across the road was quiet.

Each taking a suitcase, Jackson and Sawyer hurried to the room. Jackson opened the door and flipped on the light to reveal a no-frills layout. But it was at least reasonably clean.

"One king," Sawyer said, nodding at the bed.

"Oops. I'll sleep on the floor."

She nodded.

They made three return trips to the Jeep, again avoiding apparent detection, and returned to the room with seven suitcases of gold. Jackson locked and deadbolted the door. Sawyer plopped onto the corner of the bed. "I am beat."

"Unfortunately, we have more work to do."

She looked up at him.

"Your Jeep is conspicuous."

She raised an eyebrow.

"One of us should take it to my hotel and exchange it for my car. Not untraceable, but at least a little less likely to be recognized than a maroon Jeep."

The eyebrow went higher. "You're serious?"

He nodded.

"You have watched way too much TV."

"We want to be inconspicuous."

"For all we know, Louviere and Baldwin and whoever are digging up the Bahamas right now."

"I don't want to take any chances."

She exhaled. "Okay, so what does the other one of us do?"

"Catalog what's here. Pictures, descriptions. We don't need to count every doubloon, but I want a record of what we found. Just in case."

Another sigh. "Okay, who does what?"

"I don't know. I hate to leave you all alone with the gold, but going to the hotel could be dangerous too."

"Well, whoever goes needs to get us something to eat."

"And clean clothes."

"Yes."

"You go," he said. "I don't know where you live and I don't really feel like raiding your underwear drawer. All my stuff's in a bag in my suitcase. Just bring the whole thing."

"And if Louviere's henchman are lying in wait for me?"

"Take my phone and have 9-1-1 dialed and keep your finger on the send button."

"Way, way too much TV," she said. "Why your phone?"

"Because I'll use your phone to take pictures while I catalog everything that's here."

"Okay."

"You want me to order pizza or do you want to pick up something?"

"I'll pick it up."

"Okay."

"Can I sleep when I get back?"

"Until noon if you want."

"I want."

Jackson nodded. "Be careful. Get in and out as fast as you can, and if anything doesn't look right, abort and call me."

"I sure hope all this cloak-and-dagger is unnecessary," she said, taking her and Jackson's keys and heading for the door.

"Me too," he said as it closed behind her.

He went to the bathroom to wash his hands and splash some water on his face. He also made a cup of coffee and slugged it as he got to work, rifling through the suitcases and taking pictures of everything with Sawyer's phone. Gold coins, artifacts, implements. He also estimated the number of doubloons at over a thousand and tried to note every other object. Not a big texter or messager, Jackson found typing on her smartphone's screen to be impossible, so he resorted to motel-provided pen and paper. Seven goblets, two plates, three bowls, one cross, a couple of idols, six different animal figurines, and one big medallion-like object later, he concluded he was done. The clock beside the bed read 1:23.

Sawyer had been gone almost ninety minutes, and Jackson quickly computed travel time to his hotel, to her place somewhere on Key West, and to a twenty-four-hour restaurant. He concluded it wasn't quite time to worry.

Eight minutes later, a knock on the door shook him from a half-asleep trance. He got up and peeked out the peephole and saw a bedraggled Southern woman with slumped shoulders holding two duffels and a fast food bag. He quickly opened the door.

"You ever see the sort of people who hit up a McDonald's in the middle of the night?"

He shook his head.

"I was the normal-looking one."

"You look fine," he said. She wore a pair of sweats and a black T-shirt. Her hair was still damp, and when the smell of the burgers wore off, Jackson also sniffed a trace of shampoo. She had taken the time to shower, which he wouldn't have advised under the circumstances. But he wasn't about to critique her. He closed the door behind her, again smelling the whiff of hamburgers and suddenly having trouble caring about anything else.

Sawyer dropped Jackson's duffel bag and a small travel bag of hers on the floor and flopped onto the same corner of the bed. He pulled up a chair, and they shared four Quarter Pounders and a pile of French fries. Nothing had been out of place at the hotel or her place. No signs of being watched or surveilled. Jackson gave her his count on the treasure, saving an internet-based estimate until morning.

It was two o'clock by the time they were done eating, and Sawyer was yawning between words. "Are you sure you don't mind sleeping on the floor?"

"No. Knock yourself out."

She was already pulling back the covers. Jackson announced he was going to shower and, grabbing his duffel bag, killed the lights and ducked into the bathroom. For the first ten minutes, he just let the warm water pour over him, washing away the sand and grime and sweat of the day. His mind had grown as weak as his body, and instead of plotting and planning and processing, he decided to sleep and let a clearer head prevail in the morning.

Despite his sleepiness, the water felt so good that Jackson might have stayed in the shower all night had he not feared the sound of the running water would keep Sawyer awake. He needn't have worried. When he emerged in a clean T-shirt and a pair of shorts, Sawyer was fast asleep.

She'd left a pillow for him on the floor, along with the comforter from the bed. He curled up by the door, more to be out of her way if she needed the bathroom in the middle of the night than as any measure of protection. A thousand thoughts fought against his brain's desire to shut down, but sleep soon won out.

Jackson woke suddenly to a chime of sorts. He couldn't place it, and his initial inclination that it was still the middle of the night was destroyed by the light streaming around the curtains and through the crack under the door.

He sat up as the chime repeated itself. Sawyer pushed herself up in bed and looked around, fighting to keep her eyes open. "Jackson," she mumbled before her eyes settled on him. The chime sounded again.

"What is that, a hurricane alert? Tsunami warning?"

"Ugh, my phone," Sawyer answered, reaching for the nightstand. When she pulled her arm back, Jackson's eyes focused on the clock. 7:13.

"Hello," Sawyer said. "Yes." Her countenance darkened, and she lowered the phone, tapping the screen once. "What did you say?"

A thick, deliberate male voice answered. "We have Ben. We will trade him for the treasure."

"Wh . . . What? You have Ben?"

"Crescent Point, midnight tonight. You bring the treasure, or he dies. No cops."

"How do we know he's alive?"

The phone clicked off.

Chapter Forty-Eight

Saturday, May 25
7:14 a.m.

SAWYER TURNED HER eyes to Jackson. He jumped up, fighting through a tangled mass of comforter, and scrambled over to her.

"What are you—"

He cut her off by taking the phone. He quickly powered it off and pried off the cover.

"Jackson, what are you doing?"

"Making sure they can't trace our location," he said, finding and removing the battery and the SIM card. He set the phone and all of its components on the table, then located his phone and repeated the procedure.

Sawyer threw off her covers and got out of bed. "What about tracking the number?"

"Maybe later," Jackson said, already peeking out the window. Bright sunlight lit the ocean across the road, sending long shadows from the palm trees lining the street. They partially darkened an empty parking lot.

"Do you think it's possible?" Sawyer said, joining him by the window. "Is Ben alive?"

"I don't know."

"They never found his body. He could be alive."

"I know."

She turned his shoulder and stepped in front of him. "We give it to them—every last coin—if it will save him."

"Agreed."

She nodded. "Okay."

Jackson paced back and sat on the bed. "We need to think this through carefully. No rash decisions. They could get us killed. Ben too, if he's not already."

"I agree. Where do we start?"

"We have until midnight and we only slept about five hours. We should rest some more."

"No. No way. We're using every minute to prepare. Besides, there's no way I could sleep anyhow."

"Yeah, me either. It was worth a try."

"How do we know if they're telling the truth, if he's alive?" she asked.

"We don't. That's the big problem. They know we have a weakness and can't afford to call their bluff."

"So what do we do?"

"We call their bluff."

"What?"

"We have to figure out a way to take back the advantage."

"How?"

"I don't know yet."

Sawyer leaned against the door and shook her head. "How did they know we found the treasure?"

Jackson shook his head. "Could be a shot in the dark or could be the same way they knew we'd found a map in the Bahamas."

"Louviere must have people everywhere."

"The girl at Ace knew we bought digging tools. The clerk at Sears or wherever saw you buy luggage. Maybe Jackie or the librarian. I don't know. I'm weighing the odds you're a mole."

"For real?"

"No. But almost."

"We should call the police," she said.

"Maybe."

"Maybe?"

"We can't give them anything hard—no proof, no names for sure, just a phone call. Plus, it makes the treasure public."

"I don't care about the treasure, Jackson."

"Even if Ben's dead and this is all a ruse by Louviere or Baldwin or whoever?"

She looked down.

"I'm not saying no," he said. "We just need to think about it."

"Fair enough."

"I'm going to go for a walk."

"A walk?"

"Clear my head. And I want to see if anyone's watching us."

"Can I use my phone while you're gone? I want to find out where Crescent Point is."

"You don't know?"

"Over seven hundred keys. I don't know them all."

"Okay. Just be quick, and take it apart when you're done. I'll be back in fifteen minutes."

He laced up his shoes and peeked around the curtain again before stepping outside. The air was already warm and carried the thickness of the tropics. Jackson surveyed the parking lot, road, and beach. All was quiet. He crossed the parking lot and the street to the wide sidewalk that ran along the beach, separated from it by a short concrete wall and some planted, tall grass. He began jogging.

There were three possibilities. The caller didn't have Ben and was bluffing in a desperate attempt to get the treasure. He had Ben and would exchange him for the treasure. Or he had Ben but was going to double-cross Jackson and Sawyer and not trade him for the treasure. If that was the case, Ben was as good as dead. So it was really two choices. A bluff or a genuine exchange.

If it was the latter, not a lot of planning was necessary. If the former, Jackson really hated to lose out on millions in gold. Almost as much, he hated to see the people responsible for Ben's death cash in. Then again, this had been their plan—bait the bad guys with the treasure. So could he somehow spin this to their advantage? And then convince Sawyer to go along with the idea?

As he mulled, Jackson kept an eye out for anyone who could have been watching the hotel. Pedestrians on a bench, someone with a camera, a person in a parked car. He saw nothing suspicious. He didn't really expect to, but somehow, he and Sawyer had been followed or monitored. And what were the odds that Louviere just happened to have a girl working in the right store at the right time to know that they purchased a couple of shovels?

But what else could it have been? Jackson couldn't think of a way that Louviere or his minions could have bugged either of them. Unless they had done something to their phones during the break-in at the Hotel Sir

Donovan. GPS tracking? Then they hacked a satellite feed and watched them dig up the treasure, and instead of taking it from them on the beach, they had waited to set up an exchange? That didn't wash. Yet somehow they knew.

After a few hundred yards, Jackson turned back and returned to the Sunrise Inn. He slowed as he made his way back across the parking lot. The smells from the Mom & Pop restaurant adjacent to the motel were appealing, and Jackson added meal-planning to his list of things to think about.

Sawyer had changed into jeans and a clean shirt, her hair clipped up. She sat on a made bed. Her phone was in her hand.

"Figure out anything brilliant?" she asked.

"Not yet."

She nodded. "Well, I'm no expert at this, but it looks like they picked a good exchange point."

"Oh?"

"Crescent Key is located north of Big Pine Key. One road in, one road out. Gravel the last few miles to Crescent Point."

"Which is?"

"Not much. Just a little isthmus of land that probably makes a good place to watch a sunset. There's a small fishing pier but no buildings, no residences. It should be vacant."

Jackson sat down beside her, and they reviewed the area from Google's satellite image. Crescent Key was technically a separate island from Big Pine Key, but the bridge that connected them only spanned a few dozen yards of shallow water. About two miles in length, Crescent Key was shaped like a sliver of the moon with a pier at its northernmost tip pointing northwest. The road that crossed from Big Pine Key led to a few homes at the southern end of the island before it turned to gravel. It snaked its way around some trees and inlets before ending in a gravel cul-de-sac just short of the pier.

"What's around it?" Jackson asked.

Sawyer zoomed out to reveal a half dozen other islands in the vicinity, all of them uninhabited. Crescent Point was indeed isolated.

"What do you think?" she asked.

"I think I'm hungry."

"Hungry. Really, right now?"

He nodded. "If I try to force ideas or force a plan, I crap out. I work best by gathering intel and letting the idea come to me."

"What if ideas don't come by, say, midnight?"

"Then we wing it."

Sawyer rolled her eyes.

"Trust me," he said. "I've been here before."

"Here, really?"

"Pretty stinking close." He elbowed her. "The smells from the place next door are divine. Let's go grab a bite to eat, let our minds unwind. We'll think of something."

With a sigh, Sawyer nodded. "You really feel okay leaving the gold here while we both go eat?"

"We can get a table by the window and keep an eye on the door. And if they haven't figured out where we are and made a grab for the gold yet, I think they're willing to rely on an exchange. Besides, I think we both could use a stretch of our legs."

"Okay. Just don't forget the Do Not Disturb sign. I'd hate to leave our maid a million-dollar tip."

*   *   *

11:53 p.m.

JACKSON CROSSED the bridge onto Crescent Key. He counted two driveways on the right before, as expected, the road soon turned to gravel. Like a bobsled driver, Jackson had memorized the turns in the road, and he counted them as he went. He'd spent the thirty-minute drive from Key West praying and going over his plan and praying some more. His stomach was doing flip-flops as millions of dollars and, more importantly, possibly Ben's life hung in the balance.

The plan had first started to hatch in Jackson's mind on the walk back to the motel after breakfast. He'd refined it throughout the morning as he and Sawyer did more research and replayed the events of the last week, looking for any clues to confirm Louviere's involvement or indications that Ben was or wasn't still alive. They had also tried turning her phone back on briefly to check the number of the morning's caller. Jackson had called Mouse to have him run it, but it had come back empty. They'd tried calling it twice, hoping to make some deal for proof of life. Both calls had gone unanswered.

The afternoon had been spent planning. They had debated driving out to Crescent Key, but since the caller had picked the spot, it stood to reason he might have it already staked out. So they had remained in the motel, running scenarios, thinking, praying, debating. Ultimately, because Jackson convinced Sawyer to go along with his plan, they had not called Sheriff Hawkins. Not yet.

After dinner at the Mom & Pop place, Jackson had made a quick run to the nearest convenience store to purchase three burn phones—two for communicating with each other and a third for communicating with Louviere's people—and to Home Depot to pick up a few things he would need later. He'd returned to the motel and gone over the details of their plan with Sawyer one last time. Then they had prayed.

As Jackson made the final turn and approached a half-mile straightaway leading to Crescent Point, Sawyer's words repeated in his head.

"Jesus, we are trying to do the right thing," she had prayed. "We recognize the blessing this pile of gold could be. But we recognize how much more of a blessing each human life is. We pray that if Ben is still alive, that You would see him safely through this ordeal. Like I said, we're trying to do the right thing. Please guide us, either to accomplish Your will or out of the way so we don't impede it."

Simple words from a Southern girl with a twang, but all Jackson had been able to add was an, "Amen."

As much as her prayer had encouraged him, her question before they left the motel had served the opposite purpose. As Jackson had reached to open the door, she had put her hand on his arm. "Remember the Bahamas?" she had asked.

"Yeah. What in particular?"

"Baldwin, the kidnapping. All a ruse to get us away from the room. What if that's the case again?"

He had reasoned that if the caller had known where they were and where the treasure was, he probably would have been more direct in trying to get it. But he also couldn't argue with her fears. Nor with leaving millions in gold sitting at a forty-five-dollar-per-night motel on the coast. But it had been too late to change plans.

Locking the door behind them, they had driven into town, where Jackson had dropped Sawyer off at the northern end of a very festive Duval

Street, a few blocks from her apartment. It was Memorial Day weekend, and Key West was a destination. All the happy revelers and partiers were unaware of the life-or-death game Jackson and Sawyer were playing.

That had been at nine-thirty. Hungry, he'd grabbed some food and waited until shortly after eleven to start for Crescent Key. When Sawyer had called him on her burn phone at 11:26, the plan had officially been green-lighted. No turning back.

As Jackson bounced over a few ruts in the road, his headlights illuminated a pair of pickup trucks, both newer model, parked at the end of the cul-de-sac on either side of a narrow, wooden pier. The larger of the trucks had a covered cab, presumably for transporting treasure.

Four men stood by the trucks. Two were big and muscular, both with their arms crossed. A third held a rifle in his hands. Casually, aimed at the ground, but it sent the message. The fourth had his hands in his pockets. All but the man with his hands in his pocket wore caps or hats, none of their faces easily identifiable. Not that Jackson knew who to identify anyhow.

"Sawyer, I'm here," he said quietly into his phone. Leaving the call active, he slipped the phone into his pocket as he parked the car. He killed the lights, leaving the engine running, and slowly got out, hands raised.

The moon was high in the sky, not quite full, but shining enough light for Jackson to see the four figures in front of him. One of the pickups had a lantern on the hood, one of the modern LED models that would shine through the apocalypse.

Jackson took a few steps forward. The man who'd had his hands in his pockets did as well, stopping when they were about fifteen feet apart. He was dressed in black and wore a matching dark expression on a plain face that was scarcely illuminated by the moon. Something about the face bugged Jackson, but he couldn't quite place it. And now wasn't the time.

"You have the gold?" the man asked, eyeing Jackson's rented Chevy Aveo. His voice matched the caller's that morning.

"You have Ben?"

"In the truck."

"Let me see him."

"The gold first."

Jackson swallowed hard, then whistled. A few quick notes.

"What the heck—"

Wisssss-pttt.

The man looked down at the ground ten feet to his right where a small cloud of sand had been kicked into the air. It slowly floated back to earth, and the man opened his mouth. He never said a word.

KA-BAMMMM.

A rifle shot reverberated through the night air, floating across the water and lingering in the darkness. The man in front of Jackson looked from the sand where the bullet had hit, up to Jackson, back to his crew, and back to Jackson.

Jackson purposefully kept his eyes locked on the man's head, making eye contact when he turned back. Forcing a smirk to his face, Jackson said, "That was Lou, a local sharpshooter I hired. I figured, since I had the money . . ."

The man glared at him but didn't respond immediately. Behind him, the trio had tensed, one of the heavyset guys reaching for a pistol while the man with the rifle raised it.

"The way I figure it, you're asking yourself two questions right now," Jackson said. "A, was Lou firing a warning shot or is he just a bad marksman who missed about ten feet wide and six feet low? And B, is he the only sharpshooter I hired? You know, there are a surprisingly large number of former Navy guys down here."

"What are you trying to pull?"

"The rug out from under your feet. I don't like to be bullied. So I'm giving you two options. Either you have one of your other brother Darryls over there open the truck and let Ben out, or we deal on my terms."

The rifleman raised his gun, and Jackson couldn't help but turn his eyes to the man who'd taken aim at him. He realized for the first time as she moved in the moonlight that it wasn't a man but a woman with curly brown hair. Not unlike the woman at the Ace Hardware the previous day, but Jackson didn't have time to figure out if it was her or not. Right now, it didn't much matter.

"Yeah, you can have one of your stooges shoot me right now," Jackson said. "But I'm going to do you a solid and answer one of your questions. Lou didn't miss. So before my body hits the sand, your brain's going to splatter. And even if by some chance Lou misses, there's not a penny in the car."

The man swore, then turned back and barked a command to the woman. She lowered her gun.

"What's it going to be?" Jackson asked.

He swore again, unleashing a string of epithets at Jackson that made him blush. "You will die for this. You and the girl," he said.

"And you will stay poor for the rest of your life, you and your group of morons and everybody but Martin Louviere. He'll just use his money to hire someone smarter whose first priority will probably be to eliminate the incompetent bozos who had the job first. So, I guess we're in the same boat, sweet cheeks."

If looks could kill, Jackson would have dropped over dead. Instead, the man curled his lip and snarled, biting off his words. "What terms?"

Jackson fought off a smile. The lack of confusion on the man's face at the mention of Louviere's name indicated Jackson had hit the nail on the head. "You got Ben in the truck?" he asked.

"No," he spat.

Jackson nodded. "Then here's the deal. I'm leaving. I'll call you tomorrow morning on the number you called us with. I'll tell you when and where. You bring Ben, and I will bring one-fourth of the treasure."

"No chance. The whole treasure or Ben dies."

"Funny how you think this is a debate," Jackson said. "You ever watch *Deep Impact*?"

"What?"

"*Deep Impact*. Morgan Freeman, Téa Leoni, little Frodo, that girl who looks like Helen Hunt?"

"What are you talking about?"

"Morgan Freeman tells Téa Leoni that while it seems like they're each holding the other one over the same barrel, it only seems that way."

"Are you crazy?"

"No. You've made your threat. If I don't comply, you'll kill Ben. My threat, you don't comply, you don't get your quarter of X million dollars. Thing is, you can't up your threat. You can't kill Ben twice. But I can up my threat. I can cut you off completely. *Bupkis*." He smiled. "Call."

"There's more that you can do than kill a man."

"True. But you see, for the last few days, we've pretty much figured Ben was dead. In fact, I think he still is, and you're full of crap. Anything better than dead is a win for me. Besides, he and I are friends, but we're not BFFs. And five million dollars soothes a lot of pain."

"You are crazy," he said, adding another curse.

"And you are starting to get on my nerves with your insults and foul language. Want me to make it twenty percent?"

"I'm going to . . ."

"Hmm, what's that? I didn't hear you?"

"One-fourth for Ben."

Jackson smiled. "Now we're talking. And I should stipulate, a healthy Ben. If you plan to rough him up as punishment and then turn him over, I just might change my mind. If you've already roughed him up, I suggest you find a twenty-four-hour ER and get him medical attention. *Kapish?*"

He nearly spit a, "Yes."

"Tomorrow. I'll call you. And I wouldn't recommend trying to follow me."

The man said nothing and Jackson slowly backed up to the car and found the door with his hand while eyeing the man and the trio behind him. He got in and put the car in reverse, using the taillights to find his way as he backed up a quarter of a mile to a place where he could turn around. Every few seconds, he checked to make sure the man hadn't moved. He had rejoined the other three, but they still stood by the trucks.

Around the corner, Jackson had room to make a Y-turn. He stopped in the middle of it and tossed out six "spike strips" he'd made with two-inch screws and a box of shingles that he'd bought that afternoon. Spinning his wheels in the gravel, he left them in a cloud of dust.

As he drove, he reached for his phone. "Sawyer, I'm out. Get moving."

"Copy that."

Chapter Forty-Nine

JACKSON SAT IN the front seat of the Aveo, watching the clock on the dashboard. He had been parked in the lot of Cayo Hueso Charters for over an hour, waiting and waiting and waiting. He had driven back to Key West with his eyes on the rearview mirror as much as the windshield. He had seen nothing to indicate he had been followed, but just to be sure, he had zig-zagged a dozen times once reaching the city. He had backed into the vacant lot, quickly reattached the front license plate on the Aveo, and remained inside ever since, watching and waiting. All was quiet.

Sawyer had called at one to report that she was safely on her way back with no signs that she was being followed. Jackson wouldn't feel safe until the small powerboat she had rented was back in its slip. Until Sawyer was back in the car. In fact, until they were both back in the Sunrise Inn, with the gold, with the doors locked.

Even then . . .

Jackson passed the time by reconstructing the day in his head. First, he'd had to convince Sawyer his plan would work, that he could out-bluff the caller. He had done it before, using his overly macho, cocksure, make-the-other-guy-mad routine, and it had always worked. Still, Sawyer had had her doubts.

"Someday you're going to run up against someone who won't back down," she had said.

He had nodded.

"You're just hoping it's not today."

"That's where you come in."

"Me?"

"Yep. Assuming you still have that Ruger M77 Hawkeye you shot at that Auburn fan with."

Sawyer raised her eyebrow hesitantly. "Why?"

"Because you have to make them think we have the upper hand."

"I'm not shooting anyone so you can save your gold."

"Would you shoot near someone to save Ben's life?"

"Yeah."

"Okay."

"One problem."

"What's that?"

"It's going to be midnight," she said.

"Don't you have a night scope for hunting critters?"

"Yeah, back in my room in Tuscaloosa."

Jackson sighed. "There'll be a full moon."

"I'm a good shot, Jackson, but not that good."

"If everything goes to plan, I won't need you to be that good. Just good enough to scare them."

Sawyer shook her head. "And where am I going to shoot from?"

Jackson turned her phone, on which he had been plotting, so she could see. He tapped at a small island, the southernmost point of which was approximately an eighth of a mile from Crescent Point. "I've got it at two hundred twenty-five yards. Tell me you can make that shot."

"Sure. Probably. But how do I get there?"

"Look here. There's a channel between some of these smaller keys. With a shallow-hulled boat, I figure you can get in close on the north side, out of sight, then walk around the perimeter and set up down here. Just watch out for gators. Or crocodiles."

"Um-hmm."

"Look, you want out, I get it. You want to try something else, I get it. But you asked earlier if I thought they had Ben." He looked her in the eyes. "Honestly, no. I think he's dead, and I think they're using exchanging him as a last, desperate ploy. Unfortunately, we can't risk it and not show up because he could still be alive."

"So why not call Sheriff Hawkins?"

"Not yet. I've got a plan to get Ben—if he's alive—and the gold and, if I'm reading this right, get the caller and his cronies. That was our original plan . . ."

Sawyer had been dubious at first, but Jackson had convinced her. He'd conveyed full confidence in his plan, but now as he sat in the parking lot waiting for her to return—even after the first part of his plan had worked perfectly—he was dubious too. What concerned him most was the lack of a tie—at least that would hold up in court—to Louviere. Unless he was implicated by people lower on the food chain, he would likely never be held responsible for what he had done. But Jackson was still working on that.

Then there was the caller, the guy who'd done the talking at the exchange. Something about him bugged Jackson. He wasn't sure that he had seen him before, but he had seen someone who looked like him. Not the way a guy might look like his brother or even cousin, but the way two unrelated people might share a physical feature or gesture. But who, and where? Jackson wasn't sure he would recognize the caller if he saw him on the street in broad daylight, having only seen him for a few minutes in dim moonlight. And yet . . .

A moving light in the side-view mirror caught Jackson's attention. He turned over his shoulder to see a white and blue Bowrider puttering into the harbor. He waited until it came around a tree and the moonlight shone on the name on the side. It was Sawyer.

Jackson got out and walked to the dock, where he spotted her as she pulled into the slip. He helped her tie off. She was dressed head to toe in black, including a stocking cap and sweat-streaked grease paint on her face. She held a backpack slung over one shoulder and carried her guitar case in the other. It did not contain a guitar.

"No trouble?" Jackson asked.

"Wrong. Sand fleas. How'd it go on your end? I couldn't hear a lot on the phone."

"Their spokesman was spitting bullets, but he backed down."

"You were right," she said as they walked toward the building at the end of the dock. "They went for it."

"Yeah. They bit. Now we have to reel them in."

"You weren't followed?" She dropped the boat key through the night deposit box.

"Nope. You police your brass?"

"Huh?"

"Your shell casing. You pick it up?"

"Yes."

"Then let's get out of here."

They got into the car and headed for the Sunrise Inn. Key West had quieted, with even the last revelers returning to their hotels. Sawyer removed her stocking cap and tousled her hair. "I was worried there for a few minutes," she said. "Just as I got into position, the moon went behind the clouds. I was blind."

"Were they there already?"

She nodded. "Good thing the breeze was from the south or they would have heard my engine. I hardly dared to breathe as it was."

"You did great."

"I just hope we didn't foul things up."

Jackson recapped his conversation for her, including his stipulation that Ben had better be delivered unharmed.

"So who were these guys? You recognize any of them?"

"I think one of them was Serena."

"Who's Serena?"

"The check-out lady at Ace."

"You remember her name?"

"I'm good with names. And she was cute-ish."

"Why would the check-out clerk be involved?"

"The same reason a Bahamian crook and a reasonable-looking Bahamian woman in a green dress would be," Jackson said.

"You think she was Louviere's sleeper?"

"I think he's got a web of people all over."

"At a hardware store in the middle of the Keys?"

He shrugged. "Could have just been a lookalike. But think about it. He has people stationed in strategic locales where there are rumors Brackett's treasure was buried. If Baldwin gets wind of someone asking around or Serena reports someone buying a couple of shovels and pickaxes, he sends a goon or two to look into it."

"That's a stretch."

Jackson didn't answer. He was thinking about the caller again. What was it about him?

"I just don't get it," Sawyer said. "Louviere is a millionaire. Why does he care about this treasure? He's expending as much to get it as it's worth."

"Not quite."

"Maybe it is worth it," she said.

Jackson looked her way.

"Louviere is French, right?"

He nodded.

"And his great, great grandfather was a shipping mogul, right?"

"You missed a few greats, but yeah."

"And he had Toussaint's journal." She turned to face him. "Maybe this isn't so much about greed as it is about reclaiming something he feels tied to. Maybe he traces his lineage back to Toussaint somehow. Or even . . . to Brackett. We hit upon that theory before. Maybe it's true. For all we know, Great, Great, Great, Great-Granddaddy Louviere owned the *Missianna*."

Jackson thought for a moment as he turned onto Atlantic Boulevard. "Could be. He did seem to react sharply when I made up a story about being hired by a descendant of Brackett's." He shrugged. "Who knows at this point?"

Sawyer leaned her head back against the seat. "The guy you talked to didn't identify himself?"

"No, but there's something about him."

"Something how? He look familiar?"

"Yes and no. I can't place it. But I got the feeling he was more than just a peon. Especially when he agreed to my terms without having to run them up the ladder."

"You didn't give him much of a choice."

Jackson grinned. "True."

A few minutes later, they arrived at the motel. Jackson drove past it without slowing, checking for any signs that something was off. There were none, the parking lot quiet at two-thirty in the morning. He turned around near the airport complex and returned to the Sunrise Inn.

Jackson parked right in front of the door, and they hurried inside. The room was unchanged, their duffels right where they had left them, stacked behind the bed. "I am beat," Sawyer said, peeling off the damp outer layers she had worn. "I'm going to take a shower and sleep until . . . When do we have to call whoever tomorrow?"

"I told him in the morning. I plan to meet at noon and call him an hour before. I don't want to give them any more time than I need to."

Sawyer smiled. "Yeah. We know what happens when you give a resourceful guy a day to plan."

*　　*　　*

10:27 a.m.

JACKSON AND Sawyer stood in the parking lot of the Sunrise Inn. It was a beautiful morning, bright sunshine, a light breeze, just a few soft clouds on the horizon. Sawyer wore the same Kelly green T-shirt she'd worn when she'd shown up at Ben's house two weeks before. How things had progressed since.

They had been up since nine, when they had driven to the airport to rent another vehicle, a silver Nissan Rogue. Six of the seven suitcases were packed in the back, weighing the rear wheels down considerably. The black Aveo was parked in the next stall. One bag, loaded to the gills with doubloons, was in the trunk. It contained roughly one-third of the doubloons, which Jackson estimated to be about a quarter of the treasure. He'd thrown in a few bird statues for good measure.

"You have everything?" he asked.

"I do."

"You know what to do?"

"I know," she said with a resolute nod.

"Don't speed," Jackson said.

"I won't," she said, looking away. If Jackson didn't know better, he'd think she was holding back tears. When she looked back, a forced smile was on her face. "Thank you, Jackson. For all you've done to find justice for Ben, to find the truth, to protect me. You've been . . ."

"A perfect Southern gentleman?"

A small laugh escaped her mouth. "Yes."

"You deserve nothing less."

She reached her arms around his shoulders and embraced him. "Be careful," she whispered as she stepped back.

"I will. You'd better get going."

Sawyer nodded. She flipped sunglasses down over her eyes and used the key fob to unlock the Rogue. She opened the door and turned back to Jackson.

"I'll see you in a few hours," he said. "This will work."

Sawyer smiled and got into the car. Jackson stood in place until she had backed out of the parking spot and turned east onto Roosevelt Boulevard. He returned to their room, made a check for any belongings or scattered doubloons, and wiped down all surfaces. Then he checked out and got into the Aveo.

He drove to the corner of South and Whitehead Streets, where he got out and walked to the large concrete buoy anchored in the sidewalk. Eight feet tall, painted red, black, and yellow, it marked the southernmost point in the United States and claimed Cuba was only ninety miles away. On a Sunday morning, a handful of tourists were posing for pictures and checking out the view. Jackson wandered to a railing a few feet away and looked out at the ocean as he pulled out his third burn phone.

Dialing from memory, he placed the phone to his ear and waited.

"Hello?"

There was no mistaking the voice. It was the caller/spokesman. He did not sound happy. Jackson decided to make it quick.

"Mallory Square," he said. "Noon. Bring Ben to the pavilion by the three flags in the middle of the Square. Come alone, no weapons. I will do the same. Once I verify that he's safe, I'll tell you where to find the gold."

"That's not the deal."

"I'm giving you one-fourth of a treasure you have no right to," Jackson said. "And I give you my word I won't have any cops with me. It's actually quite a deal."

"Your word," the man spat.

"Noon, Mallory Square. You and Ben."

Jackson closed the phone, turned it off, and disconnected the battery. Then he heaved them both into the ocean.

"Hey!" a skinny guy in Birkenstocks hollered. "What are you doing?"

Jackson smiled at him as he turned toward the car. "Bad reception."

Chapter Fifty

11:57 a.m.

MALLORY SQUARE WAS located on the northwestern tip of Key West, just north of the cruise ship terminal where a Carnival cruise liner had just moored. Jackson stood beside the aluminum pole supporting the Florida state flag. To his left, the American flag and the "Conch Republic" flag were on similar poles. In front of him was a small pavilion supported by four brick columns. All around him, a wide brick plaza was filled with pedestrians, artists, vendors, and street performers. Known primarily for its "Sunset Celebrations" each evening, Mallory Square was home to eateries, entertainment venues, museums, a military memorial, and plenty of shopping. Jackson and Sawyer had both figured it would make a good point of exchange with minimal danger.

Jackson had parked in the lot at the north end of the Square, and from where he stood, he could see the trunk of the Aveo. He checked the time on his burn phone. 11:58.

He did not expect anyone to show. He didn't think Ben was still alive and in the clutches of Louviere's people. And if that was the case, they had nothing to gain by walking up to Jackson and trying to bargain with him or admitting their bluff. No, they would try another tactic.

If they did have Ben but objected to the terms, Jackson didn't know what options they had. He had made it pretty clear the night before and on the phone an hour earlier that he wasn't negotiating. If they tried to raise the stakes, Jackson would have to play it by ear. But given the "negotiations" thus far, Jackson didn't expect that either.

The one condition he had to prepare himself for was a legitimate exchange. He'd planned it out as best he could, but he still had to be ready for double-crosses and contingencies.

To Jackson's right, a juggler had a small crowd around him. A man dressed in black emerged through it, but as he drew closer, Jackson realized it wasn't the man from the night before. He glanced down at his phone again. It was noon.

The sun had grown hot, accompanied by a very faint breeze that was refreshing when it found its way through the buildings in front of Jackson. Up above, the clouds had grown, still taking up only a small portion of the sky. They reminded him of the clouds that had dotted the horizon as he'd driven from Miami two weeks ago. His thoughts drifted to Sawyer, and he said a quick prayer for her safety.

There had been no reason to think their location at the Sunrise Inn had been compromised. She had left undetected in a new car. Unless Louviere had a roadblock set up at Seven Mile Bridge or had enough contacts to put out an APB for a tall, refined Southern woman, she should be safe. Still, Jackson wouldn't rest easy until he knew she had arrived without incident.

12:02. No one had approached Jackson. He looked over his shoulder at twenty-some feet of plaza between him and the water. A guy on stilts was passing. Just stilts? No fire juggling too?

Jackson looked back in front of him, scanning the comers and goers at the Square. A guy in a gray shirt was hanging out by the memorial, as if waiting for something too. Unlike Jackson, he did not appear to have a care in the world.

Jackson waited a few more minutes, thinking back on waiting for Ben that first night. He'd given his old friend an hour then. Under these circumstances, he settled on fifteen minutes. He kept his eyes on the phone. At a quarter after twelve, he concluded the caller was a no-show. Either Ben was dead, or he soon would be.

Still keeping his eyes peeled, Jackson walked to the car and got in. The guy in gray was nowhere to be seen. Jackson started the car, waited a minute, and then drove slowly out of the lot. He concentrated on navigating downtown Key West, taking Whitehead Street to Olivia, Olivia to Center, and Center to Truman Avenue, a.k.a. U.S. 1. When he'd made the turn east, he withdrew his phone and called Sawyer's burn phone.

She didn't answer. He fought the panic that something had happened to her and figured she was driving and hadn't heard the phone ring, or hadn't felt comfortable answering it. So he left a message.

"It's me. They were a no-show. I'm headed your way."

Vague, in case anybody happened to be listening. If they were listening, they had bugged a phone or the car and were playing chess to Jackson's checkers, and being vague would serve no purpose. Still, it felt like the thing to do.

As he drove through Key West, Jackson couldn't help but wonder what his two weeks would have been like if Captain Brackett had just escaped with his treasure and spent it on pleasures of the flesh. Ben would have been waiting for Jackson Sunday night, and they would have spent a long weekend fishing, sightseeing, and chilling. Instead, he'd met Sawyer, gotten involved in another case, and chased across the Caribbean after buried treasure that only maybe would help them bring down Ben's killers. If not, Louviere and his people would likely never answer for what they had done.

Jackson crossed the short bridge to Stock Island, passed the golf course, and came to Key Haven. He hadn't known Ben well enough in recent years to be devastated by his death, but he was saddened by it. The thought that Ben might have suffered turned the sadness to anger and had Jackson fine-tuning the final details and contingencies of his plan as he drove past Boca Chica Airfield and through the Saddlebunch Keys.

He kept an eye on the rearview mirror in case a couple of familiar pickup trucks showed up. U.S. 1 had narrowed to two lanes just east of Boca Chica Key and stayed that narrow as he drove across a variety of north-south keys. The narrow road caused traffic to bunch, making Jackson's task easier and also giving him more time to think. Crossing Sugarloaf Key, he reflected back on dinner with Sawyer at The Point the previous Friday night, then on finding the treasure a couple of days ago. His adventures seemed surreal and completely real at the same time.

Jackson took a casual glance in the rearview mirror and saw a navy Ford F-150 pickup barreling down on him. He pushed the accelerator over the forty-five-mile per hour limit but soon ran up on the rear of the car in front of him. A steady stream of westbound cars kept him from passing. He looked in the mirror again; the truck was right on his tail.

Jackson reached for his phone, but before he could grab it, the truck tapped his bumper. The Aveo skidded for a moment, and Jackson needed both hands to keep control. Spotting a slight break in traffic, he punched the accelerator and veered into the westbound lane. Reaching sixty-five miles per hour, he raced past a pair of cars and swerved back into his lane just before an oncoming delivery truck would have killed him.

With a shriek of the horn, the truck raced by, and Jackson's quick peek in the mirror revealed that the F-150 had not tried to pass. He crossed a short bridge over shallow water, forced to slow down to the speed limit as he encroached on more eastbound traffic. Westbound traffic was steady again, giving him no opportunity to pass, but also keeping the F-150 at bay. Jackson again reached for his phone and started dialing.

He heard the truck before he saw it. It was accompanied by a swirl of dust, appearing on his right. The old Flagler railroad had run parallel to the current Highway 1, and the bridge it had used to cross Park Channel was now a pedestrian bridge. Evidently, the F-150 had gone off the road and taken the bridge. Now it had charged up an extra wide shoulder and pulled even with Jackson.

Dropping the phone mid-dial, Jackson surveyed his options. He couldn't win a drag race, not with cars in front of him. And there were enough cars behind him that slamming on the brakes would likely cause trouble. Besides, that would only buy him a moment's relief. Oncoming traffic was still steady, so there was no chance to pass. His only hope lay in the fact that the shoulder narrowed maybe a hundred yards ahead, and the F-150 would be forced into the brush that grew between the shoulder and the backwaters of the Keys.

But it never came to that. The F-150 drew closer to Jackson's Aveo, then surged ahead so that its rear wheels were side by side with Jackson's front wheels. Suddenly, the F-150 swerved onto the road, forcing Jackson to stomp on the brakes, at the same time veering left.

The Aveo shook and skidded, and Jackson's eyes went wide as he saw a sedan approaching from the east. He jerked the wheel hard left, spinning across the westbound lane and onto the far shoulder, the back of his car making a one-eighty as he ended up facing west. The sedan and several trailing cars whooshed by, missing his front fender by inches.

Jackson exhaled, then looked for the F-150. It had stopped on the far side of the road. Two men were getting out. Jackson tried to accelerate, but his spinning maneuver had grounded the Aveo on the sloped shoulder of the road, and he merely spun his tires.

Traffic continued to race by in both directions, slowing slightly, but passing by nonetheless. Only one vehicle altered its course, that a black, small model pickup that pulled off the far shoulder fifty feet ahead. Two more men got out, and as the Aveo's wheels continued to spin, Jackson got a sinking feeling in his stomach.

Dodging traffic, the men crossed the road. Jackson reached for the phone again. As he dialed 9-1-1, he looked up. He was just in time to see a gun aimed at his head. He dove down over the center console and onto the passenger seat just as his window exploded into a million shards of glass.

Chapter Fifty-One

1:03 p.m.

"NINE-ONE-ONE emergency response," a muffled male voice declared.

"I'm on Upper Sugarloaf Key just east of the bridge and somebody's shooting at me," Jackson shouted at the phone that had fallen onto the floor when he dove onto the passenger seat. "Black Chevy Aveo," he added as two more shots took out the windshield, sending glass everywhere. Jackson heard a car horn and screeching of tires. He also heard the male voice ask if he was in immediate danger.

Jackson found the buckle and pressed it a few times before it unclasped. He lunged for the passenger door, opened it, and expelled himself onto the shoulder of the road as more bullets riddled the car. There was nothing but thick brush for a hundred yards in either direction. But thick brush beat onrushing gunmen, so Jackson crawled across the gravel and practically dove into the bushes.

He heard two more gunshots, and a bullet may or may not have whistled over his head. It didn't track, why they were shooting at him. Dead men told no tales, including the location of the remaining three-fourths of the treasure. Unless they thought he had the entire treasure with him in the car.

The bushes were thick and scratched at Jackson as he fought through them. His first few steps were solid, but then he felt himself sinking into moist sand and eventually water. He emerged to see a wide, shallow lagoon. There was nothing on the other side but a pair of radio towers in the distance. Jackson turned west along the bushes, slogging through knee-deep water. If the gunmen followed him, he could duck back into the bushes. It beat being an easy target in the lagoon.

Police sirens reached Jackson's ears, and he realized the gunfire had died out. He stopped and listened. The sirens were close, and against his own better judgment, he ducked back into the bushes. He was halfway through them when a volley of shots exploded over the sound of the sirens. Jackson ducked down, hoping a stray bullet didn't find its way through the bushes. It wasn't likely.

After less than a minute, the shooting stopped. Tentatively, Jackson fought through the bushes. When he peeked out on the other side, a pair of Monroe County Sheriff's Department squad cars had surrounded his Aveo. Four officers, guns drawn, had two men over the hood of the Aveo. Another lay in front of it, his right hand holding his left arm as he writhed in pain. The fourth man was AWOL.

Traffic was at a standstill, blocked by two Sheriff's Department cars on the west and by a string of cars on the east, one of which had spun into the wrong lane and crashed into the F-150 that had been chasing Jackson. An officer was already headed to check on the car's occupants. A second officer spotted Jackson.

"Don't move!" he shouted, and Jackson immediately raised his hands. "I've got him," the officer said, training his gun on Jackson and striding toward him.

"I'm the victim," Jackson said as he got on his knees. "I called 9-1-1."

"Quiet."

"Jackson Douglas. Sheriff—"

"I told you to be quiet!"

"—Hawkins knows me," Jackson finished quickly.

"You're Douglas?" he asked as Jackson's words finally registered.

Jackson nodded.

"You have ID?"

"In my pocket."

"Get it for me, thumb and forefinger."

Jackson gingerly removed his wallet and held it out to the officer. He checked it, then nodded. "You want to tell me what the heck is going on here?"

*   *   *

Two hours ago . . .
11:14 a.m.

"THIS IS Sheriff Hawkins."

"Sheriff, it's Jackson Douglas."

A slight pause. Then, "What can I do for you, Mr. Douglas?"

"I have a proposition for you. What if I hand you the men responsible for Ben O'Reilly's death and evidence of their involvement in it?"

Another pause. "You have that?"

"Not yet, but I will."

"Maybe you'd better come on in, and we can talk about this."

"I'm afraid I don't have time. You're going to have to trust me, Sheriff."

"Um-hmm. Well, do you have time to at least give me a few of the particulars?"

"That I can do." For the next ten minutes, Jackson sat in his parked Aveo a few blocks from Mallory Square and recapped the majority of the events that had taken place over the last few days. Primarily, he focused on the call he and Sawyer had received the previous morning demanding the treasure for Ben, his meeting on Crescent Key with four thugs, and the scheduled rendezvous at Mallory Square. Hawkins listened quietly, a few groans his only sounds. When Jackson was finished, that changed.

"Why didn't all y'all call my office right away?"

"We thought about it," Jackson said.

"Y'all thought about it?"

"We had no proof, other than a phone call. I wanted to draw them out a little."

"And now all y'all're in a mess and need help, is that right?"

"More or less."

"Um-hmm. You think these fellas have Mr. O'Reilly?"

"No, I think he's dead. I think they're using the possibility that he's alive as bait to get the treasure. But I can't afford to take that chance, and that's why I didn't hand you everything right away, and it's also why I'm not back in California right now."

Hawkins paused again. "And y'all have this treasure?"

"They think so."

"Mr. Douglas, this ain't the time to be cute. I don't give a flying hoot about some buried treasure and I sure as heck ain't going to try to take it from y'all. But you gotta give me the truth."

"Fair enough. Yes, we found the treasure."

"Sizeable?"

"We estimate millions in gold coins, artifacts, etcetera."

"And you have it with you?"

"I have approximately the one-fourth I promised them in exchange for Ben."

"Well, where is the rest of it?"

"On its way to Miami."

"Collins?"

Jackson nodded but kept silent.

"You're playing with fire, boy."

"Yes, but I've got a pretty good pair of oven mitts."

"I'm not even sure what that means."

Neither was Jackson.

"So what exactly do you want from my office?"

"On the off chance they do bring Ben to the exchange, I think it wouldn't hurt to have someone undercover there to make sure things don't go sideways and to follow them back to whatever hole they crawled from. But like I said, I don't think they have him. I think they'll try to tail me as I leave and follow me to wherever they'll think I have the rest of the treasure, where they'll attempt to take it by force."

"But it's with Collins en route to Miami?"

"Right."

"And you think they won't find her?"

"We were careful."

"I see. What kept them from following you from your little clandestine meeting last night?"

"A homemade spike strip."

"I don't even want to know. Where do you plan to lead them?"

"There's a self-storage facility on the north side of the highway on Big Pine Key, just east of Key Deer Boulevard. I've reserved Unit 7, and the combo is five-one-one-three. Have a couple of uniforms waiting inside in the shadows, and when I throw open the door, they can arrest whoever's behind me."

"Arrest 'em for what?"

"Threat of homicide, attempted blackmail, etcetera."

"On what evidence?"

"Their own admission, which I will provide, and the testimony of a reliable witness."

"You?"

"That's right. And Sheriff, if you can get these guys to talk, they'll link back to a New Orleans businessman named Martin Louviere. I'll spare you all the details now, but Sawyer and I believe Louviere is responsible for the death of Damon Villars and is ultimately behind Ben's death. Now we're talking about a federal crime, and you've got the lynchpin that starts the whole thing rolling."

Hawkins was quiet for a moment. "That all sounds great, Mr. Douglas. Only, what if y'all have this all figured wrong? What if these boys don't follow you? Or don't show themselves at the storage facility? What if they just plan to tail you for days until they're sure you ain't got police protection? You're asking a lot of me, and my force, without evidence. On Memorial Day weekend, no less."

"I appreciate that, Sheriff. All I can do is ask you to trust me and ask you to trust Sawyer. And if that won't do it, I'll write you a blank check to cover whatever expenses your department incurs from a potential wild goose chase."

Hawkins was silent for another minute. Finally, he consented. "I'll have an unmarked car at Mallory Square by noon. And I'll send a unit to the self-storage place over on Big Pine Key. But I want your word, Mr. Douglas, that you will tell me everything. I find out you're holding anything back from me, I'll run you in for obstructing justice 'fore I do anything."

"That's fair."

"Gimme that unit number and password again."

Jackson repeated them, and Hawkins coughed. "Five-one-one-three?"

"Yeah."

"That your kid sister's wedding date or something?"

"USC's last three Heisman winners."

"Hmm."

"I appreciate your help, Sheriff. I promise you my full cooperation."

"You had better."

"I've got to get going," Jackson said. "The meeting's set for noon at the pavilion in the Square." He gave Hawkins the Aveo description and plate number and apprised the sheriff of the route he planned to take through town, just in case they tried to take him down along the way.

It was twenty to twelve, and Jackson wanted to be in place early. So he said goodbye to Sheriff Hawkins and headed for Mallory Square.

*   *   *

1:38 p.m.

"WELL, THAT went about as planned," Sheriff Hawkins said with his typical drawl. Jackson sat on the back bumper of the second ambulance to arrive at the scene. The first had carted off one of Jackson's assailants, the one who had been grabbing his arm when Jackson emerged from the bushes. The bushes were the reason Jackson was receiving medical assistance, the bushes and the shards of glass from the Aveo's windows. He'd been cut and scratched on his face, neck, and arms, and some of the cuts were semi-deep.

"Yeah, but we caught them," Jackson said.

"We?"

"How'd your guys get here so fast, anyhow?"

"Officer Petty saw a pair of pickup trucks pick up your tail right after you left Mallory Square. When they followed your little zig-zag pattern, he thought something might be up and radioed me. I dispatched a couple of cars to follow you, just in case something went down."

"I appreciate it."

The officer who had originally held Jackson at gunpoint crossed the road from the south. The Aveo had been moved farther onto the shoulder, as had the car that had crashed into the F-150. Traffic was again moving in both directions, albeit under the supervision of two officers who were stationed a quarter mile up the road to warn people to slow down. Two more of Jackson's assailants were handcuffed in the backseat of one of the squad cars. The fourth was at large.

"We still don't have him, sir," the officer reported to Hawkins. "The chopper's on the way."

"You circulate the description?"

"APB out, but it was pretty slim."

"All right, thanks. Get those boys back to the office."

"Yes, sir."

Hawkins turned back to Jackson. "You know who these guys are?"

"I was just about to ask you the same thing."

"IDs have them as Robert LaFleur and Gary Harris," he said, nodding at each of them. "Guy with the bullet in his arm is Keith Hoffman. Harris had a DUI a few years ago, but otherwise they're clean."

Jackson nodded. "LaFleur's the one I talked to last . . ."

Suddenly the wheels were spinning in Jackson's head. The name Robert. The look on his face he couldn't quite place. The snarl. Where had he heard it?

"We got 'em for reckless driving and attempted murder," Hawkins said with an odd look at Jackson. "But you mentioned a link to Ben?"

Jackson nodded and wiggled free from the medic attending him. He reached into his pocket, his brain still churning. His phone wasn't there.

"Something wrong?" Hawkins asked.

"My phone. It's in the car. I dropped it when these clowns ran me off the road. But there's a recording on there in which LaFleur will threaten to kill me, Sawyer, and Ben. It was in my pocket, but you should have good enough equipment to identify and match his voice. We listened to it earlier, and it's pretty clear."

"That's your evidence?"

Jackson's mind was spinning again. The voice. Something about it was familiar, yet not quite.

"You all right, Douglas?"

"Uh, yeah."

"That all you got for evidence?"

"Plus my sworn testimony. As soon as I'm done here, I'll give you a full statement." He looked at the medic. "I'm good, man. Thanks."

"All right."

Jackson stood up, and he and Hawkins walked a safe distance away. His eyes processed the crash scene, traffic, the bright sunlight, the distant caw of a gull. It was all white noise compared to the shouting in Jackson's head. Robert. The snarl. The voice.

He suddenly stopped.

"I think maybe you'd better sit back down," Hawkins said. "You don't look so hot."

Jackson shook his head. "I know who LaFleur is."

"What do you mean?"

"When we were in New Orleans, Sawyer and I met a woman named Ruby Mae Patterson. She's the daughter of a Congressman Patterson. And she mentioned a brother named Bobby who worked for Louviere. We never saw him, but something about this LaFleur guy has bugged me. His look, his voice, particularly his angry little snarl. I'll bet my share of the treasure that Robert LaFleur is Ruby Mae's brother Bobby. She said he was a driver or a courier or something, but he's clearly been promoted."

Hawkins shook his head. "What's all that got to do with our situation here again?"

"LaFleur's your link to Louviere. Or the feds' link, or whoever's. Just remember the name Patterson. Congressman Lucas Patterson, I think. His daughter Ruby Mae."

"And her brother with a different last name."

"Trust me, Sheriff. The resemblance is there."

"This Ruby Mae . . . Will she testify?"

"Against her brother, I don't know. But if you get anything on Louviere, she'll corroborate what she can."

Hawkins sighed. "This is the most confounding mess . . ."

Tabbing one of his deputies to coordinate the search for the fourth man, Hawkins gave Jackson (and his gold) a ride back to the Sheriff's Office. Once there, he offered him a sandwich and a soda, both of which Jackson accepted. Then, after checking in with two of his deputies, Hawkins sat back and listened to Jackson's tale.

He told him everything. Almost. Leaving out the few instances where he and Sawyer had skirted the law, Jackson went over everything from their initial research into the Brackett treasure up to the point when they discovered it under the sand of Sugarloaf Key. He covered New Orleans, the Bahamas, and their research back in the Keys. Dixon, Louviere, Baldwin. He had to get creative a few times to avoid implicating himself or Sawyer, but otherwise, he came clean.

Hawkins took notes and followed up with a few questions when Jackson was done. Finally, the sheriff concluded that he knew as much as he could at the time. He promised to interrogate LaFleur, Harris, and Hoffman and to check in with the authorities in New Orleans and on Lazarus Island, as well as to call Ruby Mae Patterson. Jackson gave Hawkins his cell number and promised to be of any help if at all possible.

"What are you going to do now?" Hawkins asked.

"Meet up with Sawyer."

"And then?"

"Lay low for a few days. Then, find someone who will pay cash for doubloons."

"If you're right about this Louviere guy, he'll come after y'all."

"Yeah, maybe. Once the gold's money in a bank account, it will be harder. Especially if you can get any of his thugs to roll back on him." Jackson shrugged. "I'm more worried about him coming after Sawyer."

Hawkins chortled. "I wouldn't worry about Collins. That is one lady that can take care of herself."

Jackson smiled. "So I've learned."

Chapter Fifty-Two

Two and a half weeks ago . . .
Wednesday, May 8
7:01 p.m.

JACKSON SAT ON his deck watching the day fade into night. It was a fade, instead of the more dramatic sunset that Southern California was famous for. The sky had remained overcast all afternoon, rain falling intermittently. It was falling now, and Jackson was soaked. He didn't care, except for the fact that his iced tea was getting watered down.

First Maggie, dating the pastor's son. How could you ever compare with a pastor's son? Then, within a month, Sam and her unnamed beau. Talk about kicking a guy when he was down. Ashley, who he'd never thought of in *that* way was getting married and moving away. Then to top it off with that awkward bit with Walker . . .

He had it coming. He'd been "seeing" two women for almost two years, not to mention flirting with every reasonable-looking woman he came in contact with, almost falling for clients, treating women and dating and relationships so casually . . .

He thought about what Zach had said, that he needed to do some soul-searching as to why his relationships failed. Was it a prosaic fear of commitment? Did it have to do with his job? Was there something else beneath the surface? Was something wrong with him? It would explain why he was sitting outside in the rain.

"Jackson!"

He turned his head to see whose shrill voice had hollered at him. But he already knew. Connie. His rotund, red-haired neighbor. She wore an outlandishly bright top, Capri pants, and galoshes. An umbrella protected her head from the rain, keeping her abundant makeup from running.

"What in the name of Noah are you doing out here in the rain?" she asked, doing a fast waddle across the lawn to his deck.

Jackson turned his head. "Hi, Connie."

"Jackson, you're getting soaked."

"I'll dry. I get soaked every morning in the shower."

Connie, although she could be a bit blustery and meddlesome, was also reasonably perceptive. "Is something wrong?"

"In a manner of speaking."

"Well, honey, let's go inside. There's no sense drowning yourself."

"Thanks, Connie, but I'm fine."

She stood for a moment as if debating whether she should go back home or sit down. Jackson's patio chairs were wet, and after nearly turning around twice, she finally stayed where she was. "Jackson, what's going on?"

"I'd really rather not talk about it," he said, following with a drink of tea/rain.

Connie stood in place for another minute, then finally turned and walked back to her house without a word. Jackson watched her go, then turned his eyes to the horizon. He certainly had a way with women.

*   *   *

Sunday, May 26
6:36 p.m.

JACKSON WAS exhausted by the time he reached the city limits of Miami. He had spent over an hour with Sheriff Hawkins, then another with various hotels and car rental agencies. He was now driving his third rental car in the last week, this a nifty blue Ford Fusion.

He had not spoken to Sawyer since leaving Mallory Square. He had tried calling her burn phone from Hawkins' office since his burner was now in evidence. She hadn't answered again, and again he'd had to quell panic that something was wrong. Maybe she was still driving. Maybe she had stopped for a snow cone on her way to Miami and left her phone in the SUV. Or maybe Louviere's Bravo team had run her off Seven Mile Bridge, and her dead body would float in the Straits of Florida until colliding with Ben's dead body. Jackson had thought about calling her smartphone with his own cell, but had advised they both keep them off and disassembled, just in case anyone was still tracking them. So he'd done his best to alleviate his nerves by praying for her safety yet again.

Jackson had finally departed Key West a little before four o'clock. He'd made good time, stopping just once for a fast food supper. Throughout the trip, as was the case now, his mind had been occupied with the loose ends of the case.

What was Louviere's motivation? Was he just greedy or did he feel he had some tie to this treasure—some family connection? How had he known so much? How many resources did he have? How many Frank Baldwins were out there? Jackson hoped that Hawkins' interrogation of the three men apprehended this afternoon would provide a tie to Louviere and also some answers. He also hoped the FBI would get involved, since Louviere and Baldwin and Dixon were outside of the Monroe County Sheriff's Department's jurisdiction. Despite what he'd told Hawkins, he didn't relish the thought of Louviere coming after him—or Sawyer—someday.

He also wondered what specifically Ben had known and how it had led to his demise. Jackson's working theory was that after stumbling upon Damon Villars, likely through colleagues and college acquaintances who had blabbed, Louviere had learned of his association with Ben and decided to silence him too. He'd dispatched a team that included Ted Ryker, and they had somehow lured Ben out onto a boat and killed him. Somehow, things had gone awry, and Ryker had bought it too. But what exactly had transpired was still a mystery.

Jackson hoped Hawkins and the proper authorities could figure that out, and realized he maybe should have involved them sooner. Then again, they had been involved since Ben's chartered boat had capsized. And while Jackson and Sawyer's little investigation had led them to the treasure, it hadn't proven much more.

One other thing plagued Jackson as he drove through suburban sprawl. Why hadn't Louviere pulled the trigger on Jackson and Sawyer too? After escaping Dixon's clutches at the hunting shack in the swamp and eluding Louviere's people at Pontchartrain Manor, they had to be considered at least as much of a threat as Ben and Damon. So why, once they had been located on Lazarus Island, had Louviere's motive seemed to turn from eliminating them to following them? Maybe when his people stole the map, Louviere thought the chase was over? Or maybe he had taken out Damon and Ben because they got too close to something he already knew, whereas Jackson and Sawyer had uncovered new information, and killing them would have kept Louviere from getting that information. Maybe he'd let them live long enough to lead him to the treasure?

It was frustrating. On TV, the loose ends always got tied up in a quick recap or a convenient confession at the end of the hour. In real life, oftentimes investigators were left with a lot of unanswered questions.

That, and a pile of gold.

Jackson and Sawyer had chosen the Excelsior Hotel in downtown Miami because of its location, and frankly, because of its caliber. They wanted to stay somewhere they could go unnoticed, and while some out-of-the-way "fleabag" motel would provide that, Jackson thought it was time for a change of pace. He figured they could hide out in plain sight, surrounded by thousands of other people. Plus, the Excelsior was the kind of place they could count on for discretion, Jackson thought. The desk clerks would be immune to bribery and coercion. He hoped.

The hotel was situated on the Miami River a few blocks west of the bay. Contrary to popular belief, Miami itself was not on the beach. Rather, it sat on the edge of Biscayne Bay, which itself was speckled with a number of islands—natural and manmade—that were home to condos, resorts, and cruise terminals. The famous South Beach, known for its party scene, was actually on the Atlantic Coast, on a barrier island a few miles east of downtown.

Even so, the Excelsior boasted excellent views of the bay, the barrier islands, and ultimately the ocean, along with the rest of downtown. If they were going to lay low, Jackson and Sawyer both preferred ocean vistas to views of a cracked parking lot. And it wasn't like they couldn't afford it.

Wheeling his one suitcase of gold and carrying his duffel of mostly dirty clothes, Jackson went to the lobby. An atrium looked out on the river, with thirty-foot palm trees stretching toward the glass ceiling. A rain shower had moved through a few hours ago, but now a beautiful sunset colored everything in a soft orange hue. That included the marble floor and gold countertop at the front desk.

"Can I help you, sir?" a petite Latina woman with short black hair asked.

"My friend checked into our suite earlier this afternoon," Jackson answered. "She was going to leave me a key here at the desk."

"Your name, sir?"

The Excelsior would not let them reserve a room without a credit card, so Jackson and Sawyer had been forced to use their real names. He gave his to the clerk, whose nametag identified her as Esmeralda.

"Yes, I see that here. Can I please see some identification?"

Jackson set his driver's license on the desk.

"Thank you, Mr. Douglas." She checked the license quickly but sincerely. Then she handed it back. She also handed him a keycard in a small envelope. "Room 2318. You can take the second or third elevator on your right. If you have any questions, please do not hesitate to ask, and please enjoy your stay at the Excelsior Hotel."

"Thank you," Jackson said, pocketing the key. The elevators had gold doors to match the countertop. Inside it was more comfortable than many hotel rooms Jackson had stayed in. It whisked him to the twenty-third floor in a matter of seconds, and Jackson stepped out onto plush carpeting. At the end of the hallway, a giant window looked out at the Miami skyline. The buildings were white, shaded in orange, their windows reflecting various angles of another paradisiacal sunset.

Jackson and Sawyer's suite was on the east side, overlooking the mouth of the river and Biscayne Bay. Jackson rapped on the door before inserting his key and swinging it open.

The sight took his breath away. He and Sawyer had reserved a two bedroom suite, on James Brackett's tab. Pristine white carpet ran the length of the suite, except for where white tiles surrounded a white fireplace with seating that allowed occupants to look from a fire to the view out sliding glass doors that led to the balcony. The view wasn't much, just the bay, cruise ships steaming toward the ocean, barrier islands, and the wide-open Atlantic.

A kitchen with an island and a small dining area were on his left, along with a powder room, and a stub hallway that led to a pair of bedrooms on the right. There was a reason the room cost $399 a night, but what were a few less doubloons?

The door swung shut behind Jackson, latching with a quiet click. He set down his duffel. "Sawyer?"

She didn't answer. Leaving his suitcase of gold by the door, Jackson peeked into the first bedroom. It was completely empty, the door to its bathroom wide open, the light off.

Jackson tried the other room, lit only by the amber light of sunset. The room was stacked full of suitcases—six of them. It too was unoccupied, and scenarios began running through Jackson's head. Sawyer had made it to the hotel, as evidenced by the suitcases and the response of the front desk clerk when he'd mentioned her. Had something happened to her after she arrived? Had she simply gone to dinner? Had she left a message explaining everything on the cell phone he'd left in the Aveo and that was now part of Hawkins' investigation?

Jackson returned to the living room. That's when he saw a manila envelope on the glass coffee table in front of the fireplace. His name was printed on the envelope, which was clasped but not sealed. A ransom? He was suddenly sweating, and he carried it out onto the balcony.

The eastern sky had turned a gradient of blue and fuchsia. A few rays of sun found their way through the Miami skyline to reflect off the waters of the bay and the white buildings on distant islands. Jackson subconsciously admired the view while he opened the clasp on the envelope.

He reached inside and pulled out three sheets of paper. The first was a penciled portrait of Jackson and Sawyer, an incredible re-creation of the selfie she had taken on her phone after dinner at The Point. The detail and the authenticity of the drawing were striking. From a distance, it could be mistaken for a black and white photo. Up close, the strokes of the pencil added depth and character to it that were amazing.

As Jackson studied the photo, his heart began to pound. Sawyer's absence, the suitcases, the drawing . . . and the emotion in her eyes in the parking lot of the Sunrise Inn all told Jackson something. He just couldn't figure out what. So he switched the sheets of paper in his hand.

He held a handwritten note, also in pencil, covering both pages. He leaned his forearms on the balcony railing and began to read, the evening breeze fluttering the corner of the paper.

Jackson,

I need to start by apologizing to you for telling you this in a letter instead of in person, but I didn't know if I had the courage otherwise. Anyhow, I don't know quite how to say this, other than to just say it. So here goes.

419

You are unlike any person I've ever met, Jackson. I've never seen someone with your determination, your wisdom, your confidence, and frankly, your luck.☺ Over the last several days, I found myself amazed that one person could be so intrepid and daring and brash, and yet so sincere and compassionate. I've learned that even though your heart may not always be in what you're doing, you do it anyhow because it's the right thing to do. I can't tell you what an admirable quality that is. Call it loyalty, call it duty, call it just being a good man. I've also seen you battle your demons, I've seen you wrestle with your questions and frustrations, and I've seen you standing bloodied and scarred but still standing, still fighting, still clinging to Truth. I can tell you have a Bedrock that keeps you anchored, even when the winds and waves of life try to blow you astray. Don't get me wrong. I know you aren't perfect. But you are special. And you are special to me, Jackson. I have no doubt that, over time, I would have fallen for you. In fact, in a way, I think I already have. Not in the swooning schoolgirl sort of way, but in the way a Southern woman who drives a Jeep and shoots a gun and wears boots—real boots, I mean—knows when she's found the real deal.

And that's why I think it's best that we part ways, Jackson. I can't see myself ever leaving the South and I can't see you ever leaving California. You have your life there and I have mine. And I love the journey I'm on and I'm not ready to be at my destination just yet. I'm the kind of person that, when I get to my destination, I'm going to up and settle down right there. But I'm not ready for that yet. There's too much of my life that needs to unfold first, things I need to do and try and experience and . . . I'm not ready yet. Does any of this make sense? Am I way too presumptuous? It's why I'm writing this instead of talking to you on the balcony at sunset.

Anyhow, as you might have already figured out, I'm leaving you Brackett's treasure. All of it. Except for one doubloon I took as a souvenir. I can't imagine my life with all that money. I can't see myself living the life I would end up living, the Southern socialite. It isn't me. It might sound strange, but I'm more comfortable—I'm happier—without it. So it's yours.☺ Do with it whatever you think is best. I trust you to make that decision.

I imagine that you'll have questions, Jackson. Maybe this letter will make you mad. Maybe it will make you sad. Maybe when you reread that third paragraph to see if I really said what you think I did, it will make you glad I'm not standing there in front of you. But please don't come looking for me. I don't have any answers for you, other than what I've written. And please don't think that if you can just talk to me I'll reconsider splitting the treasure. I won't. If you send me a check, I'll tear it up. Oh, and please don't establish the Sawyer Collins fund for this or that. I don't want my name associated with it. It's all yours, Jackson.

I cannot thank you enough for being a perfect gentleman these last two weeks. Thank you for your efforts to find Ben, to find truth, to find justice. I saw the look in your eyes when we found the treasure, the allure it had on you and on me. But I also saw the look in your eyes countless other times, and I know where your heart truly was. And for that, I commend you.

I'm running on, so I'll just say that I hope you like the drawing. I had some spare time on my hands. I'm keeping the photo, like I said, to remember people and experiences. I hope you'll do the same. Maybe someday . . . just maybe, our paths will cross again. If not, I will see you on the Other Side.

Your refined Southern woman,
Sawyer

Jackson reread the letter three times. By then, darkness had fallen, and he had to strain his eyes to make out the words. It was even harder to identify his emotions.

There had never been any romance between him and Sawyer. Not that he wasn't attracted to her. She was beautiful physically, as well as being fun, witty, clever, confident, and well . . . refined and dignified. Most importantly, she had sound, biblical character. As he watched darkness fall over the barrier islands separating Biscayne Bay from the Atlantic Ocean, Jackson realized he probably felt the same about Sawyer as she did about him. She was the real deal.

And she was gone.

Chapter Fifty-Three

Wednesday, May 29
9:17 a.m.

SHE STOOD BY a vending machine in the middle of the concourse, her back to Jackson. He paused, did a double-take, and wondered if it was possible. She bent down to retrieve her purchase, then stood and turned his way. She was strikingly beautiful, possessing the kind of face that stayed in a guy's head all day.

But she wasn't Sawyer.

Jackson resumed walking, a complimentary newspaper under his arm. One of the headings had grabbed his attention when he'd checked in for his flight. "FBI Targets NOLA Mogul."

Security had been a breeze, and Jackson sat down at his gate nearly an hour before his nonstop flight to L.A. He had no carry-on bags, just the paper and an Orange Julius. After taking in his surroundings for a moment, he opened the paper.

The morning before, he'd read on Keysnews.com that three men had been arrested for brazen attempted murder on U.S. 1 Sunday afternoon. A fourth was still at large. The same three men were also under suspicion in the death of a local history teacher, according to the paper. As he read the article, Jackson realized that his best-case scenario had played out.

According to the newspaper, the FBI had officially charged New Orleans businessman Martin Louviere with murder, kidnapping, and a host of other crimes. Louviere's lawyer claimed it was all a witch hunt, that the evidence was circumstantial and hearsay. But according to Special Agent Christopher of the FBI, an investigation launched when the FBI received a tip from the Monroe County Sheriff's Department had been augmented by the FBI's "outstanding intelligence gathering" and "diligent pursuit of justice." He complimented Sheriff Hawkins by name, as well as the district attorney, for their cooperation and for making his office aware of the connection between an incident in their jurisdiction and Martin Louviere.

The article also cited a piece from the *The Times-Picayune* in New Orleans that alleged that Martin Louviere was a distant relative of Captain James Brackett. The article didn't lay out the full genealogy, nor did Jackson have access to *The Times-Picayune*, so he didn't know if that connection was by blood or marriage. Ultimately, it didn't matter. What did matter was that Louviere *was* apparently going to answer for his crimes.

Jackson couldn't believe it. LaFleur, Hoffman, or Harris had to have incriminated Louviere. He guessed LaFleur, as Keysnews.com had indicated that Hoffman and Harris were local muscle. There was nothing in the paper confirming that LaFleur was indeed Congressman Patterson's son, but the more Jackson thought about it, the more he was sure it was the case. At any rate, as the leader of the group, LaFleur was the only one to have contact with Louviere, Jackson guessed. And he had apparently rolled.

Jackson was also surprised by Hawkins and the district attorney. He would have expected a Southern sheriff and D.A. to hold a big press conference, strut their feathers, and try to take as much of the glory as possible. Instead, they had apparently quickly contacted the FBI, who in turn had worked remarkably fast. Less than seventy-two hours after LaFleur and company had been arrested, Jackson was reading about Louviere's arrest in the paper. Not bad.

In addition to citing the work of Hawkins and the district attorney, the article also made an offhanded reference to an additional witness who had provided incriminating testimony. As Jackson skimmed the rest of the paper, he couldn't decide if he thought that other person was Ruby Mae or Sawyer.

Sawyer.

Jackson had read her letter a few more times over the last couple of days when he hadn't been busy doing online research, making phone calls, and meeting with people. It had not been easy to find the right people to whom to turn over what came to just short of fourteen million dollars in gold.

Fourteen million!

That total staggered him. He was still trying to process exactly what it meant for his life. He was now rich beyond belief. So why didn't he feel rich? Was it just the newness of it? Was it the loss of an old friend? Was it Sawyer's departure? Or was it the fact that no amount of money could bring back what he'd lost?

An announcement came over the speaker. His plane was boarding, and Jackson got up. He left the paper on his seat for the next guy and trudged onto the plane. No carry-on. Only one checked bag, containing his clothes. And a handful of doubloons. The rest of the gold had been brokered through a bank. The conditions had been simple. Jackson gave them the gold; they gave him a rather lowball estimate of its worth in the form of money wired to several banks. One in the Caymans, one in Florida, and one in California.

As for the original bank, they would likely turn the gold over to a museum, collectors, an assortment of governments, or maybe private buyers. Jackson didn't care. He also didn't care if the gold and jewels turned out to have increased cultural significance and ended up being worth double what he had been paid. The deal was struck, he was filthy rich, and he was content with that.

As he walked down the Jetway, Jackson pondered for the hundredth time what he might do with his newfound wealth. A new car? A new house? A small private island? Would he retire? Buy his grandpa a working houseboat? Bribe Maggie and/or Sam to come back to him? The only thing he knew as he took his window seat in first class was that half of the money was set aside in the Florida bank for Sawyer, just in case. He was still debating trying to get a message to her somehow, just letting her know that she could always change her mind. But he knew she wouldn't.

Jackson remained lost in thought—mulling over how to spend the money, contemplating the events of the past two weeks, and rereading Sawyer's letter in his mind—until the plane backed away from the gate. He watched out the window as it taxied to the end of the runway, sat idling for just a moment, and then thrust forward. The plane screamed down the runway and lifted into the air almost indiscernibly. Jackson watched Miami's skyline as the plane banked to the left and the coast disappeared.

He sat back, his thoughts turning to Sawyer again. He still didn't quite know what to make of her letter—what she'd said about him, her rejection of the treasure, her reason for disappearing. He wondered what she would do with her life, if she would be safe from the wrath of Louviere. He could buy an ADT home security system, guard dogs, or a private militia for protection.

He smiled. Sawyer had her rifle and the resourcefulness of a refined Southern woman.

Jackson closed his eyes. Until he'd read her letter, he hadn't been aware of any feelings for her. Now he wasn't sure if it had made him aware of what existed below the surface or if he was just reacting to an emotional experience. In the end, he guessed it didn't really matter. She'd made it clear that she didn't want him tracking her down and talking her into anything, and he was going to respect that. She was gone, just a memory in pencil.

It was turning into the story of his life. His parents were gone. His brother was gone. Maggie and Sam were gone. Ashley. Walker. Now Sawyer—brief as their time together had been and irrespective of the potential nature of their friendship—was gone too.

Fourteen million dollars. Jackson realized right then and there that it was true.

Money did not buy happiness.

Acknowledgements

AS ALWAYS, I must thank a few people who have been instrumental in getting *Golden Key* published. To my wife, Sierra, thanks for supporting this endeavor, encouraging me when I'm down, listening to all my novel ideas and drafts, and enduring my poor reception of criticism. To my parents, Doug and Jean, thanks for your proofing efforts and words of advice and cheer. To Mark and Tiffani, thanks for editing, serving as sounding boards for my ideas, and providing suggestions and analysis. To Chris, thanks for catching what the rest of us missed, as well as for your enthusiasm and high praise. Also, a special shout-out to the staff at Beacon Books, LLC for all the hard work shaping a manuscript into a published book.

Lastly, to my fans, thanks for reading, thanks for encouraging, thanks for still being there. I'd love to hear your feedback, whether via an Amazon review or a personal message. Check out my website to see how to get in touch with me and to see what's coming next. With Jackson Douglas, it's all adventure all the time!

www.ingramcontent.com/pod-product-compliance
Lightning Source LLC
Chambersburg PA
CBHW030348030726
47497CB00002B/243